D1033094

Green for Danger

with contributions from

ANDREA BADENOCH
ROBERT BARNARD
ANN CLEEVES
MAT COWARD
JUDITH CUTLER
CAROL ANNE DAVIS
MARTIN EDWARDS
KATE ELLIS
REGINALD HILL
EDWARD D HOCH
BRIAN INNES
MICHAEL JECKS
PETER LEWIS
PETER LOVESEY
KEITH MILES
GWEN MOFFAT
AMY MYERS
RUTH RENDELL
ZOE SHARP
JERRY SYKES

Green for Danger

edited by

Martin Edwards

CPL

THE DO-NOT
PRESS

First Published in Great Britain in 2003 by
The Do-Not Press Limited
16 The Woodlands
London SE13 6TY
www.thedonotpress.com
email: gfd@thedonotpress.com

C-format paperback: ISBN 1 904316 29 8
Casebound edition: ISBN 1 904316 28 X

British Library Cataloguing in Publication Data. A catalogue record for this book is available from the British Library.

1   3   5   7   9   10   8   6   4   2

Green for Danger

LIST OF CONTENTS

Foreword

Hilary Bonner

All right, I'm biased. But it seems to me that there is no greater accolade that any writer can be paid than to be described as a fine story-teller. And that, of course, includes winning the Booker prize!

The Crime Writers' Association, by the very nature of what its members do, positively overflows with fine story-tellers. And there is probably no purer form of the art than a short story, with the tight disciplines its length necessarily imposes.

In this latest CWA anthology editor Martin Edwards has yet again assembled a marvellous collection of such offerings, this time with a rural theme.

Story-telling is an ancient craft, almost as old as man himself. Before we could write or read we told each other stories verbally, many of which entered into folklore and became passed on from generation to generation. For myself I always think that short stories are rather like mini crossword puzzles. Among the many skills required to produce them effectively is a quite extraordinary degree of precision. There can be no loose use of adjectives or rambling descriptions. Instead every idea must be cut to the bone, while every character has to jump off the page after no more than a sentence or two at the most, and yet the plot must unfold before the reader in such a way that both its construction and its relation seem quite effortless.

It is a wonderful privilege to be able to tell stories. On a good day I would even go so far as to say that it's a thrill. It can also, hopefully, be a thrill to read them.

Within the pages of this book are some of the best, written by writers at the very top of their craft. I am more than proud to be introducing their work, which is actually something of a master class, and equally proud that they are all members of the CWA.

Hilary Bonner, Chairman, Crime Writers' Association

Introduction

Martin Edwards

T his, the latest anthology produced by members of the Crime Writers' Association, is published in the year of the CWA's Golden Jubilee. In the 50 years since John Creasey and a small group of fellow authors joined together to found the CWA, the regular publication of anthologies – at a rate of almost one a year – has highlighted the diversity and quality of members' work. My predecessors as CWA anthology editor have included such notable names as Julian Symons, Michael Gilbert, HRF Keating and Peter Lovesey and the books have included many prize-winning stories, several of which have achieved classic status. Most of the major crime writers of the past half-century have made contributions, but equally important for the long-term health of the genre has been the presence of stories by younger writers whose work is deserving of a wide audience. Since I took over as editor in 1996, each annual collection has had a distinct theme. And in this special year for the CWA, we are publishing in addition to the present volume a collection which represents the best crime writing of the past 50 years, *Mysterious Pleasures*.

Gathered together in *Green For Danger* are 20 stories, all but two of which were written specially for this book. As ever, I have in selecting from the manuscripts sent to me aimed for variety and entertainment. Four of the contributors have received the highest award given to authors in the genre – the CWA Cartier Diamond Dagger, marking a career of outstanding achievement – while another has produced her very first short story (and most enjoyable it is.)

The main title of this collection is borrowed from a classic detective novel by the late Christianna Brand; 30 years ago, she was a distinguished chairman of the CWA, so I trust she would approve! The guiding theme, of crimes in countryside settings (not confined just to the UK), seemed a natural choice to follow *Crime in the City,* which was the first in the current series of anthologies published by The Do-Not Press. In these days of eco-terrorism and rural revolt, there could hardly be a more topical subject for crime writers to explore.

Of course, the potential for murder and mayhem in an apparently peaceful setting has long been recognised. One thinks of a justly famous passage from *The Copper Beeches* in which Sherlock Holmes expounds his views:

'It is my belief, Watson, founded upon my experience, that the lowest and vilest alleys in London do not present a more dreadful record of sin than does the smiling and beautiful countryside... the pressure of public opinion can do in the town what the law cannot accomplish. There is no lane so vile that the scream of a tortured child, or the thud of a drunkard's blow, does not beget sympathy and indignation among the neighbours, and then the whole machinery of justice is ever so close that a word of complaint can set it going, and there is but a step between the crime and the dock. But look at these lonely houses, each in its own fields, filled for the most part with poor ignorant folk who know little of the law. Think of the deeds of hellish cruelty, the hidden wickedness which may go on, year in, year out, in such places.'

There is a good deal of insight in that passage, and yet the allure of a green and pleasant land is hard to resist. Holmes himself eventually forsook the comforts of his rooms at 221b Baker Street for a retirement spent keeping bees in Sussex and said: 'I had given myself up entirely to that soothing love of nature for which I had so often yearned during the long years spent amid the gloom of London.' It is this contrast, between the charms of the countryside and the shocking crimes that are sometimes committed there, that exerts a continuing appeal to crime writers.

One of the delights of editing the CWA anthology each year is the opportunity it gives me to see brand new stories from the pens of gifted fellow writers. I am sure that readers will find as much here to enjoy as I did. I should like to thank Hilary Bonner, the current Chair of the CWA, for contributing the foreword and to her colleagues on the CWA committee, including in particular Fiona Davies, the Treasurer, for their continuing support and enthusiasm for the annual anthology. My thanks also go to Jim Driver and his team at the Do-Not Press for making the book possible. I am also most grateful to Joan Edwards and Helena Edwards for their continuing help and support.

Martin Edwards

ANGEL'S SEAT

Andrea Badenoch

Many of the best tales of crime in the countryside deal with the arrival of a stranger who disturbs the rural calm. This beautifully written story is a good example. In its first form it was much longer, verging on a novella. Andrea Badenoch wrote it while battling serious illness but, although I thought the story splendid, it was simply too long for this book. Of course I was delighted when Andrea, racing against the clock this time, came up with a re-write, which is to my mind even better than the original.

*F*rom the diary of Jennifer Wadham Richardson, Angel's Seat Farmhouse, 1938.

August 31st

I have spent my whole life, all of twenty-two years, imagining this landscape, but now I'm here, nothing about it is a surprise. Oh, England! The meadows and the flood plains and the endless flat fens with their watery ditches marked by willow and above all the vast pale sky – everything reminds me of familiar paintings from a half-century ago. My newly adopted countryside is a delicate wash of grey and green and silver horizontals. It's called East Anglia and it is the England of everyone's dreams. I'm so glad to be here.

September 1st

So, I am relocated. I sit at *my* desk, in the window of *my* house, overlooking *my* enchanted garden. I keep telling myself I am embarking on a *Fresh Start* and the relief and optimism contained within these two words is a rush of adrenaline through my veins. My old home is nothing but a bad memory of difficulty, regret and hardship. Only the startling twang of my Canadian tongue serves here as a reminder of my origins and my former disappointments.

Peter Howlett, the agent, has proved to be most courteous and helpful. Today I met him for the first time. He tells me there has been no problem leasing my fields to neighbouring landowners. 'Angel's Seat is such a beautiful farm,' he explained in the soft local accent. 'It's south-facing, productive, well-managed to the last...'

He's an attractive man. To my dismay, he seemed nervous. He kept looking about as if expecting someone to arrive. He glanced at his pocket watch, checking the time.

'Are you in a hurry?' I inquired.

'Hurry? No, no, forgive me, I'm in no hurry.'

'Well then, please come inside.' I wanted to make a friend of him. I said, 'I come from a big, cold, windy city.' An unwelcome vision of my rooms on the fifth floor of that grim downtown block possessed me as I uttered these words. The sky was visible from only one place in that dismal apartment, and that was lying on my back in the tub under the bathroom window. Moreover, there was grinding traffic day and night. I smiled again at Peter Howlett. 'The most *I've* ever grown is an aspidistra in a pot. And that died on me!' I invited him to sit down.

'There's no bathroom here,' he admitted, as if reading my mind. He stared at his watch again. I felt he was anxious to depart but nevertheless unwilling to rebuff me.

I hung up his hat and filled the kettle. I kept going with the prattle. 'But I've found the tin bath and the boiler next to the fire!' I didn't tell him that my baths, since my arrival, have been a deca-dent luxury in front of the kitchen range. I've wallowed and soaped like a nineteenth-century courtesan.

Peter Howlett sat on the edge of the sofa and ate two pieces of shop cake. He went on to explain that the house and garden are mine, that the fields are rented out and that everything else is sold. Most importantly, he insisted, all outstanding debts have been paid. Curiously, he did not mention my cousins by name, let alone their untimely end.

For this is the situation – as the only surviving Richardson, I've inherited the farm. My dead cousins were two brothers and a sister, all unmarried. Alec Richardson died two years ago, but then, more recently, Frank and Dora Richardson were both killed. It was a great surprise to me to learn that I own property in England.

'Debts?' I felt a tingle of anxiety, unsurprising since I've known what life's like on the margins. My father, God rest him, left me penniless.

Peter Howlett was adamant. 'There's nothing to worry your pretty head about. I've taken care of everything.' He handed me a sheaf of cheques. He dusted the crumbs off his lap but didn't meet my eye.

I felt grateful. 'I want no worries, no more debts.'

There was a long silence.

'Mr Howlett?' I said, affected by his lack of cordiality. 'Is there anything to do with this farm that I *ought* to be worrying my pretty head about?'

He blushed. 'No, Miss. Everything is in order. And your daily woman, Elsie. She'll look after you.' He stood up, ill at ease, still glancing about in an odd way. 'She's a treasure.'

I felt the need to reassure him 'There's nobody here but myself.'

He was embarrassed. 'Of course. I'm sorry.' He took his hat from me and blurted out 'You see, your cousin Frank and myself, we weren't...'

'Friends?'

'That's right. We weren't... friends.'

'But that's no reason for us to be enemies, is it?'

He took his leave. Outside, as he mounted his horse, he insisted that despite the circumstances of my inheritance, I'd come to the most peaceful place in England.

Now, as I sit here and write, I realise I am rather offended by his lack of interest in me.

Just as Mr Howlett avoided mentioning the true cause of my arrival on these shores, I myself have not wasted thoughts on my poor, dead cousins. They seem unreal. Perhaps because several months elapsed before my final departure, I never experienced the publicity, nor the voyeurs whom, I understand, travelled from far and wide. Nor had I anything to do with the police and the coroner's investigations. By the time I arrived, the furore had all died down.

As it is, I know very little. I understand that Alec's death remains a mystery while the other two met with a frightful end. I also know that Frank was intestate but that Dora left a cryptic will, causing the lawyers to hunt my foreign whereabouts. So this is the cause of my life taking an unlikely turn and causing me to make my *Fresh Start*. I am quite determined that the past means nothing to me.

September 4th

Elsie is most trying. There has never been any question about her staying on – she has continued with her regular duties and clearly has no inclination to change. I've considered dismissing her but I must admit I am a coward. So there it is – this persistent Elsie arrives too early, with my newspaper and provisions, she dons her house slippers and an apron and then proceeds to light the range, prepare my breakfast and clean the dwelling. She does the laundry, in fact she does everything. She is very religious and sometimes I hear her praying as she goes about her tasks.

I've never employed a servant, until now. During the sixteen months between the death of my father and the leaving of my native land, I managed without. Fortunately, in my newly-improved circumstances I can afford her, the wages are nothing. I confess it's pleasant being waited on like a lady. I've never been adept at the domestic arts. However, I am finding Elsie to be a bully and a gossip and her company – all the company that I have – is proving rather arduous.

Elsie would agree with Peter Howlett that she is a treasure, but really I don't think she cares for me. My decision to lease the fields and break up the farm is repugnant to her and she talks about my cousins 'turning in their graves'.

I have begun making improvements to the house and of course Elsie condemns all change, as if any departure from 'the old ways' represents some form of dangerous North American heresy. I've disposed of all Cousin Frank's ghastly hunting trophies and I've sold all the guns, rods and the other paraphernalia of death. Using income from my rents, I intend to replace the pony and trap with a motor car. Today the builder called and we discussed the demolition of the stables and the construction of a sun room. Elsie busied in and out while this conversation was in progress, pretending to be dusting. Her face was a picture. There will be all hell to pay when the workmen arrive.

For the time being, I'm using my cousin's furniture, their carpets and household equipment. Temporarily, I am sleeping in a small boxroom while I sort out and dispose of their personal effects. Meanwhile, I make plans for *many* alterations. In response, Elsie punishes me. She does this by intruding upon me with revelations about my dead cousins, her employers for a quarter of a century. The more I plan to exorcise them from Angel's Seat, the greater her efforts become to keep their memory alive.

'The past is nothing to me,' I informed her again, today.

Ignoring this, she said she and Dora spent evenings together in Bible study. 'I was her comfort,' she said, 'she was my inspiration.'

This made me feel wretched. How could I compete?

She carried on talking about the church, the family pew, empty save for Dora.

I was barely listening.

She went on, '…because it was after that very last service, see?'

I tried to take no notice.

'It was that Easter Sunday.'

Suddenly, I understood what was coming.

She stared past me, her eyes bleary. 'Mind, the church was beautiful. Stuffed with cherry from behind the byre and our gilly flowers as spicy as pepper.'

I didn't want to know. She was going to tell me what happened here and I didn't want her to sully my new and perfect home.

Once aware of the truth, it would become part of my experience here. I moved to another room.

Elsie was determined. She followed me. 'The service, it were a joy, Miss, it were. And the choir sang praise the Lord fit to bust. But she came back early, Miss Dora did.' She rubbed her eyes and sniffed but there were no tears. 'Then everything was blood.'

'Don't tell me!'

She looked me straight in the eye. 'His head was blown off. Mister Frank's *and* her head was blown off – both. Blood and brains all over the yard. Splatter up the wall. Splatter all over the pony's trap. And they's both lying atop one another see, him under, her over, and the shotgun in the middle o'em. I found 'em. No one knows who did it, see?'

I felt sick. 'What?'

'No one knows. Who pulled the trigger? Was it him or was it her? Who killed who? We don't know and I dessay we'll never know.' She gave me a hard unreadable look before she put on her coat and headscarf and went off, leaving me alone.

After a while I crept outside and examined the yard for blood. I checked the trap and the walls for splashes. I found nothing.

September 5th

Today I discovered that Alec, the youngest of the three cousins, was an unwilling farmer. Elsie spoke of his hobby, which was sketching birds. She also told me of his love of dancing. It became clear that she had, at one time, been his partner. Despite my new resolution to pay no attention to Elsie, I was intrigued by this detail.

'He was a pretty dancer,' she insisted. 'Quite the most dainty dancer the world has ever seen! And such a charmer! Black hair, exactly like your own, Miss, if you'll excuse my being so familiar, and your black eyes. The Richardson eyes.'

Elsie *had* once been sweet on Alec.

'Mind, we went all over the county for these dancing competitions. The two of us waltzing around, chasing after prizes. It was the biggest thing in his life. But Mr Frank, he used to get into a terrible sweat with Alec not pulling his weight around the farm. There were rows, see. And poor Miss Dora, she used to try and cover for Alec and me. She weren't too proud to scrub floors.'

I looked away.

'She could plough and milk and dig ditches as well as any man. But I'd feel bad, right, with Mister Frank driving Miss Dora like a carthorse while Alec and me, we were twinkle toes-ing about in our finery like... like our ex-king and his Yankee divor-see.' Her eyes snapped. *Here* was the change of mood! Just like Elsie!

Again, I regretted listening to her. I walked away. 'I'm not a Yankee,' I called out. 'I'm a Canadian.'

September 8th

I'm sitting up in bed in my little boxroom and I'm cold. It's the middle of the night. I'm shivering so much I can hardly hold this pen, even though the room is warmed with Indian summer and the curtains stir in a fragrant draught from the dark garden. Close to the small gleam of my little night-light, I crouch here and try to write.

I *must* have been dreaming for my gown hangs neatly on its hook behind the door and my candle's wick has never been illumined. It's perfectly clear I've never even left my bed. I will record this nightmare then, if I can, I will attempt to say a few prayers.

I thought I heard a noise coming through the wall, from Dora's room. It was the sound of desperate weeping. I arose and lit my candle from the night-light and I pulled on my gown. I crept along the landing, my heart racing. The noise grew louder and as I reached Dora's room I knew it was a woman, crying most pitifully. With my fingertips, I touched the handle of the door but as I did so, I suffered a dreadful shock. It was as if my whole being had been plunged into a vat of ice, so cold did I become. I was unable to move and the anguished wails continued. A gust of air extinguished my candle. Suddenly I was back in my own little bed, trembling with both chill and fright.

All is quiet now. I sit here picturing my house from afar, Angel's Seat, all by itself, tiny within the wide flat sweep of fields that roll away into the distance and eventually join the sea. My little lamp is the only glimmer for miles under a moonless sky. Where are the angels? So much is black and empty. For the first time I am uneasy, being here alone.

September 9th

I sit at an open window in my morning room and the sun streams in, as mellow and golden as melted butter. Martins sweep across the lawn and the dahlias nod in a breeze that caresses the borders. Last night the fields seemed so hostile and empty. Now they fold away like a glorious patchwork of summer.

'Up early Miss?' inquires Elsie from the kitchen, a note of sarcasm in her voice.

I breathe the luscious air and I am quite recovered. My dream can be explained away. I'm sure it resulted from an unpleasant incident of yesterday.

As I mentioned, I am slowly going through my cousin's bed-rooms with the intention of commencing wholesale redecoration. I discovered a collection of sheet music in Dora's room, and yesterday I felt a desire to rekindle my musical interests. There is a piano in the drawing room and although in need of tuning it is a superior kind of instrument. I sorted the music, selecting from the easier pieces.

Elsie felt it necessary to interrupt. 'Miss Dora never allows anyone to touch her piano.'

I ignored her.

'Miss Dora is most particular that no one should interfere.' She muttered something about my cousin's playing. 'As sweet as a fen thrush,' I believe she said.

I felt a surge of irritation. 'I'm sure Dora was matchless on the pianoforte, but my aim is recreation and enjoyment, not competition.'

'Miss Dora hates it when anyone goes near…'

'It is *my* piano.'

She took out a kerchief and dabbed her eyes.

'It's *mine*. And however *ill* my efforts might sound, I shall bang on its keys when ever I like.'

She gave me a bleak look before turning to go.

'I'll be darned if I don't play it at midnight,' I called out for good measure, 'should I feel like it.'

Thinking about the ghostly weeping at the dead of night, I wonder if the raised voices in Dora's room have somehow awakened her spirit. On reflection, it seems more likely that it is *my* psyche that is disturbed, given that yesterday, I made that mistake of revisiting old emotions. For the truth is, as a girl, my father made me feel useless, playing the piano. For the first time since coming here, I conjured up his thin disapproving face, the shake of his head, the way his lips would narrow into something approaching a sneer. Nothing I did was ever good enough. I believe my quarrel with Elsie was the result of troubles carried from my past. I was too touchy, too like my *old* self. For, as I keep insisting, the past is nothing to me. I am making a *Fresh Start*. There is no need for any bitterness at Angel's Seat. I shall apologise to Elsie and all will be well.

September 12th

My days are as smooth and lovely and pleasant as my dream of England promised to be. The sun filters through the leaves of the aspen outside my boxroom as I awake from an afternoon nap. Shadows tremble and light flickers in random patterns across the walls. This prolonged hot weather has prevented the proper season from declaring itself. Everything is warmed through to the bone. At this moment I'm relaxed and almost happy.

But my nights! Sleep is disturbed and it's making me so weary. Every night I try and extinguish Dora's lament. Is it a dream or a visitation? It seems to drag me to consciousness, always in the deepest, quietest part of the night. How much I want this wearisome ghost to quit and go! Intruding on me from the past, she hauls in old hurts, old unresolved conflicts from my former life. She is spoiling my *Fresh Start*. She insists on ruining the sublime peace I have found here at Angel's Seat, destroying my fantasy of security, tranquillity, home.

September 19th

I am keen to move into a proper bedroom. Firstly I considered cousin Alec's room. Lined with books and paintings, it is gracious and welcoming. Underfoot there is a jewel-like oriental rug of some antiquity and value. There are velvet drapes across all apertures and a fine marble washstand with a white jug and bowl. A painter's easel rests in a corner while a small telescope is trained on the garden. His sketchpad, full of drawings of birds, lies undisturbed on the window seat.

I sat at his writing desk today and read all of his correspondence. Most interesting was a scribbled note in a feminine hand, undated but judging by the yellowing of the paper, rather old. 'Loved one,' it reads, 'it's impossible. I could never live at Devil's Seat.' At the bottom is an initial, which is undecipherable, scrawled within a heart.

Cousin Frank's former upstairs quarters are very different. They are untidy and unloved and today I began clearing them.

His is the largest bedroom running across the front of the house. It has generous proportions and from its high windows it's just possible to perceive, below the pale blue horizon, the deeper azure of the sea. I found some sacks in the barn and I filled them with Frank's clothes, his boots and shoes. I added his cufflinks his shaving gear and his hair oil. His only other possessions are mountains of ledgers, business documents and letters appertaining to the farm. They're all minutely kept and filed. I examined the most up to date and it is clear that Frank had serious debts and a shortfall in income. There are lawyers letters and a tentative suggestion in writing from Mr Howlett saying that he knows of the difficulties faced by Mr Richardson, and can he be of assistance in the disposal of some of the land? All of this seems to be without value or significance to me. Consequently I have gathered all the papers and files together with the other possessions and I have thrown them all away. After Elsie leaves I intend to light a bonfire behind the stables.

September 21st

Elsie said less than I anticipated about the disposal of Frank's belongings. Instead she punished me with an exposition on the recent history of the farm and its problems. Despite my attempts to appear uninterested, she told me that Frank was obstinate in the face of failure and worked like a slave on the place, eighteen hours a day, determined to keep it going. He believed that to lose the farm would be to let down his father. Unable to afford help, he drove poor Dora out in all weathers, laying hedges, harvesting, cutting hay. She was never allowed a holiday. Once, just once, she proposed a trip to Holland to see the bulb fields but he refused to let her go. Poor Dora. She was up before dawn each morning to see to the milking. 'And what did she have to show for it?' Elsie held up and examined a fine silk blouse of mine, which she was busy ironing. 'She had to make do with *worn out* clothes.'

I looked away.

September 22nd

Phew! Elsie has been very garrulous again. Today she talked about Alec, saying he was much less 'pliable' than his sister and that Frank was less successful in bullying him. She said that after his 'disappointment' he became more and more morose and his depression (my word, not hers) deepened to such a level he never left the farm. Instead he painted, worked a little, read. He foreswore all company.

'What did he die of?' I asked. I knew there was no point in trying to change the subject. I remembered that odd yellowing note I'd found in his writing desk.

'A broken heart.'

I was interested again, my resolve weakened. Try as I might to shut out the past, I can't help but be intrigued by Elsie's history of my cousin's personal relationships.

She sighed. 'He lost his lady love.'

I felt the urge to tease her. 'I thought you were his lady love, Elsie.'

She blushed and when pressed admitted that she'd loved him. 'Yes Miss, I did as it happens, but that's neither here nor there.'

As usual, she was very keen to tell the story. To my surprise, I discovered that Alec, years ago, had been in love with Patricia Howlett, the mother of the agent who'd handled the leasing of my fields. I thought about the mysterious note but I didn't mention it. For some reason I didn't want to admit I'd been reading Alec's letters.

I referred to Peter Howlett's visit. Elsie shrugged. 'He got what he wanted. He got them fields in the end.' She told me years before, Frank had refused to break up the farm for the sake of Alec's relationship with his mother.

'Alec wanted money from the farm?' I asked.

'Yes, he wanted to get out of here and marry Patricia. She was a flighty thing then, bonny mind, in a useless yellow-haired sort of a way, and a good dancer. Alec and her, they wanted to set up home in the town. He gave her his mother's ring. A beautiful diamond and emerald cluster. By rights it was Miss Dora's.'

I imagined a fashionable pair, well dressed and sophisticated. Patricia, no doubt, would have been as out of place on a farm as Queen Mary, in her fox fur and high heels. But Frank refused to buy Alec out, refused to give him his share. They had a fight about it in the lane. 'A real fight. Alec got a busted rib and a broken nose.'

'So what happened?' I thought about the note again. 'She broke it off?'

Elsie said that Alec's bones healed but he never got over it. Patricia, on the other hand, quickly married someone else. 'You see, Miss...' Elsie seemed to be opening up to me in a new and confidential way. 'Alec loved Patricia like men do. But Frank, he *loved the farm*. It only makes sense if you understand that. He loved this place more than... more than...'

'More than life?'

'You don't understand, Miss. This place was his heart and soul, it was...'

'Oh, I do understand,' I assured her. 'I feel the same. There's nothing in the world I want more than Angel's Seat. Coming here has made me... it's made me absolutely happy and complete.'

She stared at me, astonished.

I wanted to add 'I was lost and now I'm found' but at that moment I remembered my nights, so I said no more.

September 28th

Alongside the sorrowful noises, my father now interrupts my nights. My father! Stern and unlovable he stares at me from the depths of my imagination and his face is full of disappointment. He asks, 'Why are you so weak, so talentless, so irresolute? Why are you so inept?

My contemptuous, my dismissive father is *here*. God help me! I thought I had escaped him. He wanted a son of course, but my brother, my twin died at birth and then my mother followed him. That paternal accusatory stare haunts my dreams, reminding me that I was a poor substitute. With no proper heir and his wife cruelly taken – he never forgave me.

September 29th

Today I ventured into Dora's room. It's so ordinary, I can hardly believe it's the source of my anxiety. Unlike Frank's bright room (soon to be my new room!) it faces north. Built into the eaves, the ceiling slopes at one side. Dora used a single bed, a narrow wardrobe and a delicate dressing table that stands in the window. A crucifix is nailed to the wall and the floorboards are bare. Impersonal and bleak, the most comfortless area of the house, it smells of damp, despite weeks of hot weather.

I opened her wardrobe and looked through the clothes. They are old and dowdy. I fingered the folded underwear and stockings in a chest of drawers. My cousin was a woman with clean, neat habits. Moving over to the dressing table I sat in front of its triple mirrors. I touched the plain hairbrush and comb. Dora's hair was grey.

Regarding myself critically in the glass, I see that I've lost weight. There are dark circles around my eyes through lack of sleep. I opened the little drawers and found two brooches, not to my taste and an old envelope, folded over. Inside were a photograph and a ring. The latter is valuable. It is an antique cluster of diamonds and emeralds set in gold. I remembered what Elsie had told me about such a piece. The photograph is definitely Alec and Patricia because their names are pencilled on the back. They look as I imagined them. She is blonde and pretty with knowledgeable eyes and a firm mouth, while Alec looks like me. We are almost identical. I am a true Richardson!

I believe that Dora requested the ring back, after Alec's funeral. Why do I think this? Because Alec, with his proud, broken heart would never have asked and acquisitive Patricia would never surrender anything unless approached directly. Another thing... I feel that Patricia (this sharp-faced little blonde woman) never wore the ring. Unlike Alec, she doesn't look like a person prone to nostalgia, sentiment or regret.

October 2nd

For the first time since my arrival in England the sky is persistently cloudy and grey. The weather report tells me it has been an unusually long summer but now I look out on a wall of rain. The yard is a small sea and beyond the flowers droop and totter. The sky is no longer wide open, but heavy and clogged and ominous.

Marooned indoors, I decided to practise the piano. I began with Beethoven's *Moonlight Sonata* and because I know it very well, I was able to invest my playing with much emotion. When I'd finished I was startled to find I had an audience. Both Peter Howlett and Elsie were standing in the doorway! They began applauding. I covered my burning cheeks with my hands.

'Bravo!' he declared.

'That was *beautiful* Miss,' said Elsie, wiping a tear from her eye. 'I never imagined...'

'She's been hiding her light under a bushel, has she?' expostulated Peter Howlett. 'Well, we'll have to put a stop to that!'

'Oh, I'm no good,' I stuttered. I was mortified. 'Please come in and sit down.'

Elsie took away Mr Howlett's raincoat and sou'wester. He seemed less reserved than last time. His trousers steamed as he stretched out his legs to the huge fire, warming his toes on the fender. He was pleased to accept a reviving glass of brandy. We discussed business, or should I say he told me about leases, tenures and emoluments while I nodded and watched patterns in the flames. Eventually, he asked me about Canada. He seemed less desirous of leaving than on his first visit and I thought at first it was because he was unwilling to face the rain. After we'd talked a while I decided it was because he enjoyed our conversation.

Indoors all was cozy and comfortable. Warmed by the heat and the brandy I became confidential. I told him that I'd never loved my father. He said he felt the same way about his mother. We discovered that they died on the same day, sixteen months ago, on different sides of the world.

I reminded him of his nervousness on his previous visit. He told me that he was terrified of Frank. Once, when he'd called and suggested the sale of land, Frank assaulted him and broke his arm. 'I was only trying to help. Everyone knew how it was for him here. I wasn't speaking out of turn!'

'He loved this place,' I interrupted. 'He loved Angel's Seat.'

He sighed. 'I suppose so. It's a beautiful farm'

'That's why he wouldn't let Alec marry your mother.' The words slipped out. I put my hand on my mouth, wishing I hadn't said them.

'So you *do* know about all that!' He didn't seem put out.

I poured him another drop of brandy.

He spoke with feeling. 'I'm sure Frank Richardson behaved disgracefully back then, too.'

I was cautious. 'I guess your mother couldn't face it. Taking on Alec without any money or property... I don't suppose she was used to...'

He was at once indignant. 'Who told you that?' He gulped his drink and grasped the arms of the chair. He stood up, preparing to go.

I apologised over and over. I knew that his mother's photograph, with its tight, greedy expression had influenced me. I smoothed the air in front of him. I was contrite. 'I really am very sorry.'

Mollified, he sat down again. 'I can tell you what happened.'

I picked up the tongs and laid some more coals on the grate. I sat on a low footstool, leaning towards him against the sofa. I smoothed my skirt in a ladylike way.

He talked of Frank's tyranny and his treatment of Alec and Dora.

'I know all this,' I murmured.

'I don't suppose you know the worst of it.'

I frowned, thinking of my nightmares. 'Murder, suicide, how bad can it get?'

He gave me a long look, as if trying to decide something.

I told him I'd tried to shut out the past since arriving at Angel's Seat, but that it had proved to be impossible. 'I know there's something wrong here. Something terrible. I've tried to make a fresh start... but maybe I've made a big mistake.' Thinking about my high hopes and the misery of my nights, I was emotional.

He took my hand for a moment then let it go. He didn't refer to recent events and the shotgun deaths. He went back again to the past. He said that his mother broke off the engagement with Alec, not because of his poor prospects, but because she hated Frank so much. When it became clear that Alec could offer no alternative but the farm, she finished with him once and for all. 'My mother wasn't a sentimental woman. She met my father quite soon afterwards.'

I thought of the note, of the words 'Devil's Seat'. 'Why was she... so vehement about Frank?'

Peter Howlett touched my arm once more, very delicately, then withdrew his hand. His explanation was shocking. He said that at the time when the quarrel with Alec was at its height, the harvest wasn't in. Frank was desperate. 'He called on Patricia and said that Alec wasn't fit to marry her, that he wasn't fit to marry anyone. He said that Alec was having unnatural relations with his sister Dora.' Peter Howlett put down his glass and bowed his head, as if ashamed.

I felt a jolt, a movement, as if the house shook. The terrible wailing and sobbing started up, louder than ever. I closed my eyes and tried to block my ears with my hands. 'You hear that?' I whispered. The cries pounded inside my head.

'What?'

'Someone crying?' Ice cold again, shivering and shaking, I thought I might collapse. I moved from the stool to the hearth rug. Trembling I picked up my glass and swallowed some brandy. It cut through me and made me shudder. I held my hands up to the fire.

Peter Howlett knelt down next to me and encircled me in his arms.

My mind raced and the dreadful crying continued, wretched, woebegone and insistent. 'Can you hear that? You must hear it!' I whispered. At that moment I had a vision of their rooms – Dora's bare, puritanical and neat, Alec's lived-in and pleasing, full of his hobbies his books. 'No!' I shouted loudly. 'Those two? Impossible!' The crying stopped. There was a silence. I could hear the flames in the hearth, the ticking of a clock, rain. I prodded my ears.

'Of course it was,' agreed Peter Howlett.

I freed myself from his embrace. The rain was easing. I felt an overwhelming sense of relief. 'You don't believe it?'

'No. Most certainly I don't.'

I stood up and straightened my hair. I blew my nose. 'Did your mother... believe him?'

'Not for a moment. She slapped his face.'

'Did she tell Alec what Frank had said?'

'No.'

Another wave of relief swept over me.

He coughed and hesitated. 'But then she made a terrible mistake. It was years later, after we went to Alec's funeral.' Sweating, he pushed his chair back from the blaze. 'She told Dora.'

'She told *Dora*?' I was horrified.

Numbly, I listened. The story was as I'd imagined. He explained how Dora had come to see Patricia a few days after the funeral and asked for the ring. His mother handed it over without comment but Dora was upset. 'Let's face it,' Peter Howlett said, 'Her brother had just died and she wasn't herself. She accused my mother of breaking Alec's heart. It didn't go down too well. My mother wouldn't take criticism. She thought it was a cheek, this woman coming to her door in overalls, smelling of the farm. She told Dora exactly what Frank had said.'

'I suppose she spared her no details?'

'No, none. She could be cruel, my mother.'

'My father was cruel,' I whispered.

October 3rd

Last night I didn't awaken during the dark hours. There was no crying, no sobbing and I slept through until morning, as peaceful as a baby. Oh, what relief! What bliss!

Yesterday, after Peter left, I sat down on Dora's hard mattress in her bare room, and talked to her. I said that everyone had always held her in the highest regard. The Howletts never believed the story and never repeated it. I went over to the window. A pale watery sun was trying to peek out from behind clouds. Ditches criss-crossed the fields, glittering like silver silken ribbons stitched on to a patchwork of varying greens. I felt that the earth was refreshed and washed clean by the downpour.

I turned back and faced the room. 'I know you did it, Dora,' I said. 'And I don't condemn you. Frank had lost the farm. I've seen the papers and I know there was no hope. You wanted a quick release rather than a slow and tortured journey. I don't believe you acted out of malice, whatever Frank might have said or done. I know you merely spared him pain.' I walked over to her bedside table and picked up her Bible. I examined her handwriting in the front. *Dorothy Wilhelmina Richardson born May 1886.* I opened the drawer and found a pencil. *Died May 1938*, I added. *Rest in Peace.* I replaced it. I made a decision never to interfere with this room again. It would always be Dora's room. I left, closing the door firmly. Poor, dead Dora.

This evening, for the first time ever, Elsie came in to say goodbye. 'I've made you a chocolate cake, Miss.'

'Thank you,' I said, surprised.

'Miss Dora would have loved your playing,' she admitted. 'She'd be pleased to know the piano is being put to good use.' She pulled on her coat. 'It must run in the family. Music. It's a gift from God.'

I believe we have crossed a bridge together. Elsie and I are no longer enemies.

October 13th

Autumn has arrived and the evenings are drawing in. The decorating is finished and I sleep in the big bedroom. Thankfully my nights are restful and undisturbed. I leave the drapes unclosed and my windows are panoramas of the heavens. These English stars are like God's spilt treasure box, a wealth of scattered diamonds in the sky.

I misjudged Elsie. This morning we made a victoria sponge together and when Peter came to tea at four, she joined us. It was a jolly party. I have increased her wages and she now has Sundays off as well as Wednesdays. Twice a week I cook myself little meals, just as I used to do in Canada, after my father died.

He is taking up less room in my thoughts. I tried to dismiss him entirely, shut him out, erase him – but this was a failure. I was naïve in assuming I could make a *Fresh Start*, for the more I refused to acknowledge my personal history, the larger he loomed. The more I denied him, the more insistent he became. Peter and I have shared mutual confidences about our unhappy childhoods and I understand now that *I am* a person with talents and accomplishments. At Christmas I am to play the piano in the village concert!

October 16th

I have planted out hundreds of bulbs. With Peter's help I am learning to be a gardener and I look forward to my first English spring. Yes, I have started anew but I have learned an important lesson. The tragedy here is *not* forgotten. My father *is* still with me, alongside Dora, Frank and Alec. I think of them often and I no longer declare that the past is nothing to me. Indeed the past is everything to me, like the present, like the future, like the changing of the seasons. Everything is connected, for this farm belongs to all of us, to me, my cousins and those future generations lucky enough to find themselves planted on this little piece of heaven on earth. Today I told Peter that Angels' Seat is the place where angels stop to rest, whenever they are sent on their tiring journeys around the world.

The Cairo Road

Robert Barnard

It is especially fitting that this book should include a brand new story from the pen of Robert Barnard since, just four months before publication, he became the latest recipient of the CWA Cartier Diamond Dagger in recognition of a long and distinguished crime writing career. Together with Reg Hill and Peter Lovesey, both of whom have also contributed to this volume, he forms a trio of Diamond Dagger winners born in 1936 – evidently a vintage year! Justly famed for his many novels, Barnard is equally adept at the short form and his two collections, *Death of a Salesperson* and *The Habit of Widowhood*, contain many gems. He has a sharply observant eye, yet writes with a lightness of touch that is as evident in this tale as in the rest of his work.

'Trade,' said Nathan, his scowling face darkened further by the overhanging olive trees, 'couldn't be worse.'

'Trade is rock bottom,' agreed Shem, clutching the sack.

'I don't know what this government think they're doing,' muttered Ehud.

'The situation for gentlemen of the road is abysmal,' said Shem, 'but I don't suppose any of them worry about that.'

Hunched in one of the clumps of trees that dotted the Jerusalem (via Bethlehem) to Cairo highway, they presented an unenticing spectacle. Shem and Ehud were lumbering figures, useful enough in a fight, useless in a chase. Nathan was gaunt, with an acute five o'clock shadow and a brooding expression which made most people including himself think he must be the brains of the gang.

'The truth is there's hardly been a soul all evening, and those that have been were obviously economic migrants or bogus asylum seekers.'

'That sort is next to useless,' said Nathan bitterly. 'They ought to be flattered we consider robbing them at all. All you get is a couple of brass denarii and a packet of sandwiches... Mind you, who wouldn't seek asylum in Egypt, rather than stay here under King Herod's benevolent rule? I'd go like a shot if I could get a lift. There's a country that's well run, stable, with plenty of people rolling in money that they're practically asking to be relieved of. Am I right or am I right?'

'You're right,' chorused Shem and Ehud, knowing their place.

'Whereas here...'

'Here anyone with money's been picked off by Herod as a possible rival. Show him a crowd of a thousand and he sees five hundred traitors and five hundred possible rivals.'

'That's what you get,' said Nathan, 'when you have a ruler who's not even a Jew.'

Shem and Ehud thought about that.

'But he's sort of Jewish, isn't he?' asked Ehud.

'He's got the religion, but not the certificate from the Racial Purity Board,' said Nathan, who collected odd little facts.

'Pity it's not the other way round,' said Shem.

'That would suit you, wouldn't it?' said Nathan. 'I saw you two nights since dining at the White Meat Eating House.'

'So what? I just fancied chicken,' protested Shem.

'The meat you were eating had never flapped a wing,' said Nathan sardonically. 'The High Priest would have had your guts for garters if he'd considered you one of the Faithful.'

'I'm as faithful as the next man,' said Shem. 'I've just never been that worried about my diet.'

'All you worry about is getting what you fancy, which is mostly food and sleep. You'll never be a first-rate bandit because you're too soft in your lifestyle.'

Having delivered himself of this damning verdict he turned on Ehud, who had been silent for more than a minute – always a bad sign: if he was thinking he couldn't talk, and vice versa.

'So what's up with you, Socrates?'

'Nothing, what should be up?'

'You're holding yourself a bit apart. Not matey, that.'

'I'm under the weather. I haven't been too regular lately.'

'You were regular this morning. Too bloody regular. It sounded like a volcano erupting. Oh well, it can wait. You'll soon tell us what's biting you.'

And ten minutes later Ehud ended his exile and came over to the other two.

'There's talk in the souks.'

'Oh yes?'

'Talk about Herod.'

'There's always talk about Herod. If a man has had ten wives, mostly simultaneously, there's plenty to talk about.'

'This isn't sex. It's violence.'

They were unimpressed.

'Can't even say it makes a change,' said Nathan. 'Not with his record. If it was you or me it would be mass murder, but if you're a king it's called strong rule. So what's the little charmer got up his sleeve this time?'

'They say he's planning a cull.'

This took even Nathan some time to digest.

'A cull?' he said at last. 'Has High Priest Aristobulus ordered him to slaughter all pigs?'

'Not animals. Human beings – they say he's going to slaughter all the first-born sons of Israel.'

'That's rank sexism!' protested Shem. 'Why not all the first-born daughters? Or say fifty-fifty?'

Nathan had been thinking.

'When you first said violence I wondered if there mightn't be something in it for us. And you know there could be. It would be easy work.'

'Easy work!' said Shem. 'Anybody'd think you'd never met a Jewish mother!'

'If they could be persuaded to bring them to some kind of centre it would be a piece of cake. We would call it a clinic maybe.'

'With the gossip that's going round? No way. Even without the gossip they'd smell a rat. Herod and rats seem to go together.'

'True… What's behind it, then?'

'Oh, he's got hold of some magician, some soothsayer or other.' There was a general groan.

'The curse of the ruling class,' said Nathan.

'Someone called Belisarius is feeding him stories about plots and conspiracies, forecasts of future prosperity if he does this or that, future disaster if he does the other. Herod calls him his Prime Minister.'

'All these newfangled titles,' grumbled Nathan. 'Why doesn't he call him his charlatan in residence?'

'Anyway, the Prime Minister says he has become aware of a new star in the sky, which signifies that a child has been born who will rule the people of Israel.'

'I don't see a new star,' said Shem.

'Course you don't,' said Nathan. 'You never look at the sky unless you're dead drunk and horizontal. Go on, Ehud.'

'Well, naturally Herod's not best pleased. He's going to have a general cull of new-born boys, just to be on the safe side.'

'Sounds logical,' said Nathan. 'Nasty, but logical.'

'They don't call him Herod the Great for nothing.'

'He calls himself Herod the Great. Nobody else calls him anything printable.'

'He'll need a big workforce,' concluded Ehud, 'and he'll pay well for the job.'

'They always say that when dodgy jobs are in the offing,' said Nathan. 'I've experience of jobs like this, believe you me. They employ trash to do it, promising rich pickings because they're "just the men for the job." Then, when it's done they say: 'Oh no. You're just trash. We don't pay top rates to trash.'

'Are you saying we're trash?' Shem demanded.

'Of course we're trash. If we were caught on one of our usual jobs, Herod wouldn't even bother to crucify us. We wouldn't be worth the nails or the wear and tear on the timber. He'd tie us in a sack and chuck us in the Jordan.'

'Still,' said Ehud, harking back to the cull, 'it'd be money.'

'Oh yes, a bit,' conceded Nathan.

'Damn sight more than we're getting on the road.'

'True,' Nathan conceded, regretful at giving the idea the thumbs-down. 'But think of the aggro and the awful reputation we'd get. Baby-killers? Practically anyone in the country would sign up to do a bit of tit-for-tat killing. Everyone loves a baby, particularly when someone else is holding it. At best we'd probably be chased out of Jerusalem.'

'Or, worse, not allowed to leave it,' muttered Shem.

'On consideration, I'd say we shouldn't touch it with a barge-pole,' concluded Nathan. 'I'd rather bide my time, hoping for the Big One.'

'Waiting for Mr Jack Pott?' asked Shem.

'If you like.'

'Mr Jack Pott never comes, in my experience,' said Ehud.

'He's got to come some time,' said Shem.

'There you display your entire ignorance of the laws of gambling,' said Ehud.

'One day he's going to come by,' insisted Nathan. 'And then, why shouldn't it be us who picks him off?'

'And why shouldn't it be this little group coming from Bethlehem?' asked Shem.

'Because nothing worth having comes from Bethlehem,' said Ehud. 'Well, for whatever reason, they're in a bit of a hurry.'

They gazed towards the point where the road dipped towards Bethlehem. Slowly breasting the brow of the hill were a little party, a huddled group the components of which could not easily be discerned. The omens for a jackpot did not look good to the other two.

'They may be in a bit of a hurry,' said Nathan, 'but if they're having to go at foot-pace to Cairo, Herod the Great will be a couple of dates in a history book before they get there.'

'There is an animal of some kind,' said Shem, 'but they're having to go at the pace of the walker.'

'Obviously they've got a beast that can't bear two,' said Nathan. 'Probably a dromedary with a back problem.'

'We could put it out of its misery, along with the others,' said Ehud.

'Very attached to its misery is a dromedary,' said Nathan. 'Only one way of separating it from it.' He and Ehud laughed.

'We haven't decided to kill them yet,' said Shem, who had no taste for slaughter.

'Toss for what to do,' said Nathan. 'Heads we relieve them of their goods, tails we relieve them of their lives as well.'

'And rim we let 'em go in peace and brotherhood,' said Shem. Nathan tossed. The coin landed in the sand with the face of

Augustus Caesar pointing towards Ehud and the reverse pointing towards Nathan.

'Rim it is,' said Shem. 'No blood this time.'

'I vote we suspend judgment till the party gets close,' said Ehud. 'Course we do,' said Nathan. 'It was just a way of passing time.' 'Until Mr Jack Pott arrives,' said Ehud.

'This is not Mr Pott,' insisted Shem. 'He'd never ride a beast as slow as that one.'

'It's probably some poor family from some far-flung outpost of this great Roman province who've been to register in the Census,' said Nathan.

'Put your cross where the nice man tells you, and don't argue if you don't want a sore back,' said Ehud.

'All in the cause of psephological accuracy,' said Nathan. 'Which is pretty funny since we never have elections.'

'Speak for yourself,' said Ehud.

'Wait – the picture is beginning to get clearer,' said Shem. 'The man walking beside the beast is wearing a rough blanket or piece of sacking around his shoulders.'

'Surprise, surprise,' said Nathan. 'He's one of the Great Rural Unwashed. A ploughman, a carpenter, a crude metalworker.'

'That kind of person can stash away a goodly sum if he's careful,' said Ehud.

'Maybe. But he wouldn't bring it to Jerusalem for the Census, would he?'

'And he wouldn't wear his best overcoat either,' said Ehud regretfully. 'Or maybe the man holding his hand with the pen in it would decide he hadn't been paying enough taxes and he'd be justified of relieving him of his astrakhan. Either way, whether he's a rich yokel or a poor one, we're not likely to benefit.'

'That's right,' said Shem. 'And the most likely thing is that he's a poor sod with no money, hardly any possessions and... wait a bit... The one riding is a woman.'

'Figures. It's a family.'

'And she's holding a baby. The man is leading the beast – it's a donkey—'

'Just as cussed as a dromedary,' said Nathan.

'—because she can't cradle the baby and hold the reins.'

'Typical of our rural poor,' said Nathan. 'They can't adapt their meagre skills to the needs of the labour market.'

'She's feeding it. It's a nice picture, isn't it?'

'Look nice on a Passover card,' said Nathan. 'Hey – what say they've heard the rumours about a cull and are getting out in time?'

'Too bad,' said Ehud. He and Nathan laughed cynically.

'Remember the coin,' said Shem. 'It fell on the rim.'

'Oh Gawd!' said Nathan. 'We said it was just a way of passing the time.'

'Remember what you said about the popular feeling towards baby-killers.'

'I was talking about a mass cull in Jerusalem. They'd never know who did a one-off on the Cairo Road... That starlight's bright, isn't it? Never known it so bright. We'll get a good look at the bags on this side of the donkey.'

Bathed in a silver, ethereal light the little caravan approached. Ehud began to get excited.

'There's bulges,' he said.

'She's feeding the babe,' said Shem. 'You never seen them before?'

'Bulges in the personal luggage. Look, the saddlebags are just sacking like the man's coat. You can see the outline of everything they've got with them.'

'Including bulges,' said Nathan thoughtfully. 'Look at those three bulges towards the tail, will you.'

They all did, but Ehud for one expressed bafflement.

'Sort of squarish,' he ventured.

'Squarish,' agreed Nathan. 'Wouldn't you say ornamented in some way, especially the lids?'

'They're the family utensils,' protested Shem. 'Saucepans, pots, canisters – that sort of thing.'

'Would you expect a family like that to have highly-ornamented?' demanded Nathan.

'Well, why not? Maybe he's a metal-worker like you said, or has a friend who is... What do you think they are, anyway?'

'I think they are caskets,' said Nathan.

'Caskets? Well, so what? Same difference.'

'Caskets beautifully worked in rich metal, holding rich gifts.'

'Yah!' jeered Ehud. 'You've gone soft in the head. What would that couple be doing with rich gifts? Are you saying their baby will be Lord of Israel?'

'No, of course not,' said Nathan impatiently. 'How would a rural clown like that sire a great ruler?'

'She makes a lovely mother,' said Shem dreamily. He deeply approved of motherhood and apple-pie and all the sentimental ideals of the world. 'A woman like that could produce a boy who could do anything!'

'Get real!' said Nathan contemptuously. 'But what if they're travelling with it for someone else? The local big-wig, for example. He'd be an obvious target for such as us, but the local carpenter or whatever would get past unscathed.'

'What are we discussing them for, then?' asked Ehud.

'Because we're sharp-eyed and intelligent – one of us, anyway,' said Nathan. 'Trash though we are, socially speaking. And because they've packed stupidly, with the precious things pointing outwards, and showing.'

Shem wasn't taking that.

'We're so sharp-eyed and intelligent, one of us anyway, that what we saw was probably pewter boxes with a bit of fancy art work on the lid, and inside the family supply of dried mutton, matzos and dates from the family orchard. Or maybe one contains the family bible, with a family tree stretching back to King David, or another contains his mother's wedding shift. Anything is possible, so why are we guessing? I'd rather play Pass the Parcel. Anyway, it's all academic now.'

'What do you mean, "academic"?' asked Ehud.

'Useless and unprofitable speculation. They've gone past. Or do you think it's worth running after them?'

Nathan looked, surprised, at the little group progressing toward Cairo.

'Well, they've not gone far.'

'And what do you think they'd do, when three hulking men started running after them? That donkey, with the mother and babe and the three supposed caskets, would discover a surprising turn of speed and would be over the horizon in a twinkling. The best we'd get would be the man. Fancy his sacking overcoat, do you, Nathan?'

Nathan sighed.

'Give it a rest. It was just an idea. I was just passing the time. We're no worse off than we were before.'

'And no better,' said Ehud.

Perhaps. And then again, perhaps not. After all, if there is a niche in Purgatory for sinners who were saved from committing terrible sins worthy of a more dreadful place by a combination of sloth, incompetence and lack of nerve, perhaps all three had won a place in that niche that night.

Meanwhile the donkey, and the baby and the gold, frankincense and myrrh – as inappropriate as most Christmas gifts – proceeded slowly on the road to Cairo.

GAMES FOR WINTER

ANN CLEEVES

In last year's *Crime in the City* anthology, when introducing Ann Cleeves' 'A Rough Guide to Tanga', I mentioned her excellent story 'The Plater'. Just after that, 'The Plater' was one of five tales nominated for the prestigious CWA Short Story Dagger. Such recognition is well-deserved, as Cleeves has emerged in recent years as one of our most consistently entertaining crime writers. Her work derives much strength from her love of the countryside and her passion for the environment. The latest novel, *Burial of Ghosts*, is undoubtedly one of her finest achievements – and this story is, I think, another. It has a chill that matches its unusual Alaskan setting.

He flew into Stillwater in late January at sunrise on a clear day, so his first view was of flame-coloured mountains and forests heavy with snow and tinged with pink. There was no wind and the ride in the small plane from Juneau was as smooth as sailing on a lake. Although in summer there was a boat every week, in winter flying was the only way in. Stillwater was as remote as any island.

They touched down earlier than the schedule and there was no one to meet him. The pilot lifted down his bags on to the runway, then got back into the plane and took off. Mark watched until it flew away over the horizon. It was very cold standing there, and brilliantly clear. No noise, not even birdsong. The runway and a couple of huts and one road running off into the woods. A back-drop of mountain. The blinding light reflected from the ice, and sharp black shadows.

A dog barked and a woman bundled in a parka that made her look as fat as she was tall came out of the closest hut.

'Hi there.' The dog had followed her and was dancing around her legs. 'You're the new teacher.' Close to, he saw she was middle-aged but striking. Red hair under the hood, a wide Cheshire cat mouth.

'Yes,' he said, aware of how English his voice was, thought that even one word sounded clipped and pompous. 'Mark. Mark Arden.'

'Well, hi Mark. Pleased to meet you. Sally-Ann Larson. My daughter's in eleventh grade. Let's go into my office and I'll get you some coffee then phone around and find out what's happened to your ride. Welcome to Alaska.'

He met Sally-Ann's daughter the next day in school. She was sitting on the front row in the class for the older students. The school took children from kindergarten through High School. There were forty of them all together, three full time teachers. Mark was an extra, part of a cultural exchange programme. Usually he taught in an inner city comprehensive in Newcastle, not very far from the suburb where he'd been brought up. He was twenty-six and needed a challenge. There'd recently been a messy separation from the girlfriend he'd had since college.

Beth Larson was sixteen, blonde and freckled, though as she stood to recite the Pledge of Allegiance, her feet apart, her hand on her heart, she looked so earnest that he thought she seemed younger. She had the same wide mouth as her mother. As they sat down he saw a moose in the school yard, grazing leaves from a nearby tree. It shook its head and the loose skin, which hung like a collar round its neck, moved too. The kids took no notice.

He asked them to introduce themselves in a piece of writing, 'as if you were introducing the characters in a story.' When they read out their work he thought how different they were from the students he'd taught at home. One boy boasted about his skill with tractors, another described a summer fishing trip. Beth placed herself in the kitchen at home helping her mother baking for her father's birthday party. *He works most of the week in Anchorage,* she wrote, *so it's always special when he comes home.*

Mark thought it was as if he'd gone back in time. These children seemed to belong to his grandparents' generation. In some respects, however, the settlement's philosophy was surprisingly contemporary, liberal. He'd expected a backward community. Red neck. Hunting and shooting and isolationist. But many of the residents of Stillwater had moved there from the city because they were looking for a better way of living. They were idealists, who'd cleared a patch in the forest and built a house out of logs for themselves and their families. They cared about their community and their environment. In the dark winter evenings they attended book groups and nature groups. They watched arty films in the school hall and put on plays. They didn't bother much with the television because the reception was poor and anyway most of it was trash, but many did listen to the World Service on the BBC.

In the summer, he supposed it would be different. Then tourists came to camp in the National Park and took boat trips into the bay to see the wildlife. The hotel would open again. But in the dark nights of winter the people of Stillwater made their own entertainment.

Mark lived with Jerry Brown, a young man from Seattle who worked as a ranger in the National Park. They shared a little house which was reached by a track through the trees. It had a porch looking over a bit of cleared meadow to a frozen stream. Jerry had moved to the community two years before and adored it. He said it was the only ethical way to live. He had a share in the Larsons' cow and took his turn at milking her. He led the conservation group. At home he was relaxed and friendly. He liked to drink beer and smoke a little dope, play very loud rock music. After all, he said, there was no one to disturb. Only the bears and it was probably a good thing to discourage them. He seemed to Mark to be as naïve and friendly as the children.

Mark walked to and from school, unless there was heavy snow. He enjoyed the exercise, the sting of the cold against his face and in his lungs. One afternoon he walked home and stopped by the jetty to look over the bay to watch the setting sun on the glacier. Cormorants stood on the wooden railing. The lights were coming on in the scattered homesteads on the opposite shore. Despite the cold, he must have stood there longer than he'd realised, because when he turned away from the view to continue, he saw it was almost dark. There were stars and a moon like a thin, tilted smile. Someone was walking down the straight road towards him. It was Beth Larson. She stood beside him, looked out at the jetty.

'We swim from there in the summer.'

He felt uncomfortable being there with her. She was standing very close, whispering almost into his ear.

'It must be cold.' He knew he sounded ridiculous and stamped his feet to cover his embarrassment. The temperature had dropped as the light went.

'Sometimes we go skinny dipping...'

He imagined her in the summer sunshine, with her gold hair and gold skin, flashing like a fish through the water.

'You should get home,' he said. 'Your mother will be expecting you.'

'She's visiting Mary Slater. You know how they talk. She won't be home for an hour. The house is empty. Come back. You could help me with my school work.' Though her voice made it clear that wasn't at all what she had in mind.

He actually considered it for a moment. He wondered later what had stopped him and decided it had nothing to do with ethics. A fear of being caught.

'No,' he said. 'I don't think that's a terribly good idea.'

'You will,' she said. 'By the end of the winter when the boredom's set in, you'll be begging me by then. Only I might have changed my mind.'

Then she ran off, her boots making only a rustling sound in the new snow. She disappeared into the darkness and he could make himself believe that the encounter had been a figment of his imagination. Back at the house, Jerry was caring for an injured surf bird he'd picked up from the shore. He had put it in a cardboard box and was feeding it pilchards from a tin. Mark would have liked to ask his advice about Beth Larson, but he seemed engrossed in his task and the moment never seemed to arise. Although Mark's students in Newcastle had been precocious, none of them had propositioned him, and he told himself he must have misinterpreted what had occurred.

That night he dreamed of Beth Larson. In the dream it was summer and he was swimming with her. She rose out of the bay, pulling herself up on to the jetty and water dripped from her hair and ran over her body. He was about to reach out and touch her when he woke. In class the next day she was sitting in the front as usual, serious and polite. He found it hard not to look at her, to remember that she had been available to him. He lost himself in daydreams.

The following weekend it was Valentine's Day and all the community came together for a pooled supper and party. All the adults at least. The kids weren't invited. The food was supposed to have an erotic theme and they'd had fun with hot dogs and mounds of rice curved like breasts and strangely shaped fruit and vegetables. All very innocent, no doubt, but Mark felt uneasy. The evening wasn't what he'd expected. He had thought these people would lead simple and unsophisticated lives, had imagined himself even as a missionary from the civilised world. But even though they wore jeans and hand knitted sweaters and thick woollen socks they talked about artists and writers who were only names to him. They made *him* feel like the country cousin, gauche and uneducated.

It didn't help that he found it hard to concentrate on the conversation. They were talking about a student who'd drowned in a boating accident. It was almost exactly a year since his death. The water had been so cold, they said, that he'd had no chance to survive. The shock would have killed him in seconds. Jerry, who was there too, made little effort to join in. He sat on the floor, leaning against the wall, a can of beer in his hand, watching them. Even in this setting he was a scientist. Mark did try to take part in the discussion, but the party was being held in the Larson house and he was distracted. He imagined Beth upstairs in her room. When the heating pipes gurgled, he pictured her taking a shower, the water trickling over her shoulders into the tub. There was no water pressure in any of the houses in Stillwater so it would dribble slowly, across her belly and between her legs. Finally he made his apologies and left. Jerry offered to drive him, but Mark said he preferred to walk.

Outside, the cold took his breath away and he stood for a moment gasping, snorting out a white vapour through his nose. The stars were hidden by cloud and there were occasional flurries of snow. The lights from the house saw him through the trees to the road and then he switched on his torch. There was no sound except for the squeaking of his feet on the compacted snow, and that seemed very far away because of the fur hat pulled over his ears. He walked on, past the school and the gas station. Everywhere was in darkness. He was approaching the turn off, the track which led to Jerry's house when he heard the sound behind him, a roar that made him think of an avalanche or water released from a dam. Here, surrounded by trees, it didn't occur to him in that first second that the noise might be manmade.

Then he realised that it was the sound of an engine being revved very hard, revved to screaming point. Head lights flashed through the trees. In the dual beams he saw that it was snowing more heavily now. He jumped off the track into the trees just in time as a white pickup screeched past. He had stepped into a drift and the snow had gone over his boots and inside his socks. He was climbing out when the pitch of the engine changed and the headlights were turned again towards him. The truck only paused for a moment, then roared back down the road, the way it had come, spraying loose snow from the wheels, sliding when the driver touched the brakes to round a corner. Mark could not tell whether or not he'd been seen. He had the ridiculous thought that he might have been a target.

At school on Monday, he called Dan Slater back after class. The Slaters were the only family in the community to have a white pickup and the parents had been at the Valentine party. Outside, the other kids were standing around in the yard. That was unusual. It was too cold, even in daylight, just to hang out. Their presence unnerved Mark, though they couldn't possibly hear what he was saying. Dan was fourteen, very young for his age. He had problems with simple reading and writing. At home they would have said he had special needs.

'Were you driving your father's truck on Saturday night?'

Dan blinked, looked out of the window, stared at the ceiling.

'Sure,' he said. 'He lets me.'

'You were driving very fast. You could have hurt yourself.'

Outside, the kids seemed to lose interest. They were starting to drift away. Mark felt more confident. He'd worked with dozens of students like Dan. He spoke gently. 'Weren't you scared, driving like that? What made you do it? It wasn't a race.'

'Not a race, no. Sometimes we race. But not last time.'

'What then?'

'It was a game.'

'What sort of game?'

'I guess it was a dare.'

'Who dared you, Dan?'

But Dan wasn't prepared to talk any more. He pulled the strange, little-boy-faces he made when he was concentrating in class, shuffled his feet and stared out of the window. Finally, Mark let him go.

When Mark got home, Beth was waiting for him. They never locked the door and she was inside the kitchen, sitting on the rocker in front of the stove, moving backwards and forwards. He'd been surprised to see smoke coming from the chimney as he'd approached, had thought Jerry must be back earlier than usual from work. She'd taken off her boots and her outdoor clothes, put a cassette into the recorder. When he opened the door she stood up. She'd changed from the clothes she'd been wearing in school. Her jersey had a slash neck and was very tight. Her jeans could have been sprayed on.

'I thought I'd give you a second chance,' she said. 'I've seen the way you've been looking at me in class.'

He stooped to unlace his boots. He knew he should make a light hearted remark and send her on her way. Nothing too heavy. He had to live here for the rest of the year. He couldn't afford to upset her or her parents. But he was flattered too. Excited. She walked towards him, moving her hips in time with the music and she grinned, thinking in his moment of indecision, that she had him hooked.

'Is this a dare too?' he asked.

'What do you mean?'

'Like Dan stealing his father's pickup and racing round the tracks.'

She didn't answer.

'You do know Dan could have killed himself?'

She began to struggle into her coat. Although the grin seemed fixed to her face, there were tears on her cheeks. She tried to push past him, but he stood with his back against the door, pressing it shut. He took her by the shoulders, felt the bones under her thick coat, remembered other bones, another woman. He whispered into her ear, as she had whispered to him on the jetty, and his voice was seductive too. 'Just how far would you have been prepared to go, Beth? What exactly did they dare you to do?'

'Nothing,' she said. 'It was just a game.' She scrambled out of his grasp and he let her go, feeling suddenly ashamed. The last of the sun caught her hair as she ran away down the track.

That night he dreamed of her again. In the morning her school desk was empty.

'Does anyone know where Beth is today?' he said, looking around the classroom. They stared back at him, challenging him to ask more. Whatever game was being played, they were all in on it.

'Her mother phoned in to say she's sick.' It was Peter, the boy who knew about tractors. He was thick set and sullen and Mark had come to the conclusion that he knew little about anything else.

'Who told you that?'

Peter shrugged, not caring whether or not he was believed.

While the children were eating their lunch, Mark went to the Larson house. Sally-Ann would be working in the booking office on the airstrip and Beth's father was in Anchorage. On his way there he wondered why he was going. Was he looking for an excuse to see Beth on her own? He decided he was worried about her, though what on earth did he think could have happened to the girl?

He found her outside. She was in an open sided barn splitting logs with an axe. Mark watched her from the yard. The axe was heavy, and she struggled to lift it, but her aim was exact and the blow was powerful. He thought how strong she must be, stronger than him. The wood split with one go and the splinters scattered, bouncing on the concrete floor. He could smell the resin from where he stood.

'I thought you were sick,' he said. He waited until she was resting. He didn't want to scare her while she had the axe in the air. It would have been easy to cause an accident.

She didn't bother replying.

'Tell me about these games,' he said.

'Why?' Her voice was bitter. 'Do you want to play too?'

'I want to understand.'

'It's winter,' she said. 'Boring. We have to do something.'

'It has to stop. Someone will get hurt. Tell them. If it doesn't stop, I go to the principal. And to your parents.'

She turned angrily to face him, allowing the axe to crash to the floor.

'People have already been hurt,' she said. 'They won't stop.'

But the next day she was back in school and he thought he'd handled the situation well. She'd have passed on the message to her friends. There would be no more foolishness.

He stayed at school late that evening for a staff meeting, and then to prepare a lesson for the following day. He was the last to leave the building and it was already dark, though there was enough of a moon for him to follow the road. Past the gas station, Jerry's was the only house. There had been a slight thaw and he'd been aware all day of the sound of melting snow dripping from roofs and trees. Now it had started to freeze again but he felt as if he was being followed by the same persistent sound. He stopped once and still it seemed to be there, coming from the trees on either side of the road. When he shone his torch there were strings of icicles on each branch, quite frozen. It began to unnerve him and he wondered if it wasn't water after all, but the scratching of animals in the forest. There were brown bears. Everyone had stories about them, stealing food from outhouses, staring in through windows. They were only dangerous, people said, if they were cornered. He had never quite believed that. He walked more quickly. The sounds came nearer, gathering around him, closing him in.

Close to the turn off to Jerry's house, panic made him stumble. As he pulled himself to his feet, he swung the torch behind him and saw two figures on the road. They were wrapped in coats and hoods so he couldn't tell who they were. Each had a stave in one hand, a piece of wood as thick and solid as Beth's axe handle. They banged the sticks in rhythm on the frozen path.

'Hi!' he called, relieved at first to have company. 'Who is it?' But before he had finished speaking he had realised that they weren't there to help him. He turned to continue on his way, but another moving shape had appeared on the road ahead of him, blocking his path. For a moment the scarf he was wearing slipped and Mark recognised Peter, the tractor driver.

More figures approached, moving through the forest. He circled, shining the torch crazily around him, catching glimpses of them, hooded like ghosts. The noise they made didn't come from the natural sound of footsteps or crackling undergrowth. Each held a stick that he knocked against tree trunk or branch, disturbing the snow lying there and shattering icicles. It formed a strange percussion, at once hollow and brittle, which grew louder and louder. Mark jumped from the road into the trees and started running, sucking in the icy air in huge, howling gasps.

Roots tangled about his legs. The ground was uneven. There were frozen pools and outcrops of rock. Branches whipped into his face and upper body. And always he was aware of the noise around him and behind him. At last, when he was too exhausted to continue he curled into a ball behind a pile of dead undergrowth. His muscles twitched from the exertion and he was still wheezing, but he forced himself to stay silent. He listened.

The dull thud of wood against bark had stopped. There were footsteps but they seemed to be dying away. Desultory scraps of conversation grew more distant. Someone laughed. It seemed that the game was over. It was too cold and uncomfortable for them. They'd had their amusement. They'd go home to a wholesome supper, an evening of television or computer games. And in the morning they'd sit at their desks daring him to speak of what had happened. He'd over-reacted of course, which was just what they'd wanted. He'd made a fool of himself. He had believed that they meant to hurt him. He wasn't sure he could forgive them. Especially, he thought, Beth had betrayed him. She would have to pay for his humiliation.

Although it had seemed as if he'd been running for miles, he saw, when he could think more clearly, that he wasn't far from home. There was a faint light at the end of a clearing which must be their house. If he'd not panicked he could easily have made it back to safety before the children caught him up. Jerry would be cooking. He'd promised potato pancakes with apple sauce. It was the night, Mark thought, to open that bottle of Scotch he'd brought with him. What a sight he must look, all scratched and bruised. He began rehearsing a story of the incident in his head. How could he explain it? As a joke at his own expense, perhaps. The rookie Brit teacher spooked by a bunch of kids.

They were all waiting for him in the house. He didn't realise until he'd pushed open the door and by then it was too late. Peter came round behind him and wedged it shut. They were sat on the floor round the walls, the sticks and baseball bats propped beside them. They had all kept very quiet, like the guests at a surprise party. He wondered if there had been the same nervous giggling. Now nobody laughed. They looked up at him and stared.

'Come on, kids,' he said. 'This is a joke, right?'

'Not a joke,' Beth replied sternly. 'A dare.'

'You should go. Jerry will be here any minute.'

'I'm here already,' Jerry said. He slipped out from the bedroom. He looked as he always did when he got in from work. Relaxed and gentle. He wore a plaid shirt and jeans and held a can of beer in his hand. 'It's my dare. I mean, I get bored in winter too.'

'You dared them to frighten me off?'

'Oh no,' he said. 'They dared me. To get rid of you. Without too much fuss. Before you could tell anyone about our games.' He looked around at the staring children. 'What shall it be, guys? A boating accident like last time? Or something more imaginative?'

The children picked up the sticks and began to batter them, the same rhythm over and over again, against the wooden floor.

PERSONS REPORTED

Mat Coward

Mat Coward has recently published a couple of novels, *Up and Down* and *In and Out*, but (like Edward D Hoch and Jerry Sykes) he remains best known as a specialist in the short form. A regular contributor to the CWA's annual anthology, and to many other short story collections and magazines, Coward lives in rural Somerset and seized the chance to write a story with a setting in the countryside. From its wonderful opening line to the very end, 'Persons Reported' is typically fresh and distinctive.

My grandfather, for instance, created an entire religion based upon chips. He's lived just about all of his life round here, where he was born, but at the start of World War Two he found himself in London with one leg longer than the other and a slight criminal record.

He became a fireman for the duration, and on the night of the 29th December 1940 he was on duty in East London. All around him, the capital burned. Thousands of buildings were destroyed in that long night, scores of civilians were killed and hundreds injured. Entire streets were flattened; entire neighbourhoods rendered lifeless and unrecognisable.

Grandad's unit was charged with guarding a particular church. I can't tell you its name – I'm not sure if he's ever mentioned it to me, and if he has, I've forgotten it – but I do know that it was given special attention because it was a historical building of great beauty and cultural value.

He and his mates passed the time between alarms eating bags of fish and chips from a chip shop which stood next door to the church, and was open for business as usual. All night the flames came nearer to Grandad's church, and were fought by other crews, but they never quite reached it – until, late in the morning, when the bombing had stopped but the fires continued, a piece of burning timber fell from the roof of an adjacent funeral parlour, and slipped through an open transom window into the vestry. Grandad's crew went into action at last.

As dawn's revelatory light crept over a skeletonised City – a thousand years of history, they say, atomised in one night – and as that great city's people emerged from their cellars and tunnels, and looked around at their suddenly horizontal landscape and said to each other, 'If this is the worst he can do, then he's lost already.' Grandad and his comrades gazed in amazement at the scene before them, seeing it clearly for the first time. And Grandad had his moment of revelation.

The ancient church sat smoking, in ruins, its charred innards displayed, amid a street in which no building had survived above cellar level; no building but one, that is, for the chip shop still stood, even its windows intact.

'And I knew as sure as I knew the names on my ration books,' Grandad told me years later, when he was no longer sixteen but I was, 'I knew that God had spoken; that God had chosen between the sacred and the mundane; that God had let the church burn, while he saved the chippy.' He crumpled the vinegary paper into a ball and threw it on to the back seat of his ex-wife's car. 'Now, young man,' he said to me. 'Nevermore let me hear you say, 'Oh no, not bloody chips again.' For when you say that, it's not me that you hurt – it's God.'

The worst thing about being older than thirty is the knowledge that if anything exciting ever happens to you again, it'll likely be something involving an ambulance or a fire engine.

I get up at four every morning, and forty minutes later I leave the flat I share with Grandad, shutting the door behind me as quietly as I can. I walk along the balcony of our block, across the graffiti-decorated walkway and then down the piss-scented stairwell. It takes me almost five minutes to reach the outskirts of the largest council estate in the county, at which point I turn left past the garage block, across Old Meadow, where Wellington boots are essential eight months of the year, into Cheap Street – a short, snake-shaped street of sagging, mediaeval shop fronts, mostly unoccupied, and Tudor inns – over the stone bridge to my workplace where my shift begins at five.

Since I was little, I have always been mad about animals, the way some boys are about cars, and I first took employment at the poultry factory because I thought it would be fine to work with turkeys, them being such interesting beasts. The smell you get used to after the first few years, but the noise comes as a new shock every morning.

The factory stands alone, amid enough fields to cover a page in a map. From the bog window, on tiptoe, you can see across the valley to the Mendip Hills, a view uninterrupted by a single manmade structure other than the mobile phone mast.

One morning in the summer, a new man joined my shift; a young lad, perhaps in his early twenties. He had a Scots accent and a limp. There is a good deal of hauling and lugging involved in our work, and I could see the foreman watching the new boy with a sceptical and anticipatory look in his eye.

About an hour before the bell, the Scots lad appeared at my bench carrying a large box of twisters and asked me where he should put it.

'Just stick him on there,' I said, 'down the end.' When he'd done so, I offered him my hand, which he took. 'Callum Shepstone,' I told him.

'How do, Callum. I'm Joel.'

'Fancy a quick half at lunchtime, then?'

He smiled and said he did. 'I'm spitting feathers,' he said, and I chuckled – not as if I hadn't heard it before, which would be condescending, but as if he'd told it well.

At the Think Tank, not long after one o'clock, I got the first round in: for me a pint of light, one cold one not, and lager for Joel. 'There you go, mate.' I said, setting his beer before him. 'Establish a relationship with that.'

'Cheers,' he said, and we drank the first two quite fast.

He didn't have a lot of conversation to offer, but he did seem happy to be in company. I asked him where he was from, and he said, 'Can you not tell from the accent?' I asked him what brought him here, and he said, 'Oh, you know – fancied a bit of country life.' He looked around him at the pub: its low, beamed ceiling, its great fireplace, its diamond-shaped windowpanes and its dull brass. 'This is nice. Feel like I should be drinking cider, not lager.'

'Not at lunchtime,' I said.

I didn't want to talk to him about his disability, but I felt duty-bound to raise the matter. 'Listen, Joel – I don't know if you noticed, but during the shift I saw the foreman was—'

He nodded. 'Yeah, he had his eye on me, didn't he? Me being the new guy, I suppose.'

'Thing is, last couple of years, they've gone mental on what they call modernisation – which in English means fewer people doing more work for the same wages.'

'I don't mind working,' he said.

'I'm sure you don't, but – not meaning any offence – they might reckon you're not fast enough.' I nodded at his bad leg. 'Wrongly, of course, but that's the way they might think.'

'Ah, right.' He said nothing for a while, drank his beer, then he said: 'Accident, you know. Few months ago.'

'Oh, right.' I waited to see if there was anything else. There wasn't. I drank a bit more. 'You ought to see my grandad about that.'

'Your grandad? What is he, a doctor?'

'No, nothing like that. He does a kind of alternative therapy. He calls it anti-faith healing.'

'Anti-faith?'

It was a hard thing to explain, to someone who hadn't lived with it all his life. 'Anti-faith, because he says you couldn't possibly have faith in something so daft. He tells his patients, 'Now this isn't going to help you at all, understand? This is just a placebo. Can't possibly do you any good.' Charges them a token fee, then he sends them off to see their GP.'

Joel was laughing now. 'And does it work?'

'Works perfectly,' I said. 'Precisely as advertised.'

We didn't exactly decide to make an afternoon of it, but that's what we did. We went back to Joel's place, a rather flash barn conversion on the edge of the village.

'Rented,' he assured me.

'Even so – very nice. Do you live here alone?'

He didn't hear me; he was in the kitchen, getting some cans. When he came back into the living room, I repeated the question.

'No, I live with my girlfriend.'

We opened the beer. 'She at work?' I asked, at the same moment that he said she was probably asleep. 'She work nights?'

'Sorry?'

'Your girlfriend – she asleep because she works nights?'

'Oh, yeah. Does your grandfather have a beard?'

'No, he's clean shaven. Just not very often.' I didn't ask him why he'd asked; there's no law against inconsequential questions.

'No sign of a girlfriend?'

'I wasn't snooping,' I explained, 'but the bathroom shelf looked thoroughly male. Shaving foam, men's deodorant. No women's stuff at all.'

'Ah…' Grandad thought about it as he peeled the spuds.

When I was growing up we ate chips six nights a week, even after the local chippy shut down. There were various observances. Chips on Monday to give thanks, chips on Tuesday to be humble, chips on Wednesday to mark the middle, chips on Thursday to give us strength, chips on Friday for luck, chips on Saturday with a pickled egg to see off the week. On Sundays, we'd go visiting if we could, so there was generally a bit of cake.

Soon as I left school and started earning, I took over the shopping, so we eat a more varied diet now. Our nearest proper food shop these days is seven miles away, and it's open twenty-four hours a day. They call it a convenience store, which it would be if it were at the end of our road. I am especially fond of the flavours of the East, and Grandad'll have a go at anything. That's his motto: 'I'll try anything twice, I will.' Though generally a tolerant man, he has no time for those who will only try anything once. He calls them reactionaries, and even bigots.

'You could ask him round for his tea,' Grandad said as he dished up. 'This Joel boy. I'll make some chips.'

'All right. I'll ask.'

'Ask them both, Callum,' said Grandad. 'Him and his girl-friend.'

Joel lasted just under the month at the factory, before they gave him his cards. His timekeeping was satisfactory and his atti-tude was beyond reproach, they couldn't deny that, but his work rate was slow. So they said. Me, I reckon they just like to sack someone every now and then to keep in practice.

'You should sue them,' I reckoned. 'Unfair dismissal.'

'Nah, forget it,' he said, finishing his pint. 'We've not got a union, it's not worth it. You need a union for all that. Anyway, I don't need the work. It's just something to keep me out of the pub during daylight.'

'Does your girlfriend work?'

'What?'

'Has your girlfriend got a job?'

'Nope – she doesn't need to work either.'

'Can't be bad,' I said, and left it at that.

He finally came round for his tea that Sunday. He'd been asked before, but one way or another it hadn't happened. Whatever his financial position, I think losing his job had depressed him. He seemed quieter than before. The idea of spending a few hours as a guest appealed to him, I think. 'What'll we have?' he asked.

'Curry and chips.'

'First rate!'

He turned up alone, saying his girlfriend would be along later. While the curry was bubbling, Grandad entertained with his genius for pickpocketry. He would pat our guest on the back, or feign the removal of a spider from his ear, and each time he did so he would say, 'Well I always! What have we here?' and he would unfold his hand and there would be a watch, or a penknife, or a bunch of keys.

Joel enjoyed the performance immensely, and never gave any hint that the things that the master pickpocket produced from about his person were, in fact, things which he had never owned. Nobody ever does, of course. Even if we knew people capable of such rudeness, we'd hardly invite them round for their tea.

'Where did you learn to do that, Mr Shepstone?'

'Call me Stones. Ah well, I've not always been the upstanding pillar of the community I am today. Now, where's that girlfriend of yours?' By now, it was half an hour after the time we had planned to eat. 'Do you want to give her a ring?'

'In fact, she wasn't feeling too good earlier, so maybe we'll just start without her, if that's all right.'

'What did you say her name was, that you forgot to mention?'

Joel said: 'Have you a girlfriend yourself, Stones?'

'Not at the moment,' said Grandad. 'None of them round here got the energy, and I can't be bothered getting the bus.'

I passed him the cider. 'He does all right. Don't you, Grandad?'

'Oh aye?' Joel smiled. 'Bit of a ladies' man, Stones?'

'I never had no complaints.' Grandad got up to put the chips on. 'Leastways, not in writing.'

The girlfriend never did turn up, but a pleasant evening was spent with Grandad's war reminiscences. Chips went down lovely.

When Joel had gone, Grandad said: 'That boy's not heading for a good place. He's been burned, but he don't talk about it. He's had treatment before, obviously, but he won't have no more. And his girlfriend's invisible. You need to keep an eye on that one.'

'All right, I will. How do you know he's been burned? Not got rammed by a forklift, say or—'

'I seen every kind of pain, Callum, before you were born and before your parents were born. Between one birthday and the following Easter, I seen every kind of pain they ever invented. I knows which is which. That boy's been burned, and I have especially seen burns.'

'How do you tell, though?'

'We're none of us unique, you know,' he said, 'each in our own special way.'

We washed up, and finished the cider. We put the telly on for the local news.

'How do you tell?' I asked.

'You look at the mouth. If the eyes won't tell you, and the gait won't tell you, you look at the line of the lips – he'll tell you.'

'When they're eating their chips?'

The newsreader said: 'And that's all the news in the West tonight.'

'Ha!' said Grandad. 'That's all the news you know, you mean.' We turned the lights off. 'You keep an eye on that one.'

'I will, Grandad.'

'I can't do it – I'm busier than a pig with no legs.'

'Well, how busy is a pig with no legs?'

Grandad looked at me like he used to look at me when I was a kid, and a bit of a handful for an old man to look after. 'You ever seen a pig with no legs relaxing on a beach? No, well there you are, then.'

A couple of days later, I went round to Joel's place after work. I found him in the garden, reading a book.

'Any good?'

'It's about whether the Chinese discovered America.'

'Well,' I said, 'they must have discovered it by now, surely?'

He didn't have any beer in the fridge, so he made us a cup of tea. I'd spruced myself up a bit after work. 'Fancy going out?'

'Where to?'

I shrugged. 'Bristol, whatever.' He wasn't keen. 'I'll drive,' I said. 'Won't take ten minutes to fetch the car.'

'Nah, I don't fancy it. Not today.'

'Maybe you've got plans,' I said. 'With whatever her name is, your girlfriend.'

He almost lost his temper than. 'Do you want to meet her?'

'I'd love to meet her.' I didn't see any gain in backing down. Simple fact was, if he really had killed her, he needed a friend more than ever.

'Is that it? You want to meet my girlfriend?' He bashed his mug down on the patio and some of the tea leapt out. 'Have you got a girlfriend, Callum?'

'No,' I started to explain, 'I was seeing this girl from the DIY superstore, but she got—'

He interrupted me, so he never found out whether I was going to say transferred, pregnant or rabies. Perhaps he wasn't interested.

'I'll give her a ring.' He fished his mobile out of his jacket. 'Tell her to meet us here, right now, because Callum Shepstone's been asking after her.'

On the other hand, I didn't want to cause friction. 'Don't trouble her on my account, Joel, I expect she's—'

'She's in London all this this week, as it goes, but I'll get her to drop everything and rush back in a taxi because Callum bloody Shepstone and his sodding grandad—'

'Let's go for a walk,' I said. 'That doesn't cost anything.'

We walked past the empty shell of what had briefly been a DIY superstore, past the new dormitory housing development, across some fields, past the old quarry, and through a wood which is disputed common land. It was a still day, and we could hear the army exploding things off in the distance, and smell the chemicals from the barn of a farm we walked by, down an unmade road; a barn twice as big as the DIY place.

'Does your grandad do that anti-faith healing for a living, then?'

'No, he's retired now, but he used to be a TV repairman.'

Joel frowned, as if he thought I might be playing a joke on him. 'How do you mean?'

I'd forgotten how young he was. 'Well, in the old days, they used to have men drove around the place in vans fixing folk's TVs that had got busted.'

Now he nodded, slowly, and he smiled. 'I know what you mean. Like knife-grinders, and that.'

'Yeah, something like that.'

'I love the countryside,' he said. 'I think it's great. I'm glad we came here, anyway.'

We stopped by the power station, to watch the ducks. Someone at work said he'd seen an otter there a couple of weeks previously.

'Did he have a special cry?' Joel asked.

'Who?'

'Your grandad, in the old days. When he was a TV repairman with his horse and cart, did he have his own old street cry. Like, you know, cockles and mussels, alive alive-oh.'

I thought Joel seemed to be having quite a hard time lately. 'Yeah,' I said. 'He used to cry "Rediffusion".'

Grandad held up three fingers to denote the number of possible explanations he felt there were for Joel's invisible girlfriend. 'She never existed, or she's left him, or he's killed her. You got any more?'

I shook my head.

Grandad said: 'Except, maybe if she was in the fire too, she's terribly disfigured and can't stand to have people see.'

'If he was in a fire,' I said, 'why doesn't he mention it?'

'Maybe he's traumatised by it. Can't talk about it.'

'He's got no money now. When he first got the sack, he had plenty of money, but he's run out now.'

It was late evening, a hot evening, and we were sitting on the allotment, drinking gin and tonic. Grandad was smoking his pipe, and I was smoking a very small joint. It kept the worst of the gnats away. Off to the south, up on the rise, we could still see the

earthmovers and the big crane, though more as shadows now
than as solid things.

'All that down there, that used to be apples, when I was a baby.'

'I know.'

'Bloke that had that, I forget his name, he kept a donkey, and it
used to let me smooth it. She: it was a jenny. I was the only one
could smooth her, she was wild enough.'

'All gone now.'

'Then it was pick-your-own, you remember that? First wage
packet you ever had, four years old, helping that fat woman – I
forget her name – weigh the strawbs.' He tapped out his pipe.
'Too far from the main road, that was.'

'Wind farm,' I said. 'How many staff they got on one of those?
Enough so they need a supermarket, do you reckon?'

'If things are to stay the same,' said Grandad, 'then everything
must change. You know that saying?'

'Only from you.'

'Well, just because you haven't heard it, don't mean it's not
true.' Grandad stood up, flicked his slice of lemon into the black-
currants. 'You'll have to get him round again. It's time for him to
receive the chip into his life.'

'You reckon that'll save him, Grandad?'

'How can it?' said Grandad. 'It's only chips.'

He was poor and depressed, next time I visited him, and the
thing about that pair is, they stick together. They are always
there for each other. I couldn't do much about the poverty –
other than get some shopping in for him, some beer and beans
and that, and then undercharge him for it – but I hoped that a
bit of company might ease the depression.

'She's left me,' he said, not out of the blue exactly, but from
behind a can of lager, late one evening. 'I'm sorry I've been such a
misery, but it was a shock, you know?'

'When did she leave?'

'Not long after we got here. Just after I got the job at the poultry place, in fact. The thing is, I can't afford to stay here. The rent, I mean. But I really want to stay around here, I love it here.'

'There's a couple of empty flats on our estate,' I said.

He looked up. 'There are?'

'Mind,' I cautioned him, 'if they're empty, they're empty for a reason. They're not exactly out-of-town barn conversions.'

The three of us had a little flat-warming party, after I'd helped Joel squat one of the empty flats, a few blocks down from us. We drank some decent cider, and Grandad gave us his Blitz story. Joel was much taken with the fact that the chip shop stayed open all that night.

'That's true, that is,' said Grandad. 'Throughout the most sustained terrorist attack in modern history – which lasted for most of a year, and during which tens of thousands died, and many more were made homeless – the British people went about their business as if nothing were happening. Nowadays, as we know, people take a markedly less stoic attitude towards far more minor events.'

'I was in a fire, once,' said Joel.

'Is that right?'

'At my father's house. Few months ago.'

'Was your girlfriend in the fire, too?'

Joel drank some more cider, and smiled to show that he knew he was an idiot. 'There never was any girlfriend. I made her up.'

'Best sort,' said Grandad, and we all relaxed a bit.

We went back to our place and had some chips. 'The best thing about a theology based on chips,' Grandad explained, 'is that it's easy to let go of. If you live your life according to something more powerful than that, it can be hard to shrug it off when the time comes to do so.'

Along the walkway, I'd seen the pair of them from behind, both limping; walking side-by-side, the old man on the right, limping to the left, the young man on the left, limping to the right. Looked like a pantomime cow having a fight with itself.

I had to ask him. His leg obviously wasn't getting any better. 'You signed on with a doctor down here, Joel?'

He just said, 'I can't,' and wouldn't be budged on the matter.

'You could see our doctor,' said Grandad. 'He's not a bad kid, he knows his stuff.'

'Sorted out your Post-Traumatic, didn't he, Grandad?'

Grandad made a fair-enough face. 'I sleeps better than I have since I was a boy, I will say that.'

Waving a hand in front of him, shooing a fly, Joel said: 'I just want to stay here. I love it here.'

Grandad chose that moment to tell Joel that if things were to stay the same then everything must change, and the conversation diverted along a different course.

Being in the squat cheered Joel up some, and meant that he had a bit more money for the pub, but his leg wasn't getting any better, and he was beginning to find the stairs a trial. He and I spent quite a few evenings sitting on his tiny balcony, drinking cider.

He'd get either withdrawn or annoyed when I mentioned his leg, and so I stopped mentioning it. By association, I steered clear of the fire as well. I had the strong feeling that he wanted to tell me more, but since I didn't know which bit it was that he wanted to tell me, I couldn't do much except wait.

One night, about a fortnight after he'd moved into the flat, we were sitting out there as usual, when he cleared his throat and said: 'The house was a write-off. Total rebuild job.'

'Nasty. Was anyone else hurt?'

His pause was so long I thought the subject had been dropped, but eventually he said: 'My father died.' I didn't say anything. I passed him the cider and he topped up. 'I'd been up in Scotland, I'd come back to London early, and I just thought I'd pop round. See how they were doing, you know?'

'They?'

'I managed to get my stepmother out. But I took a fall, that's how the leg happened.'

'You got her out, though? That's a fine thing to have done. Saved a life.'

'What I should have done is called the Brigade first.' He smiled and passed the cider back. 'That's a lesson for you. If you've got a bloody mobile, bloody use it.'

I thought it was now or never, and never seemed far too long a time, so I said: 'If you won't see a doctor, you'll have to see my Grandad.'

'See Stones?'

'For the anti-faith healing.'

'You said that didn't work?' But he put a question mark at the end of the sentence, which made it sound hopeful.

'How can it?' I said. 'It's only chips.'

He swirled his cider round in his glass for a while. 'All right, then.'

There's no big build-up to an anti-faith healing session, because that would be contrary to the whole point of the thing. Grandad seats the patient in a chair – any chair, doesn't matter – and gives them a glass of something, while he goes into the kitchen and cooks the chips. When they're ready he sits opposite the patient, close up on a stool, and feeds them the chips, one by one. He gets them to blow on each chip as he holds it before their lips, to cool it, and he doesn't offer them the next chip until the last one has been chewed and swallowed.

Takes a fair while to eat a plate of hot chips that way, you'd be surprised.

Joel accepted the chip into his life. He was a little nervous at first, but he seemed to enjoy the chips. He kept his eyes open throughout; some do, some don't.

When the chips were gone, Grandad said, 'That's it. You've eaten a plate of chips. Big deal,' and, as always, placed the patient in the recovery position: sat in the armchair with an ashtray to his left and a glass of cider to his right.

'And that won't heal my leg?' Joel asked.

'How could it?' said Grandad. 'Potatoes, vegetable oil and salt. That's all. Got nothing to do with legs, has it?'

'Then why do people come?'

'Reckon you'd be better positioned to answer that than I would.'

Naturally, I've asked the same question myself. Because quite a few people do come. As far as I can see, they come because they've tried everything else and they are exhausted by hope. That time they spend eating the chips, they are relieved of all the burden of hope and faith; they know it won't do them any good, and so they just enjoy the chips, enjoy Grandad's gentle lack of mercy. Then they go home, and it's two birds with one stone because they've had their dinner, too. Bloody good chips; Grandad grows the spuds on his allotment.

'I hadn't really seen much of them since they got married,' Joel said, and we knew who he meant. 'They weren't expecting me. I didn't phone first.' He took a gentle sip of cider. He didn't smoke.

'Just as well you went round,' I said. 'Just as well for your step-mother.'

'Yeah.'

'You broke your leg,' I said. 'You couldn't have gone back for your father.'

'I didn't know he was in the house.'

Grandad looked at me, and I saw some of the old man's old pain on his face.

'Well, there you are,' I said.

'Lynne was delirious. Hysterical, really. I was in shock, I suppose, from the leg and that. Between us, somehow, we misunderstood. When I phoned the emergency, it went out as Persons Not Reported. You know?'

'I know,' said Grandad.

'Nobody on the premises.'

'You feel guilty about that,' said Grandad, not sympathetic but matter-of-fact.

Joel looked at him dead on and said: 'We both do.'

'Where was your dad?' I asked.

'He was in the bathroom. Had the door locked and the radio on. We never heard him, he never heard us. He was dead, of course, by the time they found him. Well dead.'

'How did the fire start?'

'She loves candles. Different scents and that.'

'Aromatherapy? Yeah, Grandad does that with chips.'

Grandad snorted. 'I do nothing of the sort. Chips are just chips.'

At the end of an anti-faith healing session, Grandad always sends his patients off to see their GP. He told Joel he had to see someone. 'You know that,' he said.

Joel said 'All right,' but neither of us thought he meant it.

When he'd gone home, I raised my eyebrows at Grandad, who shook his head. 'No,' he said. 'He can't let go of the hope, that's the trouble. He will do, but he can't yet.'

A week later, Joel fell down the stairs when he and I were on the way to the pub. He wasn't hurt, but you could see he was in pain. Grandad patched him up – plasters and TCP – but he knows a moment when he sees one, so when he'd finished he told me to bring the car round.

'You're going to have to take that leg to casualty, Joel,' he said. 'All I done is stop the blood and make the wounds sting. Last time I went on a first-aid course was 1941. That needs x-rays, I reckon.'

Joel thought about it for a long time. You wouldn't have thought there was that much to think about; it was only yes or no.

'All right,' he said. 'Callum, will you give me a lift?'

I gave him a lift down the stairs on my shoulder, and a lift into town in Grandad's car. We were still five minutes from the hospital when he said: 'This is it. Stop here, will you?'

Over the other side of the road was the police station. I turned off the motor, and waited.

'There never was a girlfriend,' he said, when he'd gathered his thoughts. He kept one hand on the door handle, as if he thought he might have to make a quick getaway. 'I didn't come down here with a girlfriend.'

'I know. You said.'

'I came down here with Lynne. My stepmother. I thought she could do with a rest cure, you know? She'd been in such a state since the fire.'

'What were you living on?' I asked, because I'd been wondering that all along.

'She had the life insurance. I had the house insurance. That was the way my father had worked it out. Before we left London, she persuaded me to turn it all into cash. Most of it.'

'That's an awful lot of cash. What if there'd been a – well, you might have been burgled.'

'She said there weren't any cash points in the countryside. It'd be simpler. We didn't want to be getting a taxi into the nearest town every time we needed to pay for something. If we had plenty of cash, we'd be able to really get away from it all, really have a rest.'

'And did you?'

'I took that job at your place, that's what went wrong. I was bored. Lynne panicked. She reckoned there was someone watching her when she went to the village shop. An old bloke with a beard.'

'Watching her?'

He was staring out of the window, at the police station. 'She hadn't told me, you see, not until then. Back in London, there'd been an investigator. For the insurance, yeah? They were trying to make out the fire was, you know, dodgy.'

'What made them think that?'

He laughed. 'Because of me.' He pointed at his leg. 'I didn't get that in the fire. All I got in the fire was a bang on the head, I got the leg years ago. I was – the expression is – I was known to the police.'

'When did she leave?'

'Like I told you, soon after I started work.' He slapped at his leg. 'She needn't have worried, eh? It's not like I had the job for long.'

I couldn't ask if he thought she'd done it. I couldn't think of a way of putting it that wasn't foul, so instead I said: 'And she took the money with her.'

He nodded. 'All of it, except what I had in my pockets.'

'Where do you think—'

'Don't know. I don't know if she had a passport, or what.' He turned to look at me, and I met his eyes as openly as I could because I could see that the next bit was the bit he wanted me to hear, more than any of it. 'You can stop your mind adding things up, if you need to. You can stop yourself seeing things if you look elsewhere.'

'I know. I know what you mean.'

'You just can't do it forever, that's all.' He got out of the car, closed the door, and spoke to me through the window. 'If I don't see you again, tell Stones – the power of the chip, you know?'

'You tell him yourself. I'll wait here for you.'

He shook his head. 'I don't know how long I'll be,' he said, and limped off across the road.

I phoned Grandad on the mobile. 'As far as I can see,' he said, 'if what he's told you is a true story, he's done nothing illegal. Why should they hold him? He's helping them with their enquiries, isn't he? Voluntarily, at that.'

'That's right, isn't it?' My grandad knows a lot about this and that, but of course he's no lawyer. 'It sounds right, doesn't it?'

'Also – the money from the house insurance, whatever's left, surely it's his by rights? He'll be able to stay round, if that's what he wants.'

Only if it's true, I thought, and I parked the car in a side street where I could watch the cop shop, and I readied myself to sit it out, to wait and see if Joel's story was true; because if it wasn't, the police would soon find the cracks in it.

It might be a long wait, but waiting itself would be no hardship. There was a chippy next to the police station and, of course, it was open for business and would be for hours yet.

STRANGER IN PARADISE

Judith Cutler

Judith Cutler began her writing career with short stories. In recent years, though, she has achieved renown as a novelist, with two distinct series detectives, Kate Power and Sophie Rivers. She has contributed once before to a CWA anthology with a fun story called 'Flying Pigs', which appeared in *Missing Persons* and attracted international attention. It is a pleasure to welcome her back.

The gates swung to and fro, to and fro, on their handsome gateposts. I closed them firmly. That was it, then. I turned and left.

There's nothing like redundancy and an unexpected bequest to make you change your ways, even when as a middle-aged widow you might be expected to be somewhat set in them. I would abandon London and go to live in my new country property. But when I looked at the cottage I'd been left, down in Withycombe Magna, where Exmoor confronts Dartmoor, I wondered if I'd made the right decision.

I'd have liked the cottage to be old-world, with one of those enigmatic names that tantalise you about their origins. In fact it was called Moor View, and wasn't at all the sort you expect to nestle between two national parks. It had neither thatch nor thick cob walls, having been built in the nineteen fifties, when English domestic architecture was not especially memorable. There were no close neighbours to settle me in and make me feel welcome.

Withycombe Magna itself was no picture postcard place. There was no romantic cluster of cottages about the village green, the church one side and the pub the other, with the flannelled fools of cricketers starting their Sunday in one, and progressing at last to the other. The rather squat church was at one end of the straggle of buildings sprawling along an unlit, unpavemented road, the pub at the other, with no green in between. There was a service just once a month: not much opportunity for socialising there. The pub was simply a drinking place for old men, with no hope of the enticing ploughman's lunches I'd hoped to enjoy after a long morning's tramping the moors. There was a village school, but that was in the process of conversion to a bijou country home for another incomer like me. At least there was a village shop-cum-post office, but that wasn't picture book either, with enticing boxes of fresh local vegetables tumbling out on to the pavement. No, it proudly proclaimed itself to be a Spar. A chain! I would have little compunction in heading for Taunton to find a proper supermarket.

One thing the village did have was a huge pair of gates. Not the sort of turreted affairs you associate with a stately home – though they would have been wide enough to drive a coach and four through – and not part of the village itself. They were supported by a most elegant pair of curved matching walls, beautifully graduated from about four feet at the outside edges to about six foot at the hinge face. In the cleanly pointed modern brick, each pier carried a granite oblong, incised with gold-blocked italic letters declaring the gates to belong to Paradise Mews. They and the wrought iron gates would have been perfect in well-heeled suburbia: in Withycombe Magna they looked plain odd. Since I knew no one to ask, I simply smiled at their absurdity every time I walked past them.

Moor View Cottage needed a lot of work doing to it, especially in the garden. It would have been easy to turn tail. But I don't like giving up. In any case, it would be a good entrée into the village to ask a local builder – if I could find one – to sort out matters of rotting window frames and drooping gutters. Meanwhile I took advantage of the remaining summer weather to tackle the profusion of greenery that shut out the light from the kitchen and dining room. The garden might resemble at a casual glance the hotch-potch cottage garden immortalised on a thousand jigsaws: in fact, any surviving perennials were tangled with couch grass and harboured a surprisingly vicious strain of stinging nettle.

I was filling my fifth plastic sack when I realised I was being watched.

Smiling, I glanced up, to see a cyclist, a rosy-cheeked woman somewhat older than myself, watching me closely. 'What are you planning to do with all that stuff?' she asked without preamble, her approach at odds with her appearance.

'In an ideal world I'd compost it,' I said, glad to straighten and hoping for a prolonged chat. 'But—'

'Oh, no. Not with all that squitch grass,' she said. 'Burn it or get it disposed of. You want to ask Mr Taylor at the bungalow by the phone box to take it away.'

'Thanks—' But I was talking to thin air.

At least if I spoke to Mr Taylor it would mean I had another acquaintance in the village. Total, two – Rosy-Cheeks and Mr Taylor, who turned out to be as cadaverous as she was rounded.

'Ah. I'll take away those Leylandii too, while I'm at it,' he said. 'No room for them in a garden that size.'

'I'll have to see if I can afford—' I began.

'I'll be round to cut them down first thing on Saturday,' he said.

And was.

'The garden feels very empty,' I ventured, meaning that I felt surprisingly vulnerable without the trees.

'Sometimes,' he said earnestly, hands on hips, 'everyone needs a good clear out. Shift all the rubbish. Be ruthless. Start again afresh.'

I nodded.

'You'll have an extra couple of hours daylight, and when you've dug in some decent horse muck you'll really start growing things. You mark my words.'

Was I surprised when four sacks of manure arrived overnight? Or when a bandy-legged old geezer, eyes mere blue slits in the crumpled face, turned up with a tape measure just as I was sitting down to my pasta supper on Monday? He stared at it disparagingly as I covered it against the flies that plagued me – they were on visiting terms from the cows in the adjoining field.

'It's no good you thinking you can have they uPVC frames,' he declared, 'because this here's a conservation area, see, and they planning folk won't allow them. So you've got to have proper wood frames, painted properly, like, none of your dark stain.'

'But the cost—' I protested.

'You can't leave them like that,' he pointed out, digging a

horny thumbnail into the hollow mess of my kitchen window frame. 'I'll order everything now and start third week in September.'

'Thank you – er—?'

'Henry,' he said enigmatically, pocketing his tape and notepad, and turning on his heel

I could afford it, whatever I'd said to Mr Taylor. The redundancy pay hadn't leapt into stocks and shares, but lurked dormant in a building society account. I'd better phone up tomorrow and to give my fifty days' notice of an intended withdrawal.

The following morning I found a freshly cut lettuce and a paper bag of late peas on my doorstep. Well, they were scarcely large enough to be a Trojan Horse. The worst the lettuce harboured was a pale green caterpillar, arguably more scared of me than I of it. All the same, it would have been nice to know who my benefactor might be. Rosy-Cheeks or Mr Taylor or Henry? I made a pilgrimage to Spar to see if I could get any hints.

Perhaps I'd been prejudiced before. Of course the prices were higher and the range much more limited than in a supermarket. But what I spent there, I'd save in petrol. Did I need ready-made dishes when I had all the time in the world in which to cook? I peered tentatively into the freezer chest.

'You don't want none of that frozen rubbish,' a voice hissed in my ear. 'You want to ask Mrs Gaye at the counter about proper meat.'

There were a couple of women peering at shelves and queuing at the post office counter – I didn't know which had spoken. Nonetheless, I acted on orders and did just that. It seemed it was possible to order local meat, delivered to the shop fresh by the farmer down the road. And chickens. Organic!

'Eggs?'

Mrs Gaye looked shocked. 'I can't compete—' she began.

I almost switched off. She was going to talk about supermarkets and bulk buying, wasn't she?

'—With the eggs sold at the roadside,' she finished. 'Mrs Collarcott's are best.'

'Where would I find them?'

She roared with laughter. 'You might find them in your garden! Her hens are the ones in the field behind your house, you see, and hens have a habit of laying where they shouldn't. Her house is along your lane – thatched, with pink-washed walls. You can't miss it, Helen.'

I didn't ask how she knew my name. I had more interesting enquiries to make. 'That'll be near those gates—' I fished.

'Now, were you wanting me to save you a paper every day?' she asked briskly. 'The *Times* is it? Or the *Telegraph*?'

I ordered the *Guardian*. Shaking her head, she gave a sad smile and wrote in her book. I might have been back with my grand-mother, watching the shopkeeper write in an identical ledger. I'd be very surprised if I got the paper of my choice.

'And what fish would you like for Friday? A nice bit of cod?'

'Salmon?'

To my amazement, she raised her eyebrows, and touched the side of her nose. 'From the river.'

I knew better than to comment. 'Tell me,' I said as I popped the few coins of change into the Air Ambulance box, 'who would have been kind enough to have left some wonderful fresh vegetables on my doorstep?'

'Could have been anyone,' she smiled.

So now I was provided with regular provisions and a daily paper, but I was still no wiser about my gifts. Or those gates.

Another inch and I'd have cared about neither, ever again. I was ambling gently home – on the correct side of the road, facing oncoming traffic – when a car approached me from behind so fast I was literally swept off my feet. Staggering, I just avoided the ditch. The car was a top-of-the-range BMW – plenty around in chic London suburbs, but a tad out of place round here, where if you went expensive you went four-wheel drive. It didn't take long to establish that Mr Beamer and Paradise Mews were intimately linked, largely because whoever I questioned would drop their eyes and fidget, like five-year-olds caught picking their noses.

A trip for autumn clothes took me into Taunton, and curiosity took me into County Hall for a look at recent applications for planning permission in the vicinity of my house. I came up with some story – largely true – about how I'd been left my home and had no idea what would happen if I tried to sell it. It must have been convincing. Despite mutterings about due written notice, the clerk produced various plans, none of which seemed especially relevant – replacement farm buildings, a new telecom mast, that sort of thing. At last I asked point blank about Paradise Mews.

'Drawings submitted by Mr Crompton Gledstone?'

'Yes. Those.' Now was not the moment to comment on his name, preposterous as his proposals. Were the plans really for a stable? Well, horses and mews had a long and no doubt honourable association, though, like the BMW, were surely more what you'd expect in an urban setting. A mews was where posh city people used to keep their carriages, horses and grooms. Well, any groom tending his equine friends in these mews would have thought he'd died and gone, yes, to Paradise. As would the horses.

I had this naïve belief that horses were outside creatures. I'd seen them, even in the dead of winter, covered by those big waterproof capes, munching away in fields. Some even seemed remarkably hairy at that time of year – presumably they did as other animals did, they grew a thick, insulating coat of their own. Any horses in Paradise Mews would probably need shaving. Unless they were some sort of Arab thoroughbred, used to warmer climes, I couldn't see how they would cope with insulated walls and double-glazing, especially as there was space in a separate section rather larger than my kitchen for a central heating boiler. I'd heard that swimming was good for horses – but to build them a swimming pool? How silly of me – that'd be for the use of whoever resided in what was labelled 'Staff Quarters'. This was a suite of first-floor rooms running the entire length of the block: four double bedrooms, two of them with en suite bathrooms, a staff kitchen, and a staff sitting room, the picture windows of which offered views on three sides of the surrounding countryside. Someone valued his staff as highly as he valued his horses. How touching.

No, the clerk assured me: planning permission hadn't yet been granted. In fact, the plans had been rejected once and were to be resubmitted soon. As someone living in the vicinity, the clerk told me, I should submit my responses to the plans in writing before the next planning committee meeting.

I certainly would.

Crompton Gledstone. A name like that would have rung bells had I ever come across it before, but it didn't. Forgetting I'd meant to hunt down good thick tweeds and cosy sweaters, I headed instead for the library. I simply couldn't wait to get home to surf the Net: I wanted information now!

If I hadn't heard of the man, the financial press certainly had. Crompton turned out to be part of his surname, his given name being Giles. I've always thought that a nice, reassuring name – but clearly it was deceptive in his case. Mr Giles Crompton Gledstone, proud owner of the latest Beamer and Paradise Mews and also a property empire I'd never heard of, was not a nice man to know. He went round the whole of the country snapping up rural properties, either selling them to the sitting tenants at an enormous price or – in cases where his heart had been more tender – waiting for the tenants to leave (for some reason it never took long) and then leasing the cherished house out to incomers at prices no native villager could afford. He bought up shops and closed them, snaffled up pubs and converted them into exclusive restaurants. What an asset to the village he and his house would be.

I must put pen to paper before the council deadline. And also do some thinking.

Fortunately the thinking fitted in well with taming the back garden. Soon there were a dozen or so bags awaiting Mr Taylor.

As he loaded the last bag, he pointed out that my apple trees were diseased. I knew they were in poor condition – the few apples the birds had spared me were bitter and tough – but I didn't realise that cutting them down and burning them was the only solution. I spread my hands in horror – there wasn't enough room in the garden for a decent bonfire.

'You want to saw up the trunks and best branches for your winter fires,' he said. 'Can't always rely on the electric, you know, not if it snows hard.'

I swallowed. I didn't know I could use logs in that grim little fireplace, and I wasn't at all sure about the chimney. But I wouldn't panic – if I knew my villagers, he'd have a perfect solution. 'And the rest?'

'November's not all that long away – you want to get on to the Scouts,' he said, hefting the last sack of assorted nettles and convolvulus. 'Over Prestcombe way.'

'There isn't a troop in the village?'

'No hut.'

At last I could come into my own – all those years of planning and guiding projects could come into their own. 'Shouldn't we get together and build one? Not just a scout hut, but a proper village hall? We could raise some of the money ourselves with craft and produce sales and get sponsorship for events. I know about lottery fund applications and—'

To my amazement, he spat. 'There's one as wants to build us one all by hisself. At least, hand over the cash for others to do the work.'

I could tell by the expression on his face that any expressions of delighted surprise would be inappropriate. He was talking Mr Paradise Mews, wasn't he? Mr Compton Gledstone.

'Throwing his money around, as if that'd make any difference. Mind you, it might to them as matter, they say.' He gestured backhanders.

'This rich person – does he live in the village?' I asked.

'No! Owns half of it, maybe, but never shall he call it home, not if I have anything to do with it!' One further spit, and he was in his cab, pulling away. He stopped. 'And I'll send Fred Babcombe over at the end of next week to sweep your chimney.'

The following morning, I found runner beans and a handful of just-ripening tomatoes on my step. Rosy-Cheeks was cycling slowly past as I picked them up.

'I've got a fairy godmother,' I said, as she came to a gentle stop by the gate. I held up the evidence.

'Ah, my dear, that's right,' she said, wincing as she put her foot to the ground to steady herself.

I pulled a concerned face and hurried towards her. No wonder she was in pain – above the bandaging round her ankle purple bruises made their way up her leg. There was a playground type scab on her left knee. I suspected she wore those cotton gloves to conceal further damage.

'Are you all right?'

'No thanks to some,' she said.

'Not a black beamer?'

She started blankly.

'A big posh car? Nearly had me in the ditch the other day.'

'Maybe,' she agreed, pushing away before I could offer any more sympathy.

Next time I went to the shop, I managed to talk to Mrs Gaye about standing up and being counted, and not taking injustice lying down. OK, we'd been discussing a prominent court case, but she knew what I meant. Not wishing to push further, I paid for my cabbage and with a final word of regret that the village hadn't started to organise its own funds for a hall, left the yeast to work.

I'd thought, as a townie, I'd find the countryside quiet. Not a bit of it. Barn owls woke me sweating in terror each night; other owls merely called a polite 'to-wit, to-woo'. Dogs barked at whatever gave them doggy nightmares; the woodpigeons cooed an inane alarm call each morning. Sometimes at dawn or dusk I heard shots. Perhaps someone was as sick of the pigeons as I was, or was incensed by rabbits. Or perhaps, I joked one morning at the shop, as I picked up my inevitable *Times*, they were shooting pheasants.

'I hope they remember there's an aitch in the word,' I laughed, 'and don't start shooting peasants.'

The shop went very quiet. I'd obviously committed a dreadful solecism. Or had I? I'll swear someone winked at me, fleetingly, before they ducked down to pick up soap powder.

The other source of noise was farm machinery. Even I hadn't been naïve enough to expect horse drawn ploughs – why, back in the nineteenth century Hardy had written about mechanised threshers – but I hadn't expected the sheer size of the vehicles and their trailers of other attachments. Apparently these days farmers didn't own such plant themselves: they'd hire it, farm by farm, in rotation. If you came on one on the move, you might find yourself reversing a mile up a narrow lane to get out of the way. So, out of consideration to other road-users, many farmers moved them round in the late dusk or early dawn: huge diggers, enormous combine harvesters, mammoth ploughs.

It was time to write to the County Council about Paradise Mews. I made up my log fire – no hint of smoke, thanks to Fred Babcome, just the wonderful perfume of apple wood – and settled down. In keeping with the ambience, I tried to employ a pen and paper, but after all my years hurling words on to a computer, the only way I could produce a well-organised letter, outlining my objections to the proposed design, was on my laptop. What I wanted to say was that any fool could see the Council was being conned. Horses might occupy the ground floor of Paradise Mews for a week or so. But inevitably they'd soon find themselves in a field, their accommodation seized by the humans who'd intended to live there all along. I wanted to add a purple PS: *if the property is built and we suddenly find ourselves the proud possessor of a village hall, we shall know what to think.*

I said all those things, but in rather more diplomatic words.

The date for the Planning Committee meeting was announced. I put a notice or two up in the shop window, just to remind everyone. And, to celebrate the arrival of a photocopier at the post office end of the shop, I leafleted every home in the parish. When the evening of the planning committee meeting arrived, villagers gathered in Taunton in force, those of us with cars ferrying those without. Some of us made it into the council chamber; those who didn't waited outside, their hostility palpable. When Mr Crompton Gledstone was late, a rumour burgeoned that he was demanding a police escort. Perhaps he was refused one. At any rate, he never appeared.

The Planning Committee conceded outline permission, but demanded some major changes – not enough, however, to make it anything other than an extremely des res with a pretentious entrance.

To my surprise – after that initial passion, I was expecting people to chain themselves to railings or organise a lynch mob – many of the older villagers were very philosophical. We drove home soberly, but gathered in the bar of the George and Dragon: it seemed there was suddenly enough room for everyone, if they moved the tables out and wedged open the doors to the snug. Fresh sandwiches appeared as if by magic. In any other circum-stances, knocking back local-brewed cider, I'd have said we were celebrating something.

During the winter, my garden subdued if not conquered, my pantry shelves full of preserves and pickles bought at the now regular fund-raising events for our own hall, and living room greeting me warmly on my return, I occasionally took long walks. I needed the exercise, after sweating over all the documentation necessary to apply for a Heritage Fund grant. Sometimes I'd tramp a whole day, sometimes seeing no one, occasionally greeted with a friendly wave, less often invited into an isolated farm kitchen for a cup of over-brewed tea. On one occasion, in a farm five or six miles from even a single-track road, I came on a field that interested me. A large patch had been dug over, tamped down and covered with turf again. It was only because we'd had such a dry autumn that the grass hadn't regrown seamlessly.

As I stared, the farmer strolled over, a touch stiff-legged, as if spoiling for a fight. But, perhaps recognising me as one of the new finance committee, he nodded curtly.

'What on earth happened over there?' I asked

'Very sad,' he mumbled, bending to scratch his dog. 'One of my horses died. Had to bury it.'

'A cart horse?'

'We'd had him a long time,' he said, still not meeting my eye.

Of course, I told myself, if you had to bury a horse or other big creature you'd need a grave at least that big.

'I'd best be turning for home,' I said. 'It'll be dark soon.'

'You want to take care, walking in those narrow lanes,' he said.

'I do.' I waved a hefty torch. 'But no big black BMW's mown anyone down for some weeks now, has it?' Nor was there any sign of its Jehu of a driver.

'City type,' he said, spitting like Mr Taylor. 'Couldn't adapt to life in the country, that's what. He'll be where he belongs.'

I tried not to look at that extra-large mound.

My route home took me past Paradise Mews. The handsome gateposts looked almost forlorn in the half-light, a couple of blackberry runners already snaking over them. The gates swung to and fro, to and fro. I closed them firmly. That was it, then. I turned and left.

There was a village hall fund-raising committee that night, and as Treasurer I mustn't be late. I should have been puzzling over figures, not speculating on the fate of Crompton Gledstone.

Gun shots. Odd looks. The righteous hatred felt by tenants blackmailed and bled dry. My encouragement to the downtrodden to fight for justice. His failure to appear at the council hearing. The burial site big enough for a BMW.

I told myself I was being too fanciful. He was probably harassing innocent people in some other part of his kingdom. If he really were missing, then surely his friends would have alerted the police. We'd all have been questioned. But perhaps men like that didn't have any friends, only dodgy associates only too glad to see the back of him. Or a cowed wife, or servants freed like slaves.

As I scraped my boots off, I looked round my territory. What was it Mr Taylor had said? 'Sometimes everyone needs a good clear out. Shift all the rubbish. Be ruthless. Start again afresh.'

Starting Over

By Carol Anne Davis

Having moved from her native Scotland to the (apparently) tranquil south of England, Carol Anne Davis is familiar with the rural way of life. Her contribution to *Crime in the City* last year was a slice of urban noir set in the seamy side of Edinburgh. A year later, she has come up with a much lighter story, but she remains fascinated by the darker side of human nature. Although primarily a novelist, she has recently published two books dealing with aspects of true crime – *Women Who Kill* and *Children Who Kill* – and her insight into human nature informs all her work.

'Y̶ou mean they've all moved here for no apparent reason?' Jennifer asked. It was her first day as a parole officer in rural Wiltshire though she had a decade's worth of experience.

Gail beamed at her. 'They have indeed.'

Jennifer had heard through the grapevine that the woman was called Gullible Gail. Hell, she didn't even have a lock on the reception room drawer which contained the Hob Nobs. Now the ex-cons were relocating to the countryside to live on her patch.

'Why would London prisoners come here?' she asked with genuine curiosity, 'There's only casual farm work on offer and there are virtually no shops.'

'There's the Spar,' Gail said. 'And the mobile library.'

'Gail – most of our clients can't read.'

For a second the older woman's mouth drooped then it curved upwards again. 'Ah, but it rents out videos of the countryside for a pound a time.'

The kind of videos her clients had been making didn't involve cute fox cubs or harvest mice – though the occasional donkey made a manually excited appearance. Hoping that the ex-cons had exited the movie business, Jennifer switched on her new computer and logged on to the Internet.

'I need to see what Wiltshire has to offer parolees,' she explained to Gail who was peering benignly over her shoulder.

'Oh, can you work that web thing? One of our clients has her own website,' she replied.

'She has? What's her name?'

Gail mentioned a prisoner who had recently spent time in Holloway for breaking and entering. 'But she's a completely reformed character. She's become a writer now.'

Further alarm bells went off in Jennifer's head. 'Writers don't make much money in their first few years.'

'Ah, but she's offering a tutoring service. You know how there's a writers group called The Nine Novelists and another called Seven Scribes? Well, she's called herself The Voluptuous One.'

A few online searches later, Jennifer found herself staring at The Voluptuous One's official site. The front page showed the former prisoner in a black blouse which she hadn't yet found time to button. The side split of her skirt was equally open to the elements. 'One to one tuition a speciality,' the wording under her nipples read.

'She must have conquered her childhood dyslexia,' Gail said with genuine admiration, 'She's come so far.'

Unsure whether to laugh or cry, Jennifer switched off the machine. She'd never thought that prostitution should be illegal, especially the behind-closed-doors type that The Voluptuous One was clearly engaged in. So she'd turn a blind eye to the woman's new career if she continued to commit a victimless crime.

But what else had been going on in this pretty part of the country? As Gail's senior officer – albeit her junior in age by twenty years – Jennifer had the right to peruse the woman's lilac-scented reports. Taking a deep breath, she started right away.

One of the first problems seemed to be the number of men who'd served time for bestiality and were now living closer to cows than might be considered proper. Jennifer made a mental note to become a vegan rather than drink the local milk.

'These prisoners who were arrested in the fields...' she said to Gail.

Gail beamed. 'No need to worry. I've fixed them all up with nice girlfriends.'

'Your girlfriends?' Jennifer asked faintly.

'No, dear, girlfriends of The Voluptuous One.'

Had the area been turned into one huge knocking shop? Should she inform the Centre For Communicable Diseases?

'Let's go to the village immediately,' Jennifer said.

Gail picked up a purple mobile with a cartoon coot on it. 'The clients gave me this and said I could phone them whenever...'

Jennifer quickly took it from her. 'I think it's time they had a big surprise.'

'You'll be so impressed when you see what they've done with the place,' Gail promised as they lurched along the country roads in her canary yellow Lada. Several sheep backed away – and Jennifer swore one crossed its back legs – at the sight of a vehicle. 'They've turned the place into an ideal village. I'll take you to the knitting group which they hold in Maggie's home.'

Maggie, as far as Jennifer could remember, was the wife of an old lag who'd served twenty years for armed robbery. And Maggie herself had managed to smoke sixty a day off a social security cheque and still have enough cash left for an ankle-length mink coat.

At Jennifer's insistence, Gail brought the Lada to a tyre-shrieking halt some distance from Maggie's villa and both parole officers entered the back door on foot. Six women were knitting busily in the plushly-carpeted living room.

'It's only me,' Gail called as they walked in.

Twelve knitting needles immediately stopped clickety-clacking. Jennifer stared at the six balaclavas they'd been working on.

'It's brass monkeys weather here in the winter,' Maggie said defensively, returning to her plain and purl.

Gail nodded understandingly. 'If you need a woollens allowance from the social fund...'

'They're up to something,' Jennifer said as they walked back to the car. Or rather they walked back to where the car had been – all that remained was the tire tracks.

'No, that's why they moved here,' Gail assured her as they started the long walk back to the parole office. 'They want to mend their ways and know that in the country there's less opportunity for crime.'

Three weeks later Jennifer wondered anew about the opportunities for crime when she gave a con-artist-turned-local-handyman cash for a steering wheel security lock. He handed her a fiver in change and it didn't seem quite dry.

'Finding enough work here to keep you busy are you Neville?' she asked, remembering how his record had involved everything from credit card scams to money laundering.

Neville looked around the empty workshop. 'Oh aye.'

Unconvinced, Jennifer drove on to the centre of the village and parked behind Fred The Fence's barn. Suddenly she heard the unmistakable clatter of a printing press. Were they actually printing their own money? Jennifer dashed into the workshop just as the press began to spew out the covers of a glossy magazine.

Fred jumped when he saw her then smiled. 'Is Gail not bringing us sultana cake any more?'

'She's gone into Salisbury to buy herself a new car – well, a reconditioned one.'

'It's a sad day when a man's so broke that he has to steal a Lada,' Fred said.

'You're doing all right yourself?' Jennifer asked. Judging by his glossy leather shoes and waxed jacket, he was doing wonderfully. She just wasn't sure how he managed it off his social security cheque.

'Aye, we've been given a small European grant to set up this magazine,' Fred explained. He held up one of the covers and Jennifer could see that it was called *Starting Over*. 'It's a magazine run by ex-prisoners for ex-prisoners,' Fred said.

'You write it all by yourself?' Jennifer queried, remembering how the man had always spelt phonetically.

'No, all the ex-cons contribute – and some are former editors,' Fred said happily.

Maybe he really had hit on something. After all, as a parole officer she had very limited time with each parolee – but if they pooled their information they could help each other find affordable housing, sympathetic new employers and even a husband or wife.

Jennifer got back to the office ten minutes before Gail arrived in an elderly four wheel drive.

'Gail, you may be right. They really are trying to turn over a new leaf,' she said and told her all about the magazine.

The following weekend, Jennifer was at a Winning Ways In Wiltshire conference and ended up having lunch with a patisserie entrepreneur from the neighbouring village. She told him how the ex-cons had impressively rewritten their own life stories by producing *Starting Over* and he suggested that she submit a copy for the annual competition to find the Local Business Of The Year.

'Nominees aren't told that they've been entered for the competition unless they reach the short list,' he added, reaching for another slice of lardy cake, 'so don't tell a soul. Just hand in a copy of the magazine to my bakery.'

It was difficult keeping her secret from Gail but luckily the woman seemed to be preoccupied with fitting new security locks to her vehicle and to her Hob Nobs drawer. (There had been several break-ins in the area which Jennifer put down to bored local children.) She casually asked Fred The Former Fence for a copy of *Starting Over* but he explained that demand was such that they were completely sold out.

'How about saving me a copy of the next issue?' she asked, keeping her tone light-hearted.

'You can bet on it,' Fred said – but when publication day arrived he claimed that every copy was earmarked for subscribers at home and abroad.

She simply couldn't get hold of a copy without arousing the parolee's suspicions, Jennifer told her new acquaintance as they sat in the ground floor tea-room of his five-storey bakery.

'Leave it to me,' he said between mouthfuls of Marlborough bun, 'I know someone in the post office who deals with the bulk deliveries.'

Jennifer winced, hating the fact that he was going to steal a copy. But she was determined that her boys would have the chance of a sheepskin fleece from the woollen mill and a side of beef from the local abattoir which together formed the top business prize.

Shortly after The Great Magazine Robbery, the bakery entrepreneur phoned her at home.

'Jennifer, you're not going to believe this.'

His voice sounded so strange that she wondered if he had
choked on a fig roll.

But when she saw the copy of *Starting Over* that he'd pur-
loined, the words stuck in her own throat. The inside front cover
offered The Dummy's Guide To Safecracking while page one
proudly displayed Jemmy Of The Month. Page two looked at
Credit Card Counterfeiting and page three featured a working
girl with her price card. Jennifer noticed that lip service was particularly reasonable but that whippings didn't come cheap.
Meanwhile the centre spread was Houses Of The Rich & Famous
which included arrows showing various windows and doors.

The classifieds were also a rich source of employment with
requests for everything from getaway drivers to doctors specialis-
ing in gunshot wounds. Not to be outdone, the travel section
offered suitcases with false compartments and ready-in-two-hours
passports while the Miscellaneous section had adverts for offshore
bank accounts, thermal lance hire and police band radios.

'My car's outside if you want a lift to the police station,' the
baker said weakly.

Jennifer hesitated. 'If we go to the police now you'll have to
admit that your friend stole the magazine. And my bosses will
think I was naïve not to have known about all of this so I'll probably get demoted.' She looked sadly at the advert from a plastic
surgeon promising that the patient's own mother wouldn't recognise him afterwards. 'Do you think we could wait a couple of
months then send it in anonymously?'

'That sounds like an excellent solution,' the man said – and
this time they both reached for a large triangle of chocolate
sponge.

The next day, Jennifer put in for a transfer back to the
Birmingham office explaining that she'd found the Wiltshire

patch hard to manage due to the distance from the office to the parolees' village. She also said that the men were running a magazine but refused to issue her with a copy and that she was slightly troubled by this.

Jennifer knew that the wheels of parole officedom grind exceeding slow, so long before anyone official looked into the magazine the police would be sent the baker's anonymous copy. She'd come out of the whole affair looking reasonable as she was the only one who had voiced her concerns.

Concern eventually spread throughout the parole system and photocopies of *Starting Over* were sent to various judicial VIPs. Several plastic surgeons and a Harley Street doctor immediately contributed to the brain drain by relocating overseas.

As for Fred The Fence and the other guys? They were forcibly relocated closer to the sea, specifically to HMP Maidstone. There they are putting their editing skills to less lucrative use by running the prison magazine. Meanwhile The Voluptuous One's tutoring is widely sought after and the suicide rate among lonely farmers has gone right down.

Melusine

Martin Edwards

No one whose life was touched by the outbreak of foot and mouth disease in rural Britain in 2001 is ever likely to forget it. Death and devastation on such a scale cast a cloud over the countryside that remains to this day, long after the smoke and smell of the funeral pyres faded away. The horrors of that spring and summer made me wonder about the effect that they would have on people who saw their whole way of life coming under threat. Crime fiction is often about the behaviour of people under pressure and 'Melusine' is my take on the tragedy of foot and mouth.

On the hillside, bodies were burning. As Jason drove down into the valley, he glanced across and saw the outlines of the bloated carcasses. Their stiffened legs protruded through the flames and pointed to the sky. On a fresh June morning, smoke and fire had turned the sky a strange purple hue that, until the coming of the plague, he had never seen before. A steamy white vapour hung close to the ground. He kept the windows of the van wound up, but the stench from the corpses on the funeral pyre was inescapable. It choked his sinuses and made his gorge rise.

The fields were deserted. Cows and sheep should be everywhere, but only their ghosts remained. All the footpaths were barred with tape and official notices; ramblers had been asked to stay at home. The winding route to Sidebottom's Farm was closed, a red sign blocking the middle of the lane. KEEP OUT – FOOT AND MOUTH DISEASE.

The grey stone cottages where a couple of the farm workers and their families had lived were shuttered and silent. When blisters were found on the tongue of one of Mick Sidebottom's bullocks, the men had been given forty eight hours to pack their bags and leave. Folk said it was worse than going on evacuation during the last war. This time the enemy drifted through the air, silent, ruthless and invisible.

His head was pounding and he kept taking the bends in the road too fast. At least there was no other traffic around; the Ministry kept warning against 'non-essential movement'. As he had driven through the smoke and vapour up top, a couple of tiny patches of unburned flesh had landed on the bonnet of his van. He clipped a hedge as he skimmed round a tight bend, but only when he struck a pothole did the bits fall off. At last he slowed as he reached the disinfected matting stretched over a cattle grid. In the distance he could see Gordon Clegg power-washing his tractor for the umpteenth time. Anything to keep the plague at bay.

Five minutes later, the squat church tower came into view. He glanced at his watch. Twelve o'clock. Time for a quick drink at the Wheatsheaf before he called home for half an hour. He had done enough killing and maybe he'd done enough drinking, too, but alcohol helped in a way nothing else did.

Dave Sharpe's rusty Vauxhall was the only other vehicle in the pub car park. He hesitated and thought about going straight to the house. Part of him wanted not to see Dave, not to speak to him, not to have to think about him ever again. But at least if he was swilling beer, he wasn't doing anything more dangerous. Jason took a breath and headed for the saloon.

Sally Binks was behind the bar, wearing a low-cut pink top and flirting with Dave. Apart from a couple of old men in the corner, no one else was in.

'Usual, love?'

He nodded. 'And one for him.'

'Cheers, mate,' Dave said.

Funny, that. They had disliked each other for years, and still they called themselves mates. They had met on the first day of school at the age of five and on that very morning, Dave had pulled his hair and made him cry, then pretended it was all some kind of joke. As they grew up together, anyone listening to their lazy banter would never have a clue about what went on inside their heads. Jason wondered if he actually hated Dave. He never cared to analyse his feelings, but he thought probably he did hate him. For many reasons, not least because Melanie had said last week that he looked like Kurt Cobain.

'All right?' he asked.

As Sally moved to pick up the tankards, Dave reluctantly shifted his gaze from her cleavage and gave a shrug. 'Feller from Padgett's was in here a few minutes ago. He said that when the rain came after they buried the sheep out Settle way, the bodies exploded. They exploded, literally exploded. He said, if you watched the ground, it looked as though the earth was sweating blood.'

'Wicked,' Sally said as she pulled the levers. Her breasts wobbled, hypnotising Dave again. 'Wicked.'

In the corner of the bar, the television was murmuring. The mid-day news. A government spokesman, carefully compassionate in a Paul Smith suit, was promising that everything was getting better. The detail of his explanation was lost as the old men in the corner hooted with scorn.

'Back under control?' one of them said. 'Tell that to Jack Wilson's widow. No wonder the poor bastard hung himself. Took him and his dad forty years to build that herd.'

'Aye,' his toothless companion said.

'Nothing even wrong with the animals. Slaughter on suspicion, that's what it was.'

The other man supped his pint. 'Aye.'

'See that bugger?' the old man said, jerking a thumb at the screen. 'Pity he's never had blood and brains splashed all over him.'

'Aye.'

Dave winced. He was a postman and his work was already finished for the day. He'd never worked on the land and was one of the few people Jason knew whose life had not been touched by the coming of the plague.

When Jason said nothing, Dave nudged him in the ribs. 'So how are you, mate? And how's the missus?'

His wolfish features gave nothing away, but was there a touch of mockery in his tone? Jason thought so. It wasn't just his imagination.

'I'm all right. So's Melanie.'

'Great. Glad to hear you're looking after Mel. Did I ever tell you how I used to fancy her when she was a kid?'

Dave would have fancied Godzilla if it had worn a skirt. His late mother had fondly described him as *incorrigible*, a favourite word. He'd finished up getting Cheryl Stringer pregnant and marrying her before the baby was born. It wasn't in his nature to do the decent thing, so everyone assumed that it was because he'd never found anyone with a sexual appetite to match Cheryl's. Jason had never cared for Cheryl – she was so in-your-face – but these days she was proving impossible to avoid. In January she had started working as a classroom assistant at Melanie's school and the two couples had fallen into a habit of seeing each other regularly. Melanie said that Cheryl was fun, but Jason couldn't help wondering if it was an excuse, an opportunity for his wife to spend more time with Dave. She said that he made her laugh.

'Yeah, you told me.'

'Course, she was too posh for me. For all of us. No offence, mate, but I never figured out how you managed to catch her eye.'

He'd often asked himself that very question, never quite worked out the answer.

Dave drained his glass. 'Same again?'

Jason hadn't finished his drink, but his headache was no better and he decided he'd had enough. Especially of Dave. He pushed the tankard across the counter to Sally and shook his head. 'Another time.'

'Off to kill a few more?' Dave mimicked the Sundance Kid firing his six-shooter.

'Later.'

Dave treated him to a knowing leer. Jason could smell the ale on his breath. 'Popping back to the nest for a quickie, then? Don't blame you, mate. Give my love to Mel, now, don't forget.'

Jason loathed the easy familiarity of that *Mel*. He turned away, not trusting himself to answer. When he reached home, Melanie was in the front room. She used it as a study and was tapping on the keyboard of her computer. It was half term, supposed to be a holiday, but she always found plenty to do. As he walked into the room, she glanced over her shoulder.

'You left early this morning.'

'I tried not to disturb you.'

'I heard the van when you set off.'

'Sorry.'

'Doesn't matter. How did it go?'

'Well, you know. The usual.'

He'd never been good with words, not like Melanie. Anyway, how could you describe what he saw, what he felt? Nothing could have prepared him for this. The terror on the face of the beasts, the staring eyes, the hoarse panting, the blood seeping from the wounds where they had in panic crashed through strands of barbed wire.

'Ready for a sandwich? There's cheese in the fridge.'

She turned back to her computer. He wondered if he should go up behind her and kiss her on the neck. At one time, that would have melted her in a moment, but they had been married four years. Four years! Time to start a family, though she had always been reluctant. Weren't teachers supposed to like kids? But she never behaved like all the other girls he'd grown up with. Always, Melanie was different.

'Good morning?'

'Not bad,' she said, still focusing on the text on the screen. 'There's such a lot of work to do with the national curriculum. By the way, I wouldn't mind a sandwich myself.'

In the kitchen, Jason found the bread knife. He hadn't expected marriage to be like this. What had he expected? He wasn't sure. Perhaps he'd never thought clearly enough about it before asking Melanie to share his life. Marriage was what people did, but he had assumed that, because Melanie was different, their life together would somehow be different from everyone else's. After all, she was his fairy bride.

He ran his forefinger along the serrated edge of the knife, remembering how young Kevin Nolan had slit the throat of a terrified lamb the previous afternoon. The lamb was healthy, like all the other creatures down Beggarman's Lane, but that was not enough to guarantee survival. Tests on blood and tissue taken from animals at an adjoining farm had proved positive and the rules of contiguous culling meant that their neighbours had to die.

'I wouldn't mind a cup of tea while you're at it,' Melanie called.

She talked like a woman of fifty, he thought, switching on the kettle. Not that she looked a day over twenty. Her face didn't have a single line. Three years older, he'd only been vaguely aware of her existence during her teens. He'd never spoken to her until the night of a dance in the village hall, a couple of weeks after she finished at college. He'd watched her, with her friends, and found himself hypnotised. She seemed delicate and aloof from their chatter, a slim, almost boyish figure in a simple dress lacking all the slits and embellishments favoured by her companions. Something prompted him to talk to her, even though he had watch her reject overtures from a number of the other young men. Including Dave Sharpe.

A couple of months later, when their unlikely romance was turning into something more than a fling, he tried to explain how he admired her, how he loved to watch her when she was watching something or someone else. There was a stillness about her that entranced him, and something more – an air of not belonging that was neither loneliness nor isolation, but a sort of serene uniqueness with which he had fallen hopelessly in love.

Of course, he found it impossible to describe his feelings. At first she had teased him, but when she realised that he meant to be deadly serious, her tone had softened and she had said that she thought she knew what he meant.

'I never wanted to be one of the crowd,' she said, squeezing his hand.

'You're not,' he said. 'You're almost – well, not quite human.'

'Thanks a lot,' she laughed, withdrawing her hand in mock indignation. 'Sort of alien from outer space, am I?'

'No, no,' he said, his voice becoming hoarse with embarrassment. 'But you're not like Dawn and Becky and all the rest. You're not like anyone I've ever met before.'

'I'll take that as a compliment, shall I?'

'You better had,' he said. 'I want to marry you.'

To his amazement, she said yes. No play-acting, no messing. He could not believe his good fortune. Why him? In the past, he'd done all right with the girls, even if he would never be in Dave Sharpe's league. At least he was muscular and fit and poor tubby little Hannah Stott had once told him that his hazel eyes were the most beautiful she had ever seen. He was never mean with money and no woman would ever feel the slap of his hand, which was more than you could say for many men, even in this day and age. But Melanie had a brain and wanted to use it. She could make something of herself.

As for Jason, he didn't think he'd ever find a job that truly suited him. Perhaps his old Maths master had been right in branding him as lazy. It went deeper than a visceral loathing of algebra. Above all, Jason admired beauty. He admired it in a landscape, in a summer sunset, in the face and body of a gorgeous woman. How easy to become lost in rapture, to pass the hours in quiet adoration. But there was no beauty in work. Routine bored him and so he moved from job to job. He had been a garage mechanic, a gardener, a farmhand, a butcher's assistant, a slaughterman at an abattoir.

A week before the wedding, he asked Melanie if she'd ever loved anyone else. Idle curiosity, no hidden agenda – but for some reason, his inquisitiveness upset her out of all proportion. She was usually calm, unworldly even, and he was surprised to see her eyes filling with tears.

'Listen,' she said gently as he stammered an apology. 'It doesn't matter. But you must promise me one thing.'

'Anything,' he said. His worst nightmare was that she would pull out of their engagement. Twice already he had dreamed of her failing to show at the church on the day itself and of his mortification as everyone in the congregation stared at him in horrified sympathy.

'You must keep this promise and never break it.' She thought for a moment. 'I don't suppose you ever heard of Melusine?'

He shook his head. She often treated him as a pupil; it amused her to teach him things. He didn't mind; he was content simply to let her words wash over him, not absorbing the lessons, just luxuriating in her company.

'Melusine was a beautiful fairy but she had a terrible secret.' A faraway look came into her eyes. 'One day each week, she became half-woman, half-serpent. A man fell in love with her and she agreed to marry him on one condition, that he never saw her on a Saturday.'

'What happened?'

'Someone poisoned his mind, and said that was the day Melusine met her lover. When her husband broke his word and found out the truth, he lost everything. Including Melusine.'

'I don't get it.'

'Listen, I'm like Melusine. I ask just one thing of you. You must promise never to be jealous.'

'So you've got a terrible secret?' His tone was jokey, but her flights of fancy baffled him. 'It's not the new vicar, is it? I saw him across the street the other day. Quite a hunk. The church shouldn't allow it.'

She put a finger to her lips. 'Shhh, darling. No, I don't fancy the vicar, but I do want you to trust me. Now, are you going to promise or not?'

'You really want me to?'

She nodded seriously and he realised that he must not get this wrong. Not now, when he was committed to her. Even though he did not know why, he had to make his promise.

'I swear.'

Her face broke into the loveliest smile and within moments he forgot about Melusine. In the years that followed, there was no hint that Melanie might have a terrible secret. She did not smoke, did not drink, and she had to be persuaded into any bedroom games that were not pretty conventional. Even now, he told himself he was crazy to believe that she was deceiving him.

He took the sandwich and cup of tea into her. 'Here you are.'

'Thanks. So when are you going back?'

'Five minutes.'

'I'll have your tea ready by half six.'

'Great.'

'No problem.'

She was still glued to the computer screen. He drank in the sight of her. Her hair was the same rich chestnut shade he had always loved, her skin was as white and unsullied as when they first kissed. Yet something had changed. He was no longer special to her; she had stopped trying to educate him to understand what appealed to her. Nowadays he featured in her life in much the same way as their shabby old furniture or the framed views of Brimham Rocks that hung on the wall of their living room.

'See you later, then.'

'Mmmmm.'

He closed the door quietly. As he rooted in his jacket pocket for the keys to the van, he wondered who had stolen her affections. Dave Sharpe? Checking the map in his glove compartment, he told himself for the hundredth time that life was not so cruel, that the only reason he was obsessed with the fear that Dave was cuckolding him was because such a betrayal would be too hard to bear.

Heading for the next Infected Premises, he couldn't rid his mind of Dave's gloating smile. As lads, they had played rugby together in winter and cricket in the summer. They had so much in common and people regarded them as bosom buddies. Dave was fun and he was generous, but there were moments when the mask of good nature slipped. Taking a short cut along a single-track lane, Jason remembered a game one July when he and Dave had batted in partnership. It was one of those days of which cricketers dream. The ball kept speeding off his bat to the boundary. Even the best bowlers on the other side were helpless in the face of such a sustained attack. When he was one run short of his century, Dave called him for a quick single. The ball was in the hands of the cover point fielder, a farmer with a famously strong arm. Jason hesitated for a second, then put his head down and ran. His stumps were shattered when he was two yards short of the safety of the crease at the far end. In the bar afterwards, Dave had bought the drinks and said he took the blame. Jason argued with him, saying that if he had set off straight away, he would have made his ground. But secretly, he knew that Dave was right. It was a reckless call, his fault. Perhaps he had been too anxious to see Jason achieve his moment of glory. Or perhaps he had wanted to deny it to him forever. Jason had never scored a ton since.

When he arrived at the site, the man from the Ministry came up as he was slipping on his white biohazard overall and rubber boots. 'You took your time.'

Jason's wave took in Kevin Nolan standing by a picket fence, supping Coke from a can and Bob Garrett sitting in the cab of his van reading the *Sun*. 'Better things to do with my day than spend hours hanging around here, waiting for the word.'

'Look here, you know the score. We have to get the go-ahead from the vet. But if you keep buggering off, we don't know where we are.'

Jason shrugged. He was freelance, and right now the Ministry needed as much help as it could get. Three million animals didn't kill themselves. None of the slaughtermen liked the Ministry blokes. They were pen-pushers, more comfortable in a warm office than on the land. Most of the slaughtermen had learned their trade on farms, they were countrymen. They didn't have to like what they were doing or the people who paid them to do it.

Bob Garrett jumped down from his cab. 'Eh up, pal. Wipe that smirk off your face. We all know you've been off giving your old lady a good seeing-to.'

Garrett's ex-wife lived across the road from Jason. The previous summer, Jason had spotted him eyeing up Melanie when he brought back the kids and she was sunbathing on the lawn. No matter how many times he told himself that other men were jealous of him, it never helped, never made him feel good. What was wrong with him? Why did he feel damaged by the way they lusted after his lovely fairy wife? And things were getting worse. He couldn't shake off the fear that people were laughing at him behind his back. They knew something that he did not.

Kevin Nolan was sniggering, but Jason didn't rise to the bait. 'How many are we doing this afternoon?'

The man from the Ministry consulted his clipboard. 'Eighty-five cattle. Not a big job. I just spoke to the vet. We should be set to go in a couple of minutes.'

Jason opened the door of his van and picked up the gun from the passenger seat. 'Better get ready, then.'

Their task did not take long. They were using captive bolt guns rather than rifles. A blank cartridge fired a four inch steel bolt into the animal's skull and a spring retracted the bolt. Once the animal had been stunned in this way, it was pithed, by means of a steel rod being thrust through the hole and into the brain.

As usual, not everything went according to plan. One bull had to be shot and pithed four times. The more he fought for life, the more Jason's temper frayed. What was the point of struggling? The bull wasn't sick, but it had to die anyway. Those were the orders. He wanted it over as quickly as possible and resented the doomed bull for delaying the inevitable. The more time you had to think about what you were doing, the worse it was for everyone.

'Where next?' he asked the man from the Ministry.

'There's a couple of dozen lambs penned up the other side of the barn at the end of the lane. You and Garrett head off there now, I'll catch up once I've had a word with the farmer.'

The farmer had turned up during the killings. He'd stayed over by the fence, watching the destruction of his herd. Jason could tell the man was close to tears. In the early days, he had talked to the farmers whose herds he shot, tried to console them. But what could you say? Most people round here reckoned that it would be enough to vaccinate the animals and claimed the culling was unnecessary. But the powers-that-be in London thought differently, and that was what mattered.

Jason held the lambs while Bob Garrett shot them. He took care not to look at the faces of the creatures, settling his gaze instead on fields in the middle distance. The countryside was full of death, but nature didn't seem to notice. Ragged robin, elderflowers and foxgloves still bloomed.

'These fellers in the Thatched Tavern were talking last night,' Garrett said. 'They'd killed fifteen hundred sheep and cattle on one farm and then they were told to disinfect round a jackdaw's nest for conservation reasons. Christ, would you bloody believe it?'

Jason grunted. Perhaps all wars were like this; everyone had an anecdote to tell. Live lambs suffocating to death under the corpses of sheep with cut throats. Wagons driven by young squaddies, carrying the carcasses to the burial pits and leaking blood all along the country lanes. Each story-teller liked to spin a yarn more absurd or more horrific than the last.

'You all right?' Garrett asked. 'You look – sort of glazed. On a promise for tonight, then?'

Jason felt his chest tightening. He wanted to grab the man, shake him by the neck until he choked, demanding to know why he kept talking about Melanie. What was going on – something that he, the poor old husband, was the last to know?

He strode away, unable to trust himself to speak. Surely he was wrong in suspecting Dave. What about Garrett himself? He was an older man and Jason supposed he was good-looking if you like that sort of thing. Or even Kevin Nolan? Kevin's last year at the school had been Melanie's first as a teacher. Jason remembered her saying that he was a rascal, but somehow she couldn't find it in her heart not to like him. That was the trouble with Melanie. She never saw through people, she was too naïve to realise that the men she liked were only interested in one thing.

'Where are you going?' Garrett demanded.

Jason pointed to the heap of bodies on the ground. 'I've had enough of this.'

'If you don't wait for whatsisname to show up and sign you off, there'll be hell to pay.'

Jason shrugged. 'So what?'

He'd walked away from jobs before. Even as he clambered out of his overall and boots, his headache was easing. Garrett give a disgusted shake of the head. Kevin Nolan was grinning. Surely, *surely*, Melanie couldn't have slept with that lad?

Even as he sped back to the village, he told himself that he couldn't confront her. It wasn't so much that he lacked the balls to do it, but he remembered what she had said about Melusine. He dared not demand to know if she had taken a lover. What he needed was reassurance.

It could still be okay, he thought, as he jolted over the disinfectant mat. We can start again. Soon, maybe, she'll be ready to try for a family. That will make all the difference.

'I didn't expect you back so soon,' Melanie said when he opened the door of the study.

'I've jacked it in,' he said. 'The money's good, but I'm sick of the smell and the faces of the animals as I kill them.'

She swallowed. 'What are you going to do?'

'Dunno. I'll find something.'

'But there's no work! Haven't you heard? The countryside is closed. No tourists, no trade, nothing. People are going bankrupt right, left and centre.'

'All right, it might take a while.' He thought for a moment. 'What's up? Don't you want me under your feet all day?'

'It's not that!' Two pink spots appeared in her cheeks. It wasn't like her to be flustered. 'We can't go on like this.'

'Me spending cash we haven't got at the Wheatsheaf, you mean?'

'Don't shout! I know you need to unwind…'

'Too right,' he said, and marched out of the house.

Ten minutes later, nursing a pint in the saloon, he was wondering if he'd been too rough with her. They hardly ever argued; neither of them were natural combatants. When Sally asked him if he was okay, he bit her head off.

'Why? Don't I look okay?'

'I only asked,' she said in an injured tone. 'And if you want to know the truth, you look as miserable as sin.'

It dawned on him that he hadn't been happy for a long time. Not since before the coming of the plague, that was for sure. Maybe he should offer Melanie an olive branch. It wasn't a Yorkshireman's habit to say sorry, but he wasn't proud. He would do anything, if it would help to recapture the love they had shared at one time. Maybe even work out his contract with the Ministry. He pulled his mobile out of his pocket and dialled home. He would apologise right now, and then go back and see what else he could do to make amends.

The number was engaged. He tried again a couple of minutes later, with the same result. Her parents were dead and she seldom socialised. The head teacher was on holiday and her two closest colleagues had taken a party of pupils to France. Who could she be talking to?

'Dave not in tonight?' he asked.

Sally shook her head to show that she bore no grudge for his sharp tone earlier. 'He said that he would be busy in the garden until it got dark. He's building a rockery, you know.'

Oh really? Jason's head was swimming and it wasn't just down to the beer. 'Same again, then.'

As darkness fell, Dave showed up. He spotted Jason and gave

him a wicked grin. 'What's up, mate? Abandoned your old lady? I dunno, you'd better take care. You know, women are like cars. You've got to keep their engines tuned.'

'You've been looking after Cheryl?' a fat man at the bar demanded.

Dave found this amusing. 'Matter of fact, I've been out in the garden.'

'Oh yeah? Planting a few seeds?'

The fat man and Dave roared with laughter and fell into ribald conversation. Jason sat glowering and monosyllabic for a couple of rounds before summoning up the energy to head for home. If Dave had been with Mel, she would need time to have a bath, make herself decent. He didn't want a confrontation this evening. He had to think things through.

Although he could hold his beer better than most, he was swaying slightly as he walked through his front door. All the lights were out. It wasn't late, but Melanie must be in bed. She would probably say she needed the sleep, after he had woken her so inconsiderately that morning. Perhaps she was already fast asleep; she was bound to be tired.

On tiptoe, he made his way into the study. At night she left her mobile on her desk. He lifted it up and checked the list of recent calls. It was the first time in the marriage that he had ever snooped on her, but he couldn't help it. A familiar set of digits came up at once. His guts lurched. The number belonged to Dave Sharpe.

He started to climb the stairs, wanting to have it out with Melanie, but half-way up he changed his mind and went back down again. Better leave it until morning. He couldn't sleep beside her, though. Not after what she'd done. *Dave Sharpe.* His thoughts were as gridlocked as an urban motorway, but he could still guess what had happened. Dave and Melanie must have had a fling, but he'd two-timed her and got Cheryl pregnant. Perhaps Melanie had been too stingy in bed for him.

Melanie must have lost her heart to Dave. Yes, that explained everything. How she had fallen for Dave's mate on the rebound, her lapses into frigidity, even the story about Melusine. She did have a terrible secret after all.

He spent the night dozing fitfully on the lumpy sofa in their living room. At about four he woke from a nightmare. A dead bullock had risen like a zombie from the pile of carcasses and come towards him, intent upon taking revenge. The room was chilly in the middle of the night, but sweat was sticking his shirt to his chest. His head was pounding and the stale taste of beer lingered in his mouth.

Why had she done this to him? Dave was no fool; he must have picked up a hint that Melanie still held a torch for him. For all Cheryl's famously voracious appetites, he wouldn't have been able to resist the opportunity to be able to turn Jason into a cuckold. Humiliating his old 'friend' at the same time as enjoying the sweet pleasures of Melanie's tender flesh would double the fun.

At ten to seven, he heard the alarm shrilling in the bedroom. Moments later, Melanie came hurrying down the stairs, calling his name. When she saw him, her face turned crimson. In that instant, he knew that she knew he knew.

'What are you doing?' Her voice was croaky, uncertain.

'You should have told me the truth,' he said. 'We never should have got married.'

'What are you talking about?' She was no good at feigning innocence. He thought she was naturally honest. Living a lie must have been a torment, but things had gone too far for him to feel a spurt of sympathy.

'Admit it. You're in love with Dave Sharpe, aren't you? That's always been your secret, hasn't it, *Melusine*? But you never had the bottle to tell me.'

No actress could have faked the horror in her eyes. 'You've got it all wrong.'

'You lied to me,' he said quietly. 'But I found you out in the end.'

'You don't understand!'

'Believe me, I do. You slut.'

Tears were dribbling down her cheeks. For a moment she seemed transfixed and then she gave a little cry and ran out of the room and up the stairs. He heard her locking the door to their bedroom. No problem. He wasn't going after her just now. There was something else – this came to him in a slap of understanding – that he must do first.

He didn't bother to wash or shave; he was past all that. From upstairs came the sound of loud racking sobs, but as he unlocked his van, he felt a strange sense of calm, as if for the whole of his life he'd been wandering aimlessly, but now he'd found a mission.

Where could he find Dave Sharpe? At one time Dave's round had covered the village and its outskirts, but now he was a floater and covered for colleagues who were sick or on holiday, so he moved around the area. He said he preferred this; he liked the variety, but more than that, there was often a chance to meet new women. Countless times he regaled the Wheatsheaf saloon bar with anecdotes of nymphomaniac housewives who asked him in while their husbands were out at work. If only his restless womanising hadn't encompassed Melanie.

As Jason turned on the ignition, he saw the bedroom curtain twitch. His wife, furtively watching him drive out of their marriage. He slammed his foot down on the accelerator and the van shot out into the road, narrowly missing a milk float. His plan was to follow a circular route, heading out west first and then up and around the hillside before returning to the village. Sooner or later, he was sure to come across Dave Sharpe.

It took longer than he expected, but five miles from home he finally spotted his target. Dave was delivering a parcel at an isolated cottage at the end of a short lane. The woman on the doorstep was white-haired and frail, so Dave would not be lingering. The lane was narrow and Jason parked his van across to block it. He watched the woman go back inside her home and Dave climb on to his bicycle. Jason picked up the bolt gun from the passenger's seat. Keeping it behind his back, he shuffled out of the van to face his enemy.

'What… oh, it's you! Christ, Jason, what are you playing at?'

Jason said nothing. Dave dismounted and leaned his bike against the hedge. He marched up and stared into Jason's eyes.

'Lost your tongue?'

'I've lost everything,' Jason said.

An odd light came into Dave's eyes. 'Is this about Mel?'

Jason showed him the gun. They were within touching distance of each other. Jason caught a whiff of the other man's aftershave. Aftershave? What sort of a postman doused himself in that muck when he went out on his round of a morning? Only one who wanted to shag anyone woman stupid enough to give him the glad eye.

Dave's cheeks lost all colour. Hoarsely, he said, 'What are you doing? Put that down.'

Jason lifted the gun and put it to Dave's forehead. 'You think I'm stupid, don't you?'

'I think you're mad. You've lost it, mate, totally lost it.'

Dave tensed. Jason knew that he was going to try to grab the gun. He would only have one chance to do this. As he fired, he tried to close his eyes, but they wouldn't shut. He saw agony in Dave's eyes as well as hearing his scream. Just like my first day at the abattoir, he thought.

The pithing was over so quickly. Even as the old lady opened her door, coming to see who or what had screamed, Jason was back in the van, reversing over the body just to make sure before turning for the village. Some of Dave's blood had splashed over him, but he didn't care. His mind was as empty as the fields as he raced along the narrow winding lanes to his home. What was he going to say to Melanie? Was she truly lost to him forever? Ought she to die as well?

Within minutes he was back. The front door was ajar. Bolt gun in hand, he kicked it wide open and strode inside. He could hear Melanie weeping. Well, now she had something to weep about. He took the stairs two at a time. The bedroom door was shut. If she'd locked it, he meant to kick it down. But when he smashed the gun against the door, it swung on its hinges.

A woman cried out. Then he heard another voice, softly murmuring. As he stepped inside the bedroom, something occurred to him. *This is all wrong.* Melanie was with someone. Yet he had killed Dave Sharpe.

Melanie was in bed. Her eyes were puffy, her cheeks wet. Her companion had wrapped a plump arm around her shoulders. They were naked, both Melanie and Cheryl Sharpe. *Yes, I got it so wrong.* Helpless as doomed lambs, neither of them able to move or speak, the lovers stared at him.

His hand shaking, he pointed the gun first at his wife and then at Cheryl, before changing his mind and raising it instead to his left temple. The cold steel nuzzled his skin. This, at least, was a necessary death.

THE ANGEL OF MANTON WORTHY

By Kate Ellis

Along with Mat Coward, Zoe Sharp and Jerry Sykes, Kate Ellis is one of the younger generation of British crime writers. Her novels featuring Wesley Peterson have attracted a growing readership and her short stories deserve equally high regard. 'The Odour of Sanctity', for instance, is a splendid modern example of the 'impossible crime mystery' and 'Les Inconnus', set in Paris, was a highlight of last year's CWA anthology. Here she tackles a mystery in a countryside setting with aplomb.

I felt his tight grip on my arm as I slumped into the passenger seat and when my hand went up to the blindfold he ordered me not to touch it. I did as I was told and clung to the soft leather of the seat, trying to work out where we were heading.

We travelled for hours on a fast, straight road and I guessed that we must be well out of London. When the roads started to wind I sensed that we were out in the country somewhere and we seemed to drive for miles before I felt the car swing sharply to the left. I heard the crunch of gravel beneath the tyres as though we were on some sort of driveway and when we stopped he told me to take the blindfold off. I could see my surprise at last.

I untied the blindfold and sat there blinking as my eyes got used to the light. I'm sure I swore when I realised where I was. But then I saw the excitement on Paul's face – like a little boy at Christmas – and I forced my mouth into a smile until the muscles began to ache. I think I managed to say what he wanted to hear. I could hardly have let him know the truth.

I managed to keep the smile in place when he told me the house was called the Old Rectory and I rushed up to the front door, forcing out enthusiastic oohs and aahs as he pointed out each new desirable feature. He expected excitement and that's what he got. He had the Merc, the million pound apartment in London and now he had the place in the country he'd been promising himself for years. To have poured cold water on his triumph would have been like snatching away a kid's birthday present… and I couldn't have done that to him. Not when I saw how thrilled he was.

He was twenty years older than me and too many business lunches meant that what he'd lost in hair he'd gained in weight. But I was fond of him – I suppose I might even have said I loved him if I believed in love, which I don't. We stayed in a hotel in Exeter that evening and he ordered a bottle of champagne to toast our new country life. After the bubbles had booted some of my inhibitions out of the window I asked him if he realised what life was really like in a place like Manton Worthy. But he just laughed and said he'd bought the best house in the village so the peasants could kiss his arse. People in the restaurant looked round and I felt myself blushing. Paul never worried about what people thought… unless he was doing business with them.

Looking back, I couldn't complain about the house itself. It was like an oversized doll's house to look at… symmetrical with long, square paned windows painted in gleaming white. Paul said it was Georgian and it had a long gravel drive and a shiny black front door you could see your face in with bright brass fittings. It had belonged to a TV executive from London who had spent a fortune on the place and only used it at weekends. Inside, the previous owners had kitted it out with gold and silk drapes and thick cream carpets. It hadn't always been like that, of course – once it had been a draughty, rambling place where the old vicar lived; where the parish bigwigs held their long, boring meetings and where the vicar's skinny wife organised her fetes and good works. But times change.

Paul had lived in London all his life and what he knew about the country came from watching old episodes of Miss Marple and reading the colour supplements. He said I should get to know the area, perhaps chat up a few locals… there was no harm in cultivating useful contacts. But I said no thanks, I had better things to do and began to paint my nails. There was no way I was going out there. Not in Manton Worthy.

I had an uncomfortable feeling that it wouldn't be long before things began to go wrong… and it turned out I was right. The cockerel next door started it: cock a doodle bloody doo over and over again at five o'clock every morning. I knew Paul would take it badly… he needed his sleep and by the third day he was threatening to throttle the bird with his bare hands. I told him that crowing is what cockerels do… that it was all part of the country experience. But there was no reasoning with Paul when something annoyed him.

He dealt with it, of course… like he dealt with everything. He stormed round to see the farmer who was called Carter – 'an inbred lump in a flat cap and waxed jacket', according to Paul. As soon as I heard Carter's name I knew I had to take care not to get caught up in Paul's little feud.

When the cockerel carried on I tried to convince Paul that you couldn't stop the forces of nature. But he said he'd have a bloody good try if they kept him awake at night. I suggested moving into one of the bedrooms at the back of the house and to my relief he agreed. I started to hint about spending more time at the London apartment but Paul said that no inbred yokel was going to drive him out of the home he'd worked his backside off for. He always had a stubborn streak.

So there we were stuck there in the middle of nowhere and, as I stared out of our old bedroom window across the rolling green landscape, the sight of Carter's farmhouse squatting there in the field nearby made me shudder. I should have got out then… I know that now with hindsight. But how could I have hurt Paul?

Another thing that spoiled the rural peace Paul thought he'd bought was the noise of the church bells. They rang on Tuesday evenings and woke us up every Sunday morning. One Tuesday Paul fetched a pair of shears from the garden shed and I feared the worst. But I thought quickly and said that I loved the sound of the bells and how glad I was that we lived so near to the church. Paul looked at me as though I was mad but the shears were returned to the shed.

When the bells stopped that evening I walked to the bottom of the garden and hid myself behind the hedge to watch the ringers leave the church. I saw Carter, leading them down the church path – probably to the pub – and my body started to shake at the sight of him. He had hardly changed. He still had the slicked down hair I remembered so well – although it was grey now rather than black – and he'd put on weight. I watched him until he disappeared round the corner then I hurried back into the house, taking deep breaths, trying to still my trembling hands. I made for the downstairs cloakroom where I threw up, scared that Paul would hear me... but he didn't. I told him that I had been outside putting something in the bin and he seemed to believe me. I hated lying to him but I had no choice.

From then on I made sure we stayed indoors on Tuesday evenings and the change of bedroom had dealt with the cockerel problem. After a couple of weeks I was becoming more confident that I could manage the situation. But being in Manton Worthy still made me nervous and I woke up each morning dreading what the day ahead would bring. And yet I put on a smile for Paul's sake.

Paul had decided to spend less time in London and run the business from the Old Rectory. I offered to act as his PA – after all, we'd met when I'd started work as his secretary... just as he was becoming bored with his first wife. And doing my bit for the business gave me the perfect excuse not to go out.

But I suppose it was inevitable that I would meet someone from the village sooner or later and one Monday morning, as I was getting dressed, the doorbell rang. I let Paul answer it while I stood hidden at the top of the stairs, peering down into the hallway to see if the caller's face and voice were familiar. Once I was sure that I had never seen the visitor before in my life, I walked down the stairs smiling graciously, and invited her in. She introduced herself as Mandy Pettifer and she seemed nice enough in her way, although she wasn't really our type... all floral dress and flat sandals. But I knew that a contact on the outside might be useful.

I took her through into the lounge – or the drawing room as Paul insisted on calling it – and offered her a coffee. This was my chance to discover the lie of the land. Who was who now and what was what in Manton Worthy.

Mandy was the chatty type. In fact once you started her on the subject of the locals it was hard to shut her up. She'd lived in

Manton Worthy for ten years and she was married to an IT consultant who worked abroad a lot. She taught part time at a primary school in the nearby town of Ashburn, the local school having closed down years ago, and I guessed that she had come visiting because she was at a loose end in the school holidays. She was one of those people who'll tell you her life story before you can get a word in edgeways.

'I expect most people in the village have lived here for years,' I said when she paused to take a sip of coffee.

She looked disappointed, as though she wanted me to reveal as much about myself as she had... but I wasn't playing that game.

'Actually the nice thing about Manton Worthy is that most of the people are newcomers like you and me.' She leaned forward, as if she was about to tell some great secret. 'To tell you the truth I don't think most of the locals can afford the house prices. I know the people who used to have our cottage live in Ashburn now. In fact I only know of one person who's lived here all her life, apart from some of the local farmers of course.'

'Who's that?' I asked, trying to sound casual.

'Miss Downey – she lives next door to me. She's in her seventies now but she used to teach in the village school when there was one.'

'Nobody else?'

Mandy shook her head.

'What about the bell ringers?'

Mandy looked surprised, as though she'd never considered that human beings rang the church bells. 'I've no idea. Perhaps they come in from Ashburn. Most of the cottages were owned by a local estate and when they were sold off the tenants couldn't afford to buy at the prices they were asking. Most of them moved to the estate in Ashburn.'

'And the cottages?'

'Bought as second homes or by people like us.'

'So there's nobody apart from Miss Downey?'

Mandy laughed... a tinkling, irritating sound. 'You'll have to meet her; she knows a lot about local history and all that. If you ever want to know what's gone on in Manton Worthy in the past, she's the person to ask.'

I smiled but didn't answer. That afternoon I went for a walk through the village. It nestled in rolling, patchwork fields; chocolate box pretty with its thatched cob cottages and ancient stone church next door to the pub – everyone's ideal English village. Perhaps I had been wrong to be afraid. Perhaps everything would be okay... as long as I avoided Carter.

Over the next weeks I became bolder. I walked through the village – well away from Carter's land – and I even took Mandy up on her invitation to call round any time for a coffee. Perhaps I needed to see someone other than Paul. Or perhaps I just felt I needed to know what was going on in the outside world.

One afternoon I found myself sitting in Mandy's front room overlooking the main village street. She had done it up nicely, I'll give her that. There was an old-fashioned inglenook fireplace and she'd taken up the carpet to reveal the original stone floor which she had promptly covered up again with a large abstract rug in shades of grey. There was a whiff of minimalism in the air which surprised me as Mandy hadn't seemed the type for that sort of thing. She talked at length about interior design... and I listened. She had gone for a fusion of old rustic and modern, she said. I nodded and let her rabbit on. But I had more important things to worry about.

She mentioned the murder just as I had bitten into a Danish pastry. I felt myself choking and grabbed at the mug of coffee. By the time Mandy had fetched me a glass of water from her new beech kitchen with its slate tiled floor, I had composed myself, although my heart was still pounding against my ribs. Who could have thought that the mere mention of it would bring back all the old terrors? But Mandy can't have noticed anything was wrong because she kept on talking, telling me how the girl had been found up by the woods, on the site of the old gallows. She'd been strangled, Mandy told me, enjoying every detail of the story. Strangled with a bell rope from the church. The police knew who'd done it, of course, but they could never prove anything. The boy had had learning difficulties and his mother had given him an alibi.

I asked her where she'd heard all this and she tapped the side of her nose. 'A woman I work with used to live here. She told me.'

'Did she mention Mr Carter who has the farm next door to us?' I regretted the question as soon as I'd asked it. But Carter was on my mind. In fact if Paul knew how scared I was of Carter he'd have done something about it, so I kept quiet. Trouble was the last thing I wanted in Manton Worthy.

Mandy looked puzzled. 'No, I don't think she did. I can ask her about him if you like.' She leaned forward, eager to please. She reminded me of a dog we had once owned, a stupid animal who was all enthusiasm and no sense. It had been put down and we'd buried it in the back garden.

'No. It's okay. It's not important.' I hoped she couldn't sense the fear in my voice.

We got through three cups of coffee before I looked at my watch and realised how late it was getting. Paul would start to worry if I wasn't home soon. Perhaps it was the age gap between us that made him treat me like a child sometimes. Mandy tried to persuade me to stay – she was probably lonely there in that cottage, that cage of rustic minimalist chic, with her husband away so much – but I had to get away. She was beginning to get on my nerves.

Now that I knew the village was full of incomers like myself I felt more comfortable walking back. But as I hurried back down the main street towards the Old Rectory I heard a voice behind me.

'Karen? It is Karen isn't it?'

I stood there frozen to the spot for a few seconds before I took a deep calming breath and turned round. I tried to smile but I felt

my mouth forming into an expression more of pain than pleasure.

The woman was small, bent with age. Her hair was snowy
white and her flesh looked like thin parchment stretched over the
bones. But her sharp eyes hinted at an agile brain behind that
mask of age. I heard myself saying, 'Sorry, you've made a
mistake. My name's Petra.'

But the woman's bright grey eyes were focussed on mine like
searchlights. She hesitated, a knowing smile playing on her lips.
'I'm so sorry, my dear, you just reminded me of one of my old
pupils. I'm Edith Downey. I live in Beech Cottage... just over
there.' She waved a gnarled finger in the vague direction of a row
of thatched, pastel painted cottages straight off a picture postcard. I shuffled my feet, anxious to get away. 'So you've moved
here recently?'

'Yes.' She looked at me expectantly. She wanted more. 'We've
moved into the Old Rectory... me and my husband... Paul. We've
come from London.' I tried to smile but I don't think I quite
managed it.

Miss Downey took a step closer. Her eyes were still on mine, as
though she was reading my thoughts. 'It's all new people now...
apart from the Carters and myself. I taught at the village school...
when there was a village school.'

'Really.' I tried to sound interested but I felt the adrenaline
pumping around my body as I prepared for flight.

'Have you been to the church yet?'

I shook my head.

'It's worth seeing. It has a medieval screen with some fine angel
carvings. Some of the people who used to live here still come for
Sunday service... most of them live in Ashburn now but they still
feel they have ties here.'

There was a hint of recrimination in her voice; a subtle criticism, as though she was hinting that I was personally responsible
for driving up the village house prices and evicting people from

their homes. But I said nothing. I wanted the encounter to be over. I wanted to get back to Paul.

I remember running back to the Old Rectory as though the hounds of hell were after me. I sank three large gin and tonics before I began the supper. Paul was busy in his office so I don't think he noticed.

It was a while before I summoned up the courage to walk through the village again. I made excuses to myself – I had to use my new Range Rover because I wanted to do some shopping in Exeter or visit a supermarket ten miles away… I didn't dare risk the one at Ashburn. I was making any excuse not to walk past Miss Downey's cottage. But how could I avoid the woman forever?

Somehow I had to persuade Paul that moving to Manton Worthy had been a mistake. But as I wondered how to go about it, I carried on day after day, driving through the village in the Range Rover wearing my dark glasses. The days passed and before I knew it the lanes were filled with farm vehicles and the fields hummed day and night with the noise of combined harvesters. When Paul complained, as I knew he would, I took my chance and said that farms were noisy places and we might be better off somewhere else. But he was determined to stay put. Once Paul had made a decision he would never admit he was wrong.

Soon after that a leaflet came through the door. It was an invitation to the church's harvest festival, followed by a hot pot supper in the church hall. Naturally I threw it straight in the bin and I had the shock of my life when Paul found it there and said he wanted to go. He said he'd decided it was about time we became part of the community. My mouth went dry and my hands began to shake. This was the last thing I wanted.

I was thinking how to talk Paul out of it when I went out into the hall and found the note lying on the doormat.

'Miss Downey was knocked down and killed on Wednesday

night… hit and run driver.' Mandy leaned forward, anxious to share this juicy piece of gossip.

'That's awful,' I said. 'Have the police any idea who…?'

'Well I've heard that an old Land Rover was seen speeding around the village earlier on that evening. Someone said the police have questioned Mr Carter who has the farm next door to you… it's said he often takes his Land Rover to the Wagon and Horses. These country people sometimes think they're above the law where drink driving is concerned, you know.'

'So they think it was Carter?'

Mandy shrugged. After virtually accusing the man she couldn't bring herself to deliver the final verdict. She leaned forward confidentially. 'Remember I told you about that murder… the girl who was found strangled? Well I asked about it and apparently she was Carter's daughter… and he was questioned about it at the time.'

'Was he?' I felt my hands shaking.

'There were rumours going round that he was abusing her but the police never found any evidence… that's what I was told anyway. Don't repeat it, will you.'

'No.' I could hear my heart beating. 'Of course I won't.' I hesitated. 'What happened to the boy the police suspected?'

'I think his family left the area. Why?'

'No reason,' I said, as casually as I could manage. 'Just curious.'

I stood up. I wanted Mandy to go. I wasn't in the mood for company. I was wondering how to stop Paul from going to the harvest supper… how I was going to keep him away from Carter. But then I realised that I didn't have to go with him. I could develop a strategic headache. As long as I didn't come face to face with Carter and the nightmares of my childhood, I'd be all right.

'You're shaking. What's the matter?' Mandy's voice was all concern.

'Nothing.' I tried to smile.

It was half an hour before she left and as she was leaving she asked me if I was going to Miss Downey's funeral. I said no. After all I didn't know the woman.

As soon as she'd gone I rushed upstairs and opened my underwear drawer. I felt underneath the layers of flimsy lace for the note and when I found it I took it out and read it.

'Dear Karen, I've been thinking about our meeting the week before last and I've been wondering what to do for the best. I do understand your feelings but I think it would be helpful to talk. Perhaps you would call on me one day for tea. Yours sincerely, Edith Downey.'

I tore it into tiny pieces and put it down the waste disposal unit in the kitchen. I was stupid to have kept it but I vowed not to make any more mistakes. That evening I told Paul that I wanted to go back to London, but his response was that it was still early days... and the harvest supper was just what I needed to get to know people.

The next day I heard from Mandy that Carter had been released without charge.

I lived in a strange state of limbo for a week, pretending to Paul that I was looking forward to the harvest supper... and all the time making plans to avoid it at all costs. The most worrying thing was that Paul seemed to have reached some understanding with Carter. He had taken to visiting the Wagon and Horses some evenings and one night when he returned, he said that he had been talking to Carter and he seemed all right really: you couldn't always judge by first impressions.

The change in Paul shocked me – he claimed that the slow pace of country life was lowering his blood pressure and making him feel calmer. Why run around like a headless chicken in London when you could enjoy the simple pleasures of a small community and open spaces? Paul seemed hooked and, like converts the world over, he began to enter into his new enthusiasm with a gusto lacking in the born and bred countryman. He talked of learning to ride, maybe joining the local hunt. To my horror he even suggested inviting Carter round for lunch one Sunday as he was on his own, an idea which sent me straight to the bathroom to throw up.

Paul was going native and with every new development I became more and more certain that I had to get back to the city... any city... anywhere away from Manton Worthy. I had to get out before it was too late.

On the night of the harvest supper I developed a headache as planned and told Paul to go on his own. He looked disappointed, like a kicked puppy, but I had no choice. After some persuasion he went and once I was alone I locked all the doors and settled down to an evening by the telly with some interior design magazines – I wanted to do something with the en suite bathroom so I found myself a pair of scissors to cut out any pictures that might provide me with some inspiration. I opened a bottle of Chardonnay too – I needed something to steady my nerves.

At half past nine it was pitch dark outside. Darkness in the countryside is nothing like darkness in the city and I could see nothing outside the windows, as though someone had hung black velvet drapes on the other side of the glass. But with the curtains drawn and the telly on I felt cosy and safe. Until I heard the noise of our polished brass doorknocker being raised and lowered three times.

I froze. The telly still babbled on, oblivious to the crisis, as three more knocks came. Then another three. I went through all the possibilities in my mind. Could Paul have forgotten his key? Could Mandy be calling to see how I was? I crept along the hall in the darkness, making for the front door. There were no windows in the door but the TV executive had installed a spy hole and security lights. I stood on tiptoe to look through the spy hole but although the front step was flooded with halogen light, there seemed to be nobody there.

I was about to return to the safe warmth of the lounge when the knocking began again. My body started to shake and I tried to peer out of the spy hole, but again there seemed to be nobody there.

I know now that I shouldn't have opened the door but it was an automatic reaction – and I suppose I assumed that I could just close it against any danger if the worst happened. But things are rarely that straightforward. As soon as I had turned the latch, the door burst open and I fell backwards. I think I screamed. I think I tried to lash out. But it was useless. It was dark in the hallway and I could see very little but I felt strong arms dragging me towards the lounge. I tried to kick but it was as though I was caught in a web like a fly… at the mercy of some monstrous, unseen spider. I screamed again but then I realised that this was the countryside. There was nobody there to hear me.

We were in the lounge now and Carter was bundling me on to the sofa. I could smell his waxed jacket as he held me… the same smell I remembered from all those years ago. And I could see his face… full of hatred.

'I saw you.' He spat the words like venom. 'I saw you run her over.'

I tried to wriggle free but he held me tight.

'But you were too late. She'd told me already that you were back.'

'I don't know what you're talking about.' The words came out as a squeak, unconvincing even to myself.

'Miss Downey, that's what I'm talking about. I got talking to that husband of yours. Funny how you didn't tell him much about yourself. He's no idea, has he?'

I felt his breath on my face and I tried to push him away. But it was no use. He was stronger than me.

'Why, Karen?' he hissed, putting his face close to mine. 'Just tell me why? What had she ever done to you?'

'I don't know what you mean.'

'My Jenny... why?'

'Luke Fisher killed Jenny. Everyone knew that.'

His hands began to tighten around my neck. 'Once you'd gone, Luke told the police what he saw. They didn't believe him – just because he wasn't all there they thought he was making it up. But I knew he was telling the truth. You were always a sly little bitch... a bully. You made my Jenny's life a misery. No wonder your mam and dad moved away so bloody quick after she died. Did they know, eh? Always looked so bloody innocent, didn't you... face like one of them angels in the church. Did they know what you were really like? Did they know what you'd done?'

With an almighty effort I pushed him off and sprang up. I don't remember much about what happened next. Only that there was a lot of blood and I felt that same strange detachment I'd felt after I had killed Jenny Carter... when I looked down and saw her dead, bulging eyes staring up at me.

The memory returned like a tidal wave, everything that had happened that day all those years ago. The bell ropes in the church had been replaced and the old ones had been left lying in the back pew, perfect for the game I'd made up... the game of dare. I dared Jenny Carter to go to the old gallows and put the rope around her neck. Luke followed us – he was hard to get rid of... older than us, big and soft and too simple to know when he wasn't wanted. But I hadn't known he was watching when I tightened the rope around Jenny's neck, just to see what it would be like to kill somebody... to have the power of life and death. Once I'd started pulling on that rope I couldn't stop. I'd watched, fascinated, as her face began to contort and her eyes started to bulge. I was all-powerful, the angel of death; just like the angels on the screen in the church... only different. As I stood over the body of Jenny's father, I felt the same elation... the same thrill. But when I heard a voice calling in the hall the feeling disappeared and my brain began to work quickly.

I began to sob and I sank to the floor. The scissors I'd grabbed from the coffee table were in my hand and I threw them to one side. I was shaking and crying hysterically by the time Paul entered the room. And when he took me in his arms I slumped against him in a dead faint.

I pretended to be unconscious when the doctor and the police arrived. I thought it was best. And when I came round, in my own good time, I told my story in a weak voice. Carter had arrived and pushed his way in then he had tried to... I hesitated at this point for maximum effect but the policewoman with the sympathetic eyes knew just what I meant. Women alone in the countryside were so vulnerable and hard-drinking men like Carter sensing weakness, knowing a woman would be alone... She was the sort of woman who believes all men are potential rapists and she believed every word I said. I was the victim, she said, and I mustn't feel guilty. I never liked to tell her that I didn't.

We left Manton Worthy soon after, of course, and made a tidy profit on the Old Rectory, which we sold to a city broker who wanted it for a weekend retreat. I told Paul that I couldn't bear to stay there after what had happened and he was very sympathetic – he even blamed himself for getting too pally with Carter. The day before we left I wandered into the church and I looked at the angel on the screen, the one with the sword, and I couldn't help smiling. I was Manton Worthy's angel of death... and nobody would ever know.

Once we were back in London I resumed my old life. I was Petra, Paul's wife; a lady who lunched and did very little else. Karen was dead.

It was six months later when Paul was found dead at the foot of the stairs in his office. He'd been working late and I'd been at the gym, working out with Karl my personal trainer. Of course when I say working out, I use the term loosely – what we were doing had very little to do with exercise bikes and weights. Karl had a girlfriend but I wasn't worried about that – he was just a bit of fun; a way of passing the time... and Paul would never get to know.

The policeman who came to tell me about Paul's death wasn't very sympathetic. He questioned me for hours about where I'd been and about my relationship with Paul. I said nothing about Karl, of course. And when he asked me how much I stood to inherit on Paul's death, I told him the truth. Five and a half million, give or take a few quid. Of course I'd assumed that Paul's death was an accident, cut and dried. But it just shows you how wrong you can be.

The police said that Paul hadn't fallen, there were signs of a struggle and fibres from my coat were found under one of his fingernails. I told the police that he'd caught his nail on my coat that morning. And I told them he had some pretty dodgy business associates... he'd even moved to Devon once to get away from them. But they wouldn't listen and when they charged me with Paul's murder even Karl turned his back on me and refused to give me an alibi because he was scared of his cow of a girlfriend.

I was convinced it would never come to trial. After all, I hadn't done anything. But every time I tried to convince the police of my innocence, they wouldn't listen. My defence barrister told the court how six months ago I'd been the victim of an attempted rape, but even that didn't seem to earn me much sympathy. The jury was full of brain-dead idiots who found me guilty by a majority of ten to two and as the police bundled me past the crowds waiting outside the Old Bailey someone flung a coat over my head and pushed me into a van that smelled of unwashed bodies and urine.

Even when they took the coat off my head the windows in the van were too high to see out of and I couldn't tell where we were or what direction we were driving in. We seemed to drive for hours on a fast, straight road then we slowed down and the roads started to wind.

I asked the sour-faced woman I was handcuffed to where we were going and she turned to me and smiled, as though she was enjoying some private joke.

'Oh you're going to Gampton Prison. You'll like it there. It's in the country… right in the middle of nowhere.'

When she started to laugh I screamed and banged on the side of the prison van until my hands were sore.

The Worst Crime Known to Man

Reginald Hill

Crime writers are generally associated in the public mind with novels rather than short stories. This is understandable, but it means that the shorter tales written by an accomplished novelist are sometimes overlooked. Reg Hill is not a prolific writer of short stories; nevertheless his work in this form is of the highest standard and he won the CWA Macallan Short Story Dagger for 'On The Psychiatrist's Couch', contributed to a previous CWA anthology, *Whydunit?* 'The Worst Crime Known To Man' won first prize in a short story contest sponsored by the *Telegraph Sunday Magazine* and Veuve Clicquot Champagne almost twenty years ago, but is curiously little known. It is good to see this 'hidden gem' back in print.

'A middle-aged man was removed from the Centre Court crowd yesterday for causing a disturbance during a line-call dispute.'

On summer evenings when I was young, I used to sit with mamma on the verandah of our bungalow and watch the flamingoes gliding over the tennis court to roost on the distant lake.

This was my favourite time of day and the verandah was my favourite place. It was simply furnished with a low table, a scatter of cane chairs, and an old English farmhouse rocker with its broad seat moulded and polished by long use.

This was Father's special chair. At the end of the day he would fold his great length into it, lean back with a sigh of contentment, and more often than not say, 'This was your grandfather's chair, Colley, did I ever tell you that?'

'Yes, Father.'

'Did I? Then probably I told you what it was my father used to tell me while sitting in this chair.'

'Life is a game and you play to the rules, and cheating's the worst crime known to man,' I would chant.

'Good boy,' he would exclaim, laughing and glancing at Mamma, who would smile sweetly, making me smile too. I always smiled when Mamma smiled. She seemed to me then a raving beauty, and she was certainly the most attractive of the only three white women within five hundred square miles. I suppose she seemed so to many others too. 'Boff' Gorton, a young District Officer from a better school than Father, used to tell her so after his third gin and tonic, and she would smile and my father would laugh. Boff came round quite a lot, ostensibly to check that all was well (there had already been the first stirrings of the Troubles) and to have a couple of sets on our lush green tennis court. I was too young to wonder how serious Boff's admiration of Mamma really was. During one of his visits, when Father had been held up in the bush, I got up in the night for a drink of water and heard a noise of violent rocking on the verandah. When I went to investigate I discovered Mamma relaxing in the rocking chair and Boff, flushed and rather breathless, sitting on the floor. Curiously, Boff's situation struck me as less remarkable than Mamma's. This was the first time in my life I had ever known her to occupy the rocker.

Father's attitude to Boff was that of an older and rather patronisingly helpful brother. Only on the tennis court did anything like passion show, and that may have been due to natural competitiveness rather than jealousy. At any rate, their games were gargantuan struggles, with Boff's youth and Father's skill in such balance that the outcome was always in doubt.

The court itself was beautiful, a rectangle of English green it had taken ten years to perfect. It was completely enclosed in a cage of wire mesh, erected more to keep wildlife out than balls in. Human entry was effected through a small, tight-fitting gate, shut at night with a heavy chain and large padlock.

Father and Boff played their last match there one spring afternoon that had all the warmth and richness of the best of English summer evenings. Mamma was away superintending the *accouchement* of our nearest female neighbour, who had foolishly delayed her transfer down-country overlong. Curiously, Mamma's absence seemed to stir things up between the two men more than her presence ever did, and Father's invitation to Boff to play tennis came out like a challenge to a duel.

Boff tried to lighten matters by saying to me, 'Colley, old chum, why don't you come along and be ball boy?'

'Yes, Colley,' said Father. 'You come along. You can be umpire too, and see fair play.'

'I say,' said Boff, flushing. 'Do we need an umpire? I mean, neither of us is likely to cheat, are we?'

'Life is a game and you play to the rules and cheating's the worst crime known to man,' I piped up.

'How right you are, Colley,' said Father, observing Boff grimly. 'You umpire!'

There was no more discussion, but even in the prematch knock-up I recognised a ferocity that both excited and disturbed me. And when the match proper began it was such a hard-fought struggle that for a long time none of us noticed the arrival of the spectators. Usually only the duty houseboy watched from a respectful distance, waiting to be summoned forward with refreshing drinks, though occasionally some nomadic tribesmen would gaze from the fringes of the bush with courteous puzzlement. But this was different. Suddenly I realised that the court was entirely surrounded. There must have been two hundred of them, all standing quietly enough, but all marked with the symbols of their intent and bearing its instruments – machetes and spears.

'Father!' I choked out.

The two men glanced toward me, then saw what I had seen. For a second no one moved; then, with a fearsome roar, the natives rushed forward. Boff hurled himself towards the gate in the fence, and for a moment I thought he was making a suicidal attempt at flight. But District Officers are trained in other schools than that, and the next minute I saw he had seized the retaining chain, pulled it round the gate post and snapped shut the padlock.

The enemy was locked out. At the same time, of course, we were locked in.

If they had been carrying guns, in, out, it would have made no difference. Fortunately they were not, and the mesh was too close for the broad heads of their throwing spears. Even so, they could soon have hacked a way through the wire had not Boff for the second time revealed the quality of his training. Father in his eagerness for the fray had come from the house unarmed, but Boff had brought his revolver, and as soon as a group of our invaders began to hack at the fence he took careful aim and shot the most enthusiastic of them between the eyes.

They fell back in panic, but only for a moment. When they realised that Boff wasn't following up his attack, they returned to the fence, but no one offered to lead another demolition attempt.

'I've got just five bullets left,' murmured Boff. 'The only thing holding these chaps back is that 'they know the first to make a move will certainly die. But eventually not even that will matter.'

'Why don't we make a dash for the house?' asked Father. 'It's only fifty yards. And once we get to the rifles…'

'For God's sake!' said Boff. 'Don't you understand? Outside this fence we're finished! And please don't talk about rifles. Once one of this lot gets that idea…'

Suddenly there came a great cry from the direction of the bungalow and I thought someone *had* got the idea. But a puff of smoke and a sudden tongue of flame revealed the truth, at the same time better and worse. Worse, because my home was going up in flames; better, because this act of arson would destroy their only source of weaponry and might even attract attention to our plight.

Father, perhaps feeling annoyed at the lead Boff had taken in dealing with the situation, suddenly picked up his racket.

'We might as well do something till help comes,' he said. 'My service, I believe.'

It may have started as a gesture, but very rapidly that match developed into the hard, bitter struggle it had promised to be before the attack. I stood at the net holding the revolver, at first keeping an eye on the enemy outside. But soon my judgment of line calls and lets was required so frequently that I had to give my full attention to the game.

But the most curious thing of all was the reaction of the rebels. At first there'd been some jabbering about ways of winkling us out. Then they fell silent except for one man, some renegade houseboy, I presume, who rather self-importantly began to offer a mixture of explanation of, and commentary on, the game, till his voice too died away; and at four-all in the first set I realised they had become as absorbed in the match as the players themselves. It was quite amazing, like watching a highly sunburned

Wimbledon crowd. The heads moved from side to side following the flight of the ball, and at particularly strong or clever shots they beat their spear shafts against the earth and made approving booming noises deep in their throats.

Father took the first set seven-five, and looked as if he might run away with the second. But at one-four Boff's youth began to tell, and suddenly Father was on the defensive. At four-four he seemed to fold up completely, but I guessed that he was merely admitting the inevitable and taking a rest with a view to the climax.

The policy seemed to pay off. Boff won that set six-four, but now he too seemed to have shot his bolt and neither man could gain an ascendancy in the final set. Six-six it went, seven-seven, eight-eight, nine-nine, then into double figures. The light was fading fast.

'Look,' said Boff coming up to the net and speaking in a low voice. 'Shall we try to keep it going as long as possible? I don't know what these fellows may do when we finish. All right?'

Father didn't answer, but returned to the base line to serve. They came hard and straight, four aces. The crowd boomed. I forgot my official neutrality and joined in the applause. Father stood back to receive service.

I don't know. Perhaps he *was* trying to keep the match going. Perhaps he just intended to give away points by lashing out wildly at Boff's far from puny service. But the result was devastating. Three times in a row the ball streaked from his racket quite unplayably, putting up baseline chalk. Love-forty. Three match points. Father settled down. Boff served. Again the flashing return, but this time Boff, driven by resentment or fear, flung himself after it and sent it floating back. Father smashed, Boff retrieved. Father smashed. Boff retrieved again.

'For God's sake!' he pleaded.

Father, at the net, drove the ball deep into the corner and Boff managed to reach this only flinging himself full length across the grass. But what a shot he produced! A perfect lob, drifting over Father's head and making for the extreme back-hand corner.

Father turned with a speed I had not believed him capable of and went in pursuit. There was topspin on the ball. Once it bounced, it would be away beyond mortal reach. The situation looked hopeless.

But Father had no intention of letting it bounce. I drew in my breath as I saw he was going to attempt that most difficult of shots, a reverse backhand volley on the run. I swear the spectating natives drew in their breath too.

Father stretched – but it wasn't enough. He leapt. He connected. It was superb. The ball floated towards Boff, who still lay prostrate on the base line, and bounced gently a couple of feet from his face.

'Out!' he called desperately.

Father's roar of triumph turned to a howl of incredulity.

'Out?' he demanded. *'Out?'*

He turned to me and flung his arms wide in appeal. Boff called to me.

'Please, Colley. It *was* out, wasn't it? It *was!'*

He spoke with all the authority of a District Officer. But I was the umpire and I knew that in this matter my powers exceeded his. I shook my head.

'In!' I called. 'Game, set and match to…'

With a cry of triumph, Father jumped over the net. And at the same moment a big black fellow with a face painted like a Halloween lantern twisted his spear butt in the chain till it snapped, and the howling mob poured in.

They were only inside the fence for about ten seconds before the first Land Rover full of troops arrived. But in that time they managed to carve the recumbent Boff into several pieces. Father on his feet and wielding his racket like a cavalry sabre managed to get away with a few unpleasant wounds, while I – perhaps because I still held the revolver, though I was too petrified to use it – escaped without threat, let alone violence.

On her return, Mamma was naturally upset. I would have thought the survival of her husband and only son would have compensated for the loss of the house, but the more this was urged, the greater waxed her grief. Later, when I told the story of the match, describing with the detail befitting a noble death how Boff had so heroically attempted to keep the final game going, she had a relapse. When she recovered, things changed. I don't think I ever saw her smile again at Father's jokes.

Not that there were many more to smile at. One of Father's wounds turned septic and he had to have his right arm amputated just above the elbow. He tried to learn to play left-handed thereafter, but it never amounted to more than pat ball, and within a twelvemonth only the metal supports rising from the luxuriant undergrowth showed where the tennis court had been.

Soon after that I was sent back to the old country for schooling, and midway through my first term the Head sent for me to tell me there'd been a tragic accident. Father had been cleaning a gun and it had gone off. Or perhaps my mother had been cleaning the gun. Or perhaps, as they both died, they'd both been cleaning guns. I never discovered any details. Out there in the old days they still knew how to draw a decent veil over such things.

I was deeply grieved, of course, but school's a good place for forgetting and I never went back. Sending me to England had been their last known wish for my future. I did not feel able to go against it, not even when I was old enough to have some freedom of choice. And I have been happy enough here with my English job, English marriage, English health. I dig my little patch of garden, read political biographies, play a bit of golf.

But no tennis. I never got interested at school somehow, and I don't suppose I would ever have bothered with tennis again if my managing director hadn't offered me a spare Centre Court ticket.

Well, I had to be in town anyway, and it seemed silly to miss the chance of visiting Wimbledon.

I was enjoying it thoroughly too, enjoying the crowd and the place and the game, here, now, with never a thought for the old days, till the Australian played that deep cross-court lob which sent the short-tempered American sprawling.

Then suddenly I saw it all again.

The white ball drifting through the richly scented, darkling air.

The outstretched figure on the baseline.

The pleading, despairing look on Boff's face as he watches the ball bounce out of his reach.

And with it his youth and his hopes and his life.

I saw the same anguish on the American's face today, heard the same accusing disbelief in his voice.

Of course, it wasn't his life and hopes and youth that were at stake. But as Father used to say, life is a game, and you play to the rules, and cheating's the worst crime known to man.

And the American and Boff did have one thing in common.

Both balls were a good six inches out.

THE WAR IN WONDERLAND

Edward D Hoch

There is no more versatile or prolific writer of short mystery stories the world over than Ed Hoch. The fertility of his imagination is quite breathtaking and it is a privilege to be able to introduce his latest story (although no doubt he will have penned several more by the time this book appears in the shops). Ed has chronicled the adventures of many series characters in the short form, but this is a stand-alone story. Unexpectedly, the backdrop is Cheshire, rather than his native USA. He took as his starting point an interesting snippet of information about the Second World War and wove around it a typically agreeable tale.

S id Jenkins was usually first up in the morning, and the others got to thinking he must be able to sense the rising of the sun because there were no windows and few clocks in their abode. Seven of them resided in their cramped underground quarters, not quite enough for two tables of bridge, but then there was always one person on guard duty anyway, every night.

They were in the north of England, in an area of Cheshire farmland remote from the bombs that fell nightly on Liverpool and Manchester. Their job was simple. The five men and two women assigned here were the entire staff of an installation known officially as Carroll Field. It had been named after Lewis Carroll, of Alice in Wonderland fame, who had grown up in the nearest village, where his father had been the local vicar.

'Everyone up!' Jenkins called out, ringing the breakfast bell in the cramped galley. Amanda stumbled from the bathroom, still half asleep, and started helping him with breakfast preparations. 'How'd you sleep?' he asked as he did every morning, more to start a conversation than anything else.

'Fitfully, dear boy.' Amanda was an attractive redhead in her mid-thirties, only a decade older than Jenkins, but since he was one of the younger men she tended to consider him as little more than a prep school lad. 'We could do with a little fresh air in this place.'

'The ventilation system—'

'Sod the ventilation system! We're buried underground like gophers, with only a little nightlight to find our way to the toilet.' She started cracking eggs in the frying pan as they heard the others coming awake.

Captain Roger Seaborn, the ranking officer in the detachment, was the first to join them. He was a handsome, quiet man who walked with a limp he'd acquired after his Spitfire made a bad landing. They'd told him the assignment to Carroll Field was only temporary until his leg healed, but he grew more impatient with each passing day. 'Good morning,' he greeted them. 'Is Private Silcrest still upstairs?'

Amanda Flower glanced at the wall clock. 'He's on watch for another ten minutes.'

'Tell him to come down for breakfast with us. The Huns aren't going to bomb us after sunrise.'

Their underground bunker was about a quarter-mile from the airfield, out of harm's way unless the German bombs were off target. It was the possibility of a bad aim that kept them underground each night, waiting for an attack that might never come. Captain Seaborn liked to say they were one of the few outposts whose mission would be a failure if they weren't bombed.

'I'll go get him,' Jenkins said, nodding toward Grace Foley and Raster as he opened the steel door and went up the spiral staircase. The guard post was just below ground level, with a periscope affording a view in all directions. As he climbed the stairs he heard voices, and recognised that of their only nearby neighbour, a farm wife named Alice Cleatworth who came by every day with fresh eggs and vegetables and milk, paid for by the government.

'Good morning, Private Jenkins,' she greeted him, handing over her usual basket of food through the raised metal door into what they all called the rabbit hole. Silcrest accepted it gently, aware of the eggs inside.

'How's the weather out today?' Jenkins asked.

'Perfect for late summer. Get out of your rabbit hole and enjoy it!'

'We'll be out soon enough.' After Mrs Cleatworth returned to her truck, Jenkins told Silcrest to come down for breakfast with the others.

The young private hesitated. 'Are you sure it's all right? I don't want to be court-martialed for leaving my post.'

'The captain said to get you. Come on.'

Grace Foley, a charming Irish lass about Jenkins's age, met

them at the bottom of the stairs and took the basket. 'Did you see any planes?' she asked Silcrest.

'Not a one. I'd have sounded the alarm if I did.'

'You were probably sleeping.' She liked to kid Silcrest and she laughed when he quickly denied the accusation.

They clustered around the dining table, which was a bit crowded for seven people. Jenkins always helped the women with the food before settling down himself. By then he was often at the head of the table because Captain Seaborn avoided showing his authority whenever possible, seating himself casually on the side. It was only after tea and coffee had been served that he shifted from small talk to the day's routines.

'Raster, how are you coming with the tank?' he asked the muscular young man who occupied the foot of the table opposite Jenkins.

'It'll be done today, Captain. Then the ladies can do a fine paint job on it.'

Amanda Flower joined the conversation. 'Camouflage?'

'The usual bit. Not too good or Jerry might not see it from the air.'

'Should we keep working on the planes?' This last question came from Sergeant Leonard. Like the captain he was recuperating from a minor injury and viewed his tour of duty at Carroll Field as a mere stumbling block in his military career. The others were all of lower rank, mainly privates like Jenkins, though ranks were unimportant at Carroll Field. All of them worked together.

'Affirmative,' the captain responded. 'Jenkins, you'll come with us. The ladies will get their paint cans ready, and Silcrest, you'll get a few hours sack time.'

'I'm on guard duty tonight,' Jenkins reminded him.

'Right you are. You can knock off when Silcrest wakes up to relieve you on the work detail.'

Twenty minutes later they emerged through the metal door with its covering of artificial grass. Jenkins squinted against the brightness of the morning sun and turned to help Grace up the last few steps of the ladder. 'I wish you were working with us today,' he told her with a smile. Behind them, Silcrest lowered the hidden entrance and locked it from inside.

'I'll bring the lunch around,' Grace said quietly.

'Is that a promise?'

'Sure!'

He watched the two women walking across the grass toward Carroll Field, wishing he was with them instead of Raster. There was something about the man that he disliked, and he distrusted him around women. Perhaps it was the odour of masculinity that seemed to cling to him. Even now he wore only an undershirt and pants, and Jenkins suspected he would shed the undershirt before long.

For his part, Jenkins walked faster to keep up with Captain Seaborn and the sergeant. Their course was slightly different, aimed at the big corrugated hanger that stood next to the landing strip. There was eight Spitfires already on view along the field, and with luck they'd add two more by the end of the day. 'After we get twenty we'll switch to medium bombers,' Seaborn told them. 'Headquarters will be sending up the templates next week.'

Passing the line of completed planes, Jenkins was struck again by the flimsy nature of their deception. These were only flat pieces of painted plywood, nailed together to form the body, wings and tail assembly of Spitfires. But photographed from the air by German reconnaissance flights, they just might fool someone back in Berlin. The long-range plan was to keep building these shabby replicas of fighter planes and medium bombers, adding occasional tanks and trucks, so that Carroll Field ultimately became not just an airbase but a possible staging area for a future invasion of France. Perhaps the Germans might risk a night raid to destroy the airfield. If so, the RAF could intercept them as they headed home.

In the hanger he set to work with Captain Seaborn and Sergeant Leonard, sawing the large sheets of plywood into their proper lengths. 'This is tough work for an officer,' Leonard remarked.

Seaborn snorted. 'I grew up on a farm before the war. I'm used to work a great deal more difficult than this. Pass me that template, will you, Jenkins?'

He handed it over. 'Still, sir, I imagine you'd much rather be back in combat.'

'And I will be, as soon as this leg heals properly.'

They worked steadily through the morning, pausing only for a bit of lunch that Grace brought around in a paper sack. Jenkins gave her a wink. He slid his hand on to hers but she slapped it gently away. 'What have you got that's good to eat?'

'The usual sandwiches,' she told him. 'Amanda made them up. Mrs Cleatworth brought a head of lettuce today so that's an extra bonus. I have hot tea in the thermos.'

Jenkins called out to Captain Seaborn and Leonard who were assembling the plywood body of the Spitfire. 'Lunch is here!'

'Ah!' the captain said, putting down his hammer and walking over to join them. 'It's our personal angel.'

Grace blushed and looked away. 'Only a delivery girl when I'm not painting plywood planes. Amanda makes the sandwiches.'

The captain took one for himself and another for Sergeant Leonard. 'I'll be back for our tea,' he said.

When they were alone, Jenkins asked, 'Is Raster giving you any trouble?'

'Oh, him! Amanda and I don't pay any attention to what he says.'

'You should report him to the captain if he makes improper advances.'

'I'm a big girl, Sid. I can take care of myself.'

'I know you can. I guess I'm a little bit jealous.'

She sighed and glanced around, making certain the other two were far enough away. 'I want to be with you, really I do. But I don't see any way we can work it. The captain never lets more than one of us at a time go on a weekend pass.'

'I'll try to work something out,' he promised.

Silcrest came out to relieve him around two o'clock, insisting he'd had enough sleep. 'Go ahead, Jenkins, get a few hours in before you have to pull guard duty. Looking through that periscope all night would make anyone drowsy.'

'I know. I've done it plenty of times.' Captain Seaborn didn't pull guard duty himself unless someone was ill or on weekend pass. That meant the rest of them had it every sixth night.

'There's a full moon tonight, a bomber's moon. Maybe they'll come after us.'

'I hope so.'

Jenkins rested for a few hours, dozing on and off without really falling into a deep sleep. The underground quarters had just three bedrooms, which meant that Captain Seaborn and Sergeant Leonard shared one, the two women shared one, and Jenkins shared one with Raster and young Silcrest. It was good being alone in the windowless room, even if only for a short time, and he almost resented the intrusion when he heard one of the others inserting a long-stemmed key into the hidden lock to open the rabbit hole.

It proved to be Amanda Flower, who glanced briefly into his room on her way to the bathroom. Peering at his watch Jenkins saw that it was nearly five. The others would be returning shortly. He got up, stretched, and went into the small galley to help Amanda with the evening meal.

She seemed surprised to see him cutting up some of the farmer's tomatoes when she came out of the bathroom. 'Dear boy, you should be getting some rest for guard duty.'

'It's not easy sleeping down here.'

'You don't have to tell me that.' She took his knife from his hand and started in on the tomatoes. 'I'll have to take a sleeping powder tonight if I'm to get any rest at all. You'd better not try waking me with the alarm while you're up there at the periscope tonight.'

Jenkins chuckled at the thought of it. 'I think we'll set out the entire war here without catching sight of a single German bomb.'

'I hope you're right.'

The others straggled in and gathered around the table. Captain Seaborn switched on the radio to the BBC so they could hear the latest war news. It was a nightly ritual with them, though the news these days was rarely good. 'They'll come one of these nights,' Raster said, downing his daily ration of beer. 'They'll come and bomb us and we'll die in our beds.'

'You almost sound as if that would please you,' Grace said.

'Not please me, no. I'd much rather die in bed with you, little girl.'

'Enough of that!' Sergeant Leonard barked. 'Or I'll have you up on charges.'

'Sorry,' Raster mumbled into his beer.

Captain Seaborn cleared his throat. 'Our rules are pretty lax in this outfit, 'but we are still subject to regulations. Any infractions will be severely dealt with. That goes for Private Raster and everyone else.'

A brief silence settled over the table. Finally, as the meal was nearing its conclusion, Amanda Flower suggested a game of bridge. They usually played two or three nights a week, so the suggestion was not unexpected. 'I'm on guard duty,' Jenkins reminded them, and Raster excused himself too.

'The rest of you play,' Captain Seaborn said. 'I'll do some reading tonight.'

So Amanda got out the cards and teamed with Sergeant Leonard against Grace and Silcrest. They'd lingered longer than usual over dinner so Jenkins climbed the spiral staircase to his periscope lookout even though the late summer sun hadn't yet set. It was a useless task, really, but someone had to do it. One of these nights the Germans just might be foolish enough to bomb the place and they'd have to scramble the RAF squadron.

He checked the alarm button and the portable toilet, then picked up one of those slim paperbound books they were printing for the armed forces. Lost Horizon by James Hilton. He'd certainly rather be in Shangri-La with Grace than here at Carroll Field.

Sometime around one he noticed that the full moon had risen, bathing the landscape in an unreal silvery glow. This was indeed a bomber's moon as Silcrest had said. He made a note of it in his log. It was a warm night and he had slipped off his shirt. The remainder of the time passed uneventfully as he nervously awaited the dawn. He hadn't slept a wink or even dozed. The early sun finally appeared in the east and through his periscope he could see Mrs Cleatworth's truck approaching along the road with her daily basket, a bit earlier than usual.

When the farmer's wife was almost up to the rabbit hole Jenkins raised the grass-covered door to greet her. 'Good morning, Mrs Cleatworth. Have you brought us anything special?'

'I don't know about special,' the farmer's wife answered, 'but these tomatoes are even better than the ones I brought yester—' Her words were cut off by a sudden shriek from below. 'My God, what's that?'

'I don't know. Stay right here. I'll be back.' Jenkins hurried down the spiral staircase as fast as he could. He paused on the bottom step, seeing that it had been Amanda who screamed. She was in the galley standing over a body and he knew it was Sergeant Leonard. Almost at once the others appeared from their rooms.

'What happened?' Captain Seaborn asked, bending to examine the sergeant's bloodied chest and the kitchen knife on the floor next to the body.

'I… I found him like this. Is he—?'

'Dead for some hours. Rigor mortis is already setting in.'

Raster and Grace and Silcrest had joined them by now, each barely able to comprehend what they were seeing. Jenkins remembered Mrs Cleatworth waiting by the open door. 'I'll be right back,' he said, hurrying up the stairs.

'What's going on?' the farmer's wife wanted to know.

'There's been an accident. I'll have to close up now.' He took the basket, his heart pounding, and tried to smile as he closed the door.

Back downstairs, Captain Seaborn was issuing crisp orders. 'Amanda, get on the radio to Headquarters, tell them what's happened.'

'What has happened?' she asked. 'Sergeant Leonard is dead but—'

'All right,' he said with some exasperation. 'Everyone gather round and we'll talk this out before she calls.'

They obeyed him, settling into chairs, and Jenkins carefully skirted the blood on the floor to join them. 'Can't someone cover him up?' Grace asked, then answered her own question by disappearing into the bedroom and returning with a sheet.

Seaborn waited until she'd settled down before he spoke. 'It's clear that sometime during the night Sergeant Leonard was murdered, stabbed to death with one of the knives we were using to cut up the vegetables. Now there are only six of us here, and no one entered through the only doorway, the rabbit hole. That's correct, isn't it, Jenkins?'

'Correct, sir. I opened the door only for Mrs Cleatworth, who arrived just as Amanda discovered the body.'

'Do you have the guards' logbook?'

'I'll get it.'

The captain flipped through it, confirming what Jenkins had said. 'So that leaves the five of us who were down here with him. I was asleep. I never heard him get up. Amanda?'

'I took a powder to help me sleep. I didn't hear a thing.'

'I was asleep too,' Grace said.

'How about you, Raster? You've had some run-ins with the sergeant.'

'If I'd killed him you'd know about it. I'd be asking for a medal.'

Silcrest, the youngest of them, insisted they'd both been asleep the entire night. 'It was her scream that woke us.'

'All right,' Captain Seaborn decided with visible reluctance. 'Obviously one of us isn't telling the truth.'

'Could he have stabbed himself?' Jenkins suggested.

'Why would he do that?'

'I don't know,' he admitted, unable to come up with a likely reason.

Seaborn shook his head. 'If he wanted to kill himself he had a service revolver he could have used. That would be much more likely than stabbing oneself in the chest and then pulling out the knife. In any event, I'll have to report this to Colonel Yardley.'

'You're saying one of us is a killer?' Grace asked. 'Who would want to kill Sergeant Leonard?' She avoided glancing at Raster as she spoke.

'An enemy agent,' Seaborn suggested. 'A spy.'

It was Amanda who spoke up then. 'Someone who's planning to kill us all, one at a time?'

'That's crazy!' Raster barked. 'You people are living in wonderland.'

'Perhaps we are,' she agreed. 'We're down a rabbit hole, at an unreal airfield named for Lewis Carroll, and we even have two queens.' She patted her hair. 'I suppose I'm the red queen, so you must be the white queen, Grace.'

'What about the kings, and the white rabbit and the mad hatter?' young Silcrest asked, entering into the game.

Amanda smiled. 'Well, I suppose the captain and the sergeant must be the kings, and you would make a nice white rabbit,

Jenkins, since you were at the top of the rabbit hole last night.' She turned to Raster. 'Would you like to be the mad hatter?'

'You're all loony,' was his reply.

'And Silcrest, you can be the mock turtle.'

Captain Seaborn was running out of patience. 'Let's not forget there's a dead man under that sheet. This isn't a matter for fun and games. I'm calling the major on the emergency frequency.' He went off to his room where the radio was kept.

When he was gone, Raster was the first to speak. 'You're all loony,' he said again. 'You're just a bunch of misfits no good for combat. That's why they have you up here building wooden planes in the middle of the woods.'

'And what about yourself?' Amanda asked. 'That uniform in your room has had stripes cut off the sleeve. A demotion, perhaps?'

Raster didn't answer, and young Silcrest spoke up. 'We don't have an Alice.'

'What?'

'An Alice in Wonderland. You've assigned parts for all of us but there is no Alice.'

'Matter of fact, there is,' Jenkins reminded them. 'Alice Cleatworth, the farmer's wife who brings us the basket each morning.'

'I don't know that we can count her,' Amanda said. 'She's never been down the rabbit hole.'

Captain Seaborn returned at that moment. 'We're to suspend all operations pending the arrival of investigating officers in a few hours. I've also been instructed to do a visual check of everyone's garments for bloodstains, and to collect everyone's footgear for testing. Including my own.'

They bent grimly to remove their shoes and slippers. The fantasy of Alice in Wonderland had burst like a soap bubble.

After dressing they wandered outside to eat their breakfast. No one wanted to eat in sight of Leonard's body. It was another perfect August day and Jenkins sat cross-legged in the grass with his toast and tea. He could see the hanger off in the distance, deserted now though he knew the captain would walk over to inspect it shortly.

'Out of the rabbit hole!' Amanda Flower announced as she reached the surface. Grace was with her and walked over to sit by Jenkins. She'd put on pants and a uniform shirt, though he was still in his undershirt. 'This is a terrible thing,' she said, 'and doubly terrible because one of us must have killed him. What will the investigators do?'

Jenkins shrugged. 'Ask a lot of questions, I suppose. Check all of our records.'

'I've got no record. I've only been in the service for six months. What about you?'

Jenkins was silent for a moment. 'I got busted once for fighting. I'm no spy.'

She glanced out at the road. 'How long will it take them to get here?'

'At least an hour.'

But he'd miscalculated badly. Just because Carroll Field was a fake, from which none of its planes would ever fly, he'd forgotten that planes could certainly land there. Fifteen minutes later, a twin-engined RAF transport settled on to the runway and rolled to a stop in front of the hanger. Captain Seaborn seemed surprised to see them that soon too, and ran out to meet them.

Three men emerged from the plane, one of them carrying a leather satchel. Jenkins couldn't tell if they were RAF or Scotland Yard investigators, though it would have been a bit too soon for Scotland Yard. Seaborn spoke with them at length, gesturing occasionally toward the rabbit hole, and Jenkins told Grace, 'You'd better round up the others. They'll want to question everyone.'

When Seaborn reached them with the new arrivals, two of the dark-suited men didn't wait to be introduced, hurrying down the rabbit hole with the satchel. The other one, a middle-aged man with a puffy face and hair graying at the temples, was named Mr Hill, with no first name or rank given. Silcrest and Raster and Amanda had joined them by this time, and Captain Seaborn introduced each of the six.

Mr Hill tried on a smile for size, found it didn't fit, and said briskly to the captain, 'Personnel files, please.'

'They're down below. I'll get them.'

'Yours too,' Mr Hill reminded him. Then he asked, 'Which one is Jenkins?'

'I am, sir.'

'Good. You were on guard duty, correct?'

'Yes, sir.'

'What are your duties at your post?'

'To watch for enemy planes. If any appear, or if any bombs are dropped on Carroll Field, the guard on duty is to ring the alarm and notify the nearest RAF squadron at once.'

'Has that ever happened?'

'Not yet, sir.'

'How long is your tour of duty?'

'From sundown to daybreak, unless relieved sooner.'

'Do you keep a logbook?'

'Yes, sir.'

'I'd like to see it.'

By that time Captain Seaborn had returned with the seven personnel folders. 'Let's go downstairs where we can sit,' Hill suggested.

The other two men had been busy downstairs. Photographs had been taken and Sergeant Leonard's body was wrapped in a canvas bag, ready for transport. 'Lots of blood around here,' one of the investigators noted. 'There were spots of it on the bottom of all seven pairs of shoes and slippers.'

'We walked around,' Grace told him. 'After Amanda found the body. Her scream woke us.'

Mr Hill thought about it. 'The killer must have got some blood on his or her clothing.'

'In the middle of the night he could have been nude,' Captain Seaborn pointed out. 'I sleep in the nude.'

'Really?' Amanda asked with a smile. 'So do I.'

Hill frowned. 'But you all took time to slip on shoes or slippers, and a robe or something when Private Flower screamed.'

'We don't run around naked,' the captain told him. 'And this cement floor is rough on bare feet. Robes and footwear are always at the ready in the event of an attack.'

The investigator made more notes. 'I'll want to talk with each of you individually, Captain Seaborn first and then the women.'

The individual interviews were held in Seaborn's bedroom, which he'd shared with the dead man. While Jenkins waited he washed his face and put on a clean shirt, trying to make himself presentable. When his turn came he entered with some trepidation to find the dark-suited investigator seated at Seaborn's little desk with a personnel folder open before him. 'Private Jenkins?'

'That's right, sir.'

'You don't have to call me sir. Mr Hill will do.'

'All right.'

'What do you know about all this?'

'Not much, Mr Hill. I was on guard duty when it happened.'

'But wouldn't you have heard the sounds of a scuffle?'

'It's not likely. That steel door pretty much blocks out the sound from below.'

'Let's see... I understand you were friendly with Grace Foley.'

'You get friendly with people when you're living and working with them day and night.'

'Is it a romantic relationship?'

'No. There's no possibility of that the way we live here.'

'The others say you all got along quite well, except for Sergeant Leonard and Private Raster.'

'I'd say so, yes.'

'Is Raster a violent man?'

'I think he could be. His language is coarse and it grates on people.'

'I note in your personnel file that you were demoted for fighting at your previous post.'

'Had a bit too much to drink,' Jenkins admitted, looking away. 'It hasn't happened since.'

'Sergeant Leonard was killed with one of the kitchen knives, probably something the killer found there.'

'They keep a little night light burning over the sink. There's always a knife around.'

Hill consulted one of his papers. 'There was a full moon last night, rising at 2355 hours, and the sky was clear. I assume you would have seen anyone approaching the bunker.'

'They was no one,' Jenkins said. 'Not until Mrs Cleatworth came this morning with our fresh provisions. That's always after sunrise.'

'I believe that's all, Jenkins. You may go. Send in Private Silcrest next.'

Jenkins went up the spiral staircase to the outer door, anxious for fresh air. Grace and Amanda were up there too, with Raster hovering nearby as usual. 'How did it go with you?' Grace asked.

'Routine. I couldn't help them.'

'Is Silcrest in there now?'

Jenkins nodded. 'He's the last of us.'

Raster strolled over to join them. 'Better not get too chummy with these ladies, Jenkins. There's a good chance one of them killed the sergeant.'

'No one had a motive to kill him, Raster, except maybe you.'

'There were only five of us down there with him,' Raster countered. 'I didn't do it, and Silcrest wouldn't hurt a fly. The captain could have got Leonard transferred if he didn't like him. That only leaves the ladies.' His voice seemed to reflect the hint of the leer on his face. Jenkins had to restrain himself or he would have punched the man.

'You don't know what you're talking about.'

'Don't I? It's always love or money, the only two motives for murder when you come right down to it.'

'This murder had no motive that I can see,' Amanda told them. 'It's almost as if Alice fell down the rabbit hole and killed him.'

Jenkins frowned. 'You mean Alice Cleatworth? She couldn't have—'

Amanda laughed. 'No, silly! I mean Alice in Wonderland. Remember our conversation earlier?'

'Someone had a motive,' Grace insisted. 'It's just that we can't see what it was.'

Captain Seaborn came up from below with Silcrest following. 'They're removing Sergeant Leonard's body and then they're going to clean up the place for us. We'd better go over to the hanger and sort this out, decide how to work our shifts until they send us a replacement.'

'Do you mean they're leaving us here?' Grace asked. 'When they know one of us is a murderer? I won't be able to sleep all night.'

'I'm sure Private Flower could give you one of her sleeping powders,' the captain replied.

Jenkins was watching Seaborn's face as he spoke the words, and he saw the captain's eyebrows rise as if he'd just come up with the answer on a final examination. The others had started across the field toward the hanger, and looking back at the rabbit hole Jenkins saw the two men in black suits lifting the canvas-shrouded body to the surface.

'I have to get something from my room,' he told the captain. 'I'll catch up with you.'

Jenkins trotted back to the entrance and slid into the little lookout box where he'd spent the night. He paused only a moment to be certain Mr Hill and the other two were all busy with the body, determining the easiest way to get it over to their plane. Hill yelled to Captain Seaborn that he needed a couple of men to help them carry their canvas burden. Seaborn called for Raster and Silcrest to help. Jenkins remained in his compartment, out of sight, watching them through the periscope. Then he turned away, bent down and carefully lifted the lid from the chemical toilet.

He was just pulling the bloody shirt from its hiding place when Captain Seaborn appeared in the doorway holding his service revolver. 'Leave it right there, Jenkins,' he commanded. 'I'm charging you with the murder of Sergeant Leonard.'

A few minutes later, downstairs in the captain's bedroom, Jenkins was confronted by Seaborn and Mr Hill. The bloody shirt was on the table between them and Jenkins moistened his lips, waiting for the first question. 'Why did you do it?' Hill asked.

'An accident…' Jenkins's voice was little more than a croak.

It was Captain Seaborn who spoke. 'Your fondness for Grace Foley was quite obvious. When Amanda Flower announced she was taking a sleeping powder last night, you saw a chance to be with Grace, in her room, while Amanda was fast asleep. You deserted your post and came down to the kitchen, and ran right into Sergeant Leonard. Leaving your post in wartime is a serious court martial offence. You'd been demoted for fighting before and you knew you had to silence Leonard. You grabbed the first weapon your fingers came upon, a kitchen knife, and stabbed him in the chest.'

'I didn't mean to kill him. I didn't know what I was doing.'

'You had to remove your bloody shirt, of course, so you stuffed it in the chemical toilet. When you knew these men would be cleaning up the place, you feared they might find it so you tried to remove it just now.'

Mr Hill nodded. 'That was good work, Captain, but how did you come to suspect Jenkins?'

'There were three things, really. The full moon rose just before midnight but he didn't record it in his log until an hour later. He didn't notice it sooner because he was down here stabbing Leonard, and after that he was probably in no shape to notice anything for some time. Also, your investigators found blood on the bottoms of all the shoes and slippers, but I remembered Jenkins stood on the bottom step when he came down, and he avoided the blood later. His shoes should have been free of it. And then there was this shirt, of course. Since there was blood on the floor it was more than likely the killer had a few spots on him too. Jenkins had removed his shirt and apparently left it in the guard cubicle instead of bringing it down with him.'

'He told me I could be shot for leaving my post,' Jenkins said, not meeting their eyes. 'I just wanted to save myself, to get away from him.'

'You did it all for the love of that woman?' Mr Hill asked, producing a pair of handcuffs.

Jenkins had to agree. He remembered Raster's words. The only two motives for murder were love or money.

Country Blues

Brian Innes

Brian Innes has a varied and intriguing CV. Check out an encyclopedia of pop music and you will find that he played percussion for the Temperance Seven, a prominent band in the pre-Beatles era. Since then, he has written extensively on the investigation of crime in real life. This private eye story is one of a series that he has penned and suggests that yet another aspect of Innes' multi-faceted career may be about to take off.

I'm not one for the country; it's full of wild animals you wouldn't trust even behind bars in the zoo, rustic retards with pitchforks and rusty twelve-bores, and happy hunting hoorays. People will tell you that the Smoke's more dangerous; but for someone like me, making tiny discreet inquiries that do very little harm – not that much harm, even, to those I'm employed to track down, nobody more sinister than slippery customers who've defaulted on their installment payments – the city offers easy concealment, and a fair degree of anonymity. Away in the sticks, a stranger stands out worse than a weights-and-measures inspector in a street market; you can almost hear the doors closing as you walk through the village, and if they still had shutters I reckon you'd hear them slamming-to as well.

So I try to keep my movements well within the confines of Greater London – the world of the A-Z Street Atlas, and the Underground. And if I hadn't toiled up the step and narrow stairs to my stark little office on that Saturday morning – something I would never normally do, but I wanted to pick up the *Melody Maker* I'd inadvertently left there the evening before – I wouldn't have got the telephone call, and some other sucker would have had to stride off into the wild blue yonder. But, as it was, I took the call: really very sorry, etc, nobody else currently available, did I think possibly? I flipped open the book. Most unusually, I was going to be tied up all the coming week. And then, supposing this would be just a local quickie, I made the foolish mistake, and said OK, I'd do the job today.

Matter of installments unpaid on a television set. Name of missing person: John Harvester. Occupation: radio repair engineer. No phone number, of course. Last known address? Boulter's Yard – aha, I said to myself, a trendy mews property in deepest St John's Wood, no doubt? – and then the rest slowly spelt out: near M-e-d-m-e-n-h-a-m... Bucks. 'Buckinghamshire?' I cried in despair. Deep in rural despond? What had I let myself in for? I looked out of the window – well, at least the sun was shining, and maybe the local mud and muck wouldn't be too widespread. Check with me Monday, I said, and cut the call.

Ten minutes with a road map and the ABC rail guide didn't improve my mood. I found the village – in the smallest type – close to the river, halfway between Marlow and Henley, each of them stations at the dead end of a branch line. A good four miles to get there along the road, I reckoned, whichever way I arrived. It not being jolly boating weather, I'd missed the only connection to Henley for two hours; if I ran, and the Bakerloo got me to Paddington in time, I could just make the Marlow train. Which I did. Lucky I had the *MM* with me: I was down to reading the last of the classifieds – 'C&W five-piece seeks bjo, vln, dms, vocalist. Prev. exp. not essential' – by the time the Flying Bucksman oozed into the terminus. No cab in the station yard – in any case, I doubted I'd get it agreed as exes this side of the millennium – and no sign of a friendly porter to point me the way.

I collared a shopping-laden biddy in the street, however, got my vague instructions, and set off trudging westward. My elastic-sided Baba boots, new-bought from Anello & Davide, weren't the best for rustic tramping, but I carried on. I might have tottered all the way to Henley if, after a half-hour or so, I hadn't spotted, low down to the left on a rickety fence, a roughly-painted sign pointing to Boulter's Yard.

A labyrinth of mud-splattered lanes led down from the road toward the river. I followed the trail marked by the deepest ruts and potholes as it wound past straggled hedges, huts that might once have bred chickens, and brooding bungalows, figuring this to be the locals' High Street. The boots began to complain, but I toiled on. Where the track split left and right I took the wrong fork, coming suddenly up short at a rusted chain-link fence, behind which crouched a shack with a corrugated sheet roof, and a snarling dog. With the gleam of the water beyond, he looked to me too much like an expectant Cerberus on the Lethe shore, and I decided that was not the way to go.

The other track, however, soon brought me to a rickety wooden arch, with the sign – I should have guessed it – 'Boulter's Yard: Moorings and Repairs'. Two upturned skiffs, a bucket, and a tangle of fraying rope, lay before a tarred hut labelled 'office', and the door was open. I knocked politely, and stepped inside.

Seated behind a desk that looked as it if had come from the bargain basement at Maples was a man's head, all that was visible above piles of yellowing comic books, empty mugs, and what were too obviously the dismembered parts of an outboard motor. Seeing me, he made the apparent motions of standing up, though the head rose no higher as it moved sideways and came round the desk end. Facing me was a Mister Five-by-Five, in a red shirt that could have served as a small spinnaker, green cords held up by a wide belt and the broadest braces I had ever seen, and turned-down wellies. His black hair was tied back in a greasy ponytail, and a full grey beard hung down so low in the open neck of his shirt that it could have proved an embarrassment during the nesting season.

'Boulter', he muttered gruffly, staring me up and down with tiny watery eyes. I explained my business, and he wheezed a chuckle that threatened the belt. 'Johnny Harvester? You won't find him here no more. Not since his boat burnt out. Go down and see for yourself.' He flapped a fist, and turned back behind his desk. I grudged a 'thank you', and followed the direction he had indicated.

Beyond the hut, a battered wooden quay stretched along the river bank, with a half-dozen shabby motor cruisers tied up. Electricity cables hung suspended from posts, and a long hose lay coiled beside a standpipe. At the far end, I could see two or three charred ribs poking above the water. As I approached, a man working with a pot of blue paint on the hull of the last boat in the line turned and grinned toothlessly at me. He wore an oil-stained yachting cap, and splashes of the paint dotted his steel-framed glasses and his khaki overalls. 'That's it, mate', he said. 'All that's left of the Saucy Sue. Poor woman, what a tragedy.' Woman? I asked. 'His wife, Nancy. Burned to a crisp, she was. Johnny was quite cut up, even if they didn't always see eye-to-eye. It was only her wedding ring they was able to identify her by – that, and her teeth. Lucky for him he wasn't aboard at the time. They'd had a bigger row than usual, I couldn't help hearing all the shouting, then there was quiet – 'cept for the telly on loud, like it always is – until all of a sudden I heard Johnny go stamping off, and he didn't get back till it was all over. Like a madman he was, then, carrying on.'

How did it happen? I wondered. 'Nobody knows for sure. Me and the police, we reckoned it was the gas bottles. They tend to leak, you know, and the gas, what is heavier than air, can collect in the bilges, and it only needs a spark – couldn't have been the telly, could it? – to set it off. Look there, I keep my bottles on the foredeck, but Johnny – I was always telling him it wasn't safe – had his aft in the well, said it looked tidier, which of course it did. When she went up, it was fortunate I was here, 'cos I was afraid the fire would spread. I slipped my bow warp, so's I could drift out into the stream away from the flames, but even so my paint-work, what I'd only just finished, was blistered. As you can see.'

When was this? 'Evening early this week. She still had the telly on when it happened. I could always hear it, morning noon and night, 'cept when it was the wireless. They had one of these new-fangled clock wirelesses, they showed me one time. Johnny got it for her, him being in the business. Nothing but pop music, rock and roll, from that pirate ship, out in the North Sea. Some of the neighbours tried turning the hose on the fire, but that was worse nor useless, and by the time the fire brigade arrived there was little for them to do. The police doctor come, and got out poor Nancy's remains, and the wash from the heavy rains a coupla days later sunk what was left.'

I explained that I would need to talk to John Harvester – did he know where I might find him? 'He's got himself in a little caravan, just temporary like, back of the pub, the Blacksmith's Arms. This being Saturday, no doubt him and his band'll be playing there in the saloon bar.' He gave me directions, I thanked him, and set off back through the slime to the road. Luckily for the boots, the pub was only a hundred yards further on, set back, with a dozen or so cars parked in front. A board outside announced 'Johnny Harvester and his Combine – Country Music' in multicoloured chalks, and I could already hear the plunk of a string bass and the whine of a fiddle.

The saloon bar was heaving, thick with smoke from a hundred cigarettes and a badly-drawing wood fire, loud with rustic banter drowning out the music, and smelling strongly of Henley Prize Ales and what I took to be pigshit. Like I've said, someone like me is a tiny bit obvious in a scene such as this, and there was a detectable fall in the level of chat, and eyes swivelled suspiciously, as I tried to ease my way nonchalantly to the bar. Even the darts players turned to look.

At least, if only for a few seconds, it was possible to hear the band, which was set up at the far end of the bar and, as near as I could make out, working its way through 'Turkey in the Straw'. There were six of them, all dressed in mock-tartan shirts and the inevitable cords: a tiny, cadaverous man, with a dozen grey strands combed across his baldness, twiddling away on the fiddle like it was the Devil's Trill sonata; a plump, crosseyed boy slackly strumming a banjo; a tall, and very thin, guitarist, staring blankly up into the rafters; a girl, rat-faced and with waist-length black hair, pumping the squeezebox; the drummer, fuzzy-chinned and wearing a tweed cap low over his eyes, otherwise hidden as he crouched at his kit; and a giant of a man, with a full rusty-coloured beard, standing with legs wide apart behind the string bass. As the mob shifted open for a moment, I saw a clutch of half-empty pint glasses clustered around the band's feet.

I reached the bar, the talk swelled again, and with difficulty I was able to make myself heard, shyly requesting a pint of best bitter and a large Grouse. The barman nodded morosely. 'Which is Johnny Harvester?' I shouted. He pointed, and leant forward so I could just hear: 'Him, with the bull fiddle.' I made deaf-and-dumb signs indicating an extra pint for the bass player, which was roughly slid along the bar and banged down on the counter beside him.

A wizened old cowherd in a stained mac, with a smouldering roll-up stuck to his lower lip, was leaning alone on the bar next to me. He looked me up and down: my best black leather jacket and rollneck sweater, the houndstooth strides, the Burberry draped from my shoulders – and the Baba boots. 'You ain't from these parts, I reckon?' he wheezed. 'On yer 'olidays, eh?' I thought it easiest to nod in agreement. He tried to chuckle, coughed throatily, and swallowed the phlegm back down again, like a competitor in an oyster-eating contest all the while the roll-up bobbing like a metronome, but not quite in time with the thud of the bass. Then he stared meaningfully into his near-empty glass, but I had no intention of offering him a refill; so he grunted, turned his back, and said no more.

The band came to the end of the number; Johnny Harvester roared 'That's all, folks', and leant across the bar, obviously to ask the barman – who flicked his head in my direction – who it was had bought him his last pint. Picking me out – not a difficult operation – he took up the glass and shouldered his huge bulk through the crowd to thank me, rearing a good eight inches over my head when he reached my side. Was there somewhere quieter where we could talk? I asked. He suggested the snug, and led the way.

The snug was indeed quieter, being empty. 'What's this all about, then?' Harvester demanded. Above the beard his heavy red face was sullen, his blue eyes piggy and surrounded by narrow creases as if the balloon of his head was beginning to deflate. His huge hands were swollen, even beyond what must have been their natural size, by his plucking of the bass strings; and his brown

cord trousers creaked in protest as he lowered his bulk on to the
settle.

I explained – a little matter of unpaid installments on a television. He shouted a brief laugh – not a pleasant sound – and
snorted derisively. 'A repossession man, are you? Well, you can
bloody well repossess that telly, far as I'm concerned. If you can
find it, that is. Went up in flames, it did, Tuesday night. And my
boat with it, and all my worldly possessions – and my wife. All I
got left is what I stand up in.' And he waved a fist vaguely at his
clothes.

In my crossest tones, I replied that I was most certainly not a
repo man – I was merely retained by the finance house to discover the whereabouts of missing clients, and it looked like I'd
come all this way on a fool's errand. If he would just inform them
of the circumstances, no doubt the insurance – 'Ha!' he interrupted. 'Effing insurance. Never had any, did I? Or I might be an
effing bit better off.' He took a slurping swallow of his beer, then
gave me a hangdog look, and grudgingly allowed he was sorry
he'd misunderstood what I was about. 'That was a nice little set,
that telly', he complained. 'I kept it all properly tuned, too, being
in the business. Bloody dead loss, that,' and he thumped the
table with his mighty clenched fist. It quivered and groaned.
Some form of peace seeming to be declared between us, I mentioned the band, how much I'd appreciated the music. Had he
played the bass long? 'I've had that fiddle ever since I was tall
enough to handle it. It's like a baby to me. Never let it out of my
sight – 'cept when I'm sitting in the snug here with you, finishing
a pint.' And he laughed – again a far from pleasant sound. Did he
know how the fire had started? 'Not a clue, mate. I'd gone off to
the flicks in Henley, leaving Nancy – my wife, rest her soul –
watching that telly. It was all gone, the whole effing lot, when I
got back. The police suggested it was gas in the bilges, but I'd
aired them out only days before. What a tragedy.' And he wiped
his eyes – unconvincingly.

All this while, little wheels had been going round in my head. Harvester was a strong and, without doubt, a potentially violent man. A particularly fierce row with the wife on the evening in question, could it have resulted in her death? I remembered the clock radio – it would have been a simple matter for a skilled radio engineer to have doctored it to produce a spark, or a succession of sparks, sufficient to ignite the gas from a gas bottle that had been left gently leaking. And it could have switched on long after Harvester was gone from the scene. My brain buzzing, I decided it was time to leave, before I asked any indiscreet questions that might provoke a further outbreak of rage. Announcing that this seemed to be the end of the matter so far as I was concerned, I asked how I could get to Henley. Harvester said there was a bus that stopped outside the pub just after closing time, 'and' – he glanced up at the snug clock and looked suitably disappointed – 'I guess that's any minute now'. I stood; I didn't want to risk serious injury, even though I no longer play the piano, so I avoided shaking his hand. Even as we came out of the pub door, the single-decker bus pulled in, its engine chugging, and I reckoned I would be able to find the cop-shop in Henley without much difficulty, and tell them of my suspicions. I waited until I stood safely on the step of the bus as the driver revved up, and then I spoke my last words to Harvester. 'That string bass,' I said. 'It wasn't lost in the fire. Tell me, do you always take it with you when you go to the cinema?'

No One Can Hear You Scream

Michael Jecks

Mike Jecks, the current Vice Chair of the CWA, is best known as an author of entertaining historical mysteries with a medieval backdrop. He has also written interestingly about the task of combining fidelity to historical fact with the need to tell a tale that present-day readers can easily enjoy. On this occasion, he has decided upon a contemporary setting; that in itself can be something of a challenge to a specialist in past crimes, but Jecks has risen to it splendidly. John Hawkwood is an appealing character and I hope that this is not the last we hear of him.

'You ever read Sherlock Holmes, Hawk?'

John Hawkwood had a mild hangover, and opened his eyes with reluctance. Rain spattered against the windscreen, almost obliterating the view of grey, grime-streaked Victorian terraces. Another perfect morning in south London, he thought. Christmas lights were going up, tinsel stars dangling between lamp posts, a massive Santa on his sleigh over a store – all added to his depression. This was a time of year for children. As it was, he'd probably spend Christmas day in the pub – unless he could wangle a day in the station. At least there would be company either way.

'He was in a train, right? Heading off into the country, just like we are now, and he says something like, "Nothing and no one in London scares me half so much as the sight of all these sodding fields," right? 'Cos in a town, there's always someone to hear you, right, but in a field nobody's goin' to hear you scream. Sounds good, that: "Nobody's goin' to hear you scream!"'

Curran sniggered. Hawkwood's driver was at least twelve years his junior, a shorter man, maybe five feet ten, and running slightly to tubbiness, with jowls that only served to emphasise the vacancy of his expression. Apparently his father was a lawyer in a big city firm, rich and very clever, but he and Curran never spoke. When Curran mentioned his old man, it was with a cold bitterness that seemed strange in such a bland man.

Bland was being generous. If there was anything in his eyes, even a tiny spark of intelligence, Hawkwood wouldn't have minded, but as it was, Curran's lean, square features under the hard-man's fair crew-cut wore only a permanent dullness like a disappointed child.

Hawkwood turned away and sighed. 'It's been used. More or less.'

'What?'

'Ridley Scott used it. The director.'

The blank expression on Curran's face made Hawkwood

grunt briefly. 'The film: Alien. They used the strapline, "In space, no one can hear you scream."'

Jimmy stared through the windscreen for a moment, a scowl of concentration darkening his features.

'Nah. Sorry, before me time, that.'

'Get a move on. You want to be late?'

'What, for the murder?' Curran said disinterestedly. 'Can't miss that.'

The house was one of very few in that wealthy area. There were five on the southern side of the road, none opposite, and all were huge. Each had sprawling grounds, Walls, trees and thick undergrowth blocking each from neighbours. It reminded Hawkwood of Curran's words – would Sherlock Holmes have been repelled? Certainly few here could witness murder.

As the car surged along the roadway beneath oaks and beeches, Hawkwood found himself staring out over a patchwork landscape, with fields and woods clearly defined. The view made any house up here worth more that Hawkwood would earn in his whole life, a fact which ignited the bitterness of his jealousy. He could have made money if he'd chosen a different career, but nothing else had appealed. There were ways to make money in the police, but he wasn't having any of that, which was why he'd retire with little more than his house. He didn't even have a family now, not since his wife left him over a year ago, taking the girls with her.

Curran muttered: 'This is it.'

'It' was an elegant building maybe sixty years old. The windows were dark wood, the walls painted white, and the driveway curved gently to a triple garage. Whoever built it expected large parties, Hawkwood thought. There was space for at least twelve cars, because that's how many were already parked, their blue lights flickering among the trees like a laser show designed by a hippy on acid.

They parked in the road. Uniformed police demanded their ID and the two had to sign the register before they could enter the large hall. The first floor was galleried, and Hawkwood hesitated. From a door on his left he heard a woman's desperate, hacking sobs. Overhead came a child's thin wailing. Hawkwood set his shoulders grimly and followed Curran.

The sitting room was at least thirty feet long, delicately decorated with a pale carpet and cream furniture. One sofa and two comfortable chairs sat about a fireplace, a second grouping faced a huge plate-glass window that looked over the view. The coffee tables were pale oak, understated but expensive. Cushions matched the floor-length curtains, with gold patterns on a red background. The whole felt comfortably wealthy, but not ostentatious.

Today strangers had taken over. A photographer stood with his camera pointing at the body, a uniformed officer slowly panned a video camera about the room, another scribbled on a clipboard and handed out evidence bags, paper or plastic depending on the materials discovered. Forensic officers squatted, studying tiny particles. A window was smashed, and tiny shards of shattered glass glittered near the window. An officer was carefully collecting it.

On the floor beside the fire there was a section of lifted carpet. When Hawkwood wandered to it, he saw it exposed the circular face of a small safe.

Curran was talking to the officer with the clipboard, who welcomed Hawkwood with a resigned air.

'Hiya, Hawk.'

Hawkwood squatted at the corpse's side. 'What's it look like, George?'

Near at hand was a large cut-glass whisky tumbler. A Glenmorangie bottle lay empty beside the sofa, and there was a stain in the carpet that stank of whisky.

'Robbery turned to murder, she says.' George's voice was toneless, like a man describing a snooker match. 'He was down here last night. She came down first thing this morning and found him like this. Window gone, safe opened, and maybe a few hundred gone. He never kept more than that in there.'

'Right.' Both he and George had been through this too often. They knew the score.

The dead man was taller than Hawkwood, maybe six one or two, and had kept in good shape. He was about forty, with a pleasant, square face, fair hair that looked as though it would have been hard to tame, blue-grey eyes that wrinkled at the corners, and a full mouth. He had the look of a man who would have been good company. His death was caused by the heavy-bladed, black handled cooking knife in his breast.

Hearing a familiar voice, Hawkwood glanced at the door.

The pathologist was a small, round-faced, balding, dapper man whom Hawkwood had never seen without a tie. He nodded at Hawkwood, and set about his work, extracting his tools from his briefcase. While thermometers took the room's temperature, and that of the body, Hawkwood asked, 'Anything obvious?'

'I'd guess he died quickly. One wound; not even defensive cuts on his hands. It must have been an entirely unexpected attack.'

Hawkwood nodded at Curran. 'Fine. Where's the wife?'

Elspeth Arnold sat at her dining table with a handkerchief held to her face, the dark-haired WPC at the window looking anxious. She looked too young to be guarding a widow. Hawkwood walked to her and muttered that she should take a seat herself. She gave him a grateful, pale grin, and slumped into a chair.

Hawkwood sat opposite Mrs Arnold. She looked up without emotion.

She was short, five one, five two at most. Perhaps on a good day she would have been pretty, but today wasn't a good day. She had a blotched, round face that looked petulant, with small eyes and a tip-tilted nose. Her mascara had run, and her hair was unbrushed.

Dressed in a pale blue sweatshirt and jeans, she was barefoot, as though she hadn't had time to shower or dress carefully.

'My name is Detective Inspector Hawkwood. This is Detective Sergeant Curran. We have to ask you some questions.'

'Anything. I've already told the others here…'

Her breath reeked from the scotch in the glass before her, a cut glass tumbler like the one on the floor beside her husband's body. The brand of whisky was the same as the empty bottle, he noticed. Perhaps they had bought it by the case. An ashtray sat on the table beside her, with stubs that had a distinctive golden band about their upper part. Each was stained with her pale lipstick.

'Yes. We are here to take your evidence. First…' he reached into his briefcase for his notepad and recorder. 'This is purely in case I miss something. Do you mind?' She waved a hand dismissively and he pressed the record button. 'Good. For the record, then, let me state that…'

He ran through the preliminary details, checking the time from his watch, giving the names of all in the room, and meanwhile he observed the woman, assessing her.

'You found him when you came down this morning?'

'Christ! He was just lying there,' she blurted, 'blood everywhere. And the Sabatier… God, I came out of there, and was sick all over the place.'

'What exactly happened? From when you woke up.'

'Well, I realised he hadn't come to bed. I came down as soon as I woke. I didn't want Amanda to… to wake him if he'd…'

'If he'd what?'

'If he'd got pissed.' She squirmed uncomfortably. It was a tiny movement, but he was aware of it, and so was she. She threw him a look, then averted her gaze, shifting in her seat. 'It happened sometimes. He'd drink a little too much and then… pass out, I suppose you'd say.'

'Had he been drinking last night?'

'Yes. A lot.'

'Why was that, Mrs Arnold?'

'He was a solicitor, Mr… sorry, Inspector Hawkwood. This morning I…' A hand flapped like a released bird.

'Just concentrate on what happened. You say that your husband was a solicitor. Last night he drank a lot.'

'Yes. He was a successful lawyer.' Her eyes rose and gazed about her at the room, up at the ceiling, at the furniture. There was a certain pride in her face then. 'He did very well. He was a company lawyer. High in the Law Society, too. But yesterday he lost another client, and he was… depressed about it.'

'Depressed? In what way?'

She flared, 'How do you think? He came here and got pissed, and… and…' As though realising she'd said more than she ought, she slumped. 'Do you mind if I smoke?'

Hawkwood watched as she took a long Rothmans International from a squashed, dark blue pack in her pocket and lighted it with a gold Dunhill. 'He got pissed?'

Already the story was pulling together in his mind. The sad, bitter, angry man arriving home, pouring himself a large one, shouting at his wife, perhaps punching her, enjoying the only control he had, the control of another person weaker than him. There was no bruising on her, but he knew wife-beaters knew where to hit so that the bruises were hidden – on the breast, the belly, the upper thighs. Abusers knew how to hide their work.

'Pissed?' she gave a bitter chuckle, smoke drifting from her nostrils. 'He was completely wasted. Out of his tree. Fucked! Is that clear enough?'

'So last night he arrived home. Was he already drunk?'

'He'd had a couple,' she said cautiously, and then gave a twisted grin. 'I suppose you aren't going to prosecute him now, are you? All right then, yes, he was several sheets to the wind when he got home. I've seen him like that before. I wasn't going to… you can't win an argument with a drunk, you know.'

'When he came home, what happened?'

'I handed him a drink at the door and made him supper. I learned that long ago. There's no point asking, 'How was your day, dear?' when he was like that.'

'And then what?'

'You aren't asking much about the robbery, are you?'

'I'm just getting a picture about the evening. I need to know everything,' Hawkwood said flatly. He couldn't tell her that the apparent robbery was already fading to an improbability in his mind compared with the other, more likely, scenario.

'Oh, all right. I left the bottle at his side. That was it. I went up to bed rather than suffer any...'

'Suffer any what?' Hawkwood asked, but he didn't need to press her. The cigarette was shaking slightly in her hand. She took a sip of her whisky, stared at the ashtray, and shook her head slowly, then lifted her chin with a certain pride.

'He was abusive. All right? He used to beat me. I took it, because I was petrified he'd turn on Amanda if I didn't let him. Christ, that was stupid, wasn't it? If I'd had any sense, I'd have left him, taken her with me.'

'But if you left him downstairs, you'd be safe?'

'He wouldn't go upstairs while there was a drink in the bottle.'

'What then? What about when the bottle was empty?'

'I hoped he'd be incapable of climbing the stairs. He'd already had a skinful and when I gave him the bottle I was fairly sure he'd sit down until he'd emptied it. I thought I was safe; I couldn't have got upstairs if I'd drunk all that. You know, when he first started beating me, years ago, I used to try to calm him with sex. It never worked. I was daft even to try that when he was drunk. He only grew more violent.'

'Was he all right when you left him?'

'What do you mean.'

'You went to the kitchen.'

'To cook.'

'The murder weapon was one of your knives. A kitchen knife.'

'I didn't...'

'You say that he could be violent. How was he when he was as drunk as he was last night?'

She looked up again, and her voice was choked. 'He was the devil. The devil himself!'

Hawkwood studied her, desperate to see a proof of sadness, a hint of regret; but all he could see was self-pity.

'No one likes a wife beater,' Curran said.

They were in the sitting room again and Hawkwood grunted, exchanging a glance with George. They both knew members of the Croydon force who who were considered 'good lads' by their colleagues, although rumours of their behaviour to their wives had spread widely. 'Maybe.'

George was about to speak when an officer appeared in the doorway.

'Sir? Thought you'd like to see this.'

'What is it?' George asked.

The officer passed him a photo. 'I was collecting the broken glass outside, and saw this.'

Hawkwood craned his neck and saw what the officer was pointing at. At the corner of the picture was a clean cigarette butt with a golden band around it, like a Rothmans International.

'It proves nothing,' Curran said. 'It could have been there for ages. Maybe she threw it out of the window days ago. Even yesterday.'

Hawkwood nodded. 'Possibly. Anything else?'

The officer nodded and handed him a second and third picture. 'Vomit. Not far from the window. Someone puked his guts up out there.'

Hawkwood was still outside, feeling marginally better, sitting on a bench in the garden and watching the forensic team, when the woman arrived.

She was a large woman – tall, strong, square-featured, with bright, intelligent eyes set in a face which had seen a lot of life. The tabloids would have characterised her as a lady of the manor, a 'toff', someone who was contemptibly unaware of the modern world. Curran appeared just as Hawkwood was introducing himself, and Curran's ill-concealed dislike made Hawkwood warm to her.

'Are you in charge here?'

She was holding two dogs, a Rottweiler and a Boxer, both straining. Curran kept his distance, but Hawkwood held out his hand to them. 'How can I help you?'

'You can't, I expect,' she said crisply. 'I want to see Mrs Arnold and her daughter to make sure that they are all right.'

'I am afraid that they are not seeing visitors. You'll understand why.'

'I live next door,' she said, jerking a thumb over her shoulder. 'I was going to offer to take Amanda away. It can't be good for her.'

'You only just realised that there was something going on?'

'Yes,' she said simply. 'I'm not one to peer between net curtains, officer.'

'Did you hear anything last night?'

'No. And these two were settled, too. Amy is a light sleeper.'

Hawkwood smiled at 'Amy', the Rottweiler. 'Was the marriage happy? In your opinion.'

She eyed him suspiciously. 'Trying to get the inside griff by plugging the neighbours? Yes, I'd say so. Wouldn't have suited me, but you can never tell what makes others happy, can you?'

'Why do you say that?'

'Well, it makes you wonder, doesn't it? In the summer it quite put us off sitting on the terrace. You could hear the shouts and screaming even when they had their windows shut. The poor child – what she had to live through.'

'Who, Amanda?'

'No, you fool. Oh! Sorry, shouldn't call an officer a fool,

should I?' she said with a glint of devilment in her eye. 'No, I meant Elspeth. It was her whom he beat. We used to hear him roaring, then her shrieking, again and again. I sent Charles – that's my husband – over there once, and Elspeth came to the door. All but drunk with pain, slurring and tottering. She said she was fine, that she wasn't hurt, and he couldn't see a mark on her.'

'But?'

'I may be older, but I can read PD James and Barbara Vine. The worst abusers can hit without leaving a mark, can't they?'

Hawkwood saw no reason to comment. 'Is there anything else?'

'I suppose I ought to tell you. A couple of times, after we'd heard them having another shouting match, neither of them went out. He stayed behind, didn't go to work. I went to make sure that they were OK, and she came to the door, but she was clearly worried.'

'What did you conclude from that?'

'That he'd beaten her and didn't want her shooting her mouth off until the bruises were gone. He wouldn't want her going to the doctor, would he? So he kept her indoors.'

'What of the child?'

'She's suffered, I think.' Her eyes went to an upper storey window. 'What a life. If we heard their rows, what did Amanda see and hear? Poor girl. It's said that they've had Social Services in here for her. I expect that's all because of the fights. She's not normal. She never even wears make-up!'

Her scandalised voice made him grin as he thanked her and walked back into the house.

'See?' Curran hissed. 'That bastard deserved it anyway. She was an angel to put up with him.'

'She may have been, but if she stabbed him, she's a murderer,' Hawkwood said uncompromisingly.

'After years of abuse? He got what he deserved, like, and I'd...'

'Whether or not he deserved something, is for others to decide. For me, she committed homicide and deliberately put clues around the place to show us a different story. It was amateur, but the sort of thing that someone who watched the TV often enough would try. She lifted the carpet, emptied the safe, maybe, smashed the window. The only thing she did wrong was, leaving that fag butt out there.'

'Like I said, that was probably days old.'

'I doubt it. The woman's house proud. She didn't routinely chuck fag ends through the window. That was the only one. No, I think she had a cigarette to calm her nerves out there, and puked because of what she'd done. She set about smashing windows and lifting carpets to throw us off the track.'

'She'd just got thumped, or was about to.'

'Maybe,' Hawkwood said. Struck with a thought, he continued, 'That's a good idea. Phone her doctor and ask if she's been prone to accidents – falling downstairs or walking into doors? Perhaps there's some mitigating stuff there. See whether she has a defence.'

There was one more potential witness whom he must reluctantly question, although he had to wait, thank God – a social worker had driven the child away. Instead, he wandered up to her room and leaned against the door jamb. Two days later, when he met her, that room would come back to him.

Only thirteen, she was already a smoker. Smoke had impregnated all her clothes. With the wide east-facing windows open, the smell would fade quickly enough, and since her mother was a smoker she probably wouldn't even detect the subtle odour. Smokers could rarely smell smoke on others.

It was a typical teenager's space. Drawers on the left, a large wardrobe, all painted white, while at her side was a bedside table with a clock radio and remote control for the large colour TV on top of the chest of drawers, next to a glass and pair of pills still enclosed in their bubbles of plastic, torn from a sheet. She hadn't taken the sedatives.

Seeing her for the first time, he thought Amanda Arnold would grow into a stunning woman. She had the best of her father's looks, with only a little of her mother's chubbiness to give her a certain softness. Calm grey eyes stared at him as Hawkwood introduced himself.

'Do you mind my asking you some questions?'

She sniffed. 'I don't know what I can say to help. Daddy's dead.'

'We'll find who did it.'

'That thief, I suppose.'

This was given in an odd, sarcastic tone of voice. It jarred on Hawkwood's ear. 'Did you hear anything odd that night?'

'The window. Yes. I heard that, I think. I didn't realise what it was at the time.'

Hawkwood nodded to himself. If what he had heard was true, she would have been used to hearing shouting and screaming through the night. 'What time was it?'

'I don't know.'

He nodded again and asked, 'Did your parents have an argument?'

'She was always on at him! Never gave him any peace. Said he was having affairs whenever he was working late, and never believed him!'

Hawkwood was shocked into silence. Beside him, he was sure that the WPC was rocked by this sudden bursting of words. It was as though the girl had bottled them up for years, and now was releasing them under an explosive pressure. The social worker at her side put a hand out, but Amanda snatched her own hand away.

'She drinks all the time, and by the time he got home, she was always out of it! She wanted more money always, just to buy stuff.'

Hawkwood was stunned into silence as the girl told of a family sinking into financial disaster. How Mr Arnold's company was failing, how Amanda had been pulled from her expensive public school and sent to a lesser one, how the cars had gone as Mrs Arnold's drinking rose to one and a half bottles of whisky a day, and how her husband tried to persuade her to go to Alcoholics Anonymous, and received more punches for his temerity.

It must have been a hell on earth for the man. Hawkwood could imagine all too clearly how he would have felt. His security gone, financial and marital, all he could do was protect his daughter. Hawkwood had done the same, in his own way. He felt the sympathy growing in his breast.

'You aren't a child, Amanda,' he said after a few moments. 'What do you think happened that night?'

'She killed him. This stuff about a robber – that's bollocks, isn't it? She lost it again and stabbed him.'

'That is a very serious...'

'Come on! She was pissed, almost out cold on the sofa when I got home. She couldn't even make it upstairs. She'd emptied the bottle. Poor dad was late home again. Not back until eight or so. She told me not to say anything, told me to support her story of a thief, but how could I? He was my dad. I loved him, I really loved him. Poor dad!'

Hawkwood stood as her features crumpled and grief washed away her maturity with tears.

'Wait!' she said as he got to the door. 'What will happen to me?'

Hawkwood glanced at the social worker. 'We'll make sure you're looked after.'

'You mean I'll have to go into a home? Why can't I go home? I can look after myself.'

Her voice had an edge of panic. Hawkwood tried to smile, but all he could see were his own daughters' faces as he admitted to those lies just to protect them. He prayed he had been right.

Curran met him in the hallway with a typewritten report. 'No mistake. The hospital confirms it. Mrs Arnold never had a fall.

If anything, it was her husband who was the clumsy one. Thought he was good at DIY and often hurt himself. Broke his thumb once, and cracked some ribs when he fell from a ladder.' His face was grim. He had learned that his idol had clay feet.

'Let's ask her, then,' Hawkwood said.

Hawkwood sat heavily across from Mrs Arnold in the interview room. Her ashtray was already full with stubs, each with their own circle of lipstick under the gold band. Next to it was a mug of tea.

He took up his pen and checked the twin tape recorder. After introducing himself and the others in the room, he began.

'Mrs Arnold, I don't need to tell you that the whole story of a thief was fiction. Amanda's confirmed it. Your story of your husband's drinking and abuse were just that, a story. You made it up to conceal your crime.'

She said nothing. As he studied her features, her eyes brimmed, but there was nothing else.

'You abused him over years, didn't you? Once or twice he couldn't even go to work because you'd beaten him so viciously. Was that because you marked his face, or because you had actually harmed him? We know you didn't let him go to the door.'

'It's not true!' She picked up her mug of tea.

'It is. Your neighbours heard the rows. You did a good job, making them think you were the victim, didn't you? But who'd believe a big, strong man like him could be beaten up by a tiny woman? Except he was a gentleman, wasn't he? And he had no idea how to control you. Perhaps that upset you. Did you find him frustrating? Was that the cause of your anger? Was that why you drank? To soothe your frustration?'

She set the mug back down, and it rattled as it met the plastic.

It was an odd, unsatisfactory story, Hawkwood thought.

She had confessed. She had been in the kitchen when he came

home, drunk again, and he sneered at her slurring and tottering. She'd reacted irrationally, grabbing a knife and going to him, screaming that he shouldn't have a go at her when it was his fault she drank – he was screwing his secretary every night. It wasn't enough that he was a failure in business, now he was trying to humiliate her. She wouldn't let a slut take her man, she said, and stabbed him.

Only later did she realise what she'd done. She woke in her own bed thinking that she'd had a nightmare, but going downstairs, seeking a hangover tonic, she found him. Rather than confess, she set up the elaborate fiction, breaking the window and lifting the carpet. She didn't even remember the cigarette end when Hawkwood mentioned it.

Curran didn't want to believe her. His face had shown his agitation, as though he wanted to grab her by the shoulders and tell her to shut up, to remember how badly she'd been treated, but still she had carried on, her voice calm apart from the occasional shudder.

'She stabbed him because she was drunk. Just because she was drunk.'

'After abusing him for years.'

'Why'd he let her?'

Hawkwood shrugged. 'He was a big man. How could he admit that he couldn't protect himself from his wife?'

'He could have defended himself.'

'Maybe he tried. But he was old school. His daughter went to public school, and I daresay he did too. Public schoolboys are brought up never to hit a woman. Perhaps that was it. It was easier to accept her violence than hurt her.'

'She was collected enough to go through the charade of the thief breaking in.'

'She can't have been all that collected,' Hawkwood said. 'She couldn't even remember that fag. Damn!'

'What?'

'I forgot to ask her about the vomit. Was she sick before or after breaking the window? How did that fit into things?'

Curran's face twisted. 'Who cares? The drunken bitch murdered her old man for sod-all reason. It's, like, completely sick, right? The whole fucking thing.'

Hawkwood nodded, but absently. He felt distaste for Curran. He'd wanted Mrs Arnold to be a heroine because that suited his own world view because his mother had been a victim of abuse. Anything that deviated from Curran's norms offended him. Mother love! It was why the Madonna and child had worked so well as Christian propaganda. For Hawkwood there was a poignant perfection about it.

Suddenly another picture presented itself to him: a cigarette butt lying in the grass; and even as he he conceived the link, he felt his stomach lurch and a cold shiver attack his spine. 'Jesus Christ!'

'What? Hawk? What's the matter?'

Hawkwood let the door crash back against the wall as he entered the room. 'So, Mrs Arnold. Tell me, where were you sick?'

'What?' Her startled gaze went from him to Curran and back. 'What is this? You've got my confession. I thought you...'

'Answer the question. Where were you sick?'

'I don't know – in the downstairs toilet.'

'And outside, while you were making up your story and smashing the windows? Where were you sick then?'

'I don't know. What does it matter?'

'We found a cigarette outside. You smoke a lot, don't you?'

'So what?'

'Perhaps that's why your daughter smokes.'

'She smokes because teenagers like living dangerously. They can't assess future risks like lung cancer.'

'You didn't see her smoking, did you? You had passed out. Did she put you to bed?'

'I... No, I was...'

'This is all a lie, isn't it?' Hawkwood said, picking up the confession. 'Is there anything you have told us so far which has been true? Any one thing?'

'You have my confession. Do I have to go through this abuse as well? Isn't that enough for you?'

'No. When kids start to smoke, they often pinch their parents' fags, you know. Just like they take booze from the cupboard.'

'So what?'

'That fag outside had no lipstick on it.'

She sneered. 'So what? It was early. Do you think all women put make-up on as soon as they get up?'

'I'll bet your daughter doesn't.'

She paled. 'That's mad!'

'There's one thing a mother will always protect – her child. Even when that child is mad and has killed her own father.'

'I... no. You're wrong.'

'Do you want a lawyer?'

She opened her mouth as though to refuse, and when Hawkwood saw her face crumple, he picked up her mug himself and went to refill it.

She confessed. When the forensic evidence was sifted, there were many traces of Amanda's crime, and the judge agreed to her plea of insanity.

Almost a year later Hawkwood met Elspeth Arnold again. He was leaving the shopping centre, parcels wrapped ready for his girls. Hopefully this year they'd actually open them. Last year they'd returned them unopened. He'd sat and stared at them for a whole morning, slowly sipping from a bottle of whisky. At lunch he'd thrown them away with the empty bottle.

'Inspector.'

'Mrs Arnold.' Here, in open territory, he felt curiously guilty and furtively looked around for an escape.

'I hoped to hear from Amanda, you know. She won't even let me phone her.'

'I'm sorry.'

'I can't understand why she did it.'

Hawkwood succumbed to his better feelings and took her to a coffee bar where he bought them large cappucinos.

'I've not touched a drop since, you know.'

He smiled. Since that whisky, he'd tried to stop too. He hadn't.

'Why did she kill him? Why not kill me? It was me she hated.'

'I think she despised him for his weakness. She helped carry you to bed but she snapped. She'd had enough of looking after you both. That was how she viewed it.'

'Something I never had an opportunity to ask you: how did you realise it wasn't me?'

Hawkwood stared over her shoulder at a mother with a pushchair at the till. 'There were some clues. I didn't think you'd be so slapdash as to invent such a good alibi and then wreck it like that. And I realised that Amanda wasn't actually so upset about her father's death. She didn't even take the tranquillisers the doctor gave her. That was odd. Then again, she wore no make-up and the cigarette didn't have lipstick on it. I didn't think you'd throw a cigarette away in your garden either. It wasn't the sort of thing you'd do even if you were drunk at the time.'

'I won't be again.'

'No, I doubt you will.'

'What else was there?'

'It was your drunkenness. Even Amanda let slip she'd had to help you to bed. If you were that pissed, he'd be able to protect himself. God, he was used to your temper, wasn't he? If you were as drunk as you and Amanda said, he'd have been able to at least throw a hand in the way and get a slashed palm but he had nothing. He obviously wasn't expecting to be stabbed, and that meant it was less likely to be you who killed him. He would have expected you to stab him. There was only one person in the house who could have stabbed him without his anticipating it.'

'I suppose.'

Hawkwood finished his coffee and the two separated. He was glad that he hadn't had to explain the last detail that Amanda had told him.

She had stabbed her father from frustration because he stopped her killing her mother, the source of, as she saw it, her father's impotence and weakness as well as her own miserable existence. Elspeth had been passed out on the sofa when he returned home. Amanda heard him weeping in the sitting room. She went to comfort him, and then fetched the knife and told him to stab Elspeth. They would explain it as a bungled murder, she said. When he refused, she snatched it back, but he stopped her killing her mother, so she struck out at him in frustration.

She carried Elspeth upstairs and put her in bed, before returning downstairs and going outside. She deliberately smashed the window and lit up a cigarette from her mother's pack, leaving it prominently on the grass. She made herself sick and left the vomit there too, making sure that her mother would be the obvious suspect.

Hawkwood stood under a street light and contemplated the scurrying crowds of people preparing for their happy Christmas. God, he needed a drink!

Her murder almost worked. Because even though the neighbours were some distance away, they still heard the screams. It almost worked because they assumed the worst of him, her father. No one could believe the little girl could have killed him. Just as they didn't realise it was her mother who was the abuser in the family.

'So what do you think of that, eh, Holmes?' he muttered and wandered through the twilight towards home and the pub.

MEDICINAL PURPOSES

Peter Lewis

Although he has yet to publish a full-length novel, Peter Lewis – an academic who has published studies of the work of Eric Ambler and John Le Carré – has written a number of enjoyably original short stories. I have had the pleasure of including his work in anthologies on several occasions, starting with 'Blood Brothers', which appeared in *Northern Blood*, a collection of regional crime writing published just over a decade ago. Together with his wife Margaret, Lewis lives in Northumberland and relished the opportunity to provide a rural setting for this breezy and distinctive tale.

'If horror be the food of lust, film on, give me excess of it.'

'What?' Penelope muttered.

'You heard.'

And indeed she had. It was just that Penelope, not being nearly as nimble with language as Diana, often needed time to figure out her best friend's wordplay.

They were travelling home on the school coach after attending a matinée performance of *Twelfth Night* at Stratford, and planning their favourite activity – curling up together in Diana's pad at the top of her mother's house to watch horror movies, which Diana either recorded from TV while telling her mother she was taping something educational, or hired from an obliging store that didn't enquire about her age since out of school uniform she could, unlike the shorter and patently adolescent Penelope, pass for twenty.

'It was the first line of the play, wasn't it, Di?' Penelope suggested.

'What? To use one of your favourite words.'

'The bit about horror being the food of lust.'

'Not exactly,' Diana laughed. 'Unless my memory's failing me, Will's music-and-love version was more… tasteful. *Le mot juste, n'est-ce pas?*' She paused to allow Penelope to work out the pun. 'Tasteful,' Diana repeated. 'Geddit?'

'Oh, yes,' Penelope replied, not quite sure whether she'd got it or not.

'And thinking about horror and lust…'

'Not that there's much else to think about,' Penelope interpolated.

'Goes without saying. What's the latest with that creepy quack of a neighbour you've got at your end of our metropolis?'

Penelope and Diana lived at opposite ends of an agricultural village, which ribboned along the ridge of a hill. There were two farms, a pub and a primary school, but the village shop and post office had been terminated in one of the periodic culls of rural England. The social composition had changed considerably in recent years with the conversion of a number of old farm buildings into executive homes for professional people who regarded commuting as the price to be paid for a toehold on the Jerusalem that William Blake promised for England's green and pleasant land.

Diana's 'creepy quack', Dr Hunter, and his wife were childless newcomers who occupied a spacious bungalow just a few houses along from the modest cottage Penelope's mother Sue had bought after her divorce, when Penelope was only five. Hunter was a consultant gynaecologist, which meant – Diana told Penelope – that he was licensed to insert his mitts into any female's pudenda much as 007 James Bond was licensed to kill.

Despite the SLOW signs on the road reinforcing the 30 MPH speed limit, vehicles entering the village past Penelope's cottage often drove too fast, and Hunter was a regular offender. Arriving at his drive, he braked as though entering a chicane on a Formula One racing circuit.

The first of Hunter's 'crimes' occurred not long after he moved into the village. Of the animals Penelope and her mother shared their home with, her favourite was the oldest cat, Catullus, whom she'd had as a kitten. Penelope was in the front garden watching Catullus walk in his magisterial manner along the top of the stone wall on the other side of the road when she heard a vehicle approaching far too fast. Old age was beginning to catch up with Catullus, but he still conducted himself as though the field he was surveying on the other side of the wall was his own private hunting ground. Although everything happened very quickly, Penelope knew instantly that Catullus had been run over. Just after the cat hopped off the wall out of sight, she heard the squeal of brakes, and Hunter's car pulled up at the garden gate. As she ran towards the road, Penelope yelled to Sue in the house to come. Hunter was already out of his vehicle inspecting Catullus who lay squashed and twitching in the middle of the road, both eyes having popped out of their sockets. It was like something out of a horror movie, only this wasn't fake, on a screen. It was for real.

'He's still alive,' shrieked Penelope, 'do something.'

'No, he's quite dead,' Hunter said, 'those are just spasms. Your cat, I presume. I'm very sorry but it wasn't my fault. Just an accident. Couldn't be helped. He just ran out in front of me and there was no way of avoiding him.'

By this time Sue had joined her daughter who was kneeling on the road beside Catullus, sobbing 'No, no, no, no, no...'

'I'll give you a hand if you like,' Hunter said. 'Help you clear up. It's the least I can do. I'll get some tools.'

'Haven't you done enough, you...' Penelope virtually spat the words at him, speaking without quite realising that she was speaking. She heard her mother thanking Hunter for his offer but declining: 'Better go now and leave us to it. We'll manage.'

And they did. Moved Catullus's remains with the help of a cardboard box. Dug a grave in the corner of the back garden. Buried him. With a brief ceremony of Penelope's devising.

It was her first experience of grief and tears came plentifully for a couple of weeks. Whenever she looked at the wall across the road, she expected to see him tiptoeing his way along the uneven stones. Feeding the other cats every morning, she couldn't believe that he wasn't among them, rubbing against her legs as though to say, Hurry up, I'm hungry.

Sue did everything she could to soothe Penelope, telling her that accidents will happen and that poor old Catullus had been slowing down for some time and had become a bit hard of hearing. But nothing she said affected Penelope's conviction that it was Hunter's fault and that if he hadn't been driving so fast Catullus would still be flicking his magnificent tail.

From time to time in the weeks after Catullus's demise, once the immediate grief had worn off, Penelope fantasised about suitable forms of revenge. She would like to... There were plenty of things she would like to... But of course she did nothing. Not a polite, well-behaved, middle-class girl like Penelope. She didn't even tell Diana what her imagination, nourished by horror movies, suggested to her. That was before Hunter's second 'crime', by which time Mrs Hunter had become the focus of gossip in the village pub and elsewhere. She was a bit of a mystery right enough, seldom seen and reputed to be somewhat sickly. Not an invalid quite, but there was something not quite right, supposedly her heart. An inherited degenerative condition, it was said. There were even rumours that Hunter had a girlfriend and that his adultery was the cause of his wife's poor health, but this was mere speculation since there was no real evidence. Indeed there were some golf widows who considered Hunter to be a very caring husband who, unlike their own spouses, devoted a lot of time to his wife.

Sue and Penelope were more feline than canine in their enthusiasm, but did their bit for the doggy kingdom, too, including Pluto, an exceedingly macho Springer spaniel with a propensity to go walkabout. Pluto was well known in the village and had quite a number of admirers who provided him with treats when he visited them on his rounds. No one had ever complained about him. To receive a call from the official dogcatcher that their dog had been reported wandering at large and had been collected from Hunter's garden therefore came as an unbelievable surprise to Sue and Penelope. Hunter had been in the village long enough to know damn well whose dog Pluto was, so why hadn't he just phoned them? What sort of bloody-minded point was he trying to make?

After retrieving Pluto, Sue decided to confront Hunter and called on him with Penelope reluctantly in tow. After Catullus, the less Penelope saw of Hunter the better. Sue expressed regret if Pluto had caused a nuisance but wasn't it over the top, she argued, to summon the dogcatcher for a neighbour's dog.

'Not at all,' he replied. 'He's lucky he didn't get a blast from my shotgun. Next time, he might not be so lucky. That dog's out of control. Seems to me you encourage him to wander far and wide. Some people round here don't seem to mind, but I do. If you don't know how to look after dogs, you shouldn't have any.'

And that, more or less, was that. Penelope was particularly upset at Hunter's threat to Pluto. How could he say something like that about a dog as affectionate and harmless as Pluto?

'Easily,' said Sue. 'He's a bloody fascist, if you ask me. Some doctors get like that. Little dictators in hospitals. And out. Think they're in charge of everything. Men in general, really. All that testosterone.'

But for some time afterwards, Penelope kept a strict eye on Pluto and curtailed his odyssean meanderings when Hunter was likely to be at home. There was something about the man that frightened her in a way she hadn't experienced before. He reeked of self-confidence and power, and seemed capable of anything. She could imagine him having a role in one of the films she watched with Diana, but *he* couldn't be turned off by pressing a zapper. *He* was there all the time. Ungetawayablefrom, in Dispeak. Angry and resentful as Penelope felt, there was no way she could get back at him except in her fantasies.

Not even Sue realised how deeply Hunter's behaviour had affected her daughter, making her anxious about even walking through the village in case she bumped into him. The only person Penelope could confide in was Diana, who said: 'Something should be done about that man. Cut him down to size. Take him down a few pegs. You'd think he owned the village, the way he carries on. Our feudal lord and master. We should cast a spell.'

'What?' Penelope said.

'You heard.'

'Don't be daft, Di. What do you think we are? The witches in *Macbeth*?'

'What's wrong with that, for hell's sake? There's nothing daft about casting a spell. Could be fun. Double, double toil and trouble. Let go a bit, Penny. It might even work. We can but try.'

And she set off briskly down the steeply sloping, gorse-ridden field behind Penelope's home, good only for grazing a dozen or so heifers. At the bottom was a copse of trees sometimes used by village children for boisterous games of hide and seek.

'Where are you off to?' Penelope called after Diana.

'Birnam Wood. Come on. You can get the eye of newt and toe of frog while I make the cauldron bubble.'

Penelope followed, as Diana knew she would. She always did.

Once in the wood Diana began to dance through the under-growth, chanting gibberish: 'Laka sangdkep marala fazun dinplat coljub...'

'What's that meant to do?' Penelope said, watching her friend pirouetting around the trees.

'Cause him maximum embarrassment at the hospital. Give him violent diarrhoea on his ward rounds with his junior doctors so that he poos his pants in public. Make him a laughing stock.'

'You're totally mad, Di. Out of your mind.'

'Why not? It's fun. Come on, Penny. You're far too inhibited. Join the dance. Walamout ranthrap gooviley...'

Penelope joined the dance, imitating Diana's steps but leaving the chanting to her friend.

'This isn't going to work,' Diana said, coming to a standstill.

'Of course it isn't, you daft bugger.'

'No, what I mean is that we're not doing it right.' Diana collected some fallen branches and arranged them in a geometric shape. 'It's a pentagram,' she told Penny, 'and we need to dance around it in a circle. Without any clothes on.'

'What?'

'You heard. You can't expect to cast a spell wearing jeans and a T-shirt. To get in touch with natural forces, witches found that nudity was best.'

'For God's sake, Di, we're not witches.'

'But we can have a go. So let's have you naked, Penny, starkers, in the buff, *tout nu,* since this is for your benefit, not mine,' Diana said as she stripped off her shirt, bra, shoes, jeans and pants in one continuous movement. 'Come on, we can't stop now we've got this far. Pretend you're in one of our films. *The Wicker Man,* or something, where they bare all.'

Penelope was familiar with odd behaviour from Diana, but never this odd. Diana seemed possessed, almost omnipotent.

'I'll give you a hand,' Diana said, beginning to pull Penelope's shirt up.

'It's OK, I can manage myself,' Penelope replied, and she obeyed Diana's command even while telling her she'd lost all her marbles. Penelope wasn't shy about taking her clothes off in front of Diana since they'd seen each other's bodies a number of times, while changing for swimming or sharing a bedroom. But out in the open was something else. Even so, they were soon dancing together around the pentagram and Penelope even joined in the crazy chanting. Despite her initial reluctance, she soon found the experience liberating and empowering. It was hardly likely to achieve anything as far as Hunter was concerned, but it did something for her.

Then suddenly Diana called a halt. 'That's enough.' She reached out to Penelope for a celebratory hug, took her in her arms and held her close. Their lips touched briefly before Penelope turned her head away and broke free to reach for her clothes.

'Yes,' Diana said, 'we'd better get dressed in case some voyeuristic dogwalker stumbles across us and accuses us of unspeakable carnal perversions.'

Hunter's third 'crime' followed soon after his second, and Penelope's immediate response was that it was the fulfilment of his threat to Pluto. One of Sue and Penelope's regular walks with the spaniel was through the field containing 'Birnam Wood' behind their house. Although there was no history in the village of flashers or men loitering with intent, Sue wasn't keen on Penelope taking that path by herself just in case something nasty came out of the copse. Penelope, of course, pooh-poohed her mother's anxiety: 'With Pluto to protect me, what could possibly happen, Mum? Get real.'

What happened one day when Penelope was walking Pluto past the copse was a sudden explosion, which made her part company with her skin. Pluto froze in panic as though thunder-struck. A few leaves and twigs fell near them. Then Penelope noticed a movement in the copse and saw Hunter armed with a shotgun looking in their direction. Her first assumption was that he'd fired at Pluto. He would hardly shoot at her, would he?

'Gave you a fright, did I?' he shouted. 'Didn't see you, I'm afraid. Looking up. Concentrating on pigeon.'

Penelope didn't believe him, even though he probably was after pigeon. The way Pluto had been racing around the field with the occasional bark when he spotted a rabbit, Hunter would have had to be blind in both eyes not to have seen them. If he'd intended to scare the pants off her, he'd succeeded. It may not have been a sexual assault, but in her view an assault is what it was. She put Pluto on the leash and headed for home, shaken and shaking.

Sue was furious. She phoned the police to report that her daughter had been terrified by Hunter's totally irresponsible behaviour in using his shotgun with people so close. A young policeman came round to take a statement, but it was obvious to Sue that nothing would come of her complaint. Hunter would swear that he hadn't realised anyone was in the vicinity. He would be advised to be a bit more careful in future, and he would agree to do so. Storm in a teacup. End of matter.

Except that Diana, when she heard about the incident, interpreted Hunter's entry into Birnam Wood as a kind of rape of her and Penelope's arena of magic and an attempt to subvert their spells. How had he known about their ritual? Could he possibly have been there in hiding?

'You're totally crazy,' Penelope told her. But when they went to the copse to investigate, they discovered that the branches forming their pentagram had been broken and scattered. 'If it's not him, it's dark forces he controls,' Diana said. 'Something to do with those goats of his, I wouldn't be surprised. I bet you anything he's a sorcerer.'

'You mean…'

'Yes, a male witch. A warlock. So we've got a real battle on our hands. We're up against more than we thought. We'll have to work out a new tactic. Cast a stronger spell.'

Hunter's fourth 'crime' differed from his others in not being a single event but an ongoing process. It concerned his four goats, which arrived shortly after he did. If it hadn't been for Hunter's killing of Catullus and his threat to Pluto, the goats would have gone down as an intermittent nuisance, which is how Sue viewed them, but for Penelope they gradually became part of his 'criminal' conspiracy against her personally.

At Penelope's end of the village, the houses were on one side of the road only. On the other side was a wide grass verge in front of the stone wall along which Catullus liked to stroll, surveying the countryside beyond. From time to time Hunter tethered his goats along this stretch of greenery, which they grazed systematically. The trouble was that they could be exceptionally noisy, bleating and roaring for no apparent reason. If residents complained, Hunter moved the goats elsewhere for a while, but before long they would be back.

Although Sue told her daughter not to exaggerate the nuisance factor, Penelope found the noise nerve-racking. If they hadn't been Hunter's goats, she might hardly have heard them, but as it was, every bleat seemed to go through her. Sue told her that she was imagining things. Animal noises were part of rural life, and while Hunter's determination to project an image of himself as a shooting-and-fishing countryman was an aspect of his pretentious pomposity, the goats were harmless enough. 'Just ignore them.' Penelope couldn't. But thinking she might be accused of being wimpish, it was some time before she let on to Diana how the goats were getting her down. When she did so, shortly before the gunshot in the copse, Diana told her off for withholding essential information in the case against Hunter.

Diana's new tactic and stronger spell meant visiting the remains of a prehistoric British hillfort overlooking the village. There, she told Penelope, they would be able to tap into ancient spirits that were bound to be hostile to the likes of Hunter. 'We'll summon up Boudicca and enlist her support. And any female deities we can access.' Penelope couldn't help laughing at all the stuff and nonsense Diana spouted, but she didn't hesitate to go along with it.

'Ideally we should do this as the sun rises,' Diana said on the way up, 'and sacrifice a virgin, but they're in short supply these days.'

'What do you mean? I'm a…'

'You don't need to tell me. But we can't sacrifice you since all this is for your benefit.'

'What about you, Di?'

'You could be accused of making unwarranted assumptions about people, Penny. I had thought of asking one of the farm boys to accompany us and do an Onan on the summit as a form of sacrifice.'

'What's Onan?'

'Who, not what. In the Bible. He spilt his seed, to speak biblically.'

'What? You don't mean…'

'Yes. But I changed my mind. Not just to spare your maidenly blushes. No, it seemed regressivly pre-feminist of me to think of relying on a mere male, even as a sacrifice. Women can manage without. When did you last see your father?'

'About ten years ago.'

'See what I mean. Mine's not much better. And when I do see him, I'm lost for words.'

'That's hard to believe.'

'True, though.'

From the top of the hill it was possible to see a long way in every direction and the two girls strolled around the earthworks to make sure no one was in sight.

'So what are we going to do this time?' Penelope asked. 'Do we have to be *tutti-frutti* like before.'

'*Tout nu*, you imbecile. I wish you'd learn to speak English. Anyway the answer to your question is yes. *Tutti-frutti*. So kit off.'

Naked, they lay side-by-side on their backs, holding hands and gazing up at the sky.

'I love these days when it's sunny and bright but you can still see the moon as a ghostly presence,' Diana said.

'So what's next?'

'I thought of recreating an Ancient Briton ceremony up here. Kind of pre-Christian black mass. Cover our bodies in woad. Tap into the occult. But if we walked back to the village painted blue, we'd hardly be inconspicuous. And we can't risk revealing our secrets or the magic wouldn't work.'

'What film did you get that from? *Boudicca Rides Again*?'

'Cheeky. Do you know about holy rollers?'

'Yes. Well, heard of them.'

'Well I thought we'd do some unholy rolling in the light of the silvery afternoon moon. Come on.'

Diana led Penelope to the steepest side of the hillfort, covered in lush grass since sheep hadn't been grazing there recently.

'Lie down on your back,' Diana said.

Penny obeyed. 'Are we going to roll down the slope like kids?'

'Sort of, but double. Together.' And with that she lowered herself on top of Penelope, holding her tight.

'What are you doing, Di?'

'I'm not going to roger you, if that's what you're worried about.'

'Who's Roger?'

'Honestly, Penny. You'll be asking me next what work working girls do for a living.'

'What?'

'What yourself, dumdum. Here we go. Hang on. I'm pushing off.'

And down they went in a tangle of limbs, whooping and shrieking like intoxicated maenads.

'That should rouse the Ancient Brits to help us,' Diana said when the ground flattened out and they stopped. With Penelope's head in her lap, Diana stroked her hair with one hand while using the other to trace patterns on her body with a long piece of grass. Then, bending over, she kissed Penelope lightly on the mouth. Penelope didn't resist but didn't respond either.

'In my saner moments I think we could be a classic case of *folie à deux*,' Diana said.

'What? Is that anything like *ménage à trois*?'

'No, but at least you've got the right language.'

Even before this hilltop frolic, Penelope noticed a change in the goats. Their decibel level was down and they sounded increasingly wheezy as though they had contracted a dose of bronchitis. They also spent more time lying down, something they'd rarely done previously. According to village gossip, there'd also been a deterioration in Mrs Hunter's condition. She was very far from well and like the goats she had been losing weight. Resembled a ghost, people said.

'Do you think we might actually have unleashed something against the Hunters?' Penelope asked Diana.

'Why not. Must be all the *tutti-frutti*.'

'I'm serious, Di. If so, we've hit the wrong target.'

'Well the goats have calmed down. That's an achievement.'

'I'm not talking about the goats. It's Mrs Hunter I'm concerned about. She's harmless enough.'

'I bet you anything that Hunter has some form of protection against magic, an invisible shield or something that deflects the powers we've released on to his wife. It comes with being a warlock.'

'You watch too many crappy films, Di.'

'So do you.'

Soon afterwards, the four goats died in quick succession and Hunter tried unsuccessfully to get a farmer to incinerate them. Not after the last outbreak of foot-and-mouth, he was told. No more animal pyres in England's green and pleasant land. But the farmer agreed to bury them in a patch of rough ground on his land. Then it emerged that Mrs Hunter had taken a decided turn for the worse. She was virtually housebound, and Hunter was employing a couple of nurses to look after her.

Penelope's anxiety was reaching panic proportions. 'Shouldn't we try to reverse the spell, just in case it is our fault?' she asked Diana.

'Quite honestly, darling Penny, it's completely out of our hands. There's nothing we can do. If he is a warlock, then he might well be using black magic against his wife.'

In a matter of weeks Mrs Hunter died at home. Her heart finally gave out.

The day before her cremation, the police arrived in the village to make an arrest. It was Hunter's mistress Cass who blew the whistle, even though it meant incriminating herself to some extent. If she hadn't found the crucial video by chance, she might have kept her mouth shut. But then again she might not.

Hunter had led Cass to believe that his wife was terminally ill with an incurable heart disease, and that in the fullness of time he would marry her. Cass was quite prepared for a long wait. But from what Hunter hinted to her, she concluded that he was willing to ease his wife's suffering even though it meant shortening her life. Cass accepted the case for euthanasia in certain circumstances, but her suspicions were first aroused when in post-coital pillowtalk he sleepily let on that he was experimenting with his goats. Injecting them with something. When the goats died not long after, she began to put two and two together. Whatever he was up to, it was sinister. Even so, she couldn't really believe that he was actively engaged in killing his wife. According to him, Mrs Hunter was on the way out anyway. It was only a matter of time. So why not let matters take their course? She didn't ask herself whether his wife was as ill as he claimed until after she'd seen the video.

She'd found it in an executive case he'd left at her flat one evening after what, trying to be funny, he called a copulatory visit to his favourite patient. She assumed the video was something medical but had a look at it anyway. She couldn't believe her eyes although she watched it all the way through. It was a poorly lit home video of Hunter and one of the nurses he employed to care for his wife indulging in a sado-masochistic orgy of bondage and flagellation, a fusion of horror and lust. The couple were cavorting with crazed demonic energy as though possessed. She was too scared to mention it to Hunter when he called round to collect his case, but for her it was the finish. He was, she was now convinced, capable of anything. His desire to have the dead goats cremated was, she decided, because he needed to destroy any evidence of his so-called experiment.

Using the excuse that her mother was seriously ill, Cass took some unpaid leave and went off for two weeks. When she returned, Mrs Hunter was very close to death and passed away the following week. Only she didn't pass away. She was murdered. Of that, Cass was sure. Whatever Hunter had tried out on the goats, he'd also used on his wife. It had to be something that was hard to detect and would not arouse suspicions. Unless she acted before Mrs Hunter was cremated, Cass knew he would get away with it. She took her story to the police just in time, not sure whether they would believe her or write her off as a jealous bitch. They believed her enough to impound Mrs Hunter's corpse and exhume the goats. The forensic evidence from the post mortems proved Cass right.

'We got him in the end,' Diana said after Hunter was charged with murder.'

'At a terrible price, though,' Penelope said. 'Someone had to die first.'

'Not quite the way we intended, I admit. But Penny darling, the gods move in mysterious ways, their wonders to perform. Especially female deities.'

The Field

Peter Lovesey

Last year's CWA anthology included an excellent story by Phil Lovesey; this time around, there is a characteristically neat contribution from Phil's father, Peter. It is noteworthy that all four of the Diamond Dagger winners represented in this book are gifted practitioners of the short story. Certainly, there is not much that Peter Lovesey does not know about economy of style and the art of the clever twist. Sometimes, it seems as if short stories 'write themselves'; on other occasions, finding precisely the best way to achieve the desired effect is a tricky task even for the most experienced author. Peter Lovesey says that 'The Field' was 'a slow-growing crop', but I am delighted to harvest it.

A field of oilseed rape was in flower, brilliant in the afternoon sun, as if a yellow highlighter had been drawn across the landscape. Unseen by anyone, a corpse was stretched out under the swaying crop, attended only by flies and maggots. It had been there ten days. The odour was not detectable from the footpath along the hedgerow.

Fields have names. This one was Middle Field, and it was well named. It was not just the middle field on Jack Mooney's farm. It was the middle of his universe. He had no life outside the farm. His duties kept him employed from first light until after dark.

Middle Field dominated the scene. So Jack Mooney's scarecrow stood out, as much as you could see of it. People said it was a wasted effort. Crows aren't the problem with a rape crop. Pigeons are the big nuisance, and that's soon after sowing. It's an open question whether a scarecrow is any deterrent at all to pigeons. By May or June when the crop is five feet tall it serves no purpose.

'Should have got rid of it months back,' Mooney said.

His wife May, at his side, said, 'You'd have to answer to the children.'

From the highest point at the top of the field you could see more than just the flat cap and turnip head. The shoulders and part of the chest were visible as well. After a long pause Mooney said, 'Something's happened to it.'

'Now what are you on about?'

'Take a look through the glasses.'

She put them to her eyes and adjusted the focus. Middle Field was all of nine acres.

'Funny. Who did that, I wonder?'

Someone had dressed the thing in a raincoat. All it was supposed to be wearing were Mooney's cast-off shirt, a pair of corduroy trousers filled with straw and his old cap.

'How long has it been like that?'

'How would I know?' Mooney said. 'I thought you would have noticed.'

'I may go on at you for ignoring me, but I'm not so desperate as to spend my days looking at a straw man with a turnip for a head.'

'Could have been there for weeks.'

'Wouldn't surprise me.'

'Some joker?'

'Maybe.'

'I'm going to take a closer look.'

He waded into his shimmering yellow sea.

Normally he wouldn't set foot in that field until after the combine had been through. But he was curious. Whose coat was it? And why would anyone think of putting it on a scarecrow?

Out in the middle he stopped and scratched his head

It was a smart coat, with epaulettes, sleeve straps and a belt.

His wife had followed him. She lifted the hem. 'It's a Burberry. You can tell by the lining.'

'I've never owned one like this.'

'You, in a Burberry? You're joking. Been left out a few days by the look of it, but it's not in bad condition.'

'Who would have chucked out a fancy coat like this?'

'More important,' his wife said, 'who would have draped it around our old scarecrow?'

He had made the scarecrow last September on a framework of wood and chicken wire. A stake driven into the earth, with a crosspiece that swivelled when the wind blew, giving the effect of animation. The wire bent into the shape of a torso that hung free. The clothes stuffed with straw. The biggest turnip he could find for a head. He wouldn't have troubled with the features, but his children had insisted he cut slits for eyes and the mouth and a triangle for the nose.

No question – the coat had been carefully fitted on, the arms pulled through, the buttons fixed and the belt buckled in front.

As if the field itself could explain the mystery, Mooney turned and stared across the canopy of bloom. To the north was his own house and the farm buildings standing out against the skyline. At the lower end to the south-east were the tied cottages, three terraced dwellings built from the local stone. They were still called tied cottages by the locals, even though they had been sold off to a developer and knocked into one, now a sizeable house being tarted up by some townie who came at weekends to check on the work. Mooney had made a good profit from the sale. He didn't care if the locals complained that true village people couldn't afford to live here at prices like that.

Could the coat belong to the townie? he wondered. Was it someone's idea of a joke dressing the old scarecrow in the townie's smart Burberry? Strange joke. After all, who would know it was there unless they took out some field-glasses?

'You know what I reckon?' May said. 'Kids.'

'Whose kids?'

'Our own. I'll ask them when they get back from school.'

The birdsong grew as the afternoon wore on. At the edge of the field closest to the tied cottages more disturbance of the oilseed crop took place. Smaller feet than Mooney's led another expedition. They were his children, the two girls, Sarah and Ally, eleven-years-old and seven. Behind them came their mother.

'It's not far,' Sarah said, looking back.

'Not far, Mum,' Ally said.

They were right. No more than ten adult strides in from the path was a place where some of the plants had been flattened.

'See?' Ally said.

This was where the children had found the raincoat. Snapped stalks and blackened fronds confirmed what the girls had told her. It was as if some horse had strayed into the crop and rolled on its back. 'So the coat was spread out here?'

'Yes, Mummy.'

'Like somebody had a picnic,' Ally added.

May had a different, less wholesome thought she didn't voice. 'And you didn't see anyone?'

They shook their heads.

'You're quite sure?'

'We were playing ball and I threw it and it landed in the field. We were on our own. When we were looking for our ball we found the coat. Nobody wanted it because we came back next day and it was still here and we thought let's put it on our scarecrow and see if Daddy notices. Was it Daddy who noticed?'

'Never mind that. You should have told me about the coat when you found it. Did you find anything else?'

'No, Mummy. If they'd wanted to keep the coat, they would have come back, wouldn't they?'

'Did you look in the pockets?'

'Yes, and they were empty. Mr Scarecrow looks nicer with a coat.'

'Much nicer,' Ally said in support. 'Doesn't he look nicer, Mummy?'

May was not to be sidetracked. 'You shouldn't have done what you did. It belongs to someone else.'

'But they didn't want it, or they would have come back,' Sarah said.

'You don't know. They could still come back.'

'They could be dead.'

'It would still be wrong to take it. I'm going to take it off the scarecrow and we'll hand it in to the police. It's lost property.'

A full three days later, Mooney escorted a tall detective inspector through the crop. 'You'll have to be damn quick with your investigating. This'll be ready for combining soon. Some of the pods are forming already.'

'If it's a crime scene, Mr Mooney, you're not doing anything to it.'

'We called you about the coat last Monday, and no one came.'

'A raincoat isn't much to get excited about. The gun is another matter.'

Another matter that had finally brought the police here in a hurry. Mooney had found a Smith and Wesson in his field. A handgun.

'When did you pick it up?'

'This morning.'

'What – taking a stroll, were you?'

Mooney didn't like the way the question was put, as if he'd been acting suspiciously. He'd done the proper thing, reported finding the weapon as soon as he picked it up. 'I've got a right to walk in my own field.'

'Through this stuff?'

'I promised my kids I'd find their ball – the ball that was missing the day they found the coat. I found the gun instead – about here.' He stopped and parted some of the limp, blue-green leaves at the base of a plant.

To the inspector, this plant looked no different from the rest except that the trail ended here. He took a white disk from his pocket and marked the spot. 'Careful with your feet. We'll want to check all this ground. And where was the Burberry raincoat?'

'On the scarecrow.'

'I mean, where did your daughters find it?'

Mooney flapped his hand in a southerly direction. 'About thirty yards off.'

'Show me.'

The afternoon was the hottest of the year so far. Thousands of bees were foraging in the rape flowers. Mooney didn't mind disturbing them, but the inspector was twitchy. He wasn't used to walking chest-high through fields. He kept close to the farmer using his elbows to fend off the tall plants springing upright again.

Only a short distance ahead, the bluebottles were busy as well. Mooney stopped.

'Well, how about this?' He was stooping over something.

The inspector almost tumbled over Mooney's back. 'What is it? What have you found?'

Mooney held it up. 'My kids' ball. They'll be pleased you came.'

'Let's get on.'

'Do you smell anything, inspector?'

In a few hours the police transformed this part of Middle Field. A large part of the crop was ruined, crushed under the feet of detectives, scenes of crime officers, a police surgeon, a pathologist and police photographers. Mooney was depressed by all the damage.

'You think the coat might have belonged to the owner of the cottages across the lane, is that right?' the inspector asked.

'I wouldn't know.'

'It's what you told me earlier.'

'That was my wife's idea. She says it's a posh coat. No one from round here wears a posh coat. Except him.'

'Who is he?'

Mooney had to think about that. He'd put the name out of his mind. 'White, as I recall. Jeremy White, from London. He bought the tied cottages from the developer who knocked them into one. He's doing them up, making a palace out of it, open plan, with marble floors and a spiral staircase.'

'Doing them up himself?'

'He's a townie. What would he know about building work? No, he's given the job to Armstrong, the Devizes firm. Comes here each weekend to check on the work.'

'Any family?'

'I wouldn't know about that.' He looked away, across the field, to the new slate roof on the tied cottages. 'I've seen a lady with him.'

'A lady? What's she like?'

Mooney sighed, forced to think. 'Dark-haired.'

'Age?'

'Younger than him.'

'The sale was in his name alone?'

'That's right.'

'If you don't mind, Mr Mooney, I'd like you to take another look at the corpse and see if you recognise anyone.'

From the glimpse he'd had already, Mooney didn't much relish another look. 'If I don't mind? Have I got a choice?'

Some of the crop had been left around the body like a screen. The police had used one access path so as not to destroy evidence. Mooney pressed his fingers to his nose and stepped up. He peered at the bloated features. Ten days in hot weather makes a difference. 'Difficult,' he said. 'The hair looks about right.'

'For Jeremy White?'

'That reddish colour. Dyed, isn't it? I always thought the townie dyed his hair. He weren't so young as he wanted people to think he were.'

'The clothes?'

Mooney looked at the pinstripe suit dusted faintly yellow from the crop. There were bullet holes in the jacket. 'That's the kind of thing he wore, certainly.'

The inspector nodded. 'From the contents of his wallet we're pretty sure this is Jeremy White. Do you recall hearing any shots last time he was here?'

'There are shots all the time, specially at weekends. Rabbits. Pigeons. We wouldn't take note of that.'

'When did you see him last?'

'Two weekends ago. Passed him in the lane on the Sunday afternoon.'

'Anyone with him?'

'That dark-haired young lady I spoke of.'

The inspector produced the wallet found on the body and took out a photo of a dark-haired woman in a blue blouse holding up a drink. 'Is this her?'

Mooney examined it for some time. He eyed the inspector with suspicion, as if he was being tricked. 'That wasn't the lady I saw.'

There was an interval when the buzzing of insects seemed to increase and the heat grew.

'Are you certain?'

'Positive.'

'Take another look.'

'Her with the townie was definitely younger.'

The inspector's eyebrows lifted. 'How much younger?'

'A good ten years, I'd say.'

'Did they come by car?'

'There was always a sports car parked in front of the cottages when he came, one of them BMW jobs with the open top.'

'Just the one vehicle? The lady didn't drive down in her own?'

'If she did, I've never seen it. When can I have my field back?'

'When I tell you. There's more searching to be done.'

'More damage, you mean.'

Mooney met Bernie Priddle with his dog the same evening coming along the footpath beside the hedgerow. Bernie had lived in one of the tied cottages until Mooney decided to sell it. He was in his fifties, small, thin-faced, always ready with a barbed remark.

'You'll lose the whole of your crop by the look of it,' he said, and he sounded happier than he had for months.

'I thought you'd turn up,' Mooney said. 'Makes you feel better to see someone else's misfortune, does it?'

'I walk the path around the field every evening. It's part of the dog's routine. You should know that by now. I was saying you'll lose your crop.'

'Don't I know it! Even if they don't trample every stalk of it, they'll stop me from harvesting.'

'People are saying it's the townie who was shot.'

'That's my understanding.'

'Good riddance, too.'

'You want to guard what you say, Bernie Priddle. They're looking for someone to nail for this.'

'Me? I wouldn't put myself in trouble for some pipsqueak yuppie. It's you I wouldn't mind doing a stretch for, Mooney. I could throttle you any time for putting me out of my home.'

'What are you moaning about? You got a council house out of it, didn't you? Hot water and an inside toilet. Where's your dog?'

Priddle looked down. His Jack Russell had moved on, and he didn't know where. He whistled.

Over by the body, all the heads turned.

'It's all right,' Mooney shouted to the policemen. 'He was calling his dog, that's all.'

The inspector came over and spoke to Priddle. 'And who are you exactly?'

Bernie explained about his regular evening walk around the field.

'Have you ever seen Mr White, the owner of the tied cottages?'

'On occasion,' Bernie said. 'What do you want to know?'

'Ever seen anyone with him?'

'Last time – the Sunday before last – there was the young lady, her with the long, black hair, and short skirt. She's a good looker, that one. He was showing her the building work. Had his arm around her. I raised my cap to them, didn't speak. Later, when I was round the far side, I saw them heading into the field.'

'Into the field? Where?'

'Over yonder. He had a coat on his arm. Next time I looked, they weren't in view.' He grinned. 'I drew my own conclusion, like, and walked on. I came right around the field before I saw the other car parked in the lane.'

The inspector's interest increased. 'You saw another car?'

'Nice little Cherokee Jeep, it was, red. Do you want the number?'

'Do you remember it?'

'It was a woman's name, SUE, followed by a number. I couldn't tell you which, except it was just the one.'

'A single digit?' The inspector sounded pleased. 'SUE, followed by a single digit. That's really useful, sir. We can check that. And did you see the driver?'

'No, I can't help you there.'

'Hear any shooting?'

'We often hear shooting in these parts. Look, I'd better find my dog.'

'We'll need to speak to you some more, Mr...?'

'Priddle. Bernard Priddle. You're welcome. These days I live in one of them poky little council bungalows in the village. Second on the left.'

The inspector watched him stride away, whistling for the dog, and said to one of the team, 'A useful witness. I want you to take a statement from him.'

Mooney was tempted to pass on the information that Bernie was a publicity-seeking pain in the arse, but he decided to let the police do their own work.

The body was removed from Middle Field the same evening. Some men in black suits put it into a bag with a zip and stretchered it over the well-trodden ground to a small van and drove off.

'Now can I have my field back?' Mooney asked the inspector.

'What's the hurry?'

'You've destroyed a big section of my crop. What's left will go over if I don't harvest it at the proper time. The pods shatter and it's too late.'

'What do you use? A combine harvester?'

'First it has to be swathed into rows. It all takes time.'

'I'll let you know in the morning. Cutting it could make our work easier. We want to do a bigger search.'

'What for?'

'Evidence. We now know that the woman Bernard Priddle saw – the driver of the Jeep – was the woman in the photograph I showed you, Mrs Susan White, the dead man's wife. We're assuming the younger woman was White's mistress. We think Mrs White was suspicious and followed them here. She didn't know about him buying the tied cottages. That was going to be his love-nest, just for weekends with the mistress. But he couldn't wait for it to be built. The wife caught them at it in the field.'

'On the raincoat?'

'That's the assumption. Our forensic people may confirm it.'

'Nasty shock.'

'On both sides, no doubt.'

Mooney smiled. 'You could be right about that. So that's why he was shot. What happened to the mistress?'

'She must have escaped. Someone drove his car away and we reckon it was her.'

'So have you arrested the wife?'

'Not yet. She wasn't at home when we called.'

Mooney grinned again. 'She guessed you were coming.'

'We'll catch up with her.'

In a tree in the hedgerow a songthrush sounded its clear notes and was answered from across the field. A breeze was cooling the air.

On the insistence of the police, Mooney harvested his crop a week before it was ready. He'd cried wolf about all the bother they'd caused, and now he suffered a loss through cutting too early. To make matters worse, not one extra piece of evidence was found, for all their fingertip searches through the stubble.

'Is that the end of it?' he asked the inspector when the final sweep across the field was made. The land looked black and bereft. Only the scarecrow remained standing. They'd asked him to leave it to use as a marker.

'It's the end of my work, but you'll be visited again. The

lawyers will want to look at the site before the case comes to court.'

'When will that be?'

'I can't say. Could be months. A year, even.'

'There won't be anything to see.'

'They'll look at the positions where the gun was found, and the body and the coat. They map it all out.'

'So are you advising me not to drill next spring?'

'That's an instruction, not advice. Not this field, anyway.'

'It's my livelihood. Will I get compensation?'

'I've no idea. Not my field, if you'll forgive the pun.'

'So you found the wife in the end?'

'Susan White – yes. She's helping us with our enquiries, as we like to put it.'

'How about the mistress? Did you catch up with her?'

'Not yet. We don't even know who she is.'

'Maybe the wife shot her as well.'

'That's why we had you cutting your crop, in case of a second body. But we're pretty certain she drove off in the BMW. It hasn't been traced yet.'

Winter brought a few flurries of snow and some gales. The scarecrow remained standing. The building work on the tied cottages was halted and no one knew what was happening about them.

'I should have drilled by now,' Mooney said, staring across the field.

'Are they ever going to come back, do you think?' his wife said.

'He said it would take a long time.'

'I suppose the wife has been in prison all these months waiting for the trial to start. I can't help feeling sorry for her.'

'If you shoot your husband, you must get what's coming to you,' Mooney said.

'She had provocation. Men who cheat on their wives don't get any sympathy from me.'

'Taking a gun to them is a bit extreme.'

'Quick and merciful.'

Mooney gave her a look. There had been a time before the children came along when their own marriage had gone through a crisis, but he'd never been unfaithful.

The lawyers came in April. Two lots in the same week. They took photos and made measurements, regardless that the field looked totally different to the way it had last year. After the second group – the prosecution team – had finished, Mooney asked if he could sow the new crop now. Spring rape doesn't give the yield of a winter crop, but it's better than nothing.

'I wouldn't,' the lawyer told him. 'It's quite possible we'll bring out the jury to see the scene of the crime.'

'It's a lot of fuss, when we all know she did it.'

'It's justice, Mr Mooney. She must have a fair trial.'

And you must run up your expenses, he thought. They'd driven up in their Porsches and Mercedes and lunched on fillet steak at the pub. The law was a good racket.

But as things turned out, the jury weren't brought to see the field. The trial took place a year after the killing and Mooney was allowed to sow another crop. The first thing he did was take down that scarecrow and destroy it. He wasn't a superstitious man, but he associated the wretched thing with his run of bad luck. He'd been told it had been photographed for the papers. Stupid. They'd photograph any damned thing to fill a page. Someone told him they'd called his land 'The Killing Field'. Things like that were written by fools for fools to read. When a man has to be up at sunrise he doesn't have time for papers. By the evening they're all out of date.

An evil thing had happened in Middle Field, but Mooney was determined to treat it as just a strip of land like any other. Personally, he had no worries about working the soil. He put the whole morbid incident to the back of his mind.

Until one evening in September.

He'd drilled the new sowing of oilseed, and was using the roller, working late to try and get the job finished before the light went altogether. A huge harvest moon appeared while he was still at work. He was thinking of supper, driving the tractor in near darkness along the last length beside the footpath, when a movement close to the hedge caught his eye.

If the figure had kept still he would have driven straight past. The face turned and was picked out by his headlights. A woman. Features he'd seen before.

He braked and got down.

She was already walking on. He ran after her and shouted, 'Hey!'

She turned, and he knew he wasn't mistaken. She was the woman in the photograph the police had shown him, Sue White, the killer, the wife of the dead man.

'What the devil are you doing here?' he asked.

'Walking the footpath. It's allowed, isn't it?' She was calm for an escaped convict.

Mooney's heart pumped faster. He peered through the fading light to be certain he wasn't mistaken. 'Who are you?'

'My name is Sue White. Are you all right?'

Mooney wasn't all right. He'd just had a severe shock. His ears were ringing and his vision was going misty. He reached out towards the hedge to support himself. His hand clutched at nothing and he fell.

The paramedics attended to him by flashlight in the field where he'd fallen. 'You'll need to be checked,' one of them said, 'but I don't think this is a heart attack. More of a shock reaction. The blood pressure falls and you faint. Have you had anything like it before?'

Mooney shook his head. 'But it were a shock all right, seeing that woman. How did she escape?'

'*Escape*? Just take it easy, Mr Mooney.'

'She's on the run from prison. She could be dangerous.'

'Listen, Mr Mooney. It's only thanks to Mrs White that we got here at all. She used her mobile.'

'Maybe, but she's still a killer.'

'Come off it. You're talking about the man who was shot in your own field, and you don't know who did it? It was all over the papers. Don't you read them?'

'I don't have time for the papers.'

'It was his mistress that killed him. She's serving life now.'

'His mistress? But the wife caught them at it.'

'Yes, and that's how the mistress found out for certain that he had a wife. She'd got her suspicions already and was carrying the gun in her bag to get the truth out of him, or so she claimed at the trial. She saw red and shot him after Mrs White showed up.'

His voice shook. 'So Mrs White is innocent?'

'Totally. We've been talking to her. She came down today to look at those cottages. She's the owner now. She'll sell them if she's got any sense. I mean, who'd want a home looking out over the Killing Field?'

They helped Mooney to the gate and into the ambulance. Below the surface of Middle Field, the moist soil pressed against the seeds.

FITTING IN

Keith Miles

Keith Miles writes stories set in the past or the present with equal facility. His pseudonyms include Edward Marston, and a book forthcoming in the USA under that name will be well worth looking out for. It is *Murder – Ancient and Modern*, and it will showcase the talents of an author whose versatility and flair for the short story form deserves to be widely recognised. For this book Keith Miles, like his real-life partner Judith Cutler, has given a fresh spin to the 'stranger in paradise' theme.

Dove Cottage was too good to be true. Having bought it on impulse, Derek and Alison Wilmer waited for the house to reveal its dark secrets, those major defects that had been cunningly concealed behind the glib prose of the estate agent. Why was such an attractive property being offered at such a reasonable price? Did it harbour a ghost? Was it riddled with dry rot? Had the previous occupants made a bizarre suicide pact to hang themselves from the beam in the living room? The Wilmers entered their new home warily, bracing themselves against the possibility of discovering the hideous truth about Dove Cottage. But disillusionment never came. The estate agent had been uncharacteristically honest.

What the newcomers had bought was a charming three-bedroomed Tudor thatched cottage, set in half an acre of garden (complete with dovecote) and adjacent to a working farm. Advertised as being in need of sympathetic renovation, it had some obvious structural problems and lacked such niceties as central heating, mains drainage and a gas supply. The garden was a positive jungle. Local amenities were poor – one pub and a village shop with erratic opening hours – and the private road that served the cottage was little more than a succession of ever-deepening potholes. The Wilmers were well and truly off the beaten track.

Yet that was the main appeal for them. After years of teaching in a tough, unyielding, inner-city comprehensive, Derek yearned for a quieter life without the daily pitched battles in the classroom. His left-wing colleagues had been horrified to learn that he was taking up an administrative post in a famous private school in Canterbury but he was prepared to endure their scorn. Alison, too, was ready for a change. Now that their children had left home, she wanted to escape the multi-cultural tumult of Wolverhampton and enjoy the benefits of rural seclusion. Having made a handsome profit on the sale of their house in the Midlands, they decided that Alison could afford to give up her job as manager of a travel agency and concentrate – at least for the first year – on licking Dove Cottage into shape.

On their first night at their new abode, the doubts began to surface. They were lying in bed, adjusting their ears to a whole battery of new sounds. The constant traffic that passed their house in Wolverhampton was now replaced by the lowing of cattle, the hoot of an owl and the high-pitched screech of a vixen. There was also a rustling noise directly above their heads. Alison nestled into her husband's arms.

'Have we done the right thing?' she asked nervously.

'Of course,' he said with more confidence than he felt. 'This is a dream home.'

'Then why was it on the market for so long?'

'People were put off because it needs so much doing to it.'

'I'm worried that they knew something that we don't.'

'That's a silly idea,' he said, ruffling her hair. 'By the time we've finished all the restorations, everyone will be green with envy.'

Alison sighed. 'There's so much to be done, Derek.'

'That's why we took it on, love. It's a challenge.'

'I suppose so.' She looked upwards. 'What's that noise in the attic?'

'A bird, probably. I'll clear out the nest in the morning.'

'You don't think it's a rat, do you? Or even a squirrel?'

'I don't care if it's a flock of long-horned sheep,' he said with a chuckle. 'First thing tomorrow, out they go. My wife is not going to have any disturbed nights here.'

She kissed him. 'Actually,' she whispered, 'I was rather hoping that I would.'

Derek responded at once. Ignoring the strange sounds from outside and inside the house, they celebrated their move to the country with renewed passion. Alison fell asleep soon afterwards. Her husband needed time to get his breath back.

'Welcome to Dove Cottage!' he said.

The first discovery they made next morning was that they would never need an alarm clock to wake them up. Henry Clout, the farmer, started milking the dairy herd at exactly 5.30am. Though it was over thirty yards away, the milking machine was very audible when it kicked in, jerking Derek and Alison out of their slumbers. Light was already peeping around the edges of the curtains. When she got up to draw them back, Alison saw that they now had doves in the dovecote. It looked as if it was going to be a glorious summer's day. She gazed out across rolling fields that were splashed with trees and mercifully free from ugly pylons. It was a scene of beauty and tranquillity. Her faith in Dove Cottage was revived.

Other discoveries quickly followed. By way of a welcome, a huge bunch of wild flowers had been left on their doorstep by Joan Clout, the farmer's wife, a bustling woman in dungarees who helped her husband with even the most onerous chores. The Wilmers also learned that they had a garrulous postman called Vernon ('Wolverhampton, eh? That where you come from? Suppose that means you support Wolves. Man United fan myself. They play my kind of football.'); a mobile library that came once a fortnight; an irascible milkman who complained about the pot-holes in their road; an affable vicar who dropped in to introduce himself; and Nan Raybone, a decrepit old lady in tattered clothing, who seemed far too frail and ill to have walked the hundred yards from her own cottage. One hand on her walking stick, she carried a basket of fresh eggs over her other arm and told Alison that her chickens would always provide free eggs for her new neighbours.

'What a dear old soul!' said Derek as their visitor hobbled away.

'She looks as if she can hardly stand up,' observed Alison.

'I did offer to give her a lift back home.'

'I know. And Mrs Raybone said the only vehicle she'd ever

agree to get into was a hearse. I hope she meant that as a joke, Derek. She struck me as a delightful character.'

'A real countrywoman. You wouldn't meet anyone like that in Wolverhampton.'

'I think we've made our first friend.'

It was not long before they met their first enemy. After a productive morning's work, they had lunch at the table in the rear garden, noting the way that it was a natural sun-trap and making plans for a large vegetable patch. Derek was still enthusing about the prospect of growing his own potatoes, carrots and courgettes when they heard hooves drumming up their drive. Three wild-eyed cows suddenly appeared, trampling madly across the flowerbeds before disappearing around the other side of the house.

Alison leapt up in alarm and rushed back into the safety of the kitchen, but Derek pursued the invading animals into the front garden. After scattering the doves, one of them had the temerity to lift its tail and leave a series of large, glutinous brown calling cards all over the lawn. Scampering feet etched fleeting autographs in the thick grass. Derek's first thought was that Henry Clout had let some of his herd escape but he soon realised his mistake. The owner of the runaway Frieisians was a big, brawny, foul-mouthed man in his forties, who was yelling at his wayward beasts through the open window of an ancient Triumph Herald, using the vehicle as a four-wheeled cow dog as his front bumper prodded the back legs of the fleeing animals.

Forgetting the damage done to his garden, Derek watched in amazement. He had never seen anything so cruel, reckless and disturbing. It was almost as if the driver were trying to run his cows down. Henry Clout appeared at the fence in time to hear the car horn being pressed violently. He spat on the floor with disgust.

'Who was that?' asked Derek.

'Colly Raybone,' said Henry. 'You should have been warned about him.'

Everyone in the village had a Colly Raybone story. When she called at the shop that afternoon, Alison heard a selection of them. Raybone was a maverick, a brutal and uncaring man who eked out a living as a tenant farmer and who was the bane of the area. His first wife had left him in terror yet, in spite of his reputation, Raybone had no difficulty is finding other women to warm his bed. Though they rarely stayed long in his dilapidated farmhouse, they were instantly replaced. At one point, it transpired, he had had two mistresses living with him simultaneously.

Raybone was a law unto himself. If people annoyed him, he assaulted them. If bills needed paying, he tore them up. When food ran short, he poached rabbits, deer and other game. When dogs trespassed on his land, he shot them. Few people dared to take him to court and those that did soon regretted it. Alison gave her husband one example.

'He fell out with someone at the pub,' she explained, 'and beat him black and blue. The police became involved but Mr Raybone somehow got off with a fine. A week later, the farmer who'd pressed charges against him had his barn burned to the ground.'

'Didn't they arrest Raybone?'

'They had no proof, Derek.'

'Well, we've got proof,' he said, pointing to the garden. 'We both saw his cows churning up our flowerbeds and ruining our lawn. He should pay compensation.'

'The man at the shop said you'd wasting your time in trying to get it.'

'Why?'

'Because it's happened before to other people and nobody's ever got a penny out of Mr Raybone. In our case, he'd argue that it was our responsibility to protect our property by having a gate at the bottom of the drive.' She pulled a face. 'I suppose that there's something in that.'

'We can't let him get away with it, Alison. I'll speak to the man.'

'No,' she protested. 'I don't want you to end up with a broken nose.'

Derek stuck out his jaw. 'I'm not afraid of Colly Raybone.'

'Everyone else is,' said Alison. 'Except for his Aunt Nan, that is.'

'What – old Mrs Raybone, who gave us those eggs?'

'She won't hear a word against him, apparently. Mrs Raybone thinks that he's a wonderful nephew. He looks after her, does all her shopping, calls regularly. She's the one person in the village who speaks up for Colly Raybone.'

'He's a complete menace.'

'That's why we have to watch him carefully.' Alison brightened. 'However, there's one ray of hope.'

'Is there?'

'Yes,' she said. 'It's not his farm. It's a tenancy and the contract is coming up for renewal soon. The County Council hates him. Since he's broken just about every term of the agreement, they have the excuse they need to kick him out. Colly Raybone may have to sell his stock and leave the area. If that happens, the whole village will celebrate.'

'I'll be there to lead the cheering.' There was a thunderous knocking at the front door. Derek was startled. 'Who the hell is that?' he asked, getting up from his chair. 'We're not deaf in here.'

When he opened the door, he found himself face to face with the very man they had been discussing. At close quarters, Colly Raybone was a fearsome individual. Towering over Derek, he had broad shoulders, a barrel chest that was matted with hair and the bulging forearms of a working farmer. His face was flat, snub-nosed and craggy. His piggy eyes glared with hostility. Assessing Derek at a glance, he was not impressed.

'How much do you want for Dove Cottage?' he grunted.

Derek was taken aback. 'It's not for sale,' he replied.

'Like this place. Always have. They asked too much. What's your price?'

'We don't have a price, Mr Raybone.'

A sly grin. 'Know who I am, then, do you?'

'Yes,' said Derek. 'You're the man whose cows damaged our garden.'

'Your fault,' said Raybone levelly. 'No gate on the drive. First thing I'll put up when I move into Dove Cottage. Want to be close to Auntie Nan, see? Keep an eye on her. How much would you take?'

'Nothing, Mr Raybone. My wife and I are staying here.'

Raybone scowled. 'See about that, won't we?'

'You had your chance to buy the property when it was on the market.'

'They wanted too much. Your price will be much lower. I know that.'

'Do you?'

'Yes,' said Raybone, putting his face inches away from Derek. 'You're town, I'm country. You don't belong here. I do.' He gave a harsh laugh. 'You'll soon learn.'

The campaign of intimidation began almost immediately. When they woke the following morning, Derek and Alison were horrified to see that their dovecote had vanished. That night, as they retired to bed, they heard two of their downstairs windows being smashed. The next outrage was the attack on Derek's car, a blue Mondeo. It was covered with graffiti, some of it so obscene that he would not even let Alison see it, driving the vehicle off to the nearest garage to be cleaned. A load of manure was dumped on the doorstep of Dove Cottage, a stoat somehow got into their kitchen and ran riot, then the five-barred gate that Derek bought to hang at the end of the drive simply disappeared into thin air.

Everything pointed to Colly Raybone but, when the police were called in, they could find no evidence. The intervention of the law only served to escalate the attacks. All four tyres on Alison's car were slashed, garden implements were stolen from the shed and the hedges that bordered the front garden were set alight. The Wilmers felt increasingly alarmed and alienated. One of Raybone's comments proved to have a ring of truth about it. They were townies, who did not belong there, resented interlopers who would never be accepted in the village. Everyone offered them tacit sympathy but nobody stepped in to help them. Derek and Alison were comprehensively on their own.

Fearing that worse was to come, they turned to the one person who might be able to save them. Nan Raybone agreed to see them even though she was ill in bed, and she listened to the grim litany of incidents that they recounted. Genuinely sorry about the way that they had been plagued, the old woman refused to believe that her nephew was in any way involved in the persecution.

'Colin would never do such things,' she argued. 'He has too sweet a nature.'

'He threatened me, Mrs Raybone,' said Derek. 'He wants to drive us out.'

'Oh, I'm sure that was only said in fun, Mr Wilmer. It's something that people don't understand about Colin. He has a lovely sense of humour.'

'Is that why he slashed the tyres on my car?' asked Alison.

'Or set fire to our hedge,' added Derek.

'I don't believe that he did either of those things,' said Mrs Raybone, 'and I'll prove it. I'll speak to Colin. He's an honest boy. He won't lie to his aunt. Leave it with me,' she suggested. 'I'll have a word with him.'

The Wilmers never heard what that word was but Colly

Raybone obviously responded to it. There were no more attacks. A fortnight of complete calm ensued. Dove Cottage slowly began to feel like the place that Derek and Alison had coveted. As they entered a third week without incident, they believed that their troubles were over and ascribed their good fortune to Nan Raybone. They sought for a way to thank her but they were too late. Dogged by illness and wearied by fatigue, the old lady died peacefully during the night. The Wilmers were shocked. Since she had been the one person to befriend them, they felt obliged to attend her funeral. It was a gruesome occasion.

As her only surviving relative, Colly Raybone had pride of place. Dressed incongruously in an ill-fitting charcoal grey suit, he arrived at the little church with a pert young woman in red velvet on his arm. His features were arranged into an expression that was halfway between grief and triumph. Raybone insisted on reading the lesson, stumbling through it as if he had only just become acquainted with the English language. The vicar spoke movingly about the affection in which Nan Raybone had been held by all, then the full congregation moved out to the graveside.

It was there that the horror occurred. Fred Skears had known the deceased for nearly sixty years and, though he had retired as the official gravedigger, he volunteered to prepare the last resting-place of his dear friend. Poor eyesight and failing energy had taken their toll. Skears's grave was barely deep enough and it tapered sharply towards the bottom. When the coffin was lowered into it, therefore, the lid only went down to ground level before the whole thing jammed. They heaved, shoved and used a spade as a lever but it would not budge. Colly Raybone lost his patience.

Leaping into the air, he came down on to the coffin lid and stamped hard with both feet, dancing on the timber until it suddenly gave way and went down into the grave. Like most of the mourners, Derek and Alison were aghast at what they had witnessed but

Raybone's female companion roared with laughter and clapped her hands in approval. Raybone himself grinned from ear to ear.

'Auntie Nan could be an awkward bugger when she wanted to be,' he declared.

The Wilmers entered a new phase of misery. In losing a kind neighbour, they had gained a deadly threat. Colly Raybone inherited everything owned by his aunt and promptly took possession of her cottage. Derek and Alison were sleeping only a hundred yards away from their tormentor. He still had designs on Dove Cottage but he was content to bide his time while he wound up his enterprise at the farm before he was replaced by a more responsible tenant. The lady in velvet, meanwhile, started to use Nan Raybone's little house for professional purposes, creating yet another scandal in the village. When the vicar unwisely tried to remonstrate with her, she gave him such a mouthful of abuse that he rushed off to the church and knelt in prayer for an hour.

Alison was in despair. Over dinner one evening, she pleaded with Derek.

'We can't stay here any longer,' she said.

'Nobody is driving me away, Alison.'

'We were so much better off in Wolverhampton.'

'We need time to settle in, that's all,' he reasoned. 'We haven't picked up the rhythm of country life yet.'

'I'm not sure that I want to, Derek. This place is a nightmare. Our garden has been ruined, our cars vandalised and our windows smashed. And the man who did all this,' she stressed, 'is living just up the road with a common prostitute. What upsets me most is that there's nothing at all that we can do about it.'

'Yes, there is, love. We fight back.'

'Against *him*?'

Derek was defiant. 'Colly Raybone will get Dove Cottage over my dead body.'

'Don't say that!' she begged. 'He'd dance on your coffin as well.'

'Only if I give him the opportunity. We're here to stay, Alison,' he assured her. 'The scaffolding arrives tomorrow. At the weekend, I'll start painting the house. That will send a signal to Colly Raybone. Dove Cottage is *ours*.'

The police raid was well-timed. Swooping on the house in the middle of the afternoon, they not only caught Raybone's mistress in bed with one of her clients, they found two others queueing outside and speculating on what services were on offer. The most telling find was a battered exercise book in which she recorded the day's receipts, clear proof that Raybone was keeping a disorderly house. He and the woman, Fleur Addis, were hauled off to the police station to be interviewed. They had such a violent row during the journey that they came to blows. By the time he got to his destination, Raybone faced additional charges of inflicting actual bodily harm both on Fleur Addis and on the policeman who tried to restrain him.

A night in a police cell did not improve Raybone's temper. He had lost a mistress and a regular source of income. The least he could expect was a heavy fine. Someone had betrayed him and he wanted revenge. Nobody in the village would have dared to report him to the police. It had to be the work of the newcomers. Raybone resolved to drive them out of Dove Cottage for good. He was given police bail next morning then released, pending an appearance at the magistrate's court in Canterbury. He did not even listen to the conditions of the bail when they were read out to him by the custody sergeant. All that he could think about was getting back to confront the Wilmers. He vowed to make them wish they had never gone anywhere near Dove Cottage.

It was Saturday morning and, true to his promise, Derek was painting the house. Scaffolding had been erected at the back of the building because the ground fell sharply away, making a double ladder necessary if the top of the cottage was to be reached. A DIY enthusiast, Derek knew that thorough preparation was the first requisite. Everything he needed had therefore been carried up to top deck so that he could clean, sand, seal, spot prime, re-putty and apply fungicidal wash. He had taken other precautions as well. Beside his array of tools and tins were a few spare scaffolding poles. Derek had the feeling that they might come in useful.

He heard the car long before it actually reached the cottage. The rasping exhaust of the Triumph Herald was matched by its squealing tyres as it tore along the unmade road. Colly Raybone, it seemed, had been released and had returned to his farm to collect the vehicle. Though it shot up his drive as if leaving the starting grid in a Grand Prix race, Derek did not even look around. He worked calmly on with his spot priming. Bringing the car to a juddering halt, Raybone leapt out and charged around to the rear of the house. He pointed a finger of doom at Derek.

'*You* did it, didn't you?' he accused. 'You rang the coppers.'

'Somebody had to,' replied Derek without even turning round.

Raybone was puce with fury. 'Come down here!'

'No, thank you. I'm painting my house.'

'It's not your bloody house,' roared the other. 'It's mine. Now, come down.'

'You're trespassing on my property, Mr Raybone.'

'I'll trespass all over you in a minute. You watch.'

Enraged by Derek's composure, Raybone grabbed one of the scaffolding poles and tried to dislodge it, making the whole structure shake. If Derek was not going to come down voluntarily, he would be hauled down and beaten to a pulp. Alison's face appeared at the bedroom window as the scaffolding rattled even more. Throwing the window open, she begged Derek to climb inside before he was hurled to the ground.

'Don't worry, Alison,' he said, picking up one of the loose

poles. 'I anticipated this.' He brandished the pole. 'Stop that, Mr Raybone,' he warned, 'or I'll drop this.'

Raybone laughed. 'You haven't got the guts,' he sneered. 'Know what I'm going to do to you? I'm going to come up there and shove that pole right up your arse. Yes,' he went on, leering at Alison, 'and when I've finished with you, I'll start on her. I'll show her what it's like to have a real man in her bed for a change.'

Alison screamed and retreated from the window. Raybone started to ascend the ladder. Derek Wilmer was a peaceful man but he had been goaded into action. He was not merely guarding his house, he was protecting his wife's virtue. The only way to deal with a bully like Colly Raybone was to teach him a lesson. Fired by the memory of all the anguish he had inflicted on them, Derek felt a surge of anger that smothered all trace of fear. As Raybone's head appeared over the edge of the boarding, Derek poked the end of pole at him, intending to prod him hard in the chest to keep him at bay. Instead, he struck his attacker in the middle of the forehead, drawing a cascade of blood. Raybone's eyes widened in disbelief then he trembled violently for a second, let go of the ladder and fell backwards through the air. There was a loud crack as he hit the ground and his head twisted at an unnatural angle. Colly Raybone would not be able to tyrannise the village any more. Dove Cottage was no longer within his grasp.

Realising what he had done, Derek dropped the pole and brought his hands to his face. He was full of remorse. In trying to repel the man, he had contrived to kill him. It was Henry Clout who came to his rescue. Leaning over the fence, he gazed down at the dead body with quiet satisfaction.

'It was an accident, Mr Wilmer,' he said with a grin. 'I'll swear to that.'

Derek was amazed how many other people claimed to be witnesses. Delighted to be rid at last of their scourge, over a half-a-dozen people came forward to give evidence that Colly Raybone had climbed up the ladder, dislodged one of the loose scaffolding poles and been knocked backwards. It was a version of events that the police were only too happy to accept. At the inquest, the coroner announced a verdict of death by misadventure. The whole village rejoiced.

The death of Colly Raybone was more than a blessing. It was a passport that took Derek and Alison into the very heart of village life. They were welcomed, thanked and accepted by everyone. When the house was painted, it looked exactly as they had hoped it would. The Wilmers stood proudly in their garden and looked up at Dove Cottage, confident that nobody could shift them from their dream home now.

'You see?' said Derek, an arm around his wife. 'I told you, didn't I?'

'Told me what?' she asked.

'This place is idyllic. It was only a matter of time before we fitted in.'

The Eighth Sin

Gwen Moffat

Along with Ann Cleeves and the prolific veteran Gerald Hammond, Gwen Moffat is a crime writer whose work has for many years shown a passion for the environment. Her enthusiasm for the outdoor life is evidenced by her love of mountaineering and the backdrops for many of her novels. This story, too, exudes that same strong feeling for and empathy with a countryside that is far from 'chocolate box' but rather rugged and wild.

Ivan throttled down as they approached his lobster pots under the big bird cliffs and now the chuckle of the engine was no louder than the crooning of guillemots and gulls. A fulmar floated down to the boat, regarding the occupants with soft cat's eyes. Ivan and Sue had been debating the seven deadly sins, agreeing that, although in the third world eating lobsters might be viewed as gluttony, here on a Hebridean island where living, at least in a good summer, was sweet and secure and the sea so productive, the only argument against consuming two lobsters at a sitting had to be satiety not sin.

'I never thought the seven sins were all that deadly anyway,' Sue said, and Ivan spluttered with laughter. 'Now what?' She looked on her elderly landlord as a father figure but she didn't share his sense of humour.

'It's not funny,' he admitted, schooling his face, pausing as he hauled in the first pot. 'Just typical. You never experienced those sins: pride, lust, covetousness, the rest, so you deny them.'

'I covet,' she said stoutly. 'I want a Jersey cow. I want rich cream and proper butter.'

'Not to eat but to make a living.' She sold her dairy produce in the village. She lived at subsistence level and thought she was comfortably off because she didn't starve and her roof didn't leak.

Ivan took a pair of hen lobsters from the pot, eyed them speculatively and dropped them in a bucket. He threw out the old bait, the gulls swooped, and he reached for a mackerel. All around the boat the gannets dived, hitting the water like miniature depth charges.

'I saw a documentary once,' Sue said. 'In the old days a criminal was put in the water alive and shackled, with a herring tied to his head. Your ancestors were a bloodthirsty crew.'

'Impalement by gannets?' He grinned. 'It was the punishment for betrayal: the eighth sin.'

'How primitive can you get?' There was sudden confusion and distress on the bird ledges. 'There's a raven stealing eggs. The bastard!'

'Ravens have to live too.' He grimaced as the next pot broke the surface, empty. 'These remote communities could work only with everyone pulling his weight. Betrayal upset the apple cart.'

She was puzzled. 'What on earth could anyone betray here?'

He sighed. He was twenty years her senior; he admired her youthful spirit, was even somewhat in love with her but he deplored her blinkered attitude. Married to a feckless drone, she was confirmation of the belief that the wife is always the last to know (or admit?) that the husband is playing away from home.

'Is this your land?' she asked suddenly.

He followed her gaze to the top of the cliffs. 'It's all mine, for my sins.' He smiled. 'Meaning I have responsibilities.'

'You're not meeting them then. That fence is falling over the edge.'

'The cliff's eroding. There's a path along the edge but cracks have appeared. You can see light through a hole – below that patch of gorse. I've lost sheep there; they fell right through and landed on the rocks. So I fenced it to be on the safe side.'

'That's not going to stop hikers—'

'There's a notice on the road saying the cliffs are dangerous.'

'Just the thing to encourage the idiots.'

'Idiots are no loss to society. Hand me the bait bucket, will you?'

They finished lifting the pots and motored gently home to Ivan's mooring in the cove below his croft. Once he cut the engine the air was full of larksong and the turf below his house was alive with small blue butterflies. Westward the water faded from jade through turquoise to cobalt while on the horizon the stacks of St Kilda were a frieze of spiky fins. Beyond St Kilda there was nothing until America.

'You'll stay for a dram,' he said, knowing she wouldn't. She had to get back to prepare her husband's supper.

She hesitated, then accepted. 'Milking can wait a few minutes longer, and Joe's away. These long evenings he stays out late.'

'Oh yes.' It was too casual.

She shrugged. 'You know he's hopeless with animals. Can you see Joe milking a cow? I prefer it this way, Ivan; I'm good at farming – OK, it's a smallholding, but you know what I mean. We each do our own thing.' There was a pregnant silence. The query, And what is *his* thing? hung in the air. She caught it. 'He's finding his feet,' she stated defiantly. 'He never had a chance; overqualified. Where does a guy like Joe find work nowadays?'

'Difficult, without a degree.' He couldn't be so cruel as to ask what the qualifications were, let alone a superfluity of them. 'You managed,' he pointed out.

'Anyone can farm!'

And anyone can find a labouring job in the islands, he thought as she rattled away in her ancient Land Rover. The sin of sloth was amply demonstrated by Joe Maxwell who had tried everything over the years, but in descending order of status, from chief instructor at an outdoor activities centre to lorry driver at the local quarry – and the situation was dodgy there. More time spent in bars than behind the wheel, ran the gossip. The fellow was brash, handsome, charming, not just an incomer but alien. Sue now, she had been absorbed by the island after only a couple of years, helped, of course, by her friendship with himself Ivan Sinclair, was strapped for cash but he was still the laird. Joe Maxwell despised him but he was wary. Ivan wore dungarees and was subject to ringworm but he owned the Maxwell croft and Joe set great store by his creature comforts.

Their two crofts were all that remained of an old settlement. The houses stood apart, nestled under rocky outcrops, and between them were the scattered ruins of the folk who lived here before the Clearances – the time when people were evicted to make room for more productive sheep. It was poor land, with scarcely enough pasture for Sue to run two cows, and Ivan didn't even try, confining himself to sheep. The good land was on the other side of the peninsula where long sweeps of pale shell sand were backed by the grassy flats they called the *machair*, and the village of Scandabaig was dominated by the Victorian pile of Castle Sinclair, which Ivan leased to Daniel Clay to run as an hotel.

A road meandered for ten miles round the coast from Scandabaig to the settlement and although it was beset by sheep, and thistles were pushing through the tarmac, it was known as the new road. Before it was built the only way out of the settlement other than by sea was the route they took the coffins. There wasn't enough soil at the settlement for a graveyard. The old coffin track ran for four miles across the moor; it wasn't too boggy, on the wettest stretches there were the remains of raised dykes marked by cairns. On a spring evening and in good visibility it was a reasonable place to exercise a horse but, more than that, it was an ideal place for clandestine meetings.

Eve Clay was in her twenties, arresting in a pale, mystical fashion, like the Mona Lisa without the smile, and her husband adored her, called her his 'belle dame sans merci'. It had been child's play, once she had met Joe Maxwell, to persuade Daniel to buy her a pony. She had little more ability than to sit tight and grip but it was enough to stay on this steady animal on those evenings when, increasingly reckless, she left her husband sweating in the kitchen and took to the moor. Her affair with Joe was at white-heat and if the pony had been sick she would have walked the four miles. Except that it wasn't four miles. They met halfway.

This evening she came to the highest point and pressed on, not stopping to rest the pony, in any event she would be stopping shortly, at last out of view of anyone spying on her from home. Daniel would be occupied with dinner but there were others, women for example. Joe said people would wonder why she always rode in one direction, MacLeod for one. MacLeod was the policeman and he was always on the watch for poachers. Eve said MacLeod wouldn't risk antagonising her and Joe didn't ask her how she could be so certain. You didn't question Eve.

She approached the ruined bothy, its beams collapsed, the walls still standing. He didn't step out at the sound of hooves and she stopped at the doorway, looking to see if he'd come and gone, leaving some indication. There were only nettles and the stench of sheep.

She glanced at her watch. It was turned seven-thirty. He was seldom punctual and she found waiting a trial. There was no reason why she shouldn't go on, meet him and turn aside. There were huge boulders under the crags, the pony would be hidden, but no one came this way, not in the evening. She rode on.

A cuckoo called – a tinny sound among the rocks. She could see ahead for some distance but there was nothing except heather, so tall it hid the cairns until you were on them. She passed a lochan with yellow water lilies and something splashed heavily. Her eyes widened but the pony was unconcerned.

The sea appeared, the ground dipped and she could see all the way to the old settlement but his house was hidden. The pasture was a brilliant green enclave below the moor. There was no sign of people. He could be hidden in a fold of the ground, he might be sunbathing and had fallen asleep; he could be anywhere, he was unpredictable – part of his charm but infuriating at this moment. She wanted him, she needed him, ached for him, and he'd said seven-thirty at the bothy and he wasn't here.

She kicked the pony savagely and, startled, he leapt forward, unseating her. She lost a stirrup and slid sideways, hitting the ground, held by the other iron. The pony stopped and stood, bracing itself as she squirmed to break free. She stood up, dripping with peat, gasping with the effort and looking frenziedly for something to beat the animal with, remembering in time that he might well run and leave her to walk home. She transferred her rage to Joe, the cause of it all; she mounted and rode down to the sea, her eyes blazing, heedless of consequences.

By the time she reached his croft she was sullen but seething.

His Land Rover stood outside the cottage but he wouldn't have taken that to meet her, so where was he? She stopped.

The house stood below a little crag. Hens scratched on flowery grass in front of the open door. His wife came round the gable end carrying a bucket. She saw Eve on the road and waved with her free hand. She called something and Eve seized the opportunity. She pushed up the track. 'Sorry? I didn't catch that.'

Sue was smiling. 'I said do you need butter? I've got some to spare. The cow—' She started. 'You've had a fall! Are you all right?'

'He reared.' Eve was tense. 'Nothing broken.' Her eyes shifted, flicking to the doorway. 'Butter,' she repeated. 'We can always do with butter.'

'But difficult to carry,' Sue pointed out.

'Yes.' Eve's eyes ranged beyond the woman, thinking that there were buildings at the back – a cow-house, a stable.

'No saddlebags,' Sue murmured.

Eve focused on her. The old bat was winding her up. Her nostrils flared. 'So?'

'You're upset.' Sue was concerned. 'You'll be worried about the pony. Would you like Joe to look at him?'

'He's here?' Eagerness bloomed and was suppressed. 'What's he know about horses?'

'You'd be surprised. Joe! Come and look at Eve's pony.' She was shouting at the open door.

Eve's eyes were lidded. How the hell was she going to play this? Leave it to him? He was old, experienced; he'd know how to handle it. But why wasn't he on the hill? Why hadn't he come? *She'd* stopped him!

Sue picked up the bucket. 'Come and have a drink,' she ordered. 'Tie the pony.'

Eve followed her into the house. Sue shouted again but it was obvious the place was empty. 'Scarpered,' she said easily. 'He does that. I'm sure the pony will be all right. Where did he throw you?'

'On top.' Eve sat at the kitchen table, accepted a whisky and drank without appreciation. 'Where did he go?'

Sue raised heavy eyebrows. 'You're asking me? My dear, that man's as slippery as an eel. He's along the shore, on the hill, over to Scandabaig… Maybe he's found a new woman, who knows? That's a joke,' she added quickly, seeing the other's shock. Her tone changed. 'Look, would you like to go up and lie on our bed for a while? It won't be the first time—'

'*What?*'

'—that you've been thrown.' Sue looked at her oddly. 'But it's always a shock, isn't it? Not that I know much about these things… Tell you what – leave the pony here and I'll run you home.'

'I'll ride home,' Eve said harshly.

Sue held the pony's head as she mounted. Eve looked down. Momentarily they regarded each other, the one furious again but puzzled, the other bland. 'Messages?' Sue asked politely.

'Why?' Eve grated. 'They're superfluous. We know where we're coming from.'

'I doubt it,' Sue said.

Ivan was scything bracken when a Land Rover appeared on the road and turned up his track. He walked down the hill as Sue started towards him. She didn't waste words, but then she seldom did.

'Joe didn't come home last night.'

'But it's three o'clock!'

'He stays out sometimes. He needs space.'

'This much? When did you see him last?'

'Around this time yesterday.' She was subdued and worried.

'Where were you then?'

'In the garden, planting potatoes and salad stuff.'

'I phoned. Where were—' He stopped. 'You said: you were in the garden. Have you rung MacLeod?'

'There's no point. He didn't take the 'Rover. He went on foot.'

'But—' He looked away.

'Eve rode over about eight o'clock,' she told him. 'She was in a state; she'd fallen off her pony and she was terribly embarrassed, even hostile.' He said nothing. She shook her head. 'I know what you're thinking: that she was expecting to see him. No way, not covered with peat. Anyway, Joe would never look at another woman, he's not interested.'

'You mean he's gay?'

'Come on, Ivan! I said another woman not any woman. He's straight and macho and he's got me! I mean, it's a good marriage. Eve Clay? He'd run a mile.'

'Hardly macho then.'

'Well, she's – er...'

'Rapacious.'

'So you noticed.'

He shrugged. 'But if Joe's not up to mischief – that kind anyway, and you're sure he didn't take the 'Rover—'

'It's here! How could he have taken it?' She gestured wildly at the vehicle. 'What do we do, Ivan? Where did he go?'

They stared seaward. 'He didn't go far,' he said. 'Not on foot. He didn't give any indication? And he isn't a photographer, or a hiker. He doesn't watch birds—'

'He was interested in that eagle.' A white-tailed eagle had been sighted on sea cliffs to the north.

'He'd have taken the 'Rover.' Ivan was puzzled. 'That's one thing – you know he hasn't had a road accident.'

'Unless he was picked up by someone,' she said gloomily. 'I joked to Eve about him having found a new woman.'

He gaped. 'What did she say?'

'She looked as if I'd uttered a blasphemy. Why are you so amazed? OK, it was a joke in poor taste but she was so strung up. I was infected by it, lost my cool, you know?'

'She was looking for him.'

She gasped and reddened. 'That's the second time you've implied—' She stopped, stared at his concerned face and took a deep breath. She exhaled slowly. 'You know something. 'What is it?'

'I don't *know* anything. There's gossip.'

'Oh – bollocks! This place is alive with gossip.'

'Maybe you're right. It doesn't help us to find out where he went anyway.' If Eve's looking for him too, he thought.

They were quiet until she asked, 'What good would MacLeod be?' as if he'd again suggested contacting the police. It could be that they were both thinking that if Joe were holed up somewhere, doing something he desired to keep private, but by absenting himself for so long he was only attracting attention...

'If he was away all night at other times,' Ivan said, 'where was he then?'

'He took a sleeping bag and spent the night on the cliffs or the moor – anywhere. Not with a woman,' she added fiercely.

Not according to *him*, he qualified, but kept it to himself.

'Maxwell missing?' MacLeod regarded Ivan across his young cabbages. 'Since when?'

'Over twenty-four hours now. He didn't come home last night.'

'He'll be with her from the castle.'

They could speak freely. Ivan and MacLeod were distant cousins and there were no witnesses to this conversation. The police house stood apart from the village at one end of the strand of Scandabaig.

'She rode over to our side,' Ivan told him. 'To my mind she was looking for him. She had to be desperate to go to the house.'

'How did Sue receive her?'

'Politely. Sue would keep control – and she has no idea... I've dropped hints about the affair but she won't hear a word against him; it's a good marriage, she says.'

MacLeod snorted and reached for his cigarettes. 'Always the last to admit it,' he said.

They agreed that something should be done about a search but to take their time over it, spread the word, give the fellow a chance to show if he was up to mischief. People should be telephoned discreetly.

Daniel Clay found his wife pacing the terrace in front of the castle, a brandy glass in her hand, walking like a marionette on strings.

'Joe Maxwell's missing,' he said.

She was still, glaring at him. 'He didn't come home yet?'

'That's right.' He frowned, wondering who'd told her.

She was trying to think, a welter of sensations chasing each other – fear, suspicion, horror. 'Who called?'

'Ivan. Sue said he left the croft at three yesterday.'

'Where did he go?'

'Apparently he didn't tell anyone – well, there was only his wife to tell, wasn't there? They don't know where to start looking.' He followed her eyes to the moor where the coffin road crossed. 'Did you see him?' She stared at him with contempt. 'Well,' he spluttered, 'you wouldn't have known he was missing, I mean, going to be missing. It might help?' He was placating.

'I didn't see him.' She thrust the brandy at him. 'We have to start searching—'

'Not you! Not on your own,' he shouted at her back. 'Darling, don't go – you don't know where—'

But she did. He'd fallen in the heather, was lying out there with a broken leg, had been out all night, drowning in a bog, attacked – by what? Anything. A heart attack. She saddled the pony herself, fighting off Daniel who dared not restrain her by force, although allowing him to tighten the girths, trying to canter up the track but the pony wouldn't have it, plodding sullenly towards the pass… the realisation coming to her now that their meeting had been for seven-thirty and he'd left home at three, so in the middle of the afternoon he'd had something else in mind other than a rendezvous with her.

Daniel leaned over the bar, lowering his voice. 'You mean, he's got a girlfriend somewhere, a mistress? I don't believe it.'

'It happens.' Ivan was dispassionate. 'What's your guess as to his whereabouts?'

'Well,' Daniel's fleshy face was a caricature of perplexity, 'normally one would think of a road accident but if you say he was on foot...' He stared through the open window at the water. 'A boat?' he wondered. 'Does he own a boat?'

'He doesn't, and none of mine are missing, and he couldn't handle one anyway.'

'Could he have been picked up by someone? But that suggests something sinister if he hasn't surfaced – unless of course it *was* a lady but then he's attracting so much attention.'

'Not if she picked him up and then there was an accident.'

'We'd have heard.'

They looked at each other. Ivan saw a gross and normally genial fellow, evidently sincere and concerned but totally at a loss, both as to the problem of a missing islander and that the one person who might solve it was most likely his own wife.

On the third day the search became official. A helicopter combed the coastline, a Search and Rescue team covered the moors with dogs. Nothing was found. It was thought that he was still on the island but as time went on they had to admit that he was probably dead. People affected not to notice Eve's distress. After two more days she went to his croft.

'Déjà vu,' Sue said tonelessly as Eve rode up the track on her pony. 'Come in and have a drink.'

Again they faced each other across the kitchen table. 'You scrub this,' Eve said accusingly, fingering the bleached wood.

'It's something to do,' Sue said.

She'd lost weight. She had been meaty, obviously powerful. Eve had been sleek. Now they both looked ravaged, like women after a siege.

Eve drank and raised dull eyes. 'What happened?'

'You tell me.'

'You said that before. You knew, didn't you?'

'I have no idea. I assume he's in a cave, a cavern, somewhere the searchers missed.'

'You knew about us.'

Sue set down her glass carefully. 'Who is "us"?'

'Did he tell you himself or did you go through his pockets?'

'Are you suggesting that you and Joe were—'

'Lovers,' Eve said. 'He was going to leave you and marry me. You found out. What have you done with his body?'

'Does your husband know about this?'

Eve hesitated. 'What difference would that make?'

'I suppose he's – not unaccustomed to it.' Sue was murmuring as if talking to herself. 'But you're rather old for teenage fantasies.'

Eve looked wild. 'Where's the fantasy? We met! Almost every day – up there, on the moor.'

Sue nodded. 'He told me.'

'He – what! You did know!'

'I've known since you started.' Sue smiled kindly. 'He found it amusing actually – being stalked by a lady on a pony. It didn't bother him, he was quite flattered – as anyone would be; you've very attractive, my dear.'

'I didn't – he, *he* made a play for *me*! At the castle, in the bar. It was obvious—' She lurched to her feet, knocking over her chair. 'You fool!' she shouted. 'You stupid, patronising old cow! It was going on right under your nose and you never saw – you don't deserve him!' She was shaking, gripping the table for support.

Sue was on her feet too. 'You need help,' she said quietly.

'Daniel has to be told about this. He's a good chap, Eve, you don't need to go running after other people's husbands—'

'I don't want—' Eve hissed, poised between plunging out of this claustrophobic kitchen and throttling her tormentor.

'Men like Joe can't give you security,' Sue went on. 'He's a drifter but he's fetched up with me and there's no way he's going to give up his home and his marriage – he wouldn't even consider it. You built a fantasy round the wrong guy.'

Eve's face had set to a mask. 'I'm carrying his baby.'

'That's great!' Sue reached for the bottle and the other's glass. 'I mean great that you're pregnant. Daniel will be delighted.'

'Can't I get through to you? It's Joe's. And he's over the moon. That's why we're leaving...' Eve blinked and for a moment there was doubt in the wild eyes. 'He's away to—'

'Make arrangements?' Sue's eyes were calculating, belying the sweet tone.

'It resolved nothing,' she told Ivan later. 'We're no further forward. She's a nutcase from start to finish.'

They were strolling down to the dinghy with bait and buckets and for a while they busied themselves with rowing out to the big boat. As they left the cove he returned to the subject. 'Not a complete nutcase,' he observed.

'You mean she's obsessed just with Joe? She's not a nympho, not after anything in trousers?'

'She's obsessed with Joe,' he said heavily. 'Everyone knew that.'

'I didn't.'

He stared landwards, searching for words other than the obvious ones. 'She's a harpy,' Sue conceded. 'I teased her with it, accused her of stalking, said she terrified Joe, more or less. She would, you know; the poor guy likes motherly women, he wants – wanted his life to be ordered – by someone else.' Her voice cracked. 'Christ, Ivan, do you think he's gone, that he's not alive?

She said he'd left to make arrangements, implying she was to join him.'

'She could believe that herself.'

'You mean she's living in a total dream world? She's conjured up a complete scenario: they're having an affair, she's pregnant by him?'

'It's not fantasy, Sue. They *were* having an affair.' She opened her mouth to blast him. He held her eye. 'You're the last to know.' He was miserable but firm.

The boat chugged on. She'd turned away from him and was staring at the horizon, her hands clenched, the knuckles white. He studied her back and wondered how much Daniel Clay knew. They were passing under the bird cliffs when she said coldly, 'She was having an affair, right, but it wasn't with Joe. He told me everything, and he detested her type. He needed a good listener.' Her face slackened. 'And here I'm talking about him in the past tense. Where is he? That silly girl knows he isn't waiting for her on the mainland. She knows he's dead. She's an utter wreck.'

'What did he take with him?'

'Why, you know that. It was the first question MacLeod asked. He didn't take anything, not even his sleeping bag. That was what worried me – when I looked for it, found it and realised he hadn't intended staying out all night.'

'Not unless he was in someone's house.'

'Like the castle?' Her contempt was obvious but then she took pity on him. 'No boots,' she said. 'He left wearing sandals – shorts and sandals.'

'Leki poles?'

'What?'

'Trekking poles. Did he take them?'

'He doesn't own…' She paused. 'That's odd – *I* have a pair. That is, I should have but one's missing. Ivan? Have you found… Joe took a trekking pole? Where did you find it?'

They were at the pots and he drifted towards the floats. He nodded shorewards. 'At the bottom of the cliff. I saw it gleaming and went in.'

'Washed up, you mean? Or…' Her eyes rose from the tumbled rocks at the foot of the cliff to fence posts askew against the sky.

'It was below the hole in the path I told you about. He could very well have slipped in sandals.' She said nothing. 'There was no sign of anything untoward,' he went on. 'He'd have been taken away by the tide.'

'Maybe he fell in elsewhere and the pole washed up here. What did you do with it?'

'I was taking it home and then I thought: it was only a trekking pole, could belong to anybody, what use was it, just an unnecessary complication. I threw it overboard.'

'If he did fall there,' she said slowly, studying the cliff, 'what was he doing in that place?'

'Meeting Eve?' Her lips tightened but she responded in kind: 'She could scarcely ride, let alone take her pony near that drop.'

'She could have been on foot, or he was with someone else on foot.'

'Who would that be?'

'Did MacLeod ask you what you were doing the afternoon that Joe went missing?'

'I'm sure he did. There were all kinds of questions, like which direction did he go, and there was no way I could have seen because I was cleaning the hen-house—'

'Planting potatoes and salad stuff, you told me.'

'I did both. It was a long afternoon.'

'Where were you when I came across?'

'You didn't visit that day. You're confused with some other time. You phoned but I was outside—'

'There's a bell on the gable—'

'I'd turned it off. I hate that bell shrilling out over the cove.'

Suddenly she flared up. 'Why the hell are you asking me these questions? It's a bloody inquisition.'

'I came to your croft and you weren't there. I came because I needed a broody hen and you didn't answer the phone. I saw the Land Rover.'

'Of course you did. On the road.' He gestured to the land.

She sighed and closed her eyes. 'Let's go back. Bring the pots up and we'll go home.'

They sat outside his house, their backs to the warm wall, drinking his good malt, watching the gannets winging majestically towards the uninhabited islands. Below, on a rock bared by the tide, a troop of cormorants hung out their wings to dry.

'He was interested in the white-tailed eagle,' she said, suggested rather, adding more firmly, 'He'd talked about it.'

'It could be near the bird cliffs,' Ivan conceded. 'So he went for a stroll, taking your trekking pole. Macho man with a stick? In sandals? Hardly the gear for dangerous cliffs.'

'All the same you found the pole.'

'I found him too.'

Startled, she recovered in a moment. 'I don't believe you. You said there was no sign.'

'I lied. I needed time to think. I wanted you to tell me where you were that afternoon. I saw the Land Rover going towards the bird cliffs.'

She licked her lips delicately. 'I took him there and dropped him – dropped him off. I had to get back. There was a lot to do at home.'

'You told MacLeod you didn't leave the croft.' She looked wary. 'No one else could have seen you. No one lives here but us; there were no hikers about, no boats. MacLeod thinks you never left your place.'

'But you're saying I did; you're saying more than that.'

He didn't look away. 'I know those cliffs well; I was working there, putting the fence up. There's the hole, and the sea a couple of hundred feet below, an awesome place. Actually it's a very tight hole, he could have wedged there and been unable to get out. Struggles would only have made him sink deeper.'

'In that case perhaps he's still—'

'No, he fell through.'

'How do you know that?'

'Because I could see from the bottom. Light showed through the hole.' He continued carefully, as if instructing her: 'No one can ever know how he came to fall – or even where, come to that. It's not a case of did he fall or was he pushed. The body will be recovered eventually but it will have nothing to do with you. He was alive when you left him.'

'I did love him,' she said, and he believed her.

It had been a woman's crime. The old people could set a traitor adrift with a fish on his head but no man today could walk away and leave another wedged in the hole among the scavengers. Because Joe was still alive when Ivan found him, even after the ravens had been at work, although he'd fined down by then of course, and it was a simple matter to take a fence post and push what was left of him through the hole.

Granny Trotter's Treasure

Amy Myers

Amy Myers is, like Mike Jecks, widely acknowledged as a standard-bearer of the light and entertaining historical mystery and her novels featuring Auguste Didier have gained a loyal readership. It is good to know that the American publishers Crippen and Landru, who specialise in short story collections, will shortly be publishing a book of her tales, *Murder! 'Orrible Murder!* Again like Mike Jecks, Amy Myers lives in rural England and possesses an under-acknowledged talent for writing lively stories set in the present day.

It was all her fault. Bloody foreigner. As if the village didn't have enough trouble without her coming to plague us. Mrs Christine Nabb from London, if you please. Carving out a new role for a vicar's wife, she said she was. Carving a hunk of trouble is what she done. She wouldn't listen, oh no. St Swithin's in the Lea had done all right for the last fifteen-hundred years without having Christmas organised for it, and it could have gone on doing so for a few more thousand, I reckon.

'Now that I'm a Maid of Kent,' she told us gaily, 'I feel my task is to put this village on the map.'

I knew she'd do that all right, as true as Granny Trotter's Treasure. That's a saying we have round these parts for something you've got no evidence for, but know to be a fact. We didn't want to be on no map, though. The village was better without it, and so was The Green Man, my pub. Well, my son Mike ran it actually. I was just the old man in the corner, sipping my pint. Jack in the Green, they called me. Most excited was Mrs Nabb when she heard that.

'The old religion lives on,' she exclaimed solemnly. 'They may think you're past it, Jack, but in you dwells the wisdom of bygone ages.'

This was news to me. 'Pardon?'

I certainly wasn't past it that Christmas. I knew trouble was on the way. Mark you, a blind horse could have foreseen it when she started in on the Hoodening.

Just to show she was a modern woman and didn't mind having meetings in sinful pubs, her ladyship beamed at what she was pleased to call The Christmas Committee, of which she had appointed herself the chair, as she called it. Daft, was my word for it. Anyway, there we were gathered in the snug, fearing the worst. And it came.

'We'll still have the Christmas Eve Hoodening of course. I do so admire the way you keep up these old customs.'

There was a chorus of surprised assent, since no one had

thought of cancelling it. Thank you very much, Mrs Vicar's wife, I thought, but didn't say nothing. Give her enough rope and she'd hang herself.

But then she grew all solemn. 'We do need a fresh eye on the Hoodening, I feel. So I've decided that Sam Farthing should play the Horse this year. A signal of new blood in the tradition, especially since he is so much younger than Joe Stratton.'

There was a stunned silence. It would be the signal for blood all right. The Farthings and the Strattons had been feuding in this village for hundreds of years; every so often a new generation came along, vowing peace and friendship, but that never lasted long, and the old fights would break out again. Only at Christmas did they have a truce. Old Joe Stratton had the honour of playing the Hooden Horse, while Sam led the Wassailers on Christmas Eve. Both groups went round playing music, banging drums and what not, collecting money, and knocking at people's doors.

Each year the Farthings put up a token fight to play the horse, but everyone knew Joe would win. The nearest the Farthings ever got was to have one of them playing the Jockey instead. He's the character who has a running battle with the Horse, trying to mount him and getting thrown off. When I say the Farthings put up a fight, that wasn't Sam himself, who was a timid sort of chap, but his old father Tom and Sam's brothers. Sam was a good son of the Church, which I reckon put this stupid idea in our Fair Maid of Kent's mind. He didn't like the Strattons any more than the rest of his clan, though his ways of doing them down were sneakier than theirs.

The stunned silence soon ended with a roar of approval from the Farthings and outrage from all the Strattons, especially Harry, Joe's son.

'See here, Mrs Nabb,' I said. I likes to be polite. 'The Strattons have always been the Horse. It wouldn't be a Hoodening without it.'

'Everyone has to make way for the younger generation, Jack. Turn and turn about, you know.'

Joe put in a word for himself. 'I *always* plays the Horse,' he quavered, banging his fist on the table.

'Not this year, Joe. Be a sport.' Despite her sunny beam, Mrs Nabb was an iron lady.

'Then all us Strattons resign,' Joe's son Harry declared angrily. He played the Waggoner.

There are four main roles in the Hoodening, the Horse himself, which was Joe bent double under sacking holding the wooden head on a pole, the Waggoner who leads him along on a rope, the Jockey and Mollie. After the Horse, Mollie is the most prized role, who goes a-sweeping the ground before them with her broom.

'We'll do it,' cried the Farthing clan as one.

'Oh good,' cried Mrs Nabb. 'What fun. All fresh blood. And I'll play Mollie.'

There was an appalled silence from the Farthings, but the Strattons could hardly speak for laughing as to what the Farthings had got themselves into. Joe spoke up at last: 'Look, Missis,' he chorted, 'Mollie's always played by a man, see?'

'Not this year.' Mrs Nabb smiled sweetly at him.

We're all gentlemen in St Swithin's in the Lea, so we didn't like to say that the whole point of Mollie was that she had to be upended to show her drawers – only of course Bill Stratton, who usually played it wore his old corduroys and boots.

After the Maid of Kent had departed, we set too with a vengeance, and Mike had to call time early to prevent bloodshed. The Strattons and the Farthings spilled out into the street to battle it out (except for Sam, who encouraged his kin from the safety of the pub doorway). Even though Harry walked away top scorer, the Strattons all wiped their hands of the Hoodening.

If it had been left at that, the village might have got away with a few bloody noses. As it was, Mrs Blasted Nabb was into everything, more excited than a ferret in a smelly hole. She arranged Christmas trees, Christmas lights, old folks' parties, carol singers, and worst of all a Treasure Hunt on the Sunday before Christmas. Doesn't sound bad, does it? This one was.

She had the nerve to call it Granny Trotter's Treasure Hunt. Now I'm a Trotter born and bred, and therefore so are Mike and his kids. Granny Trotter was burned as a witch way back sometime, and the village hunted high and low for the fortune they knew she must have tucked away somewhere. There's a story she sheltered some king and saved his life by turning him into a frog for a few days, and that he rewarded her handsomely. It never turned up, but the village still believed in it. Hence our saying: As true as Granny Trotter's Treasure.

Mrs Bloody Nabb had discovered where Granny's cottage used to be – on land which is now plum in the middle of Pound Spinney on Sam Farthing's farm – and put a prize of her very own chutney there. No problem about that if you like chutney, even if she didn't have the courtesy to ask us Trotters whether we minded our name being taken over. What happened was the village took the treasure hunt seriously. Hundreds of people were traipsing over Sam's fields, and with only one prize there wasn't much Christmas cheer around. Even worse, rumours started going round that Sam Farthing had actually found Granny Trotter's Treasure, so by Christmas Eve when the Hoodeners gathered in the Green Man to get ready, there was a fair old cauldron simmering – especially since Joe and Harry Stratton had popped in to see the fun.

The Hooden Horse's head is kept at the pub during the year, and a noble thing it is with its clomping wooden jaws, leather ears, head brass and bridle. I'd brought it down to the snug all ready. The musicians came with their top hats and spangled jackets, there was an old skirt and halloween hat for Mollie and of course her broom for sweeping. Mrs Nabb was enough of an old besom without it, if you ask me. Sam Farthing was in fine form, prancing around under the sacking, and a tail wagging at the back. Harry Stratton was still smarting though, at seeing him taking over his father's beloved horse's head. Joe himself couldn't bear to come, he said.

'You found the Trotter Treasure, so I heard,' Harry growled.

'Rumour, Harry, all rumour,' Tom Farthing said jovially, grinning his head off.

'It had better be,' Mike said from behind the bar. Mike's a big man, a gentle giant of a man, so not many argue with him. Except Liz of course. She's a fiery girl is my daughter-in-law and, in my opinion, their marriage wasn't long for this world. 'That's Trotter Treasure,' Mike continued.

'No, it isn't,' said Sam piously. 'It was on Farthing land, and,' he raised his voice grandly, so we'd all know what a generous chap he was, 'I've decided to donate it to the Church.'

Well, there were a few shocked faces around then, I can tell you. His own father's for one, and his brothers'. Not to mention his wife Adele's. No wonder she'd shown such unusual wifely devotion in coming along to see her husband's glory as the Hooden Horse. She was always devoted when there was money to be had. I'd had my suspicions for some time that she rather fancied being a publican's wife, in particular Mike's, but Liz wasn't the sort to let go that easily. Not if there were a hint of Trotter Treasure around.

Harry went purple. ''Tis Dad's and mine,' he roared. ''Twas a Stratton owned that cottage Granny Trotter lived in, and I ain't giving it to the Church.' He gave Sam a push, none too friendly it was. 'First you steal the Horse from Dad, now you're making free with the Trotter treasure.'

Sam reacted automatically – which only goes to show that piety and timidity are only skin-deep. He pushed Harry back so hard he fell against the table, upsetting all the beer. Mike was just about to step in when our Mrs Nabb decided to play peacemaker.

'The treasure is coming to the Church,' she declared with a winning smile. 'Sam is quite right. It was after all a Church treasure hunt, and the village can heal its feuds and differences by uniting over this gift. What better solution than for all to help preserve St Swithin's church for future generations.'

We all stared at this barmy woman, wondering who wished this crazy lunatic on us. 'Shut up, you stupid cow,' Tom Farthing roared, and for once the assembly was indeed unified – except for Sam, who stayed very quiet.

A rich red stained her cheeks better than twenty pints of our best ale could have done, and we felt it had all gone a little too far. She was a vicar's wife after all, so we did our best to remember it was the season of goodwill. We therefore listened in respectful silence as Sam, who seemed to think he was about to wear a golden halo, not a Hooden Horse's head, announced that he would be handing over the treasure as a Christmas gift at Midnight Mass in a few hours' time.

Mrs Bloody Nabb clapped her approval, while the rest of us were working out that as Sam's farm was a fair way out of the village, and as the jollifications in the pub would go on a while after the Hoodening and Wassailing, Sam must have brought the treasure with him. No wonder Adele had followed him down here. I wondered what she'd had to say on the question of the Church's rights? I know what I'd have said – and indeed was saying – me being a Trotter.

'I'll help you on with the Horse,' Adele cooed lovingly. We all crowded round wondering where he was keeping that treasure. He wouldn't let go of it, not Sam. He would have it right there in the Horse with him.

Horses have always been special in Kent, and the Hoodening Horse was once a real dead horse's head, but folk are squeamish now. Now its wooden jaws, with hobnails inside for teeth, are pulled by a string by the man inside to open them up for contributions. There's a bag fixed at the end of the mouth to take the loot.

Inside bent double with old blankets and sacks laid over him, was Joe – beg pardon, habit dies hard – Sam clinging on with one hand to the pole the head was fixed on and on to the string with the other. Off he went, led by the rope held by the Waggoner with Mollie and the Jockey prancing along with him and the musicians following, all making a lot of noise with a concertina, drum, and handbells.

People wait to hear them approach. 'The Hoodeners are coming,' the cry goes up. Oh, it's a grand sight, though it can be creepy too. During the day it isn't, but at nights it's a different matter. With a torch or lantern held inside, the eyes seem to glow in the dark, and Hoodening has an atmosphere all of its own. We have our own traditional route, but this year, according to the gospel of Mrs Christine Nabb, it had to be different. They would start at the Vicarage, she decreed, tie the Horse to a tree with a nosebag over his jaws, and go inside for a glass of something. The horse would get his later. This revised route, according to the Fair Maid, was supposed to indicate the unity of the old religion and the new.

It didn't that night.

First of all, the Farthings had turned out in force in front of the pub to cheer their man on. Unfortunately the Strattons had the same idea, only they were intent on roughing up Sam Farthing for Joe's sake. Wassailing could start later, they had more important things to do. I wouldn't hold out much hope of Granny Trotter's treasure reaching the Church if the Strattons got their hands on it.

Mollie received a bit of jostling too, and thinking the mob believed this was the usual man, I cried out warningly:

'It's the vicar's wife, chaps.'

This just brought more eager fighters into the fray, but luckily the sight of a squad car – rare indeed round here – driving towards them, made the armies decide to melt away back to their homes before they were able to attack the Horse. The happy Hoodeners were left to get on with the job.

They did their best, but there wasn't the usual happy atmosphere. Since the Vicarage is near the pub, I sauntered over to watch, as the old tunes were sullenly jerked out.

'Isn't this fun?' I heard our Mollie squeal, as they marched up to the Vicarage door.

'Oh my goodness,' said the Vicar dutifully. 'What have we here?' Much laughter from his wife.

After he had put a token coin in the snapping jaws, the Hoodening Horse flashed his eyes at him, then galloped round the garden, with the Waggoner trying to haul him back, musicians playing, and Mollie and Jockey in full pursuit. Then the party went in to have their drink, leaving Mrs Nabb tying Sam Farthing up, nosebag and all, and looping the rope round a hook provided in a tree. I went to have my drink too, only mine was in The Green Man.

A while later I saw them come out from the Vicarage, and they didn't look that happy. The Vicarage is no substitute for The Green Man. Standing round with a mince pie and a glass of wine making polite talk isn't the same as swigging down our best ale.

The Horse had been duly collected from its tree, and off they all went to start the tour of the village. I heard later it wasn't bad. Even St Christine of Nabb had entered into the spirit of the thing, and consented to be upended. She had the vicar's checked golf trousers on ready.

By the time the Hoodeners had been to the Squire's house and got back to The Green Man to count up their loot, the Strattons' will to fight the Farthings over the Horse had worn off – chiefly because tension was rising about the handing over of Granny Trotter's treasure.

'Come on, horsey darling,' tittered Mrs Nabb, patting the horse and ready to help with the head removal. She got snapped at for her pains, much to her surprise, so we all went to help her. And what do you think?

It was Joe Stratton underneath, not Sam Farthing, but none of us could work out how this had happened.

Well, we all thought this a splendid joke – even the Farthings saw the funny side of it. That was until someone wondered what had happened to Sam, when he didn't turn up to join us all.

We found his body at the end of The Green Man garden. Santa Claus had dropped a present on St Swithin's with a vengeance. You see, Sam was still dressed as the Hooden Horse, with the nosebag drawn tight around his neck. He'd been suffocated.

St Swithin's in the Lea couldn't stay out of the public eye after that. It made the perfect Christmas headline. So would the fact that Granny Trotter's Treasure had disappeared too, except that the press and police didn't know about that. There seemed to be an unspoken agreement that it wasn't respectful to Sam to mention it straightaway, though we were all thinking our own thoughts, I'm sure.

In due course there was an inquest, but the coroner couldn't decide what caused the suffocation other than it was by the nosebag, so it was an open verdict. It could have been murder, it could have been manslaughter, or even a nasty accident. Poor old Joe told the police the switching of the Hooden Horse had all been a joke. He and the other Strattons had made a copycat Hooden Horse complete with rope and nosebag, then they had pounced silently on Sam while he was tied to his tree, and Joe took his place. Harry and the other Strattons led Sam away, docile as anything, him not being able to see and thinking this was his regular Waggoner.

Harry hooked him up at the end of the pub garden, where even if Sam kicked up a din, no one would hear him on Christmas Eve. The jukebox would see to that. He'd left the nosebag on, but only as they'd found it, over the horse's wooden jaws, and not drawn up round Sam's neck. Sam would have been to breathe perfectly well, and anyway there was nothing to stop him throwing the sacking off, letting go of the head and standing upright. So the coroner reckoned Sam might have realised he'd been made a fool of, struggled to free himself the wrong way so that the nosebag landed up round his neck, and in fighting it he made it worse so he couldn't breathe.

Once again, nothing more might have happened if it hadn't been for Granny Trotter's Treasure. Mrs Nabb eventually broke the silence. It would be her. She was set on finding it, having come to the same conclusions as we did, either Sam had taken it with him while he went Hoodening or Adele had taken it for safe-keeping. As none of us knew what it looked like that would be the last we'd ever see of it. So Mrs Nabb announced she wanted to have a meeting about maypoles and midsummer revels. You'd think the disaster of Christmas would have put her off, but not a bit of it. It wasn't just old customs she wanted to discuss this time. It turned out she now saw the treasure as the thing to put St Swithin's on the map for some good publicity instead of bad.

'Before we hold our little meeting, I thought I'd come to you first, Jack,' she said to me flatteringly one Saturday lunchtime, just as I was thinking I had the place to myself, 'because only you can help.'

I took a swig of my beer. 'How's that, Mrs Nabb? I don't do dancing round maypoles.'

I meant it seriously, but she gave a merry laugh. 'You will have your little joke, Jack. I meant I need your help in solving the mystery surrounding Sam's death.'

'What mystery?' I asked carefully. 'Seems to me it's all settled. We'll not know exactly what happened now.'

'I think we will, Jack, but only you can play detective.'

'How's that?' Amateur detectives aren't too popular round here. I remember the time one of the Strattons played detective over who was rustling pigs locally. Got himself a bullet in the leg for his pains. It kept the rustlers away, but it put me off playing detective myself.

'If you think Sam was murdered, Mrs Nabb,' I continued plainly, 'best go to the police. We can't go investigating it ourselves. St Swithin's won't take kindly to Inspector Morses prowling around even if they are disguised as vicar's wives or old men in corners.'

'It's not Sam's death itself I'm concerned with. After all, that's the police's responsibility. It's the disappearance of the treasure. Now you have an interest in that, don't you?'

I couldn't deny she was right, though since we'd all heard Sam say he was going to give it to the Church, it was good of her to remember the Trotters still existed.

'You see,' she continued, 'everyone is certain that Sam wasn't joking and that he had it with him that night.'

'Then Adele will know where it is.'

'She denies it. I heard one of the Strattons accusing her. She says Sam took it with him in the bag used to collect the money. She says she quite agreed with him over giving it to the Church, however.'

I snorted. 'You don't know Adele Farthing too well, Mrs Nabb.'

'Now, now, Jack. Don't speak ill of a widow.'

She should have heard the ill our Liz could speak of the merry widow. I decided to keep my mouth shut though. I told Mrs Nabb I'd think it over, and think it over I did. Me being a Trotter with a claim on it, I could go to talk to Adele. I agreed it wouldn't do to have Mrs Nabb storming around with her big feet (even though she hadn't expressed it quite that way). She was right. I could do the job tactfully. I could get a general idea of who had been in a position to both murder Sam and collar the Trotter treasure. For I was certain that murder it was and that the murder was on account of the treasure. I couldn't see Harry Stratton going so far as to do Sam in just so Joe could play the Hooden Horse. There'd be no need for a start, once he'd led Sam away.

Adele, as Mrs Nabb had said, was the key to the problem, and

I reckoned I was on the same side as Adele wanted her bread to be buttered on. Mike's. She wouldn't risk upsetting me. I waited till she came into the bar one day, and that wasn't long.

'How do, Adele. What are you drinking?' As if I needed to ask. The most expensive drink in the place of course. Still, it meant she had no option but to spend a few token minutes with me.

'You know there are rumours going round about the Trotters' treasure, me darling. You sure about Sam taking it with him inside the Horse?'

'Oh yes, Jack. As I told Mike,' she sighed, a loving tone in her voice, 'he took it with him so that he could have the pleasure of handing it to the Church on Christmas Eve. That meant a lot to him. If I hadn't been of the same mind myself, it might have looked to nasty minded people as though Sam didn't trust me.'

'Can I ask what this treasure was.'

'You can ask, Jack. But I can't answer. He didn't show it to me.' Butter wouldn't have melted in her mouth.

'Then you can't be sure there was any treasure.'

'There bloody well was, the old skinflint.' Adele's mask slipped somewhat. 'I could show you the old box it came in, if you want. I've got it at home.'

'I'd like to see that sometime, Adele.' I put on my old man's pathos.

'Suit yourself when.' She shrugged. 'Call in at the farm any day.'

'What made Sam decide to give it to the Church?' I asked curiously, not that I thought I'd get the truth. She was right about Sam being a skinflint, though. He only drops twenty pence in the collection plate on a Sunday. I've seen him.

She stole a look at me and giggled. 'Poor dear old Sam could get funny delusions at times. I think he might have done it to spite me, under the impression I had someone else in tow.'

'I'd never believe that of you, Adele,' I lied. 'Now you were in the pub with us that night, didn't you see where he put it?'

'Nope. He took it with him and it didn't come back. He only had twenty quid thirty pence with him when he was found. You can't kid me that was the Trotter treasure.'

'Did you go home while the Hoodening was on, m'dear?'

'Yes.' She fluttered her eyelashes mockingly at me. 'And, do you know, Mike kindly drove me back there while Liz looked after the bar.'

Had he indeed. I didn't like the sound of that, and wondered if either of them had known about the switch of horses. I couldn't see the Strattons telling her though. It was worrying knowing Mike had been away from the bar – if he was of course. Adele might be making it up. But if he had, and knowing that Mike would have thought the same as me about who was entitled to the Trotter treasure, I had to knock this theory on the head and make sure that Mike couldn't have done it.

It was a knotty one, though. If Mike had reclaimed the Trotter inheritance, he'd have told me, though it's true he wouldn't have done so if he had murdered Sam to get it. Could have been an accident, I ruminated.

'Son,' I said to Mike when I could get him on his own, 'I want to talk to you.' This was all very well when he was a lad of eight or so, because I was bigger than him then. Now he towers above me. He's always very good though, never treats me as though I'm past it. So he agreed readily enough.

'What is it, Dad?'

'It's about Adele. You planning to run off with her?'

Mike flushed. 'What's it to you?'

'I don't want to have to run a pub again at my time of life.'

'Lizzie could run it,' he muttered.

'Aiming to move into Farthings' Farm, eh? You're a fool, Mike. What do you think folk will say?'

'Nothing. It's none of their business.'

'Maybe no, but you're in a sticky position,' I told him honestly. 'I can say you were here with me all that night, even if you did take Adele home, like she claims. But all of us have to take a pee at times, so I couldn't swear I saw you here *all* the evening and the toilets are out the back, which folks might think was very handy.'

'You saying you think I rushed down the garden, pinched the treasure and killed Sam? Blimey, you've some imagination, Dad.' He didn't quite bring it off, and there was an uneasy note in his voice. 'Remember I didn't know he was down there.'

'You could have seen Harry and Joe set off and watched what happened.'

'Even if I did, and I'm not saying that, I couldn't have known Harry would bring him back here, could I?'

'You could have seen him, Mike.' I was getting desperate for him to prove to me he couldn't have done it, but he said nothing for a while. Then suddenly: 'But I couldn't have known Sam was inside and not Joe, could I?'

This was true. He and Adele might know where the treasure was, but how could they have known for sure it was Sam was out at the back yelling his head off with the Hooden Horse on him. Maybe Adele found him though... My thoughts ran away with me, and then I remembered of course.

'Harry,' I cried. Harry, who hated Sam Farthing for taking away the horse from his father. Always hot-headed was Harry, always in trouble at school, always in trouble after school. He might not have gone so far as to kill Sam for taking Joe's place, but add the treasure in as a motive and Harry could be a suspect. Who was better placed than Harry to commit the crime and pinch the treasure for the Strattons. He was Joe's Waggoner, he was the one who led Sam back here and tied him up. He had most time, he had most knowledge and he had been present while Sam was boasting about giving the treasure to the Church.

It was a conundrum, but I was beginning to see daylight. I decided to have a talk with Harry. He was one of the village postmen, so this wasn't difficult. As we sauntered along, it was easy to raise the question of the Trotter treasure, or as he would see it, the Stratton treasure.

'We've got all the evidence we need that it would belong to us Strattons,' he told me. Never a thought did he give to the fact it was called Trotter treasure, not Stratton. 'We owned the land then.'

'And the Farthings now.'

'Sam Farthing's dead and he didn't have no right to give it away.'

'He is indeed dead, Harry. Was it by your hand?'

'You have to be joking.' He roared with laughter. 'I'm stronger than he was. I could just have taken it, since it was ours by right.'

I could have argued the toss over ownership, but it wasn't worth it. The treasure had disappeared, and when it was found would be the time to argue that. So who had it? My money was on Adele. She would get the treasure and with Sam dead, the farm too, and probably Mike thrown in. She was there at the pub, she could have seen Joe slink off in his Horse's head, and followed him and Harry till she saw what happened.

It was time to see Mrs Nabb again to try this theory on her, so I called in at the Vicarage.

She was all over me. 'I knew I could trust you, Jack,' she gushed, as I carefully explained my reasoning that it was Adele, and that we ought to have a united front to get the treasure back (and a united share-out).

She nodded gravely. 'Whoever stole the treasure must have killed Sam Farthing, isn't that so?' she twittered.

'Oh yes, I said grandly. 'Adele could have found out about the switching of the Hooden Horses, and known exactly where Sam was hiding it on his person.' I thought this sounded very Hercule Poirot, and was proud of myself.

'Just one moment, Jack.'

She went out of the room and came back with a plastic bag, which she emptied on the table in front of me. Out fell a very old dirty collection of old stones; they were very dull, but I could make out what they were. Cleaned up a bit, there would look a very classy set of diamonds. I was beginning to get a very nasty feeling about all this.

'This is Granny Trotter's treasure.' She beamed at me very sweetly indeed.

'You mean,' I grappled with this, trying to hold on to the sense of it, '*you* killed Sam Farthing?'

'No, Jack. Sam gave me the bag when I hitched him up to the Vicarage tree and put the nosebag over the horse's jaws. He was afraid he might lose it with the Jockey playing so roughly with him. He said it was for the Church anyway, so I might as well have it now. That's as true as Granny Trotter's treasure.'

They were beginning to wink at me, those diamonds, as I tried to get my old brain to work.

'You see, Jack,' Mrs Bloody Nabb continued, only she wasn't beaming now, 'there was one more person who was eager to have the treasure and could have seen the switching of the horses.'

'Who's that?' Who had I missed out?

'You, Jack.'

She was right of course, and here I am in the corner. A cell corner, this time. I said that woman was trouble.

Weeds

Ruth Rendell

Few authors can match the critical and popular acclaim
that Ruth Rendell has achieved. Rendell has lived for many
years in the English countryside and has a real feeling for
landscape and the environment. A rural backdrop is inte-
gral to fine novels such as *A Fatal Inversion* and *The
Brimstone Wedding*, both of which appeared under the
pen-name of Barbara Vine. This story, which comes from
one of her finest collections, *The Copper Peacock*, illus-
trates her talents to perfection.

'I am not at all sure', said Jeremy Flintwine, 'that I would know a weed from whatever the opposite of a weed is.'

The girl looked at him warily. 'A plant.'

'But surely weeds are plants.'

Emily Hithe was not prepared to enter into an argument. 'Let me try and explain the game to you again,' she said. 'You have to see if you can find a weed. In the herbaceous borders, in the rosebeds, anywhere. If you find one all you have to do is show it to my father and he will give you a pound for it. Do you understand now?'

'I thought this was in aid of cancer research. There's not much money to be made that way.

She smiled rather unpleasantly. 'You won't find any weeds.'

It cost two pounds each to visit the garden. Jeremy, a publisher who lived in Islington, had been brought by the Wragleys with whom he was staying. They had walked here from their house in the village, a very long walk for a Sunday afternoon in summer after a heavy lunch. Nothing had been said about fund-raising or playing games. Jeremy was already wondering how he was going to get back. He very much hoped to catch the twelve minutes past seven train from Diss to London.

The Wragleys and their daughter Penelope, aged eight, had disappeared down one of the paths that led through a shrubbery. People stood about on the lawn drinking tea and eating digestive biscuits, which they had had to pay for. Jeremy always found country life amazing. The way everyone knew everyone else, for instance. The extreme eccentricity of almost everybody, so that you suspected people, wrongly, of putting it on. The clothes. Garments he had supposed obsolete, cotton frocks and sports jackets, were everywhere in evidence. He had thought himself suitably dressed but now he wondered. Jeans were not apparently correct wear except on the under-twelves and he was wearing jeans, an old, very clean, pair, selected after long deliberation, with an open-necked shirt and an elegantly shabby Italian silk cardigan. He was also wearing, in the top buttonhole of the cardigan, a scarlet poppy tugged up by its roots from the grass verge by Penelope Wragley.

The gift of this flower had been occasioned by one of George Wragley's literacy anecdotes. George, who wrote biographies of poets, was not one of Jeremy's authors but his wife Louise, who produced bestsellers for children and adored her husband, was. Therefore Jeremy found it expedient to listen more or less politely to George going on and on about Francis Thompson and the Meynells. It was during the two-mile-long trudge to the Hithes' garden that George related how one of the Meynell children, with appropriate symbolism, had presented the opium-addicted Thompson with a poppy in a Suffolk field, bidding him, 'Keep this for ever!' Penelope had promptly given Jeremy his buttonhole, which her parents thought a very sweet gesture, though he was neither a poet nor an opium addict.

They had arrived at the gates and paid their entry fee. A lot of people were on the terrace and the lawns. The neatness of the gardens was almost oppressive, some of the flowers looking as if they had been washed and ironed and others as if made of wax. The grass was the green of a billiard table and nearly as smooth. Jeremy asked an elderly woman, one of the tea drinkers, if Rodney Hithe did it all himself.

'He has a man, of course,' she said.

The coolness of her tone was not encouraging but Jeremy tried. 'It must be a lot of work.'

'Oh, old Rod's got that under control,' said the girl with her, a granddaughter perhaps. 'He knows how to crack the whip.'

This Jeremy found easy to believe. Rodney Hithe was a loud man. His voice was loud and he wore a jacket of loud blue and red checked tweed. Though seeming affable enough, calling the women 'darling' and the men 'old boy', Jeremy suspected he was the kind of person it would be troublesome to get on the wrong side of. His raucous voice could be heard from end to end of the garden, and his braying unamused laugh.

'I wouldn't want to find a weed,' said the granddaughter, voicing Jeremy's own feelings. 'Not for a pound. Not at the risk of confronting Rod with it.'

Following the path the Wragleys had taken earlier, Jeremy saw people on their hands and knees, here lifting a blossoming frond, there an umbelliferous stalk, in the forlorn hope of finding treasure underneath. The Wragleys were nowhere to be seen. In a far corner of the garden, where geometric rosebeds were bounded on two sides by flint walls, stood a stone seat. Jeremy thought he would sit down on this seat and have a cigarette. Surely no one could object to his smoking in this remote and secluded spot. There was in any case no one to see him.

He was taking his lighter from his jeans pocket when he heard a sound from the other side of the wall. He listened. It came again, an indrawing of breath and a heavy sigh. Jeremy wondered afterwards why he had not immediately understood what kind of activity would prompt the utterance of these sighs and half-sobs, why he had at first supposed it was pain and not pleasure that gave rise to them. In any case, he was rather an inquisitive man. Not hesitating for long, he hoisted himself up so that he could look over the wall. His experience of the countryside had not prepared him for this. Behind the wall was a smallish enclosed area or farmyard, bounded by buildings of the sty and byre type. Within an aperture in one of these buildings, on a heap of hay, a naked girl could be seen lying in the arms of a man who was not himself naked but dressed in a shirt and a pair of trousers.

'Lying in the arms of' did not accurately express what the girl was doing but it was a euphemism Jeremy much preferred to 'sleeping with' or anything franker. He dropped down off the wall but not before he had noticed that the man was very deeply tanned and had a black beard and that the girl's resemblance to Emily Hithe made it likely this was her sister.

This was no place for a quiet smoke. He walked back through the shrubbery, lighting a cigarette as he went. Weed-hunting was still in progress under the bushes and among the alpines in the rock garden, this latter necessarily being carried out with extreme care, using the fingertips to avoid bruising a petal. He noticed none of the women wore high heels. Rodney Hithe was telling a woman who had brought a Pekinese that the dog must be carried. The Wragleys were on the lawn with a middle-aged couple who both wore straw hats and George Wragley was telling them an anecdote about an old lady who had sat next to PG Wodehouse at a dinner party and enthused about his work throughout the meal under the impression he was Edgar Wallace. There was some polite laughter. Jeremy asked Louise what time she thought of leaving.

'Don't you worry, we shan't be late. We'll get you to the station all right. There's always the last train, you know, the eight forty-four.' She went on confidingly, 'I wouldn't want to upset poor old Rod by leaving the minute we arrive. Just between you and me, his marriage hasn't been all it should be of late and I'd hate to add to his troubles.'

This sample of Louise's arrogance rather took Jeremy's breath away. No doubt the woman meant that the presence of anyone as famous as herself in his garden conferred an honour on Rodney Hithe which was ample compensation for his disintegrating home life. He was reflecting on vanity and authors and self-delusion when the subject of Louise's remark came up to them and told Jeremy to put his cigarette out. He spoke in the tone of a prison officer addressing a habitual offender in the area of violent crime. Jeremy, who was not without spirit, decided not to let Hithe cow him.

'It's harmless enough out here surely.'

'I'd rather you smoked your filthy fags in my wife's drawing-room than in my garden.'

Grinding it into the lawn would be an obvious solecism.

'Here,' Jeremy said, 'you can put it out yourself,' and he did his best to meet Hithe's eyes with an equally steady stare. Louise gave a nervous giggle. Holding the cigarette end at arm's length, Hithe went off to find some more suitable extinguishing grounds, disappeared in the direction of the house and came back with a gun.

Jeremy was terribly shocked. He was horrified. He retreated a step or two. Although he quickly understood that Hithe had not returned to wreak vengeance but only to show off his new twelve-bore to the man in the straw hat, he still felt shaken. The ceremony of breaking the gun he thought it was called was gone through. The straw-hatted man squinted down the barrel. Jeremy tried to remember if he had ever actually seen a real gun before. This was an aspect of country life he found he disliked rather more than all the other things.

Tea was still being served from a trestle table outside the french windows. He bought himself a cup of tea and several of the more nourishing biscuits. It seemed unlikely that any train passing through north Suffolk on Sunday evening would have a restaurant or even a buffet car. The time was coming up to six. It was at this point that he noticed the girl he had last seen lying in the arms of the bearded man. She was no longer naked but wearing a T-shirt and a pair of shorts. In spite of these clothes, or perhaps because of them, she looked rather older than when he had previously seen her. Jeremy heard her say to the woman holding the dog, 'He ought to be called a Beijingese, you know,' and give a peal of laughter.

He asked the dog's owner, a woman with a practical air, how far it was to Diss.

'Not far,' she said. 'Two or three miles. Would you say two miles, Deborah, or nearer three?'

Deborah Hithe's opinion on this distance Jeremy was never to learn, for as she opened her mouth to speak, a bellow from Rodney silenced all conversation.

'You didn't find that in this garden!'

He stood in the middle of the lawn, the gun no longer in his hands but passed on for the scrutiny of a girl in riding breeches. Facing him was the young man with the tan and the beard, whom Jeremy knew beyond a doubt to be Deborah's lover. He held up, in teasing fashion for the provocation of Hithe, a small plant with a red flower. For a moment the only sound was Louise's giggle, a noise that prior to this weekend he would never have suspected her of so frequently making. A crowd had assembled quite suddenly – surely the whole population of the village, it seemed to Jeremy, which Louise had told him was something over three hundred.

The man with the beard said, 'Certainly I did. You want me to show you where?'

'He should never have pulled it out, of course,' Emily whispered. 'I'm afraid we forgot to put that in the rules, that you're not supposed to pull them out.'

'He's your sister's boyfriend, isn't he?' Jeremy hazarded.

The look he received was one of indignant rage. 'My sister? I haven't got a sister.'

Deborah was watching the pair on the lawn. He saw a single tremor shake her. The man who had found the weed made a beckoning gesture to Hithe to follow him along the shrubbery path. George Wragley lifted his shoulders in an exaggerated shrug and began telling the girl in riding breeches a long pointless story about Virginia Woolf. Suddenly Jeremy noticed it had got much colder. It had been a cool, pale grey, still day, a usual English summer day, and now it was growing chilly. He did not know what made him remember the gun, notice its absence.

Penelope Wragley, having ingratiated herself with the woman dispensing tea, was eating up the last of the biscuits. She seemed the best person to ask who Deborah was, the least likely to take immediate inexplicable offence, though he had noticed her looking at him and particularly at his cardigan in a very affronted way. He decided to risk it.

Still staring, she said as if he ought to know, 'Deborah is Mrs Hithe, of course.'

The implications of this would have been enough to occupy Jeremy's thoughts for the duration of his stay in the garden and beyond, if there had not come at this moment a loud report. It was, in his ears, a shattering explosion and it came from the far side of the shrubbery. People began running in the direction of the noise before its reverberations had died away. The lawn emptied. Jeremy was aware that he had begun to shake. He said to the child, who took no notice, 'Don't go!' and then set off himself in pursuit of her.

The man with the beard lay on his back in the rose garden and there was blood on the grass. Deborah knelt beside him, making a loud keening wailing noise, and Hithe stood between two of the geometric rosebeds, holding the gun in his hands. The gun was not exactly smoking but there was a strong smell of gunpowder. A tremendous hubbub arose from the party of weed-hunters, the whole scene observed with a kind of gloating horrified fascination by Penelope Wragley, who had reverted to infantilism and watched with her thumb in her mouth. The weed was nowhere to be seen.

Someone said superfluously or perhaps not superfluously, 'Of course it was a particularly tragic kind of accident.'

'In the circumstances.'

The whisper might have come from Louise. Jeremy decided not to stay to confirm this. There was nothing he could do. All he wanted was to get out of this dreadful place as quickly as possible and make his way to Diss and catch a train, any train, possibly the last train. The Wragleys could send his things on.

He retreated the way he had come, surprised to find himself tiptoeing which was surely unnecessary. Emily went past him, running towards the house and the phone. The Pekinese or Beijingese dog had set up a wild yapping. Jeremy walked quietly around the house, past the drawing-room windows, through the open gates and into the lane.

The sound of that shot still rang horribly in his ears, the sight of red blood on the grass was still before his eyes. The unaccustomed walk might be therapeutic. It was a comfort, since a thin rain had begun to fall, to come upon a signpost which told him he was going in the right direction for Diss and it was only a mile and a half away. There was no doubt the country seemed to show people as well as nature in the raw. What a nightmare that whole afternoon had been, culminating in outrageous violence! How horrible, after all, the Wragleys and Penelope were and in a way he had never before suspected! Why were one's authors so awful? Why did they have such appalling spouses and ill-behaved children? Penelope had stared at him when he asked her about Deborah Hithe as disgustedly as if, like that poor man, he had been covered in blood.

And then Jeremy put his hand to his cardigan and felt the front of it, patted it with both hands like a man feeling for his wallet, looked down, saw that the scarlet poppy she had given him was gone. Her indignation was explained. The poppy must have fallen out when he hoisted himself up and looked over the wall.

It was a moment or two before he understood the cause of his sudden fearful dismay.

A Bridge Too Far

Zoe Sharp

Believe it or not, this entertaining short story is the very first to have been published by its author. I am sure it will not be her last. Zoe Sharp is a relative newcomer to the crime scene, but she has quickly established herself as a notable talent. Like a number of contributors to this volume, she is also a member of a group of crime writers who have joined forces to promote their work to a wider audience. This trend began three years ago when Margaret Murphy formed 'Murder Squad' and has proved an effective way of achieving collective publicity at a time when publishers' marketing budgets are often over-stretched. Zoe Sharp's own gang of four, formed earlier this year, is known as 'Ladykillers' and they appear at gigs up and down the country.

I watched with a kind of horrified fascination as the boy climbed on to the narrow parapet. Below his feet the elongated brick arches of the old viaduct stretched, so I'd been told, exactly one hundred and twenty-three feet to the ground. He balanced on the crumbling brickwork at the edge, casual and unconcerned.

My God, I thought, *He's going to do it. He's actually going to jump.*

'Don't prat around, Adam,' one of the others said. I was still sorting out their names. Paul, that was it. He was a medical student, tall and bony with a long almost Roman nose. 'If you're going to do it, do it, or let someone else have their turn.'

'Now now,' Adam said, wagging a finger. 'Don't be bitchy.'

Paul glared at him, took a step forwards, but the cool blonde-haired girl, Diana, put a hand on his arm.

'Leave him alone, Paul,' Diana said, and there was a faint snap to her voice. She'd been introduced as Adam's girlfriend, so I suppose she had the right to be protective. 'He'll jump when he's ready. You'll have your chance to impress the newbies.'

She flicked unfriendly eyes in my direction as she spoke but I didn't rise to it. Heights didn't draw or repel me the way I knew they did with most people but that didn't mean I was inclined to throw myself off a bridge to prove my courage. I'd already done that at enough other times, in enough other places.

Beside me, my friend Sam muttered under his breath, 'OK, I'm impressed. No way are you getting me up there.'

I grinned at him. It was Sam who'd told me about the local Dangerous Sports' Club who trekked out to this disused viaduct in the middle of nowhere. There they tied one end of a rope to the far parapet and brought the other end up underneath between the supports before tying it round their ankles.

And then they jumped.

The idea, as Sam explained it, was to propel yourself outwards as though diving off a cliff and trying to avoid the rocks below. I suspected this wasn't an analogy with resonance for either of us, but the technique ensured that when you reached the end of your tether, so to speak, the slack was taken up progressively and you swung backwards and forwards under the bridge in a graceful arc.

Jump straight down, however, and you would be jerked to a stop hard enough to break your spine. They used modern climbing rope with a fair amount of give in it but it was far from the elastic gear required by the bungee jumper. That was for wimps.

Sam knew the group's leader, Adam Lane, from the nearby university, where Sam was something incomprehensible to do with computers and Adam was the star of the track and field team. He was one of these magnetic golden boys who breezed effortlessly through life, always looking for a greater challenge, something to set their heartbeat racing. And for Adam the unlikely pastime of bridge swinging, it seemed, was it.

I hadn't believed Sam's description of the activity and had made the mistake of expressing my scepticism out loud. So, here I was on a bright but surprisingly nippy Sunday morning in May, waiting for the first of these lunatics to launch himself into the abyss.

Now, though, Adam put his hands on his hips and breathed in deep, looking around with a certain intensity at the landscape. His stance, up there on the edge of the precipice, was almost a pose.

We were halfway across the valley floor, in splendid isolation. The tracks to this Brunel masterpiece had been long since ripped up and carted away. The only clue to their existence was the footpath that led across the fields from the lay-by on the road where Sam and I had left our motorbikes. The other cars there, I guessed, belonged to Adam and his friends.

The view from the viaduct was stunning, the sides of the valley curving away at either side as though seen through a fish-eye lens. It was still early, so that the last of the dawn mist clung to the dips and hollows, and it was quiet enough to hear the world turning.

'Hello there! Not starting without us, are you?' called a girl's cheery voice, putting a scatter of crows to flight, breaking the spell. A flash of annoyance passed across Adam's handsome features.

A young couple was approaching. Like the other three DSC members, they were wearing high-tech outdoor clothing – lightweight trousers you can wash and dry in thirty seconds, and lairy-coloured fleeces.

The boy was short and muscular, a look emphasised by the fact he'd turned his coat collar up against the chill, giving him no neck to speak of. He tramped on to the bridge and almost threw his rucksack down with the others.

'What's the matter, Michael?' Adam said, his voice a lazy taunt. 'Get out of bed on the wrong side?'

The newcomer gave him a single, vicious look and said nothing.

The girl was shorter and plumper than Diana. Her gaze flicked nervously from one to the other, latching on to the rope already secured round Adam's legs as if glad of the distraction. 'Oh *Adam*, you're never jumping today are you?' she cried. 'I didn't think you were supposed to—'

'I'm perfectly OK, Izzy darling,' Adam drawled. His eyes shifted meaningfully towards Sam and me, then back again.

Izzy opened her mouth to speak, closing it again with a snap as she caught on. Her pale complexion bloomed into sudden pink across her cheekbones and she bent to fuss with her own rucksack. She drew out a stainless steel flask and held it up like an offering. 'I brought coffee.'

'How very thoughtful of you, Izzy dear,' Diana said, speaking down her well-bred nose at the other girl. 'You always were so very accommodating.'

Izzy's colour deepened. 'I'm not sure there's enough for everybody,' she went on, dogged. She nodded apologetically to us. 'No one told me there'd be new people coming. I'm Izzy, by the way.'

'Sam Pickering,' Sam put in, 'and this is Charlie Fox.'

Izzy smiled a little shyly, then a sudden thought struck her. 'You're not thinking of joining are you?' she said in an anxious tone. 'Only, it's not certain we're going to carry on with the club for much longer.'

'Course we are,' Michael said brusquely, raising his dark stubbled chin out of his collar for the first time. 'Just because Adam has to give up, no reason for the rest of us to pack it in. We'll manage without him.'

The others seemed to hold their breath while they checked Adam's response to this dismissive declaration, but he seemed to have lost interest in the squabbles of lesser mortals. He continued to stand on the parapet, untroubled by the yawning drop below him, staring into the middle distance like an ocean sailor.

'That's not the only reason we might have to stop,' the tall bony boy, Paul said. 'In fact, here comes another right now.'

He nodded across the far side of the field. We all turned and I noticed for the first time that a man on a red Honda quad bike was making a beeline for us across the dewy grass.

'Oh shit,' Michael muttered. 'Wacko Jacko. That's all we need.'

'Who is he?' Sam asked, watching the purposeful way the quad was bearing down on us.

'He's the local farmer,' Paul explained. 'He owns all the land round here and he's dead against us using the viaduct, but it's a public right of way and legally he can't stop us. That doesn't stop the old bugger coming and giving us a hard time every Sunday.'

'Mr Jackson's a strict Methodist you see,' Izzy said quietly as the quad drew nearer. 'It's not trespassing, that's the problem – it's the fact that when the boys jump, well, they do tend to swear a bit. I think he objects to the blasphemy.'

I eyed the farmer warily as he finally braked to a halt at the edge of the bridge and cut the quad's engine. The main reason for my caution was the elderly double-barrelled Baikal shotgun he lifted out of the rack on one side and brought with him.

Jackson came stumping along the bridge towards us with the kind of rolling, twitching gait that denotes a pair of totally worn-out knees. He wore a flat cap with tar on the peak and a tatty raincoat tied together with orange bailer twine. As he closed on us he snapped the Baikal shut, and I instinctively edged myself slightly in front of Sam.

'Morning Mr Jackson,' Izzy called, the tension sending her voice into a high waver.

The farmer ignored the greeting, his eyes fixed on Adam. It was only when Michael and Paul physically blocked his path that he seemed to notice the rest of us.

'I've told you lot before. You've no right to do this on my land,' he said gruffly, clutching the shotgun almost nervously, as though suddenly aware he was outnumbered. 'You been warned.'

'And you've been told that *you* have no right to stop us, you daft old bugger,' Adam said, the derision clear in his voice.

Jackson's ruddy face congested. He tried to push closer to Adam, but Paul caught the lapel of his raincoat and shoved him backwards. With a fraction less aggression the whole thing could have passed off with a few harsh words but after this there was only one way it was going to go.

The scuffle was brief. Jackson was hard and fit from years of manual labour but the boys both had thirty years on him. It was the shotgun that worried me the most. Michael had grabbed hold of the barrel and was trying to wrench it from the farmer's grasp, while *he* was determined to keep hold of it. The business end of the Baikal swung wildly across the rest of us.

Izzy was shrieking, ducked down with her hands over her ears. I piled Sam backwards, starting to head for the end of the bridge.

The blast of the shotgun discharging stopped my breath. I flinched at the pellets twanging off the brickwork as the shot spread. The echo rolled away up and down the valley like a call to battle.

The silence that followed was quickly broken by Izzy's whimpering cries. She was still on the ground, staring in horrified disbelief at the blood seeping through a couple of small holes in the leg of her trousers.

Paul crouched near to her, hands fluttering over the wounds without actually wanting to touch them. Sam had turned vaguely green at the first sign of blood, but he unwound the cotton scarf from under the neck of his leathers and handed it over to me without a word. I moved Paul aside quietly and padded the makeshift dressing on to Izzy's leg.

'It's only a couple of pellets,' I told her. 'It's not serious. Hold this against it as hard as you can. You'll be fine.'

Michael had managed to wrestle the Baikal away from Jackson. He turned and took in Izzy's state, then pointed the shotgun meaningfully back at the shaken farmer, settling his finger on to the second trigger.

'You bastard,' he ground out.

'Michael, stop it,' Diana said.

Michael ignored her, his dark eyes fixed menacingly on Jackson. 'You've just shot my girlfriend.'

'*Michael*!' Diana tried again, shouting this time. She had quite a voice for one so slender. 'Stop it! Don't you understand? *Where's Adam?*'

We all turned then, looked back to the section of parapet where he'd been standing. The lichen-covered wall was peppered with tiny fresh chips but the parapet itself was empty.

Adam was gone.

I ran to the edge and leaned out over it as far as I dared. A hundred and twenty-three feet below me, a crumpled form lay utterly still on the grassy slope. The blood was a bright halo around his head.

'Adam!' Diana yelled, her voice cracking. 'Oh God. Can you hear me?'

I stepped back, caught Sam's enquiring glance and shook my head.

Paul was already hurrying towards the end of the bridge to

pick his way down beneath the arches. I went after him, snagged his arm as he started his descent.

'I'll go,' I said. When he looked at me dubiously, I added, 'I know First-Aid if there's anything to be done and if not, well—' I shrugged '—I've seen dead bodies before.'

His face was grave for a moment, then he nodded. 'What can we do?'

'Get an ambulance – Izzy probably needs one even if Adam doesn't – and call the police.' He nodded again and had already started back up the slope when I added, 'Oh, and try not to let Michael shoot that bloody farmer.'

'Why not?' Paul demanded bitterly. 'He deserves it.' And then he was gone.

It was a relatively easy path down to where Adam's body lay. Close to, it wasn't particularly pretty. I hardly needed to search for a pulse at his outflung wrist to know the boy was dead. Still, the relatively soft surface had kept him largely intact, enough for me to tell that it wasn't any shotgun blast that had killed him. Gravity had done that all by itself.

I took off my jacket and gently laid it over the top half of the body, covering his head. It was the only thing I could do for him, and even that was more to protect the sensibilities of the living.

When I looked up I could see half of the rope dangling from the opposite side of the bridge high above my head, its loose end swaying gently. The other end was still tied around Adam's ankles. It had snapped during his fall, but why?

Had Jackson's shot severed the rope at the moment when Adam had either lost his balance and fallen, or as he'd chosen to jump?

I got to my feet and followed the rope along the ground to where the severed end lay coiled in the grass. I used a twig to carefully lift it up enough to examine it.

And then I knew.

The embankment seemed a hell of a lot steeper on the way up

than it had on the way down. I ran all the way and was totally out of breath by the time I regained the bridge. But I was just in time.

Diana was crouched next to Izzy, holding her hand. Paul and Sam were standing a few feet behind Michael, eyeing him with varying amounts of fear and mistrust. The thickset youth had the shotgun wedged up under Jackson's chin, using it to force his upper body backwards over the top of the parapet. Michael's face was blenched with anger, teetering on the edge of control.

'He's dead, isn't he?' He didn't take his eyes off the farmer as I approached.

'Yes,' I said carefully, 'but Jackson didn't kill him, Michael.'

'But he must have done.' It was Paul who spoke. 'We all saw—'

'You saw nothing,' I cut in. 'The gun went off and Adam either jumped or fell, but he wasn't shot. The rope gave out. That's why he's dead.'

'That's ridiculous,' Diana said, haughty rather than anguished. 'The breaking strain on the ropes we use is enormous. No way could it have simply broken. The shot must have hit it.'

'It didn't,' I said. 'It was cut halfway through. With a knife.'

Even Michael reacted to that one, taking the shotgun away from Jackson's neck as he swivelled round to face me. I could see the indentations the barrels had left in the scrawny skin of the old man's throat.

Chances like that don't come very often. I took a quick step closer, looped my arm over the one of Michael's that held the gun and brought my elbow back sharply into the fleshy vee between his ribs.

He doubled over, gasping, letting go of the weapon. I picked it out of his hands and stepped back again. It was all over in a moment.

The others watched in silence as I broke the Baikal and picked out the remaining live cartridge. Once it was unloaded I put the gun down propped against the brickwork and dropped the cartridge into my pocket. Michael had caught his breath enough to think about coming at me, but it was Sam who intervened.

'I wouldn't if you know what's good for you,' he said, his voice kindly. 'Charlie's a bit of an expert at this type of thing. She'd eat you for breakfast.'

Michael favoured me with a hard stare. I returned it flat and level. I don't know what he thought he saw but he backed off, sullen, rubbing his stomach.

'So,' I said, 'the question is, who cut Adam's rope?'

For a moment there was total silence. 'Look, we either have this out now, or you get the third degree when the police arrive,' I said, shrugging. 'I assume you *did* call them?' I added in Paul's direction.

'No, but I did,' Sam said, brandishing his mobile phone. 'They're on their way. I've said I'll wait for them up on the road. Show them the way. Will you be OK down here?'

I nodded. 'I'll cope,' I said. 'Oh and Sam – when they arrive, tell them it looks like murder.'

Nobody spoke as Sam started out across the field. He eyed the quad bike with some envy as he passed, but went on foot.

'I still say the old bastard deserves shooting,' Michael muttered.

'I didn't do nothing,' Jackson blurted out suddenly. Relieved of the immediate threat to his life he simply stood looking dazed with his shoulders slumped. 'I never would have fired. It was him who grabbed my hand! He's the one who forced my finger down on the trigger!'

He waved towards Michael, who flushed angrily at the charge. I replayed the scene again and recalled the way the stocky boy had been struggling with Jackson for control of the gun. It had looked for all the world like a genuine skirmish but it could just as easily have been a convenient set-up.

When no one immediately spoke up in his defence, Michael rounded on us.

'How can you believe anything so *stupid*?' he bit out. 'Adam was a good mate. I would have given him my last cent.'

'Didn't like sharing your girlfriend with him, though, did you?' Paul said quietly.

Izzy, still lying on the ground, gave an audible gasp. I checked to see how Diana was taking the news of her dead boyfriend's apparent infidelity but there was little to be gleaned from her cool and colourless expression.

A brief spasm of what might have been fear passed across Michael's face. 'You can't believe I'd want to kill him for that?' he said and gave a harsh laugh. 'Defending Izzy's honour? Come on! I knew right from the start that she's not exactly choosy.'

Izzy had begun to cry. 'He loved me,' she managed between sobs, and it wasn't immediately clear if she was referring to Michael or Adam. 'He told me he loved me.'

Diana sat back, still looking at Izzy, but without really seeing her. 'That's what he tells – told – all of them,' she said, almost to herself. 'Wanted to hear them say it back to him, I suppose.' She smiled then, a little sadly. 'Adam always did need to be adored. The centre of attention.'

'You're just saying that, but it wasn't true,' Izzy cried. 'He loved me. He was going to give you up but he wanted to let you down gently, not to hurt your feelings. He was just waiting for the right time.'

'Oh Izzy, of course he wasn't going to give me up,' Diana said, her tone one of great patience, as though talking to the very young, or the very slow. 'He used to come straight from your bed back to mine and tell me all about it.' She laughed, a high brittle peal. 'How desperately keen you were. How eager to please.'

'And you didn't *mind*?' I asked, fighting to keep the disbelief and the distaste buried.

'Of course not,' Diana said, sounding vaguely surprised that I should feel the need to ask. She sighed. 'Adam had some – interesting – tastes. There were some things that I simply drew the line at, but Izzy—' her eyes slipped away from mine to skim dispassionately over the girl lying cringing in front of her '—well, she would do just about anything he asked. Pathetic, really.'

'Are you really trying to tell me that you *knew* your boyfriend was sleeping around and you didn't care at all?'

Diana stood, looked down her nose again in that way she had. The way that indicated I was being too bourgeoise for words. 'Naturally,' she said. 'I understood Adam perfectly and I understood that this was his last fling at life while he still had the chance.'

'What do you mean, while he still had the chance?' I said. I recalled Michael's jibe about Adam having to pack in the dangerous sports. 'What was the matter with him?'

There was a long pause. Even Jackson, I noticed, seemed to be waiting intently for the answer. Eventually, Izzy was the one who broke the silence.

'He only told us a month ago that he'd been diagnosed with MND,' she said. Her leg had just about stopped bleeding but her face had started to sweat now as the pain and the shock crept in. When I looked blank it was Paul who continued.

'Motor Neurone Disease,' he said, sounding authoritative. 'It's a progressive degeneration of the motor neurones in the brain and spinal cord. In most cases the mind is unaffected but you gradually lose control of various muscle groups – the arms and legs are usually the first to go. You can never quite tell how far or how fast it will develop because it affects everyone in a different way. Sometimes you lose the ability to speak and swallow. It was such rotten luck! The chances of it happening to someone under forty are so remote, but for it to hit Adam of all people—' he broke off, shook his head and seemed to remember how none of that mattered any more. 'Poor sod.'

'It was a tragedy,' Izzy said, defiant. 'And if I gave him pleasure while he could still take it, what was wrong with that?'

'So,' I murmured, 'was this a murder, or a mercy killing?'

Diana made a sort of snuffling noise then, bringing one hand up to her face. For a moment I thought she was fighting back tears but then she looked up and I saw that it was laughter. And she'd lost the battle.

'Oh for God's sake, Adam didn't have Motor Neurone Disease!' she cried, jumping to her feet, hysteria bubbling up through the words. 'That was all a lie! He *wanted* you to think of him as the tragic hero, struck down at the pinnacle of his youth. And you all fell for it. All of you!'

Paul's face was blank. 'So there was nothing wrong with him?' he said faintly. 'But he said—'

'Adam was diagnosed HIV positive six months ago,' Diana said flatly. 'He had AIDS.'

The dismay rippled through the group like the bore of a changing tide. AIDS. The bogeyman of the modern age. I almost saw them edge away from each other, as though afraid of cross-contamination. No wonder Adam had preferred the pretence of a more user-friendly affliction.

And then it dawned on them, one by one.

Izzy realised it first. 'Oh my God,' she whispered. 'He never used...' She broke off, lifting her tear-stained face to Michael. 'Oh God,' she said again. 'I am *so* sorry.'

Michael caught on then, reeling away to clutch at the bridge parapet as though his legs suddenly wouldn't support him any longer.

Paul was just standing there, staring at nothing. 'Bastard,' he muttered, over and over.

Michael rounded on him in a burst of fury. 'It's all right for you,' he yelled. 'You're probably the only one of us who hasn't got it!

'Ah, that's not quite the case, is it, Paul?' Diana said, her voice like chiselled ice. 'Always had a bit of a thing for Adam, didn't you? But he wasn't having any of that. Oh, he kept you dangling for years,' she went on, scanning Paul's stunned face without compassion. 'Did you really not wonder *at all* why he suddenly changed his mind recently?'

She laughed again. A sound like glass breaking, sharp and bitter. 'No, I can see you didn't. You poor fools,' she said, taking in all of their devastated faces, her voice mocking. 'There you all were debasing yourselves to please him, hoping to bathe in a last little piece of Adam's reflected glory, when all the time he was spitting on your graves.'

Michael lunged for her, reaching for her throat. I swept his legs out from under him before he'd taken a stride, then twisted an arm behind his back to hold him down once he was on the floor. *Come on Sam! Where the hell were the police when you needed them?*

I looked up at Diana, who'd stood unconcerned during the abortive attack. 'Why on earth did you stay with him?' I asked.

She shrugged. 'By the time he confessed, it was too late,' she said simply. 'There's no doubt – I've had all the tests. Besides, you didn't know Adam. He was one of those people who was a bright star, for all his faults. I wanted to be with him, and you can't be infected twice.'

'And what about us?' Paul demanded, sounding close to tears himself. 'We were your friends. Why didn't you tell us the truth?'

'Friends!' Diana scoffed. 'What kind of friends would screw my boyfriend – or let their girlfriends screw him – behind my back? Answer me that!'

'You never got anything you didn't ask for,' Jackson said quietly then, his voice rich with disgust. 'The whole lot of you.'

Privately, part of me couldn't help but agree with the farmer. 'The question is,' I said, 'which one of you went for revenge?'

And then, across the field, a new-looking Toyota Land Cruiser turned off the road and came bowling across the grass, snaking wildly as it came.

'Oh shit,' Paul muttered, 'it's Adam's parents. How the hell did they get to hear about it so fast?'

The Land Cruiser didn't stop by the quad bike, but came thundering straight on to the bridge itself, heedless of the weight-bearing capabilities of the old structure. It braked jerkily to a halt and the middle-aged couple inside flung open the doors and jumped out.

'Where's Adam?' the man said urgently. He looked as though he'd thrown his clothes on in a great hurry. His shirt was unbuttoned and his hair awry. 'Are we in time?'

None of the group spoke. I let go of Michael's wriggling body and got to my feet. 'Mr Lane?' I said. 'I'm terribly sorry to tell you this, but there seems to have been an accident—'

'*Accident?*' Adam's mother almost shrieked the word as she came forwards. 'Accident? What about this?' and she thrust a crumpled sheet of paper into my hands.

Uncertain what else to do, I unfolded the letter just as the first of the police Land Rover Discoveries began its approach, rather more sedately, across the field.

Adam's suicide note was brief and to the point. He couldn't face the prospect of the future, it said. He couldn't face the dreadful responsibility of what he'd knowingly inflicted on his friends. He was sorry. Goodbye.

He did not, I noticed, express the hope that they would forgive him for what he'd done.

I folded the note up again as the lead Discovery reached us and a uniformed sergeant got out, adjusting his cap. Sam was in the passenger seat.

The sergeant advanced, his experienced gaze taking in the shotgun still leaning against the brickwork, Izzy's blood-soaked trousers, and the array of staggered faces.

'I understand there's been a murder committed,' he said, businesslike, glancing round. 'Where's the victim?'

I waved my hand towards the surviving members of the Dangerous Sports' Club. 'Take your pick,' I said. 'And if you want the murderer, well—' I nodded at the parapet where Adam had taken his final dive, '—you'll find him down there.'

Cowboy Mouth

Jerry Sykes

Jerry Sykes has established himself as one of the most talented of the new generation of crime writers. Like Mat Coward, he has defied conventional publishing wisdom by focusing especially on the short story. The strategy has paid off, as he is a past winner of the CWA Short Story Dagger (in the illustrious company of the likes of Reg Hill, Ian Rankin and Julian Rathbone). Like all good writers, he is not afraid to experiment and 'Cowboy Mouth' is a story which he describes as 'a little different to anything I've done in the past'.

Kenny Harris had seen the actress before some place, but for the life of him he couldn't remember where. Probably some skunk Channel 5 film he had tuned into on a slack afternoon out here at the petrol station, although pretty much every afternoon was slack up here on the top of the world at this time of year. He couldn't remember the last time there had been more than a handful of customers his entire shift, probably some time around the back end of summer, couple of months back. The actress looked hot in an airbrushed kind of way, her blonde hair all knotted up on top of her head like that, but he couldn't see her all steamed up and bent out of shape on some motel mattress.

The bell over the door tinkled and Kenny hit the mute button on the remote, thankful for the distraction.

A man in a battered blue suit entered the store, trailed a cold front in behind him. The loose soles of his shoes slapped on the cracked lino floor, a spectacle that made it look like he had just stepped out of the circus. Under the suit he sported a thick jumper that strained at the buttons of the jacket. Thick curls of iron-coloured hair boiled on his scalp and his face burned a deep red from a life out in the open. Cold-loosened tears fell from his eyes and left faint tracks on his thick parchment skin. He shuffled to the chill cabinet at the back of the store, his fist clenched out in front of him.

'Another round, Coco?' Kenny called across the store.

Every afternoon the man would sit on the bench in front of the store and drink cans of Red Stripe and stare out across the moors. He would buy four cans from the store one at a time and then around four thirty head back to where he had come from. Some afternoons, Kenny would slip a pack of Silk Cut from the display rack above the counter, pick up a Coke from the chill cabinet and head outside and join him. The old man had once told Kenny that because he could hold on to such a routine, the drinks one at a time, he didn't feel like such a loser. He could see himself in some flash beer joint, the sun and alcohol loose in his muscles just like as if he had a real job and a real home and all the stress and shit that came with a real job and a real home. The way he spoke, Kenny was sure that the man'd had all that stuff in a previous life and that he now missed it like mad, the reason for the drink. It had happened to a lot of people in this part of the world. The man had never told Kenny his name and so Kenny had christened him Coco on account of the shoes. He had no idea where the man lived, there were no houses within a couple of miles of the petrol station, but he made the trek out to the store every day.

'You seein' that little honey of yours later on?' said the old man. 'I hope you're lookin' after her, takin' care of her?'

'Don't you be worryin' about that now, Coco,' said Kenny. 'She's more than capable of takin' care of herself.'

The old man nodded and turned to open the chill cabinet, and Kenny drifted back to the mute TV and a close-up of the blonde actress screaming like the TV was a glass cage and she wanted to be let out. He hit another button and dropped her into darkness.

Coco shuffled up the aisle, a can of Red Stripe in his left hand and his other hand still clenched into a fist and held out in front of him. 'I ever tell you that I used to know her mother,' he said. His shoes slapped on the lino, like cracks in the cold air. 'Oh sure, it was way back now, of course, but the memories are still there.' He tapped the side of his fist to his temple. 'Fire, she was. All red hair and red cheeks and red hot passion. Fire.' He stopped in front of the counter and tilted his head to the side, peered into some other time just out of reach and for a second pale fire seemed to flicker deep inside his pupils.

Moments later the coldness returned to his eyes and the old man lifted his arm and dropped a pile of coins on the counter. 'I think you'll find that's correct,' he said.

Kenny watched the old man walk out of the store and climb up on the bench. He pictured Janie's mother, her pale thin frame and timid manner, and tried to shoehorn her reality into the old man's spoken memories and failed. He looked at the old man some more as he popped open his can of beer, and the trace of a sad smile flickered on his lips. He shook his head and the smile faded back into his face and disappeared.

'In the States you can drive all day and drive all night and still be in the same state when the sun comes up the following morning,' said Joel, and tapped at the bottom of the wheel to hold the car in line. 'Over here, keep on driving and you're more than likely to splash into the North Sea before the sun comes up again.'

Neville stared out at the primal roll of the Pennines, marbled in monochrome under the shift of the dark clouds, a thin curtain of rain. His mind had drifted in and out of the conversation but he could see that Joel had a point – from Liverpool to the North Sea and all the buried seaside haunts of his childhood was little more than a couple of hundred miles.

'The trick is not to let that short distance limit your ambition. To the British, roads are nothin' but strips of dead tarmacadam, the shortest routes between A and B, but across the Atlantic the road is still the last frontier. You only have to look at all the top tunes and top films that have come out of the States to realise that there's more life out there on the road than there is in most towns and cities. *Bonnie and Clyde, Wild at Heart, The Searchers, Night of the Hunter, The Wild Bunch*... All those outlaw stories to inspire you, man, there's just no fuckin' reason whatsoever to not succeed at just about anythin' you care to try. Let it roll, let it roll, let it roll...' Joel trailed off and shook his head, turned to Neville with a loose smile on his face. 'Still, I suppose it's better if you have a decent set of wheels under you,' he said, and tapped the dash of the pale blue Metro that he had lifted from the car park behind Victoria Station earlier that day.

Neville sniffed and continued to stare out across the Pennines, lost in the sudden freedom of it all, the endless possibilities before him. He scratched at the acne scars on his cheek, blinked at the sunbeams that broke from the clouds and flickered on the steel pylons that sat on the earth like skeletons of ancient peaks that had been eroded over the years by the brutal assault of the elements. But almost at once he felt flattened by the burden of history. Here he was, thirty minutes out of jail and already his old friend had started in on his pitch about his latest job. Jesus, sometimes it felt like he had been strapped to the wheel of a car the day he met Joel and every couple of months after he would be crushed under the wheel as it trundled across one broken plan of Joel's after another. And every time without fail Joel would come out of the crush unscathed, his head and heart already on to his latest slice of cheese. It was as if he had no sense of failure, a sense that transmitted itself to those that tracked him and blinded them to his true involvement in criminality. Let all the bad shit fall on his friend's head as he walked on, his head up in the air.

They had cut across the eastern side of Manchester, up on to the back end of Saddleworth Moor and then out on to Snake Pass, the old road that crossed from Yorkshire to Lancashire. The road had been there decades before the M62 had been built at the end of the '60s, and for most of the year the road was still the quickest route from Manchester to Honley, the place where he had been born and raised. Late autumn and the road was still open, but it took no more than a bad storm for the narrow road to become impassable, and it was not unheard of for the road to be closed for days at a time when the snow blanketed the hills. To Neville, it looked like that day was not too far off. Most of the colours of nature had been bleached from the landscape and the dark cotton clouds looked ready to burst across the jaundiced bracken and heather.

The flat rhythm of the land lulled Neville into daydreams.

From as far back as he could remember he had embraced the freedom of the open road, cruised the dark roads of the Pennines in a stolen car, the radio pitched to a hush backbeat. The solitude made him feel that he could project his dreams into the deep reflected darkness of the windscreen, and for some time the nocturnal journeys had been the one true freedom that his life had offered. Deep inside, he knew that now this would never be more than a memory to him, a picture of lost innocence that he could roll up under his arm and take out and pin to the wall as and when it was needed.

They passed an abandoned farmhouse crumbled under the pressures of time and in the far distance black rock formations rose out of the heather like ancient creatures. Thick clouds crashed into the farmhouse and the rocks and tore apart in a fine mist.

'You should listen to this,' said Joel, and pointed at the stereo deck. Some kind of country music shit bleated out of the speakers. 'That's Steve Earle there, one of the best players to have come out of the States in the last twenty years. But the man's also been a junkie, he's been in and out of rehab and he's also done a stretch inside – oh, and he's been married about five times, you believe that, and two of those times to the same woman. Check out the other tapes: Johnny Cash, Willie Nelson, John Prine, Guy Clark – shit, I reckon the fella that had this Metro before us must've reckoned that he was some kind of outlaw himself, some kind of cowboy or somethin'. Shit, he's probably really from Bolton, some dark satanic place like that.'

'I never heard of any of them,' replied Neville.

'Your problem, you need to open your mind,' said Joel, and looked across at the kid all bundled up inside about four sets of clothes as if he felt the cold a season ahead of most other people. 'This is a land of opportunity just like the States, and you have to take your chances where you find them. You need to ditch that loser state of mind or you'll be stuck in that yo-yo rut of crime and punishment the rest of your life.'

They drove in silence for another couple of miles, crested the peak where Lancashire became Yorkshire. Some sheep had strayed on to the road and Joel had to slalom to avoid them, hit the brake as the mist became thicker and closer to the earth.

'You have any money?' said Joel at last.

Neville leaned into the door and turned to look at him. Suspicion buckled his face, some kind of smile behind the caution. 'What, there some left from the last job?'

'You must be jokin',' said Joel. 'Your cut – you think your old lady'd let me hold on to it until you came out, live on fresh air and donuts for ten months? No, what I meant was, d'you need some pocket money to keep you tickin' over, like that?'

Neville hiked his shoulders, looked off. 'Reckon so,' he said softly, ashamed that he had to rely on his old friend for financial support.

'Okay, I'll hit the first cashpoint we come across,' said Joel.

Kenny held the phone out from his ear. His head bobbed with the monotonous rhythm of her speech. He looked out at Coco on the bench, the can of Red Stripe beside him like a little tin pet. In the distance he could see the speck of a car as it came down the hill, the first vehicle he had seen in thirty minutes. It had become a habit with her, Janie on the line just before he left at the end of his shift with a list of stuff she wanted him to fetch over, boost from the store like he was a shoplifter and not the hired hand. He let the clack of her demands roll around his ear until it became no more than a thick hum deep inside his head.

A pale blue Metro turned into the crumbled ashphalt forecourt and a couple of minutes later the bell tinkled and two men stepped inside. The old man turned on the bench and tracked them with rheumy eyes.

The man in front wore a black T-shirt over black jeans, a baseball cap pulled down low over his eyes. He held both his hands curled behind his back, looked around the store with cool detachment. The other one looked like he had stuffed himself inside three or four layers of clothes to pump himself up from stickman, and his face poked around the corners of the store with kinetic snaps. He jumped around behind the man in the baseball cap as the pair of them approached the counter.

Kenny pointed into the phone and then held up his hand. 'Be with you in a mo,' he mouthed, and tilted his head back and stared up at the far corner of the store.

Seconds later, he sensed a flash of blue steel out of the corner of his eye as the man in the cap leaned across the counter and snatched hold of the front of his Polo shirt and pressed a cold and blunt instrument to his temple. 'Put the phone down,' said the man in the cap, calm and hard. 'Don't speak. Just put the phone down. Now.'

Kenny paused for the briefest of seconds, bravery on the cusp of action and inaction, and the man hit him across the temple with a solid thump. He jerked as if he had been hit by a cattle prod and the phone clattered to the floor.

Joel jabbed the tip of a steel rod into the clerk's face and held him with a hard stare. The air pressure in the store seemed to rise and the room filled with a tense silence, the echo of a small metallic voice from the cracked receiver the only break in the silence.

'Open the till,' said Joel.

The clerk stared at Joel, incomprehension in his eyes. Heat and perspiration burst from his skin and lacquered his face in a dull mask of fear.

'C'mon, c'mon, we don't have all fuckin' day,' said Neville from halfway down the centre aisle. His tunnel focus jumped around the room, out across the forecourt and back like the beam of a torch. 'Just do like the man said and open the fuckin' till.'

Some deep and heroic pulse passed across the clerk's eyes, and bravery started to tick in his blood. He slipped his left hand under the counter and pushed the alarm button. Metallic screams tore loose from the front of the store and ripped out across the moors. The old man lifted his head and peered into the store, squinted into the reflection of the pale autumn sun.

Shock turned to fury and Joel pulled back his hand and lashed the clerk across the face with the steel rod. He heard the dull collapse of bone and the clerk fell to the floor behind the counter. Blood spilled around his head in the shape of a buffalo, spread across the cracked lino.

'Fuckin' local heroes,' spat Joel, and jumped the counter and punched open the till, slipped the steel rod into his back pocket and started to pull out stacks of notes. Neville backed up to the door and scanned the forecourt, lifted a tube of Smarties and a Snickers bar from the rack on the centre aisle and dropped them into his pocket.

Seconds later, his pockets heavy with cash, Joel climbed back across the counter and ran out of the door that Neville held open for him. Neville ran after him and they climbed into the car. It roared into life and left a cloud of burnt dust behind as it ripped out of the forecourt.

The old man watched the Metro tear down the road towards Marsden, trailed it with open eyes until it disappeared around a thick formation of dark rocks, a dense sheet of mist. The alarm continued to tear at the cool air of the day, but as he hurried into the store he knew that it would be at least an hour before anyone made it out here.

He pulled open the door of the chill cabinet, lifted four cans of Red Stripe from the shelf and stuffed them into his jacket pockets. He plucked another couple of four packs by the plastic snaps from the back of the cabinet and bunched them up under his arms. He could always hide them out on the moors, keep them cool in one of the streams that cut around the thick tufts of heather.

Behind the counter, a small metallic voice continued to echo from the broken receiver.

AUTHORS' BIOGRAPHIES

Andrea Badenoch has published many articles, reviews and short stories and for several years edited the magazine *Writing Women*. Her first two novels were contemporary urban thrillers. More recently she has drawn on her native North East for inspiration. *Blink* is a story of secrets, set against a grim Durham coalfield. *Loving Geordie* is the tale of a boy's love for his autistic brother, a suspect in a murder reminiscent of the Mary Bell case with its backdrop of slum clearance, social upheaval and corruption.

Robert Barnard was born in 1936 and brought up near Colchester in Essex. After Balliol, he worked for the Fabian Society, then went to teach in an Australian university in 1961 (it was later used in his first crime novel, *Death of an Old Goat*). He and his wife Louise went to Norway in 1966 where he taught English at the universities of Bergen and Tromsø, and began writing crime fiction. He returned to England in 1983, becoming a full time writer. He has now written over forty mysteries, as well as books on Agatha Christie, Dickens, Emily Brontë and a Short History of English Literature.

Ann Cleeves lives in West Yorkshire with her family. She is best known for her Inspector Ramsay novels set in Northumberland, but she has recently turned to non-series novels of psychological suspense and both *The Crow Trap* and *The Sleeping and the Dead* have earned considerable critical acclaim. As a member and bookings secretary of the collective 'Murder Squad', she works with other Northern writers to promote crime fiction.

Mat Coward was born in 1960 and became a full time free-lance writer and broadcaster in 1986. Having written all manner of material for all manner of markets, he currently specialises in book reviews, magazine columns and short stories – crime, SF, humour, horror and children's. His first crime story was shortlisted for a CWA Dagger and he has also published two novels: *Up and Down*, and *In and Out*.

Judith Cutler, now based in rural Kent, draws on the murkier depths of Birmingham for her two acclaimed series of crime novels and for many of her short stories. Sophie Rivers, her feisty amateur sleuth, made her debut in *Dying Fall* and has been Dying to right wrongs ever since. Police officer Kate Power burst on to the scene in *Power on her Own*, and has continued to live up to her surname. Judith has also published romantic novels set in Devon. Until recently the Secretary of the Crime Writers' Association, she has now turned her attention to organic vegetables.

Carol Anne Davis writes both crime fact and fiction. Four reviewers chose her mortuary-based novel *Shrouded* as their debut of the year in 1997 and its successors include *Safe As Houses*. Most recently, she has published *Women Who Kill* and *Children Who Kill*. Carol's short stories have appeared in anthologies and magazines and have been placed in national competitions. Her dark crime collection is available for publication and she says that no reasonable offer will be refused.

Martin Edwards has written seven novels about the lawyer and amateur detective Harry Devlin; the first, *All The*

Lonely People, was shortlisted for the CWA John Creasey Memorial Dagger. He has published a collection of his short fiction, *Where Do You Find Your Ideas?* and other crime stories, and has edited thirteen crime anthologies. He is also the author of seven non-fiction books on legal topics and *Urge To Kill*, a study of homicide investigation. In 1999 he was commissioned to complete the late Bill Knox's police novel *The Lazarus Widow*. His latest book is a non-series novel of psychological suspense, *Take My Breath Away*.

Kate Ellis was born and brought up in Liverpool and studied drama in Manchester. She has worked in teaching, marketing and accountancy, and first enjoyed literary success as a winner of the North West Playwright competition. Keenly interested in medieval history and 'amateur' archaeology, she lives in North Cheshire with her family. Her novels featuring Detective Sergeant Wesley Peterson include *The Merchant's House*.

Reginald Hill is the author of over forty books, including the internationally acclaimed Dalziel and Pascoe series, which has been successfully adapted for BBC television. His other series character is the Luton private eye Joe Sixsmith. His many awards include the CWA Cartier Diamond Dagger and the CWA Gold Dagger for *Bones and Silence*.

Edward D Hoch is a past president of Mystery Writers of America and winner of its Edgar award for best short story. In 2001 he was honoured with MWA's Grand Master Award. He has been guest of honour at the annual Bouchercon mystery convention, two-time winner of its Anthony Award, and 2001 recipient of its Lifetime

Achievement Award. Author of some 875 published stories, he has contributed to every issue of *Ellery Queen's Mystery Magazine* for over thirty years.

Brian Innes has enjoyed a varied career as a popular musician, on percussion with the Temperance Seven, as a research biochemist, and as an author of crime fact and fiction. His book *Bodies of Evidence* includes over 100 case histories explaining how forensic evidence has been used to solve crimes.

Michael Jecks gave up a career in computing to write. Inspired by the demise of the Knights Templar, he created a series of medieval crime stories, launching Sir Baldwin of Furnshill, Keeper of the King's Peace in Crediton, and his friend Simon Puttock, Bailiff of Lydford Castle, responsible for justice over the tin-mining Stannaries of Dartmoor. Living in, and writing about, Dartmoor, he is delighted to have found a career that is more stable, better managed and, even better, more enjoyable.

Peter Lewis has lived in the North-East for more than 30 years. He is an academic and teaches courses in crime at one of the institutions for which Durham is famous. Among his books are critiques of Eric Ambler and John le Carré; the latter received an Edgar Allan Poe award from the Mystery Writers of America. He and his wife Margaret run Flambard Press, which has published *Northern Blood 2*, an anthology of regional crime stories, collections of the work of Chaz Brenchley and HRF Keating, and novels by crime writers such as Maureen Carter and Meg Elizabeth Atkins.

Peter Lovesey's short stories have been honoured with a number of awards, including the CWA Veuve Clicquot prize, the Ellery Queen Readers' Award and the Mystery Writers of America Golden Mysteries Prize celebrating their 50th anniversary. Five collections of his stories have been published, the latest, *The Sedgemoor Strangler*, in 2001. Many have also been read on radio and adapted for TV in the *Tales of the Unexpected* series and the BBC Schools Service. As a crime novelist, he has been the recipient of Silver, Gold and Diamond Daggers. His latest novel, *The House Sitter*, was published this year.

Keith Miles was born in Wales and educated at Oxford; he has written over forty plays for radio, television and the theatre. His published work includes biography, literary criticism, short stories, children's fiction and sports books. The majority of his crime novels are historical mysteries, written under the pseudonym of Edward Marston – the Domesday Books; the Nicholas Bracewell series, set in the Elizabethan theatre; and the Redmayne Mysteries, featuring an architect who is helping to rebuild London after the Great Fire of 1666. The latest addition to the Redmayne series is *The Frost Fair*. Miles is a former Chairman of the Crime Writers' Association.

Gwen Moffat was an army deserter and mountain guide. She published her autobiography, *Space Below My Feet*, and sequels in the '60s, subsequently turning to crime fiction. Commissioned to write an historical/travel book on the California Trail, she wrote two, including *The Buckskin Girl*, involving violent deaths in a nineteenth-century wagon train. These were followed by nine modern crime novels set in the American West and alternated with others featuring upland areas of Britain from Snowdonia and the Pennines to Cape Wrath. *Man Trap*, set in the Scottish Highlands, was published in 2003. She lives in the

Lake District with a cat and her interests are mountains, music and malt whisky.

Amy Myers has had short crime stories published in many anthologies and in *Ellery Queen's Mystery Magazine*; a collection of them is shortly to appear under the title *Murder 'Orrible Murder* from Crippen & Landru. She is also the author of a series of eleven crime novels featuring the Victorian chef sleuth Auguste Didier and, under the pseudonym of Harriet Hudson, historical sagas and romances. Before becoming a full time author in 1988, she worked in publishing, editing fiction and non-fiction. Married to an American car-buff, she lives in Kent – not far from where 'Granny Trotter's Treasure' is set.

Ruth Rendell, under her own name and as Barbara Vine, has won both critical and popular acclaim for her achievement in showing the rich potential of the crime novel. Her first book about the Kingsmarkham policeman, Reg Wexford, *From Doon with Death*, appeared in 1964. Her non-series novels under her own name include *A Demon in my View* which won the CWA Gold Dagger in 1976 and *A Judgement in Ston*e. *Lake of Darkness* won the Arts Council National Book Award for Genre Fiction in 1981. The much-praised Vine novels include *A Fatal Inversion* (another CWA Gold Dagger winner) and *The Brimstone Wedding*.

Zoe Sharp spent most of her childhood living aboard a catamaran on the north west coast of England. She opted out of mainstream education at the age of twelve and wrote her first novel when she was fifteen. She went through a variety of strange jobs in her teenage years, before becoming a freelance photo-journalist in 1988. Receiving threatening letters through her work inspired her to write *Killer Instinct*, the first of her series of thrillers featuring ex-army heroine, Charlie Fox, which was published in 2001. Zoe lives in Cumbria and is married, but would rather have a motorbike than children.

Jerry Sykes's stories have appeared in diverse magazines and anthologies, including *Cemetery Dance*, *Crime Time*, and *Love Kills*. He edited the collection *Mean Time – New Crime For A New Millennium* and in 1998 he joined the ranks of such illustrious writers as Reg Hill, Ian Rankin and Julian Rathbone by winning the CWA Short Story Dagger.'

Grief by John B Spencer

'*Grief* is a speed-freak's cocktail, one part Leonard and one part Ellroy, that goes right to the head.' George P Pelecanos
When disparate individuals collide, it's Grief. John B Spencer's final and greatest novel.
'Spencer writes the tightest dialogue this side of Elmore Leonard, so bring on the blood, sweat and beers!' Ian Rankin

No One Gets Hurt by Russell James

'The best of Britain's darker crime writers' – *The Times*
After a friend's murder Kirsty Rice finds herself drawn into the murky world of call-girls, porn and Internet sex.

Kiss It Away by Carol Anne Davis

'Reminiscent of Ruth Rendell at her darkest' – Booklist (USA)
Steroid dependent Nick arrives alone in Salisbury, rapes a stranger and brutally murders a woman.
'A gripping tale of skewered psychology... a mighty chiller,' *The Guardian*

A Man's Enemies by Bill James

'Bill James can write, and then some' *The Guardian*
The direct sequel to 'Split'. Simon Abelard, the section's 'token black', has to dissuade Horton from publishing his memoirs.

End of the Line by K T McCaffrey

'KT McCaffrey is an Irish writer to watch' RTE
Emma is celebrating her Journalist of the Year Award when she hears of the death of priest Father Jack O'Gorman in what appears to have been a tragic road accident.

Vixen by Ken Bruen

'Ireland's version of Scotland's Ian Rankin' – *Publisher's Weekly*
BRANT IS BACK! If the Squad survives this incendiary installment, they'll do so with barely a cop left standing.

The Do-Not Press
Fiercely   Independent   Publishing

Keep in touch with what's happening at the cutting edge of independent British publishing.

Simply send your name and address to:
The Do-Not Press (GFD)
16 The Woodlands, London SE13 6TY (UK)

or email us: gfd@thedonotpress.com

There is no obligation to purchase
(although we'd certainly like you to!)
and no salesman will call.

Visit our regularly-updated websites:
www.thedonotpress.com
www.bangbangbooks.com

Mail Order
All our titles are available from good bookshops, or (in case of difficulty) direct from The Do-Not Press at the address above. There is no charge for post and packing for orders to the UK and Europe.

(NB: A post-person may call.)